CHASING THE ALPHA'S SON

Penny Jessup

Tiny Ghost Press

*actual size

For every queer person looking for community and family.
For my pack...xxx

One pack under the moon.

ICE QUEEN

"Watch out!" Todd calls, careening across the ice rink on a collision course with my face. I brace for impact as he swerves, missing me by less than an inch, then skates away.

Unsteady on his feet, he skids around a mitten-clad couple holding hands, almost taking out a child and her fiberglass penguin before purposefully ramming into Simon. Simon, who is much less confident on skates, loses his footing. His legs slip out from under him and he tumbles backward, but not before grabbing hold of Todd's jacket collar.

The bros end up wrestling in a heap in the middle of the ice, neither letting the other back to his feet. Around them tourists and families skate in circles, trying to give the pair a wide berth.

I sigh and lean against the barrier, staring up at the too-brightly-lit Christmas tree. I used to love coming to skate at Rockefeller in the lead-up to the holidays, but this year it just seems kind of lame. The tree is way over the top—it's garish and unnecessarily large. The other skaters are annoyingly chipper despite most of them fumbling about like baby deer learning to walk. And it's way too crowded.

I shiver and glance back at the phone in my hands. My shoulders drop.

Or maybe I'm just feeling bitter this year.

Because for the first time ever I actually want to do all those cheesy, romantic things you see in holiday movies. And for the first time there's a person I could be doing all those things with—who I want to do all those stupid things with.

But that person hasn't sent me a single text since September.

I scroll through the countless messages I've sent Jasper, the occasional unanswered phone call.

I promised myself I'd do anything to make Jasper see reason—go to the moon and back, chase him to the ends of the world if I have to. But I don't know how I'm supposed to do that if he won't even speak to me.

"If you don't stop looking at that thing someone will mow you down," Katie says, effortlessly gliding toward me and coming to a perfect standstill.

Honestly, she could be an Olympic skater if she wanted; she has the poise, the grace, and she isn't afraid to take out the competition if need be.

I shrug and slide the phone back into my jeans before shoving my bone-chilled hands into the pockets of my puffer.

Katie sidles up next to me and rests her head on my shoulder. "Still nothing, huh?"

"Nada."

She twists her feet and rotates her body so that she's standing in front of me.

"Don't get depressed," she says tugging on my elbows. "This isn't over. Operation GJA is far from complete."

I scoff thinking back to the day Katie and I conceived Operation Get Jasper's Attention. It was the day after he and I kissed on the beach and he told me he accepted me as his mate, but that we could never be together—what a load of bull, right?! Katie and I sat down in her mom's freshly wallpapered living room and made a plan. The idea was to make it impossible for Jasper not to notice me. That way, he couldn't just forget and move on, and eventually he'd give in.

Turns out I'm easier to ignore than I thought. And easier to forget.

Nothing has worked. No amount of texting, calling, or letter writing has garnered a response—yes, I stooped to Jane Austen levels of desperate. One time I showed up at his house and Melissa told me he was out of town visiting a friend at boarding school. Another time I sent him a pair of mugs I'd had our faces printed on—psychotic, I know. I stopped taking all of Katie's suggestions so seriously from that point on.

"I think OGJA is dead in the water," I say. "It was always a pretty terrible acronym anyway."

"Come on," Katie says, skating a little ways backward and spinning in a tiny loop. "There has to be something we haven't thought of. When we get to Starry B's after this, let's think it over."

With a huff I push off the barrier, my ankles starting to ache in these cheap rented skates. "There's no point, it's over. It's more than over. It's obvious Jasper was serious when he said he didn't want to be around me, and anyway I'm starting to think..."

"Max, what?" Katie tilts her head. Her pale cheeks are super rosy.

"I'm starting to think he doesn't care."

"How can you say that?! Of course, he—"

"Dude! Seriously, get off!" Simon shouts.

Across the ice things have graduated from a friendly wrestle to a heated scuffle.

"What's wrong with you, man?" Todd replies, trapping his adversary in a headlock.

Katie's shoulders drop and she sighs like an exhausted parent. "One second. I need to stop this before they take out a family right before Christmas."

With her brow knitted, Katie heads out onto the ice, chastising her man-babies and trying to pull them apart.

"Good talk," I huff.

"Cheers!" Katie says an hour later in the coffee shop, raising her festive paper cup.

Over in the corner waiting for their drinks, Simon knocks Todd sideways into the gingerbread display, causing an avalanche of cookie people.

"Way to go, dude, look what you made me do," Todd says.

Katie bites her lip and sets her cup down without bumping it against mine, which is hovering in midair. "Honestly, I can't take them anywhere."

"What *is* going on there?" I ask, only slightly stung that Katie seems to have forgotten it's tradition to *cheers* with our first festive drinks of the season.

"We've all been getting along great," Katie says. "They've seemed pretty okay with the whole double-dating thing. But just in the last couple of weeks they've started getting territorial. It starts as play-fighting and within minutes I'm worried one of them's going to lose an eye or a leg."

Simon has taken to pelting wooden stirrers at Todd, who's commandeered a plastic tray to use as a shield.

"The other day"—Katie leans in conspiratorially—"it got so heated Simon nearly shifted in the middle of the High

Line." She fiddles with some errant sugar someone spilled on the table.

I shrink a little lower in my seat, hoping no one notices we're here with the clowns throwing paper straws. It's bad enough she brought them with her to our festive-season kickoff coffee date; the least they could do is sit and stay like good pups.

"Okay," she says, gulping down a sip of toffee nut latte. "I've been thinking—what if we use the holidays as a reason for you and Jasper to see each other, like what if your parents throw a Christmas party and invite the alpha's family!"

I nearly choke on my too-hot peppermint mocha.

"You think the alpha is going to come to my house in Stony Point? He'd barely fit through the front door."

"Maybe he wouldn't come, but Jasper might—"

"I don't think—"

"Okay, well then what about—"

"Katie."

"I was thinking we could—"

"Katie!"

The old couple at the table next to us jump in their seats at my outburst and a few other heads turn to stare at the hot-faced kid disturbing their caffeinated tranquility.

"Sorry," I say.

Katie's big, concerned eyes glisten with questions and just a little pang of hurt. The rest of the coffee shop goes back to their conversations and phone screens, and I lean closer, lowering my voice.

"It's just, I don't want to do it anymore. This whole chasing after Jasper and being ignored time and time again. It isn't fair."

"I know but he's your m—"

"Don't say it. Jasper obviously doesn't care that we're mates, so why should I?"

I catch Katie glancing to where her double mates are wrestling, each trying to stop the other from collecting their drink.

"I know I said I would chase him to the ends of the world. I know I said I don't care that he doesn't want to be with me...but I do. And I should. It isn't healthy all this pining for someone that couldn't give less of a wolf's tail. I always wanted more than to be *just* somebody's mate; maybe this is fate's way of telling me I was right."

Katie sits back in her chair, her shoulders slumping forward.

"Okay," she says, just above a whisper.

"You sure?"

"Yes, okay. You're right." She perks up a little, maybe the caffeine is starting to take effect. "You deserve better, I always said that. So screw Jasper! And Merry fudging Christmas!"

"Merry freaking Christmas!"

We bump our festive cups together.

Once I've dropped Katie and her terrible twosome off at the subway, I head back in the direction of Grand Central. There's a nasty chill in the air, so I shove my hands farther into my coat pockets, but I'm happy to be walking.

It's good practice. The way I'm steeling myself against the cold is exactly what I need to do with Jasper. The Moon Gods know he's about as icy as the rink at Rockefeller and as gray and emotionless as the clouds overhead. I need to brace myself against any lingering mushy feelings, any shred of desire. I definitely need to stop picturing our kiss on the beach every time I close my eyes.

By the time I reach the station I'm almost in a good mood. I pop in the AirPods my parents bought me as a way to say, "Sorry you were almost killed by a pack of rogues, we're glad you're okay," and put on some music. I don't even think about checking my messages.

I know he hasn't texted or called. And I'm okay with that.

I'm okay with that.

How hard can it really be not to look at my phone?

About fifteen minutes into the train journey, I start to feel like an addict going through withdrawal. My foot is tapping relentlessly; my fingers are fidgeting, inching closer and closer to my pocket; I'm grinding my teeth so loud the guy in the wrinkled suit opposite me keeps glancing up from his newspaper.

And then my phone buzzes and I nearly explode. Why would the Moon Gods do this to me when I'm trying so hard to be good?

Fine, I'll look.

With trepidation and a heartbeat faster than a bullet, I pull out my phone. Maybe the new plan worked. Maybe somewhere Jasper could sense that I was over him and felt spurred into action.

Or maybe it's just Katie saying she's made it home already. I send her a quick smiley face in response and sink deeper into my seat.

Dad is waiting for me at the station when the train pulls in.

"Hey champ," he says. Why is he always so damn jolly? "Did you have a nice time?"

"It was fine," I deadpan and get into the car without looking at him.

When we arrive home I slam the front door behind me and head straight for my room.

"Is that you, kiddo?" Mom calls from the living room, but I don't answer. I stomp up the stairs like each step is Jasper's stupid face and I want to break his perfect nose. "Don't you want any dinner?"

I spend the night tossing and turning. Somehow making the decision not to care has only made things worse. I keep glancing at my phone on my bedside table, somehow expecting it to light up even though it's three in the morning and why would Jasper be awake at three in the morning, let alone texting me?

When the sun finally rises, I sit up and rub my bleary eyes. My phone sits lifeless and dark next to me.

Screw this!

I throw on the warmest clothes I can find and grab my sketchbook. It's been a while since I've gone down to my spot by the river, and I could really use some clarity right about now.

Mom is already up making coffee in the kitchen as I pass through.

"Hey, where are you off to?" she asks, clearly surprised to see me out of bed before noon on a weekend.

"To the woods to draw."

"Not without your coat and hat, kiddo, it's below freezing out there."

I sigh dramatically but she's right. Even though wolves tend to run hot, I'd still come home a human popsicle in this weather. Like a begrudging toddler I grab my coat from the rack by the front door and pull my beanie down over my ears.

I step back into the kitchen and throw my arms out. "Better?"

"You look very snug."

"So I can go now?"

"Ahuh, just don't stay out there too long; our insurance doesn't cover frostbite or moodiness."

With an obviously sarcastic laugh, I hurry for the door.

"Just one more thing," Mom says.

I wait for her to keep speaking. She's clutching her coffee mug with both hands and chewing the inside of her cheek.

"Mom? What is it?"

She sighs. "Nothing."

"Great!"

I let the screen door slam shut behind me.

The river isn't flowing when I reach it. It's frozen over. An intricate pattern of crystals dance across the surface.

Carefully, I reach out and press down on it with my boot. I want to know if it will crack under my touch—if under that ice there is still flowing water.

Nothing happens so I press harder.

Still nothing.

Man, it's frozen solid!

So this is my new plan. Be like the river. Frozen, hard, unbreakable.

Jasper doesn't care about me. I don't care about him.

That's all there is to it.

A breeze rocks the barren branches of the trees above me, and I can almost make out a hint of sun behind the clouds.

I open my sketchbook and draw. Pictures flow out of me like they haven't since before the Harvest Moon—the way they used to before Jasper consumed my every waking thought. I draw so long my nose is dripping and my lips are chapped by the time I realize I should probably head home.

There's a lightness in my step and I let my lungs fill with cold, refreshing air as I make my way back through the woods. I'm not going to chase someone who doesn't want to be chased. I'm not going to waste any more time pining like a lovesick pup.

Stepping inside feels like entering a new climate. Every winter Dad says his feet get cold and turns the heating way up, so the kitchen is always sweltering. I shed my layers of winter clothing as fast as I can and drop them in a pile by the door.

"Don't even think about leaving those there," Mom says, coming into the kitchen holding an envelope.

I gather up my coat, beanie, and two sweaters and make to pass her when she holds out the letter.

"This came for you. Must be important—we don't usually get mail on a Sunday."

She slips the letter between two of my fingers and I head upstairs with my bundle of clothes.

The second I'm in my room I drop everything except the envelope and turn it over in my hands.

My stomach drops right out of my ass.

On the front my name is written in a familiar and foreboding cursive.

And on the back is the seal of the alpha.

Gulp.

Maybe forgetting is easier said than done.

AN INVITATION

I hop from one foot to the other trying to keep warm while I wait for Aisha to get out of practice. I've been hanging around in this alley staring at the maroon-painted steel door for almost half an hour. The envelope is burning a hole in my pocket, right next to my cell. Some beefy guy in a black puffer gives me a strange look as he passes and slips in through the cast entrance of the theater.

What? You don't like my Kermit impression?

Finally, the door opens and a stream of flush-faced ballet-bun-sporting dancers flow out. Practice must be over. *Good.* Flesh-colored tights stick out the bottom of large winter coats and I'm overwhelmed by the sheer number of leg warmers. Everyone looks so fit and healthy. A couple of guys walk past—one with the most pristinely groomed eyebrows and well-coiffed hair I've ever seen, and the other with a buzz cut and shoulders wider than my arm span. They glance in my direction, and I dart my eyes to the ground.

"Hey dude." I glance back up and Aisha is standing a few feet away, hand on a hip, eyebrow raised. "This is a surprise. What are you doing here? I don't think we made plans."

"Do you know about this?" I pull the crumpled envelope out and shove it into her hand.

She turns it over, staring at it like it's some archeological artifact I've recovered from a tomb. "Know about what? What is this?"

"Open it."

She lifts the crinkled flap and pulls out the letter.

Her eyes scan the page and she pouts. "Oh."

"Yeah, oh. Is this some kind of joke? Where did this come from?"

Aisha exhales through her nose and shakes her head.

"It's an invitation to a party, not a death threat."

She's not taking this seriously enough, so I snatch back the letter.

"It's an invitation to the Yule Ball, at the freaking Plaza! The only people who get invited to this are personally selected by the alpha."

She shrugs. "Is that a bad thing?"

"Why would the alpha invite me unless *someone* asked him to?"

"I dunno," she says, trying hard not to smile too widely at my discomfort. "Maybe he likes you."

"Or maybe Jasper asked him to invite me..."

Adrenaline surges through my body in an instant, boiling the blood in my face, making my legs shaky. It's the only explanation for why I'd be invited to the Yule Ball. The only possible way *I* would have been included on the guest list of such a prestigious event. But I hadn't let myself believe it until the words were coming out of my mouth.

"It's possible," Aisha says, still acting way too cool about the whole thing. "Jasper does get to invite people. That's why I'm going."

The relief is like a cool wave sploshing over me, taking away some of the searing pain from my cheeks.

"You're going?"

"Ahuh."

"Okay, that's good." At least I'll have a friend when I go—*if* I go. *I'm not going to go, am I?*

"But why would Jasper invite me now? He hasn't spoken to me since September."

"That I can't say. Maybe he just felt like it was time."

I throw my head back and fling myself against the brick wall like a damsel in a black-and-white film collapsing against a banister.

"Calm down, Scarlett, don't hurt yourself."

Eyes squeezed shut, I press my head against the wall and try to think. I know I'm acting like a hysterical nut, but I just don't get it... Why now?

"I wanted to forget about him," I say, opening my eyes. "I was ready to move on. I'd decided to move on."

Sighing a gentle sympathetic sigh, Aisha steps to my side and leans her shoulder against the wall.

"I know things have been hard," she says. "But maybe he wants to see you."

I glare at her out of the corner of my eye. "Did he say something to you?"

"What?! No." She scoffs and pushes off the wall, turning away with her tongue pressed into her cheek. A totally sus reaction.

"He did! What did he say?"

"Nothing," she says, hands up like she's under arrest. "Honest to the Moon Gods, he didn't say anything about inviting you to the Yule Ball. I swear."

"Then why are you acting weird?"

"We hung out the other day"—she leans back against the brick, her shoulder brushing against mine—"and he told me he thinks about you."

Doesn't seem likely. "Jasper said that?"

"Scout's honor or whatever."

Now it's my turn to raise a brow at her.

"Okay, maybe not those exact words. But he said he's been checking on you, you know in that creepy wolf-sense way he does." She taps the side of her head and I think back to all the times I walked in on him meditating, opening his mind to the souls of his pack. "He wants to know you're okay."

A plume of smoke rises through a grate from the subway, like the fog in my mind, pulling my attention. People are passing by the entrance to the alley completely oblivious that a teenage werewolf is being torn in two.

"I'm the first to admit that what he did was shitty," Aisha says. "I can't explain why he turned you down the way he did—"

"He wanted to protect me," I mumble.

"The only thing I know is that Jasper was doing what he thought was right. He only ever does what he thinks is right. It's just sometimes he's a big dumbass."

She elbows me in the side, and I can't help but giggle. She's got a point.

"You don't have to go," she says pretty casually, all things considered. "You don't owe him anything after what he did."

There are too many thoughts running through my head—too many conflicting feelings, so instead I watch a nearby pigeon pecking about at the pavement. Could I really not go? After all this time and all the texts and calls, the personalized gifts! Could I really just not show up?

The boy with the pristine, angular brows turns the corner into the alley and heads for the door.

"Hey Aisha," he says as he passes. "Forgot my water bottle."

"Skylar, you'd forget your pretty head if it wasn't screwed on," she responds jokingly.

"That's the truth. Did you see the allegro Madame Emma came up with this morning? No way I'm keeping all of that in here." His eyes—piercing steel-blue of course—land on me and he pauses for the briefest of seconds, as if he's thinking something over. "Who's your friend?"

"This is Max, he's the coolest kid from Stony Point."

My cheeks are warm and I wish I could shrink all the way into my puffer.

"Hey Max, nice to meet you."

He holds out his hand for me to shake and I can't seem to get mine out of my pocket.

"Sorry...hand is...stuck." With a grunt, I finally manage to free my hand. I take Skylar's and am amazed at how firm his grip is. Strong but not painful, like he's got you. "Nice to meet you too."

Our eyes linger just a little longer than feels natural and a corner of his mouth curls upward.

"Cool," he says, retracting his soft, firm hand and heading off. "Gotta get that water bottle before Madame Em tosses it. Nice to meet you, Max. See you tomorrow Aish!"

The second the door slams shut, Aisha's mouth drops open into an unbearable grin and I have to look away. I can't help laughing as well.

"You thought he was cute!" They probably build theaters with walls thick enough so Skylar can't hear what's happening from inside, but with the way Aisha is hollering I'm not so sure.

"Stahhhhhhp," I whine.

"Hey no judgment. Skylar is super cute. I can get you his number if you want."

"I'm fine, thank you."

I lean back against the wall, huffing and unwilling to look Aisha in the eye.

"You know there are plenty of cute guys out there who aren't Jasper," she says, sidling up once more. "Nice ones too. The kind that reply to texts"

"Yeah," I say. "But that's just the problem. They're not him."

Reluctantly, I turn and face her.

"You're definitely going to this party?" I ask.

She nods.

"Can you help me find something to wear?"

It's way past my curfew when I walk through the front door, shopping bags in hand. I could've called and asked for a ride from the station but the idea of sitting through Dad's inevitable lecture about tardiness was all the motivation I needed to walk.

The lights are off in the hall but there's a dim glow coming from the living room.

"Get in here, kiddo," Mom says in her stern voice.

Gulp. I know what that voice means.

With a resigned sigh I plonk the bags down in the hall and drag my feet to the living room.

"What time do you call this, Max?" Dad asks from the armchair.

Mom is perched on the edge of the couch, her knees pressed together, shoulders back; she won't look at me.

"I texted," I say.

Color rises in Mom's cheeks, like lava in a volcano, about to erupt.

"I'm sorry."

"Do you have any idea how worried we've been?" Mom asks, her voice wavering. She still won't look at me.

"I was just shopping with Aisha. I told you where I was I—"

"Not just tonight." Her words are clipped and harsh. "Ever since you ran off with Jasper to goodness knows where and didn't answer your phone for two days."

What is she on about? That was months ago; I thought we'd moved on from that. "I told you I was sorry about that."

"And then the rogue attack at the Hamptons." Now she turns to me with red, strained eyes and lips squished into an unpleasant squiggly line. "You haven't been yourself, Max. And you won't tell us what's happening."

Dad swallows uncomfortably and clutches the armrests of his chair.

"How are we supposed to protect you, Max, when you won't let us?"

Jeez, first Jasper and now my parents; everyone is obsessed with protecting me.

"I'm fine, Mom. I was just shopping."

She bows her head and wipes at her cheek so quickly I know she doesn't want me to see her like this. Who knew shopping was such a dangerous activity?

"You used to talk to us, sweetie. You used to tell us things and now it's like...like you don't want us to know what's going on in your life."

"It's called being a teenager, Mom."

She snorts a bitter laugh and Dad reaches out to place a reassuring hand on her knee.

"Here's the thing," he says, in as authoritative a tone as he can muster, trying to bring some semblance of calm back to the room. "What happened in the Hamptons was a message to the pack, that we aren't as safe as we thought. And this is causing a lot of tension—tension between the packs and those who would undermine everything we stand for."

"You mean the rogues," I say with a huff. "I told you they're not all like that. When I was in Rogue City I saw—"

"I know," he continues while Mom composes herself, taking a breath and lifting her head to listen. "Believe me I know not all rogues are bad, and the pack system isn't perfect either. But there are dangerous people out there. And it isn't just the rogues. There is tension within the pack as well."

I furrow my brow. "I don't understand."

"There are people who feel the recent attack is proof that the alpha has lost control over our borders. There are some who think he should be deposed."

Instantly, I begin running scenarios in my head where Jericho isn't the alpha anymore and Jasper is no longer the alpha's son—just a normal wolf, like me. Would things be different then? Could we be together? Is this burgeoning mutiny part of the reason I haven't heard from him?

"What does any of this have to do with me buying clothes?"

"The pack isn't as safe as it once was," Mom says slowly, her words considered and deliberate, as she studies the coffee table. "And we need to know that you're safe. But we can't do that if you don't talk to us. Haven't we told you we can handle anything? You can tell us anything."

"I know," I say, rubbing the back of my neck. "I know."

"So then what's going on?"

Suddenly, I'm aware that I'm still wearing my coat and beanie and I'm starting to sweat. I grab my beanie and shove it in my pocket, then ruffle my flattened hair. She wants me to talk but I still don't know how to. I don't know how to tell them that I'm not what they've been expecting their whole lives. They want me to confide in them, but how can I when my very existence is in opposition to the structure of our society? Dad has devoted his life to the pack, working as a pack accountant since he left college.

On some level I know—*I know* it would be fine if I told them about me and Jasper... About me. That I'm... *Fuck!*

I can't even say it to myself! So how am I supposed to tell them? How am I supposed to tell them when doing so puts me in danger of the thing I'm most scared of—losing them.

"I...I..."

The words won't come. As much as I want them to, they won't.

Mom sighs, clutching her forehead as if I'm giving her the biggest migraine.

"At least tell me one thing," she says. "Why were you invited to the Yule Ball? They don't invite just anyone. The Moon Gods know your father and I have never been. Can you at least explain how that's happened?"

My whole body is starting to quiver—so much my skin might actually vibrate off. My head is empty and likely to float from my body. There's only one reason I can think of that makes any sense. And it's the one thing I can't say out loud. Not to my parents.

I shrug hopelessly and Mom exhales, clearly frustrated beyond belief.

"Okay, if you won't tell us that then could you at least tell us what happened the night of the Harvest Moon Celebration?"

"I told you what happened—"

"No, Max. You gave us a vague synopsis and then never brought it up again."

"You have kind of avoided the subject, buddy," Dad joins in.

"Well, it was scary, it's not something I want to talk about..."

"But there's more to it, isn't there?" Mom says, staring me down, looking into me like she knows I'm lying. "What aren't you telling us, Max?"

I feel like a hamster backed into a corner by a python. There's nowhere to run and no way I'm getting out of this without giving them something.

Maybe now is my chance to come clean. Tell them everything. They want to know. They're begging to know. The door is wide open and all I have to do is step through.

I open my mouth to speak.

UBER NERVOUS

"So did you tell them?" Katie asks.

"No, I completely chickened out."

We're in an Uber on our way to the Plaza. Through some magic of the universe—thanks to their parents' connections—both Todd and Simon were invited to the Yule Ball and they both asked Katie to be their date. Apparently, this was the cause of some angsty tension between the bro twins, but it's lucky for me. Aisha had a late rehearsal and could only meet me once the ball was underway. With Katie going I had someone to get ready with and I wasn't forced to rock up outside like some interloper.

On the back seat next to me, Katie is clutching her purse. She's wearing a red dress that shimmers like a ruby, her hair is tied up, and her eyes are shrouded in a puff of smoky eye shadow. City lights reflect on the glittery highlighter she's used on her cheeks as we crawl uptown. It's a marked difference from the frilly cocktail dresses and the pastel palette I'm used to seeing on her. The whole look is more grown-up, but it suits.

"You know they'd be totally fine with it," she says, making me roll my eyes. "Even the alpha is fine with it. That's what you said, right?"

"Yeah. He was totally cool about me and Jasper."

"So what makes you think your sweet, down-to-earth, equal-opportunity-supporting parents won't be?"

I sigh and lean my shoulder against the window. Christmas lights strung up between streetlights twinkle and the sidewalks are full of puffy-coated tourists. We pass a steak house, and my eyes linger on a family seated at a table by the window. They're laughing and smiling.

Katie is right, of course; I have no reason to think my parents would be anything but accepting and loving. But still I couldn't do it. I couldn't tell them about me and Jasper.

They gave me the opening, handed me the chance to come clean on a platter, and what did I do?

"What did you tell them then?" Katie presses.

I didn't exactly lie. But it wasn't the truth either.

"I told them I'd been acting weird because of the attack, that I didn't want them to worry so I didn't tell them the whole story."

"And they bought that."

"Ahuh."

"How much of the whole story did you tell them?"

"I told them I was kidnapped and taken to the yacht with a couple of other hostages. I neglected to tell them a mate-crazed friend of mine picked me specifically so she could replace me as Jasper's mate."

"How did they take it?"

"They ate it up. Seriously, I'm waiting for my Oscar nomination any day now."

"Really?"

The truth is Mom started biting her nails halfway through and was finished giving herself a manicure by the time my sob story ended. She sprang up and wrapped me in this massive hug, which would have been comforting under normal circumstances. But on this occasion it just made the strange humming sensation in my chest worse.

"Yeah, they bought it."

"And what about the party?"

"I said it was sort of like an apology, a way for the alpha and his family to make it up to us."

She raises an eyebrow. "Us?"

"Yeah, you know. Me and the other hostages."

"Max! I know the truth is hard but you're just lying to your parents now."

"I know! But what else am I supposed to do?"

Katie gives me this look like the answer is obvious, like the truth is that simple.

In my head I know my parents will love me no matter what, but for some reason the words won't come out. They're just stuck inside of me, like a pile of bricks, weighing me down. There's a chasm between my brain and my mouth and I have no idea how to bridge it.

"Can we talk about something else?" I ask, as the Uber comes to a stop at a traffic light.

"Of course," Katie says.

I know she's looking at me—I can feel her in my periphery but I don't look back. I just keep watching as the traffic light turns from red to green. We roll forward.

The Plaza is only a couple of blocks away. We're minutes from entering the Yule Ball, where I'm sure to feel completely at home and not at all like a weed in a bed of roses. It's the first time I've been around this many wolves since the Harvest Moon, and the closest I've been to Jasper in months.

My body is vibrating, like I'm plugged into an electrical socket and the current is jolting about in my veins. I keep fighting the nervous urge to yawn and rub the back of my neck—not that I can reach that far back in the suit Aisha picked out for me, but still. My collar is way too tight and I'm worried I might suffocate in my supposed-to-be-ironic bow tie.

"How are you feeling about...?" Katie begins to ask but trails off. She's still got her smoky eyes on me. Beneath the eye shadow and the contouring my best friend is still there, still by my side, where she'll be forever.

"Nervous doesn't even begin to cut it."

She places her hand on top of mine and gives it a little squeeze.

"For what it's worth, I'm proud of you. And I think you look very handsome in your suit."

Absent-mindedly, I run a jittery hand through my hair before remembering it took about twenty minutes to get it into a style I liked.

"Thanks," I mumble. "You look good too. Maybe too good, actually. There's a high chance Todd and Simon will shift the second they lay their eyes on you in that dress."

She smirks. "That was the idea. Although now that I think about it, you might be right. What if they go on a rampage through the Plaza?"

"A lot of rich people are going to be very upset."

"No one is safe."

"Probably best if we turn around now, head home, avoid the commotion."

The car comes to a stop.

"This okay?" the Uber driver asks.

Katie and I both stare out the window at the golden entrance. I try to swallow the watermelon in my throat.

"This'll do."

I help Katie out of the car, shutting the door behind her as she smooths out her dress.

This all seems like something from a movie. I've walked past this entrance—the shiny gold-framed doors, the checkerboard paving, the red-carpeted steps, the footmen, the lamps that look like clusters of little moons—millions of times on my way to the park, but I've never actually been inside. Never crossed this glossy threshold.

"You don't really think they'll shift and ruin the party, do you?" Katie asks, coming to stand next to me.

I cock an eyebrow and glance sideways. "You want to put money on it?"

Our glances meet and we both take a deep breath.

"We can still turn around if you want?" Katie says, sounding about as nervous as I feel.

But I can't turn around. There's a familiar sensation drawing me to the entrance. Like an invisible rope's been tied around my chest and is pulling me in.

"He's in there," I say.

And knowing what that means, Katie slips her hand into mine and together we enter the building.

Inside we're bathed in the golden light of a car-sized crystal chandelier, and I'm hit with a wave of familiar scents. Musky and sweet. They're the scents of Elite Pack wolves—my pack—and I feel instinctively at home, welcome even though I'm more uncomfortable than I was when Eleanor had a gun to my head. An older couple walks past, the man in a tux and the woman in a beaded sky-blue gown with a fir tossed over one shoulder. The dude gives us a knowing nod as he pushes through the next set of doors, as if we have some secret connection. I almost laugh. We may both be Elite Pack wolves, but I couldn't have less in common with these people.

They look like they know where they're headed, so Katie and I follow. We pass through a hall with more chandeliers, marble floors, and flower arrangements that would strike fear into the hearts of allergy sufferers. There's a sign that says we're heading toward the Grand Ballroom, because of course we are.

Two pack security guards stand on either side of white-and-gold doors, with earpieces and sunglasses and stern faces. Another wolf—a woman in a sparkling lavender gown, with her hair delicately arranged on top of her head, half-moon spectacles, and too much makeup—is a few feet in front of them holding an iPad. The elegant couple stop and speak to her like they're old friends. She smiles a wide, cheesy grin and waves them through, touching the woman's arm as they go. The security guards push open the doors and the couple disappear inside.

I catch a glimpse of what lies beyond—an overwhelming snapshot of a glittering world like something from a fairy tale—and a sneak of a scent slips through the doors...

Cherry blossom.

"Good evening, can I help you?"

Katie elbows me in the ribs and I shake myself back into the room. The woman with the updo is staring at me like I'm a stray dog trying to come inside for the night.

"We're, um, here for the party."

She squints and pouts her lips. "Do you have an invitation?"

"Oh yeah, I have it here somewhere."

I fumble around in my pockets and finally produce the crumpled envelope from inside my blazer.

She takes it like it's a used tissue and cross-references it with her iPad.

"Ah, there you are." Her expression shifts and suddenly she's all smiles and big welcoming eyes. "Welcome to the Yule Ball, Maximilian Remus. Have a gorgeous night."

"Uh, thank you."

Katie pulls lightly on my arm and we make our way to the doors.

When I was a kid *The Wizard of Oz* was one of my favorite movies, and walking into the ballroom, I'm

Dorothy stepping foot in the Emerald City for the first time. The people look so suave and sophisticated, so alien. Every surface seems to shine; the ceiling is so high it might as well be the sky. Everything is over the top but ultrachic. A central dance floor is surrounded by circular tables and golden chairs where I can picture Belle and the Beast waltzing in circles while everyone watches on. Columns line the room, each punctuated with a Christmas tree overladen with silver and gold decorations. There's a stage at one end on which a string quartet is playing gentle music, and the ceiling is lit up like the most spectacular artificial dusk you've ever seen: mind-blowing shades of violet and peach. It's a winter wonderland, a high-end fantasy—it's too much.

"Wow," Katie says, smiling as the lights dance in her eyes, her mouth hanging open.

"Seriously."

We take a few steps into the room and it suddenly dawns on me I have no idea what happens now. Are we supposed to mingle? Is there dancing? I'm very aware of my hands and have no idea what to do with them.

My eyes roam the busy ballroom expecting to meet Jasper's. My heart races. He has to be here, right? He's so duty-obsessed there's no way he'd be playing hooky. I caught his scent, so he must be here. Unless I was imagining things? Or maybe he caught a whiff of me too and ran. But no, that doesn't make any sense. If he invited me that means he wants to see me, doesn't it?

I've been so caught up in my mental paralysis I haven't moved more than two feet into the room.

"Come on," Katie says, eyeing a server in a black waistcoat across the room. "I'm starving."

She takes off and I follow, knowing I'd probably barf if I tried to eat anything right now but not knowing what else to do. We slide between clusters of party guests in expensive suits and extravagant *couture*—a word I learned from Katie on the drive over. As we make our way round the room's perimeter I keep my eye out for any familiar faces, but so far it's just faceless rich people. Still no sight of him.

"Damn, where'd she go?" Katie says, stopping short. "She must have moved on."

"There," I say, spotting the server weaving through the crowd.

Katie ducks between two women in pastel gowns and I take a step to follow her but run into a woman as she steps into my path.

"I'm so sorry!" I splutter, stepping back.

"It's fine," Olivia says, looking up and adjusting the strap of her dress which has slipped off her muscular shoulder. Surprise flashes across her face, then something cooler. "Oh, you."

"Hey Olivia! Sorry, I didn't see you there."

"It's fine," she grumbles, scowling before taking off without so much as a glance back.

"Okay, Frosty the Snow-Woman, that was weird."

I stare after Olivia, feeling like roadkill. We were never exactly close but I always thought she found me sort of amusing. Why the cold shoulder now?

Turning back, I've lost Katie in the sea of Armani, Dolce, and hors d'oeuvres. I take a few steps, trying to get a better view of the other side of the room, and as I do every hair on my body stands to attention. My lungs stop working and inexplicable tears spring to my eyes. My feet are stuck in place like someone crazy-glued them to the floor.

My eyes dart back and forth, seeking the source of my discomfort. But all I find are unfamiliar faces, bow ties, sequins, jewelry, cuff links—all swirling in a sea of tuxedos and chiffon. And then by some sort of miracle the sea parts. Like clouds rolling away to reveal a full moon, the crowd disperses, creating a path through which I can see all the way across the universe.

And there standing next to a Christmas tree, in a perfectly fitted tux, with his night-black hair slicked back and a knowing, adorable smirk on his face...is Jasper.

A NIGHT AT THE PLAZA

He's here.

My senses are alive. Multicolored fractals of light are swimming around the edges of my vision. My skin is tingling, my hands trembling. I have to bite my bottom lip to keep it from quivering off my face.

Jasper.

I haven't seen him in months and he... He looks *good*. He has one hand casually dipped into the pocket of his suit pants and the other he runs through his hair. My eyes focus in on all the small details I remember—the pale Milky Way of freckles across his nose, those peach-colored lips, the emerald green of his eyes. Has he somehow become more handsome? Is that even freaking possible?

Someone nudges me as they pass but I don't register it. I stand in the swirling crowd of fancily dressed people and stare. I've been waiting for this moment for months and now it's finally here. All of the things that were left unsaid are about to come out, if only I can make myself move. Just one foot.

But I can't. Even though my body is urging me forward, propelling me on a cellular level, I can't walk just yet. Maybe I'm in shock, my poor little body unable to cope with the adrenaline flooding my system. All I know is that every cliché is true and happening all at the same time. My heart is about to burst out of me, my stomach is stuck in my throat. I wouldn't be surprised if tiny love hearts were floating in circles around my head.

Why am I waiting?

He invited me here. He wants to speak to me—*finally,* after all this time!

I take a step and as I do the crowd parts a little farther. I stop in my tracks.

Suddenly I can see who Jasper is talking to—the person he's grinning at, leaning into, angling his body toward. It's a guy I've never seen before, and oh boy, would I remember if I had. This guy looks like a goddamn Grecian statue. His blond hair is perfectly quaffed with exactly the right amount of curl. His skin is tanned like he's just come back from summering in the Mediterranean. He's talking, smiling, probably regaling Jasper with some hilarious story from his most recent trip to the Cape.

My feet are once again stuck in cement, unable to move. My heart is no longer bursting out of my chest; now it's burning.

Who is this guy? Why does Jasper look so relaxed around him, like he's enjoying himself? Involuntarily, a low growl rises in my throat and my lips pull back ever so slightly. My fingers curl and my claws press into my palms.

Jasper stops smiling. His nostrils flare. He turns to look at me and the expression on his face is devastating.

His eyes are wide with shock, his mouth a displeased sneer. His brows arch in a way that makes it clear he wasn't expecting to see me. The truth lands on me like a grand piano falling from the sky.

Jasper didn't invite me.

His friend glances in my direction, curious as to what's drawn Jasper's attention, but he looks straight through me as if I'm not even there.

Before Jasper can turn from me, resume his conversation like I don't exist, I run.

I push through the hectic ballroom, making for the exit.

"Excuse me!" a woman says as I nudge past and burst through the ballroom doors.

I don't turn back or say excuse me. I can't right now. All I want is to be outside in the cold December air—to tear off this dumb bow tie and forget I ever came to this stupid party.

"Whoa! Dude, is there a fire or something?"

Aisha catches me by the shoulders before I can make my escape.

"Where are you heading?"

I glare at her sideways and immediately she can tell something is wrong.

"What did he do?"

My jaw trembles.

She looks around and gently guides me toward a glass-paneled door. On the other side, a restaurant is bustling with the overflow from the main ballroom. Lush palms surround an oval-shaped bar, which Aisha ushers me along, finding us a seat beneath a couple of large fronds.

"Here, sit down," she says.

I press my back into the chair and realize I'm shivering, like it's below freezing, even though the heating here is pumped all the way to eleven.

"Something to drink?" a waiter asks, swanning up to the table.

"You got champagne?" Aisha asks coolly. "We'll take two." The guy doesn't even blink before nodding and floating away. "They're never going to card two people looking as fine as us," she says. "Don't tell anyone I'm a bad influence, okay? I just thought we could use a drink."

When the waiter returns, sliding two tall bubbling glasses in front of us, Aisha takes a sip, exhales, and asks, "So what's he done this time?"

"He... He didn't do anything. I didn't even speak to him."

"So what's got you all spooked?"

"He didn't invite me."

"How do you know that if you didn't speak to him?"

"Because he looked at me like—like I was the last person in the world he wanted to see."

I'm either about to burst into tears or crumble into a million pieces, so instead I grab the champagne, gripping the glass like I'm King Kong, and down it in one gulp.

"Oh, honey." Aisha wraps a comforting hand around my wrist. "I'm sorry."

I hiccup but try to hide it with a grunt.

"Hold up—who did invite you then?"

I shrug. "No idea."

"Weird." She takes another sip. "So you came all this way, got all dressed up, and you were about to leave without giving Jasper a piece of your mind? After all this time?"

I slouch over the table and rest my head on my hands. "What's the point?"

"The point is you're a person in this too. Why is it always on Jasper's terms?"

I can't answer, so instead I turn my face away and stare at this weird little stain in the carpet.

"Don't try to freeze me out. You know who freezes people out?" Aisha asks. "Jasper, that's who."

I jerk backward, spinning my head and shooting Aisha the most incredulous open-mouthed look of disgust I can.

"Talk to me," she says.

With my eyes closed, I breathe in through my nose, and then I say it: "He was with another guy."

Aisha scrunches up her face.

"Uh-uh, nope. Not on my watch. Come on." Aisha stands, downing the rest of her drink; she pulls me to my feet and marches us toward the ballroom.

Like a stampede of rhinos, we explode through the doors, huffing and sweating. The crowd seems even livelier than before, while I'm starting to feel more and more frazzled.

"Can you see him?" Aisha asks.

I scan the room. "Nope." Then my eyes catch on a tuft of wavy blond hair. "But there's his friend."

Jasper is nowhere to be seen, but his blond Shawn Mendes look-alike friend is chatting with two girls in backless dresses over by a drinks table. Aisha takes two steps forward and stops. Her shoulders drop.

"*Him*? You don't have to worry about him." I should be relieved, but Aisha's icy tone makes me think I maybe *should* worry about him, just not for the reason I was thinking.

"Who is he?"

"His name is Clayton Bridgers. He went to boarding school with Jasper and me. But Jasper and him have been friends since they were pups. His father is Walter Bridgers, the pack's financial adviser."

"I've heard of him."

Of course I've heard of him. After the pack's defense forces—which are headed up by Olivia's father, Beta Salazar Castillo—the treasury is the next most important pack institution. The Bridgerses have been in charge of the pack's finances for centuries. Some people think they're even more wealthy than the Apollos.

"The Bridgerses and the Apollos go waaaaay back," Aisha says, glassy-eyed. "Jasper and Clayton's friendship was basically written in the stars."

"If you all went to boarding school together, are you friends with him too?"

Aisha scoffs and shakes her head.

"Sometimes Jasper can act like a pompous, privileged ass, but Clayton, he's the prince of entitlement. The very definition of a rich, white, privileged asswipe."

Aisha really doesn't like this guy, which kind of makes my cheeks warm. "He looks it too."

"Anyway, you don't have to worry about him and Jasper. Clayton is as straight as they come."

A lump lodges in my throat and I struggle to swallow it down. That word she used—*straight*—as if implying I'm the opposite, the other thing—the thing I can't even say out loud.

"Max!" I turn at the excited, high-pitched sound of my name and find Jodie running at me, arms wide, teeth showing in this big grin. "You came!"

Jasper's little sister wraps my waist in a tight hug, which I return awkwardly. Coming up behind her are Melissa and Alpha Jericho, with a trail of security guards in their wake.

"Of course I came," I say. "Wait how did you know I—"

"I invited you, stupid," Jodie says, swishing her hips from side to side. She's wearing a green gown and looks about a foot taller than when I last saw her. "I wanted to see you."

"Jodie was very insistent that you be her allocated guest," Melissa says, sounding a little annoyed about it, like she was hoping Jodie might invite someone her own age and give Melissa a night off.

"Wow!" My face is suddenly the temperature of the sun, and I just know I'm the color of a fire engine. I can't help rubbing the back of my neck. "Thank you."

Jodie gestures for me to come closer, so she can whisper in my ear. I lean down and she cups her little hand around her mouth and leans in.

"He misses you."

I start up in an instant and almost choke as I meet eyes with the alpha. Jericho has come to join our little reunion, and he doesn't look too pleased.

"Maximilian," he thunders, his deep bass drowning out the strings.

"Sir," I say, half bowing, half curtsying, and wholly losing it.

"Aisha, it's good to see you," he says.

"Good evening, Alpha," she responds respectfully.

The alpha nods before turning his steel glare back in my direction.

"A word, Max."

"You want...a word...with me?" I hold a finger pointed at my own chest, searching the faces of Melissa, Aisha—hell, even Jodie—for an explanation, pleading for an escape plan. "Uh, sure."

"I'll catch you later, Max" Jodie says.

"Good luck," Aisha says quietly into my ear as she turns her attention to Jodie: "And how have you been, Squishface?"

Casually, as if they haven't left me alone with the most powerful wolf on the East Coast, the three of them saunter away.

"Oh and Max," Jodie says, turning back, calling across the room. Don't be a bonehead."

She and Aisha can't help giggling as they make their way to a table.

"So, Max," Jericho says, commanding my complete and undivided attention, "you've disappointed me."

Gulp!

"I have? I'm—I'm sorry. I'm really sorry. I'll...wait what?"

"I told you that being mated to my son would be difficult. I thought you might have what it takes. It seems I was wrong."

"What? Sir, he... I... That doesn't seem fair."

Jericho is so tall I'm worried my neck might snap from staring up at him. What is he talking about? Jasper is the one who's been avoiding me. What am I supposed to do with that?!

"Being mated to an alpha is a challenging prospect; I had hoped you were up to the challenge." His voice is so mesmerizing I find myself swaying on the spot, staring into his striking gray eyes. "You came through for us when the rogues attacked, and I thought that showed gumption, a sort of"—he waves a large hand around in the air, searching for the right word—"stick-to-itiveness."

Is that even a real word? I have no idea, but coming from the alpha's mouth I'd believe just about anything.

"Maybe I was wrong."

"I... I..." My mouth is open but my mind is in such a frenzy I can't pick which sentence to begin or which word to start with.

"I haven't given up faith in you completely, however," Jericho continues, and I feel something like relief, although it's possible I've just wet myself. "Later tonight I'll be making an announcement. I want you to pay close attention."

"Yes, sir. I will," I squeak.

"Don't disappoint me, Max." Jericho places his mammoth hand on my shoulder, and I almost collapse under the weight. He holds my collarbone firmly and I know not to take his words lightly.

"I'll try not to."

He snickers lowly. "Good boy."

Frozen in place, I wait for Jericho and his remaining security detail to leave.

I have no idea what just happened. All I know is I've been left feeling like a domesticated dog—and that somehow, Alpha Jericho is shipping me and Jasper big-time.

Needing to offload and decompress, I spin around in search of a friendly face. I know there are at least two in here somewhere. People are dancing and it's hard to make out anyone through all the festive cheer and expensive perfume, but I spot Katie under a giant red bow and hurry over. She's leaning against the wall with her arms crossed, and as I get closer I spot why.

Todd and Simon are having a heated discussion—probably about who gets to dance with Katie first, or who she's going to sit next to later when they serve the food. Simon's shirt is half untucked and Todd's bow tie is undone, which makes me wonder if they haven't already gotten into a fight. I guess Katie went looking for a snack and got a whole meal.

Katie notices me and gives me this pleading "Come save me" look, so I square my shoulders and am about to head over when—

"Max."

His voice hits me like an arrow. My spine straightens, my neck elongates, my fingers tense. Hell! Every muscle in my body tenses. Blood begins to thud through every limb, every artery, every—okay, let's just say the blood is pumping to all the places blood pumps.

"Jasper?"

I turn around and he's just a few feet away. He's closer than he's been in months. And yet he still isn't close enough. His scent hits me and I'm suddenly thirsty for a cherry soda.

I take a step and he backs up like I'm contagious.

"Not here," he says, then turns on his heel and marches away.

Without missing a beat, I follow.

THE ALPHA'S CHALLENGE

This can't be Jasper's first time at the Plaza. From the way he navigates the confusing labyrinth of halls, pushing through doors like he knows exactly where he's going, like he owns the place, it's obvious he's a regular.

I follow like a cartoon dog who's caught the delicious whiff of a freshly baked pie. I don't even question why we're headed away from the party, away from prying eyes, from the world he doesn't want to be seen by, not with me.

We eventually reach a door with a sign reading *Private*, and Jasper, without a moment of hesitation, pushes through. I step into a small dim hallway. It's not fancy like the rest of the place. There's no cream wallpaper and lush carpet. The walls are gray concrete, the floor a checkered linoleum. The stark fluorescent lighting makes me squint.

"I don't think we're supposed to be back here," I say, but Jasper isn't facing me; he's bowing his head, rubbing his eyes with his thumb and forefinger.

"You're not supposed to be here at all," he says.

My jaw tenses and my teeth grind audibly. After months of radio silence, after everything we went through in the summer, after seeing me here dressed up like a freaking Christmas tree, he's still pushing me away. Any hopeful anticipation I may have been holding onto drops away. All that nervous excitement seeps out of me, leaving me heavy and flat.

"Is that all you can say?" I ask. "Is that all you can ever say?"

He turns and closes the distance between us in a flash, anger flaring his nostrils and creasing his brow.

"I'm trying to protect you," he says through gritted teeth. "It isn't safe here. Not here and not with me."

"Is that why you brought me back here?" I ask. "So no one would see us together."

He sighs and runs a frustrated hand through his shiny hair. His face is redder than I'm used to seeing it; tiny beads of sweat are gathered on his forehead.

"It's better this way."

"For who? You or me, Jasper?"

His piercing eyes bore into mine. "For us both."

"This is bullshit!" I explode. "Why don't I get a say in this?"

"Because this isn't a committee."

"So you're just gonna ignore me forever, act like you don't see the texts and the calls?"

"Yes," he says, "and the mugs."

Oh god.

"Okay the mugs were a step too far. But my point is still valid."

"No, Max." Jasper takes another step forward and I breathe him in. Jasper keeps tensing his abnormally square jaw. "It can't happen."

Frustration courses through me. We're going in circles on this demented merry-go-round and I'm not even sure I bought a ticket.

"The only reason it can't happen is because of you," I say, lowering my gaze and trying not to mumble too much. "Eleanor is locked up; we're safe. You say you want to protect me but what are you even trying to protect me from?"

"She's not the only one. There are other people out there who want to hurt me and the people I"—he catches himself, changes track—"the people close to me. Tensions are high in the pack, our position is vulnerable. Not to mention the threat of rogues, Eleanor's father out there somewhere." He takes another step toward me, and I can feel the warmth of his breath on my cheek. "I meant it when I said I don't want to lose you. This is the only way I know how."

Somehow we've drifted so close his face is out of focus. My eyes dart to his lips, the glimpse of straight white teeth behind them, his tongue. I reach out and grab him, pull him to me and plant my lips on his. Our chests collide and relief surges through me. It's very possible I may black out here and now. For a second Jasper is putty in my hands, but very quickly he tenses and shoves me away from him, hard.

He wipes his lips with the back of his hand.

"I'm doing this for you," he says.

"Are you? Because you looked pretty happy back there with Clayton."

Jasper shakes his head like there's a fly pestering him. "What's that supposed to mean?"

The door swings open and guess which blond-haired, privileged asswipe pokes his head in?

"Hey, I heard a commotion. Everything all right, Jasp?"

He surveys the staff hallway and raises a judgmental eyebrow.

"What are you doing back here with the staff anyway? Is this guy bothering you? Hey dude"—he turns to me—"I think we're running low on quail eggs so you might want to run off to the kitchen, let someone know. Kay, bud?"

Jasper steps forward. "Clayton, he's not—"

"Don't bother," I say, pushing past them both.

"Whoa, rude!" Clayton says. "You know we're friends with the owner, right?"

Ignoring him completely, I traipse back through the halls of the Plaza. This whole night has been a colossal fuckup. And after that little interaction I know why. I don't belong here with these people.

I should just leave, but as I pass by the doors of the ballroom the alpha's voice catches my attention. Something he said earlier reverberates in my head. *An announcement, pay close attention.* Maybe it's curiosity or some kind of hold the alpha has over his pack, but as much as I'd like to run screaming into the night, I make my way back into the ballroom.

The room is quiet except for the alpha's voice, booming unnecessarily from a sound system. "Thank you for gracing this ballroom with your magnificent presence," he says. "And thank you to the Plaza for hosting us this evening."

A small round of applause rises from the audience.

I can't see Katie or Aisha, or a spare seat anywhere, so I find a column to lean on and listen. The door behind me swings open, allowing Jasper and Clayton to slip inside. I catch Jasper's eye, but huff and turn my attention back to his father.

"For those of you paying close attention to your lunar calendars," Jericho continues, "you'll be aware of an auspicious lunar occurrence due to herald in the New

Year." He pauses for dramatic effect. "A blood moon is on the horizon, due to rise two days after Christmas." Hold for chorus of oohs and aahs.

A blood moon. They don't come along that often—less often than a blue moon as far as I know. Although, apart from glowing this spooky shade of red, there's nothing that exciting about them. Of course, being wolves we have superstitions about every lunar event. It's all childish nonsense, but people go wild for it.

"My good friend Alpha Morven Labraid from the Rocky Pack has invited a select group of Elite wolves to join them in their mountain-lodge packhouse for the event. These fortunate wolves will be treated to all the skiing, mountaineering, and hot chocolate the Rocky Pack has to offer. Then as Christmas draws to a close, they will make the journey to the stone circle of Wolf Point, the highest peak in the Rocky Pack's territory, where they will be privy to what is sure to be an amazing view of the blood moon."

Excited whispers zip through the room.

"My son Jasper will be my official representative on this trip."

I glance back at Jasper, who is tensing his jaw.

"And while I'm certain interest in this event will be unprecedented, sadly the Rocky Pack only has the space to accommodate three more wolves and their mates. To determine who will take the other six spots, I have decided to host a competition. To win a spot on this trip I am laying down a *challenge*."

Jericho's eyes land on me when he says that last word, as if it's meant just for me. Is this the challenge he mentioned earlier?

"Ladies and Gentlewolves, a competition of this nature has yet to be held in this century... To decide who is worthy of a spot in my envoy, I will be holding a race of fire and ice!"

Hands clutch pearls. Every mouth in the room falls open. A couple of women gasp audibly.

The race of fire and ice is an old-school Elite Pack tradition—so old-school there hasn't been one since Jericho took over from his father. It's extremely dangerous; people have died competing. And I, like most people in the room it seems, thought it was a thing of the past, a barbaric ritual we all pretend was discontinued long ago, a relic of a less evolved pack. For an alpha whose authority is being questioned, this is a strange move.

But what's even stranger is Jericho seemingly hinting that I should take part. Does he really think the scrawny pup from Stony Point stands a chance? Is this some dumb hazing ritual for me to prove I'm strong enough to be with Jasper? Couldn't his challenge have been something I'm good at, like cake eating or binge-watching TV?

"If you wish to compete please register your interest with Tobias Volk, who is present here tonight. You will receive instructions in the mail, and for those who simply wish to observe, the race shall be held in a week's time at Lunar Lake. Now I have spoken enough. Please enjoy tonight's festivities. And Merry Christmas to you all!"

There's a smattering of applause but mostly the room is too confused, too shocked to notice the alpha as he leaves the stage. Music chimes back in and eventually the excited murmur of the crowd returns to normal.

What is Jericho thinking? There's no way I'm competing in that death race. Not even for…

I twist my head and glance behind me. Jasper is still there. Clayton is talking excitedly beside him, but Jasper is saying nothing, he's just staring back at me. My ear twitches and I'm able to catch a little of what Clayton is saying.

"Well I suppose that answers the question of where I'll be staying for the holidays. How about it, Jasp? I don't imagine it will be too hard to win a spot and we can see in the new year with champagne and a hot tub full of Rocky Pack wolves." Jasper's expression is a mix of desperation, sheer determination, and a little pinch of queasiness. "Doesn't sound too shabby? Jasp? Jasper?"

Jasper's attention falters and he shakes his head.

"What?"

"Is some she-wolf's scent distracting you. I said it won't be too shabby, the hot tubs and the mountain girls."

I know Aisha said that Clayton is straight but even the thought of him hanging out with Jasper at Christmas, them drinking hot cocoa together, sitting in a hot tub, their shoulders bumping against each other, has my fangs ready to elongate and tear into his flesh.

Spinning on my heel without thinking, I head off in search of Tobias. If I wasn't in a jealous tailspin there's no way I'd be looking for the pack secretary, wanting to sign up for a suicide race. Sure it helps that my alpha has all but commanded me to, but part of me wants to stick it to Jasper too, to show him that I'm not so easily ignored. If I win then he'll be forced to spend time with me.

I'm halfway across the room when a cold, steel grip clasps my wrist and I freeze.

"Don't, Max"

I keep looking ahead. Party guests stream around us, oblivious to the electricity sparking where our skin is touching.

"How do you even know what I'm doing?" I ask.

"Because...I can sense you."

I turn and face him.

"Have you been sensing me this whole time?" Annoying tears spring to my eyes.

"I have."

"You're keeping tabs on me."

"Yes." His hair hangs over his eyes which won't meet mine. "To make sure you're safe."

"If I'm not safe away from you then why keep me at a distance?"

Jasper's mouth contorts, his lips press together, his neck muscles pulse. Is he shivering?

I step closer. The crowd presses in around us. No one can see when I link my index finger around his thumb.

"Isn't the safest place I could be right here with you?"

"Max, you know I want that; you have no idea how much I—"

Some couple who think they're Fred and Ginger bump into us before spinning away. Jasper retracts his hand, shoving it in his pocket.

"Your dad said the wolves who get to go to this blood moon thing can take their mates. Take me. Then I won't have to race."

"I can't," he mumbles too low for human ears to hear.

"Then I don't have a choice."

I turn and push my way through the crowd. I don't even know what I'm doing when I find Tobias Volk standing at the bar.

"Hi," I say, interrupting his conversation. "I volunteer as tribute."

"Pardon?" He stares at me with a puzzled brow.

"I want to race. Sign me up."

HOT AND COLD

"WHAT?!" Mom shouts at me from my bedroom door.

"I told you I signed up for the Race of Fire and Ice," I say from where I'm sitting on my bed, sketchbook in hand.

"But you—you don't even like sports!"

Mom's face is more flushed than that time I thought it would be a great idea to repaint the living room using peanut butter when I was five.

I dig my toes deeper into my comforter and press my head back against the wall.

"Max, what is going on?"

Honestly, I can't even think of a good lie right now. She's totally right. The most interest I've shown in competitive sports was the last Olympics when that cute British diver won gold and, thinking back, that was probably more about how he looked in a Speedo than the actual diving. Plus, no one knows better than Mom how little stock I put in the importance of lunar events—or did, until the last one turned my life completely on its head. She's waiting for an answer and all I can offer is a halfhearted shrug.

She sighs in frustration and lets her head droop forward for a moment.

"Fine," she says eventually. "You're a teenager, I get it. You need your space. But that doesn't mean I'm going to let you go running off to get injured in some death sport."

I lean forward and drop my sketchbook. "Mom!"

"No, Max! This isn't a discussion. You're grounded until after the race."

"You don't understand."

"No I don't, but I've tried to."

There's just a hint of a wild sort of anguish in the corners of Mom's eyes as she grabs the handle of my door and slams it shut.

Why can't I just speak to her when it would solve so many problems?

I grab my phone and text Katie.

Mom grounded me so I can't race.

Immediately, my phone begins to ring.

"What?!" Katie bellows when I answer. "Oh Max, I'm sorry. I know you had your heart set on it."

Something about her tone tells me she isn't so disappointed.

"Why do you sound kind of relieved?"

There's a weird staticky pause. "Look, I know why you signed up, but I wasn't exactly bowled over at the idea of my best friend being flash frozen."

I laugh. "Okay, understandable. It's just...it feels like everyone is obsessed with my safety right now."

Another pause.

"What?" I ask.

"It just means people care about you," Katie says offhandedly.

"But there has to be more to it than that."

"Well..."

"Spit it out."

"First just let me say that I am 100 percent the biggest supporter of your pursuit of Jasper. I am after all a member of the OGJA Alliance."

"You're the treasurer," I giggle.

"And you know all I want is for you to be happy, but ever since you met him you've been sort of unpredictable."

I curl my legs a little bit farther beneath me. "More than usual?"

"Kinda."

We sit quietly for a moment, just knowing the other is still there on the other end of the line.

"And some of the decisions you've made lately," Katie continues hesitantly, "I'm not sure they've been the most thought-out."

"Like what?"

"Like signing up for a sporting event with a 36 percent death rate," she retorts. "I'm not saying you can't be impulsive or spontaneous, and I know I've been right there by your side trying to get Jasper's attention, but sometimes I worry you're not using your best judgment. And I don't want you to get hurt."

"I thought people were supposed to do stupid things when they're in love."

"Maybe, but it's a big difference from the person you used to be."

"You used to organize your My Little Ponies alphabetically, and now you have two boyfriends."

"I'm not saying people can't change—I know I have. Just make sure you're changing for the better."

Katie's breaths are gentle and constant; I know she's waiting for me to say something, but I can't think of anything. And that never happens with her.

"I've gotta go," I say.

"Max, I—"

I hang up and toss my phone onto the laundry pile across the room.

The night of the race I do something I've never done before in my life: I sneak out.

Mom and Dad are downstairs watching TV and I tell them I've got homework before heading to my room. I quickly get changed into my winter running gear and open my window. This isn't like what you see on TV. There's no conveniently placed drainpipe or tree. Just a ten-foot drop onto icy grass.

I land with a heavy thud, hitting my shoulder hard against the soil, but luckily my wolf strength keeps me from breaking anything. Risking a quick glance behind me to make sure I haven't been spotted, I take off into the trees.

Aisha was reluctant but I managed to convince her to pick me up. She's parked a little ways down our street so my parents don't see her headlights. When I emerge from the bank of trees lining the road, I spot her car idling nearby.

"Hey," I say, sliding into the passenger seat.

"Hi." She eyes me curiously, and when I don't respond she huffs and puts the car into gear.

"You sure about this, kid?" she asks once we've been driving for a while.

"Ahuh," I say, trying to convince myself as much as her.

"You don't have to do this, you know? He's just a guy—he's not worth hurting yourself over."

I try and muster my most convincing tone. "I'm sure."

"Okay."

She sighs and indicates that she's turning. We head off down a narrow, poorly lit stretch of road, trees pushing in on either side. Lights become visible between a narrow gap at the far end of the trail. Lights we're heading toward.

Finally, we emerge into a gravel parking lot. Enormous trees loom all around, fire pits burn by the entrance to a path, casting long shadows. We pull into a spot, and before I can jump out Aisha grabs my wrist.

"I'm only going to ask this one more time: are you sure this is what you want?"

I pause, stare at the gear stick, and try to gather my thoughts. This is sort of reckless, more reckless than normal. Is Katie right? Have I become unpredictable? Am I putting myself in danger for a guy?

Maybe. But there's so much else at play here. There's Jericho for one, who all but commanded me to take part. There's the way Jasper wouldn't look at me as I linked my finger around his. He said he wanted me—he actually said it. And that's all the motivation I need.

"I'm sure," I say.

"Okay." Aisha nods solemnly. "I'll be cheering for you."

There's a path through the woods lit by flaming torches and Aisha stays half a step behind me as we make our way. I keep my shoulders as square as I can and don't look back at her. I know what I'm doing and I don't need any of her doubt creeping into my mind.

There are other wolves making their way through the trees, but it isn't until we emerge on the banks of the river that I realize how many people are here. The lake itself is frozen over, flat and white like a salt plain, only disturbed by a tortoise-back-shaped island a few miles from the shore. On either side of us, the riverbank is flooded with wolves wrapped up in winter coats, crammed together like the crowds at a festival, staring out at the frozen arena.

"Ladies and Gentlewolves!" Tobias Volk's voice rises over the crowd, amplified through the speakers I've only just noticed are stationed every hundred feet or so down the shore. "Could all competitors make their way to the starting line."

"That's me, I guess," I say, rubbing the back of my neck.

"May the Moon Gods light your path, dude." Aisha pulls me in for a hug and squeezes harder than I'm prepared for.

"I'm going to be fine." I'm trying to sound convinced but I'm starting to shiver a little.

"I know you are."

Pulling my coat a little tighter, I leave Aisha and push my way down toward the river's icy edge. Off to the left a rickety pier extends out over the ice, and a crowd of race-ready wolves have gathered at the far end. I grit my teeth and head toward them.

Jericho is there next to Tobias, who is twirling his expansive moustache. There're a few kids I don't recognize. And I almost turn back when Clayton spins toward me, his golden curls swooshing perfectly in slow motion. But his gaze never lands on me; instead he waves to someone coming up behind me. I glance back just in time for Olivia, waving in return, to pass, knocking her shoulder into mine.

"Ow!"

She stops and raises a brow in my direction. "Sorry." Only she doesn't sound very sorry, at least not about running into me. With a shrug she takes off again.

On either side of the pier the frozen river lies motionless, the surface hard and unforgiving. A series of black dots make a trail across the river, leading toward the island. Those must be the marker points. I've never seen a Race of Fire and Ice before and all I know is that it involves lighting a series of braziers and traversing a frozen landscape. So I guess we'll be running across the lake—the one that looks hard enough to break a bone or two if you fall.

"Hey bro!" Todd calls from up ahead. He and Simon are among the crowd of competitors. Todd is waving, Simon is staring at me with a confused expression, like I've wandered somewhere I don't belong.

"Hey guys," I say as I reach them, trying not to let my teeth chatter too much.

"You're competing?" Simon asks.

"Uh, yeah."

He nods incredulously. "More power to you, bruh"

Todd slaps me on the back so hard I nearly choke. "You'll be fine."

"Yeah, why wouldn't I be?"

"I dunno, man," Simon says, shrugging and twisting his mouth. "Maybe because we're about to race against some of the strongest wolves in the pack across an icy tundra that could crack and swallow us up at any moment."

"You can always back out," Todd says to Simon, slapping him on the chest.

"And let you take Katie to the lodge without me? Not a chance, my man, not a chance."

I force myself to laugh as my bro-y friends continue gibing each other. Then my gaze returns to the frozen river, all the way to the island. It's a gray blur from this distance. All I want is to be back at home, curled up in my covers, reading a cozy graphic novel about high school sweethearts. The last thing I want is to be out there with a bunch of roided-up wolves. I turn my attention to my fellow competitors. Other than Olivia and Clayton—definitely tough to beat—and Todd and Simon, there are about fifty wolves stretching and hopping from foot to foot on the deck. One dick is doing push-ups. Everyone's expression is a different shade of nervous or determined.

And then our eyes meet. Jasper is standing at the far end of the pier. Even in this cold weather he looks chic as hell, in a fitted black peacoat, a gray scarf, and leather gloves. Neither of us move toward the other. His stare is cold and accusing as always, but there's a hint of sadness tugging at the corners of his mouth, as if he's resigned to some undesirable fate. Once again someone is acting as if the race is lost before it's even begun.

Everyone is assuming I'm going to lose, that I'm not even going to finish this dumb race. I huff and tense my jaw. I'll show them. I'll prove to all of them I have more strength than they know. And I'll show Jasper just how determined I can be.

"All right competitors," Tobias hollers, "we will begin the race shortly. Once you've all shifted into your wolf forms, I will ask you to take hold of a torch."

A spark ignites behind Tobias as his helpers light a series of torches that have been jabbed into the ice so they stand upright.

"Each wolf will carry a flame of a different color. You need to carry this flame for the entirety of the race. If your fire is extinguished, you are disqualified. If you are the first to reach a marker point, light the brazier. It will burn the same color you have been assigned, denoting you as the leader of the pack. Be prepared for some surprising twists and turns in the journey. Once you reach the island it will be a scramble to the center, where a large bonfire sits waiting to be lit. The first person to light the bonfire is the winner."

Jericho takes an attention-grabbing step forward.

"As you know," he booms, his voice echoing across the lake, "the first three to reach the island will join my emissary to the Rocky Pack, along with their mates. They will join Alpha Morven as he travels to Wolf Point to experience the blood moon. This is a sacred experience and one not many from our pack will have the opportunity to see. Race with that thought in your heart. For most of you this is a once-in-a-lifetime opportunity. For some"—he narrows his eyes at me—"this could be a critical turning point in your lives. Race as if your lives depend on it."

"What if the ice cracks?" a particularly shivery guy asks.

"The ice is the thickest it's been all winter," Jericho responds. "My people have checked the lake and deemed it safe. I know in the past there have been casualties during this race. I assure you that will not be the case tonight."

For some racers this is comforting, but I've been doing such a good job not thinking about my impending doom, hearing about it now is less than reassuring.

"Racers, we will begin momentarily," Tobias chimes back in. "Once you've swapped your clothes for one of the robes provided by the team, please make your way to the ice. There I will ask you to shift and choose your torch."

We all begin shuffling toward the race organizers, who have matching jackets with the alpha's insignia printed on them.

I completely forgot we'd be shifting to race. Getting undressed is probably my least favorite thing about wolf culture. Some of the guys have already whipped off their shirts and are pulling the robes on. A couple of the girls have draped their robes over their shoulders and are getting undressed while trying to stay covered. If I don't get a robe now, I'll still be undressing when the race starts.

Nudging my way through the cramped pier I make my way to the end. Jasper stands off to the side, his gaze low but unmistakably pointed in my direction. I snatch a robe and turn around, looking for a place to change.

Holding the robe between my knees, I take a deep breath and unzip my jacket. The race team are wandering by with large baskets, and one stops so I can throw my clothes into it. I drop the jacket and, bracing for the cold, pull my T-shirt and sweater off with the same movement. Icy wind hits my chest and stomach instantly as I drop my clothes into the basket.

For a second I wonder if Jasper is still staring at me. Does he like what he sees? What does he think of his pale, skinny mate? Desperate for warmth, I pull the robe around me tightly. I kick off my shoes and struggle not to topple off the pier as I manage to remove my pants without exposing myself.

The other racers are in line waiting to climb down the ladder to the ice. I'm turning to join the queue when Jasper appears at my side.

"Don't do this," he mutters.

Not now, Jasper. I need to focus. I need to get my head in the game.

"Max, listen." He pulls on my arm, and I twist away from him.

"No, Jasper." A harsh whisper. "I'm doing this."

"Nothing will be different. At the Rocky Pack, nothing is going to change."

I meet his gaze.

"We'll see about that."

I turn and follow the last of the competitors down the ladder. The ice burns the soles of my feet it's so cold. It's hard but slippery. *I hope my claws are sharp enough to get some traction!*

Everyone is already standing behind a torch, each burning in a brilliant shade. Green and orange and violet and purple and every vibrant color you can imagine. There's only one spare place—the smallest of the torches, burning less bright than the others, this trippy shade of black and gray when it flickers, that's just barely visible in the dark.

Will that thing even have enough gas to get to the end?

It doesn't matter. It's the only option left so I take my place. Tobias shuffles into line with the torches, clearly less stable on the ice than he'd like us to believe. Jasper's presence is a cold shadow on my back.

"On my command you may shift," Tobias calls, "and the race will begin."

To my left Olivia is poised, one leg in front of the other, ready to pounce. Beside her, Clayton is readying himself, a smug grin on his chiseled face.

Directly to my right Todd and Simon are jostling each other, trying to put the other off. *Do they ever stop?*

All the other racers are staring forward, eyes on the prize.

I close my eyes, take a breath, and picture my goal. Jasper's face rises in my mind and at once I'm focused. I want to prove to him I'm not so easily pushed aside—that he can't control me. When I open my eyes, all I can see is the torch in front of me and the path out onto the ice.

Tobias, holding a mint-green handkerchief, lifts his hand into the air.

"Racers!" he cries. "On your mark, get set...go!"

FIRE AND ICE

We leap into action—fifty-odd wolves drop their robes, rise into the air, and shift in unison.

Bones snap. Muscles tear. Teeth become fangs. Fingers become claws.

The ice creaks as we all land, digging our nails into the surface.

I take a second to adjust to my wolf form. It's been a while and my senses need a moment to catch up. There are already wolves clutching their torches in their jaws and tearing them from the ice. Clayton's golden-coated wolf takes an early lead, heading out onto the lake. Fluorescent colors float around me. The scents of the other wolves and the overpowering smell of Jasper behind me spin my mind in circles. My wolf's instinct is to turn and pounce on him. But I take command, overriding my natural impulse.

I'm already behind; the other wolves have run on ahead. Was this a mistake? The others are stronger, faster, more accustomed to shifting. My legs are quivering.

"What are you doing?" I hear Jasper call from behind and twist my muzzle so I can see him. "Run, Bonehead!"

With a snarl, I clasp my fangs around the base of my torch and tug it free. Then I'm off. It takes another moment to get my bearings on the ice. Even with my claws it's more slippery than I anticipated. But once I've found a technique that works, landing on the tips of my paws and digging in, propelling myself forward, I'm off.

My wolf lungs fill with cool, frostbitten air, my nostrils flare, and I swear I can smell every atom floating by. Each wolf out on the ice has a different scent and, being at the rear of the pack, I'm battered by them all as I run.

Up ahead the first marker point erupts into brilliant yellow flames and the crowd behind me roars. The speakers blare and Tobias's voice reverberates in my ears. "Clayton Bridgers has lit the first of the braziers!"

Not him!

Determination floods my veins and I pick up speed. My legs stretch and push as I fly forward. My superspeed kicking in. I had thought it was a blue-moon-specific trait, but it seems anytime Jasper is involved, my physical prowess increases. I make a mental note to do some research on the subject when this is over—depending on whether or not I survive—and press on.

Gradually, I begin to overtake people, the other wolves who don't have my speedster capabilities fall behind.

Another burst of flames up ahead—this time an electric shade of blue—tells me the next brazier has been lit.

"Olivia Castillo, our beta's daughter, has lit the second fire!"

Great! Go Olivia! She's been weird and kind of rude lately, but I'd rather watch her mop the floor with Clayton than let him win.

We keep running straight, following the line of torches as more are lit. Olivia and Clayton are in a constant tie for first place, blue then yellow then blue again, one beating the other each time. I'm not even sure why the rest of us bothered bringing a torch along for the run—at this rate we won't have a chance to use them!

More of my competitors fall behind me as I make up time. I catch a glimpse of Todd and Simon, their wolves noticeably familiar, up ahead. They're matching each other's speed but constantly barging into each other, trying to knock the other over.

There's a howl from up ahead and I'm shocked to see the trail of wolves ahead of me diverging from the path. Clayton and Olivia are still in the lead, only now they're running perpendicularly to the island.

What? I thought we were heading straight there and back?! And then I remember Tobias saying there would be some surprising turns along the way. Well...surprise!

The turning point comes into view but we're all going too fast for the corner. I do my best to control my speed and slow down. Two wolves ahead of me overcompensate as they round the bend, their legs slip out from under them, and they tumble sideways, spinning across the ice before coming to a stop. One of them tries to stand and rejoin us; the other doesn't move.

I gulp and dig in my claws as I round the corner.

There are only ten or so wolves left ahead of me, but as I try to regain my pace I notice I can only see six, then five, then... They're disappearing up the bank of the river into the trees.

Where are we going?

The braziers light the path that leads to the shore and then into the snow-covered woods.

Scrambling up the boulder-laden shore is a struggle— a wolf to my side slips and disappears into a crevice—but once I'm in the forest I can really let my legs go to work.

A burst of blue flame erupts ahead and to the left, lighting up the trees and startling a family of deer. I adjust my direction and chase the light. The wolves in front of me are struggling to climb a rocky outcrop, and I know if I get stuck beneath them I'll never catch up, which is when I spot it: a fallen tree resting like a seesaw on a boulder.

I hope it can hold my weight.

Without thinking I spring onto the trunk and sprint nimbly toward the uprooted end. I pick up speed and leap into the air, arching over the wolves below and landing at the peak of the outcrop. The wolves below snarl and huff but I don't have time to help them up.

Another fire erupts between two massive oaks to my right, and I know which way to go.

For a stretch the trees spread out, giving me clearer passage through which I hurtle. Todd and Simon are just up ahead, but their constant headbutting is slowing them down. They look up, shocked, as I pass them.

It's just Olivia and Clayton ahead of me now and I almost can't believe it. I mean, I knew I was fast—or at least, I was fast sometimes. And part of me always thought I had a chance of placing high enough to win a spot on the trip. But I'm starting to believe that I could actually win this thing.

Take that, Jasper!

The crunch of paws tearing through the frosty undergrowth grows in volume until a wolf finally comes into view. He has the coat of a goddamn golden retriever but the physique of an alpha. *Clayton.*

We've never spoken—not properly—and I'm pretty convinced he doesn't know I exist. But I want to beat him so bad it hurts.

My breaths grow ragged as I speed up once more, gaining on Jasper's childhood pal.

The woods are dark, and I have no idea how Olivia knows which way she's going, but I can follow the bioluminescent trail of her scent.

Clayton glances behind and snarls when he sees me catching up. His lips curl into an unpleasant grimace and it's almost as if I can see the gears shifting in his mind. Before I know what's happening, he's digging in his paws and skidding to a stop. He spins and growls.

But I'm not put off. I keep running. If he wants to stop and threaten me into quitting, he really has no idea who I am.

When I don't stop he barks, and as I grow near he twists, digging a paw into the soil and flinging a clump of icy dirt into my eyes.

I rear back, snarling, shaking my head and pawing at my face. When I finally regain my vision, Clayton is disappearing into the forest.

That little bitch!

Who throws dirt at their competitors? What is this, kindergarten? If this is who Jasper is friends with, no wonder he doesn't know how to act like a normal person.

I growl lowly and, even more determined than before, take off.

By following the asshat's scent, I'm able to keep track of the path. Another fire erupts and I make my way toward it. Eventually the path turns back toward the lake, and I race through the tree line and down a jagged shore to the ice. We're behind the island now and Olivia is out on the ice, nearly halfway there, with Clayton only a little ways behind.

Clayton glances back only once, but he's clearly not happy to see me making up so much time. From the string of braziers burning blue, Olivia pretty much has this in the bag, yet Clayton seems determined not to let me come a distant third.

Up ahead, Olivia reaches the island; there's no shore, just a boulder-riddled path leading to a rocky wall, and finally a flat patch of grass. Olivia is stealth and agility, bounding from boulder to boulder. Clayton picks up his pace as she reaches the top and disappears. I do too but Clayton growls, huffs, and slides to a stop. He turns again, the flames of his torch reflected in his eyes.

Why is this dick so obsessed with me not winning?

Thump. One of his back paws slams the ice. Then again and again.

What is he doing?

I close the distance between us and he just stands there...thumping. I'm coming up on him but he's blocking my path. If I try to go around he'll only take off and I'll never catch him. So I skid to stop a few meters from where he stands. His lip curls and I swear, even though wolf faces don't really work this way, he's grinning.

He thumps his paw again and this time I hear a crack. The next time, a web of black lines appear under his foot— black jagged lines that spread out farther with every thump. Clayton lifts his foot again, but this time he jumps, landing with the weight of his whole body, and the black lines become full-on cracks.

This psycho is trying to kill us both!

If I don't move now, I might not make it to the island, so I leap to my right, but Clayton jumps as well, leaving more cracks where he lands. I bark at him and he snaps his jaws as a warning. *You shall not pass!*

With a huff, I jump back to the left, but Clayton mirrors my movements.

Cracks are now appearing of their own accord, starting as a thin pencil-drawn lines and opening up until they're scrawled in Sharpie.

Clayton barks and whines, baring his teeth and shaking his muzzle. And then the bonfire erupts.

We stare in the direction of the island as blue sparks fly into the clouds. Flames reach above the tops of the trees toward the pale moon. Olivia's done it—she's lit the final fire.

Clayton howls in agony. His chance of winning is slipping away. He huffs at me like it's my fault he's wasted his time antagonizing me.

I growl in response and watch as Clayton turns, sprinting toward the island, his tail whipping behind him.

Without wasting any time I take off after him, but I temper my speed when I hear the ice creaking. A large chasm opens up in front of me and I skid to stop. I try to find my balance, moving as little as possible. More cracks and more creaks ring out from all around. The ice is no longer stable.

Beside me, a patch breaks free and like a whale breaching the surface, it tips sideways. Black, deathly water flows at a surprisingly speedy pace below. The ice whale is swiftly pulled under.

I need to get to sturdier ground, but when I move another crack opens. And another. Surrounded by jagged cracks, I spin in circles as more and more patches of ice are sucked down by the undertow.

Black holes of rushing water appear between the cracks. But I can see where the ice is holding solid, closer to the island. If I can make it there I might survive. So I leap and land on an ice platform, nearly tipping it over as I do, but managing to stay upright. Again, I launch myself into the air, only just managing to land safely, and take off once more before my platform is dragged under by the current. I land scrambling for secure footing on a less than solid piece of ice. I'm one jump away from the edge, and my platform is starting to sink.

With all of my strength, I ready myself and pounce, but as I do the ice under my feet slips away and I don't move more than a foot or two. I flop forward, my legs running in the air, grasping at nothing—looking like one of those doggy-fail videos on TikTok—and I splash land in the river.

Falling into freezing water *does* feel like a thousand knives stabbing you all at once. My breath is stolen the instant I break the surface, and I'm pulled under by the rushing current. I struggle against it, flailing my limbs like it's doing any good. But I can't find the surface, I don't know which way is up. In a second I'll be pulled beneath the ice, and then there'll be no way out. I'll be trapped. And everyone will be right. I never should have entered this stupid competition.

All these thoughts are rushing through my brain as the ice seizes my body and I stop struggling. My feet stop kicking. My vision blurs and darkness closes in around the corners of my eyes.

And just when I think it's all over, I feel the pinch of teeth at the back of my neck. I'm jerked back into action. My legs take up thrashing again as the bite at my scruff tightens and I'm pulled from the water.

The wolf who's saved me tosses me across the ice, knocking any wind I still had in me clear of my body.

I lie there panting, coughing, spluttering, too weak to stand, to even lift my head enough to see who my rescuer is.

As I pass out, Jasper's midnight wolf leans over me; his green eyes stare down at me, brimming with worry.

I sit shivering in my robe, waiting for the fire to rid my body of icy chills. Jasper sits on a log across from me, on the far side of the fire. He hasn't looked at me since I came to warm up.

After being pulled from the water, the first thing I remember is waking up on the pier. Jasper was the first person my eyes were able to focus on. He was pulling a robe over his bare shoulders. Then walking away.

I sat up, my head spinning as a couple of team medics fussed about me. After they'd checked my pulse and made sure I wasn't actually a zombie, they gave me a tin mug of hot cocoa and told me to warm up by the fire.

The race was done. Olivia won, with Clayton in second place, although I personally believe he should have been disqualified for cheating. Apparently, attempted murder isn't against the rules, according to Tobias. I guess that's why so many people used to die doing this.

My whole body is aching—from the run and my icy dip, but also because I failed.

Todd and Simon came in joint third. Someone said they were still wrestling each other as they crossed the finish line.

So that's it then. I'm not going to the Rocky Pack, I won't be spending the holidays with Jasper. And he'll be farther away than he was before.

Aisha plops down next to me and leans her shoulder against mine.

"Sorry you didn't win, dude," she says. "On the bright side, you didn't die either."

"That's something," I say, still watching Jasper.

Behind him there's a smattering of the dispersing crowd. Clayton wanders out of the shadows and up to a couple of other guys. His friends slap him on the back and congratulate him as he runs a carefree hand through his hair.

"It wasn't for lack of trying though."

Aisha follows my eyeline and spots him too.

"Ugh, he's always been ridiculously competitive. He thinks winning is his birthright."

"Hey Max," Katie says, appearing out of nowhere.

"Hi, I didn't know you were here."

"I sort of kept it quiet." She's having trouble making eye contact as well. *Do I have a massive zit or something?* "I came to support Todd and Simon."

"You could have said."

"I know." She sighs. "I thought if I let you believe I wasn't coming you might be less likely to race. I guess I was wrong."

"Well, thanks for the support." My words are more bitter than I mean them to be, but I almost died, so Katie should probably let it slide.

"I'm glad you're okay," she says, fidgeting with one of her bracelets. "And sorry, you know, about the Rocky Pack and all."

Then it dawns on me. Todd and Simon get to go and bring their mate.

"I hope you have a nice time," I say, and this time I mean every bitter syllable.

"Max..."

I turn away from Katie and focus on the bonfire. She waits for a moment but I ignore her, waiting for her to run back to the terrible twosome.

"Max, I..." She trails off and I've had it.

"What?" I ask. "Why can't you finish a sentence?"

Katie's mouth is clamped together, her eyes darting from me to a towering figure I'm only just now realizing is behind me.

Alpha Jericho steps over my log bench and stands in front of the fire; the flames light one side of his face in orange and leave the other in shadow.

Automatically, Aisha and I stand out of respect.

"Please accept my apologies, Max," Jericho says, every eye in a ten-meter radius staring in his direction. Even Jasper glances up. "I had not intended to put anyone in danger."

"I'm okay…" My jaw is quivering more than when I was drowning in a frozen river. "Really, it's okay."

"You nearly had it, too," Jericho says with a grin. "You've impressed me once again."

I don't really know what to say. I'm not sure being a drowned rat is that impressive—and I mean, it's sort of his fault. He's a big part of the reason I entered the race in the first place. If he wasn't pressuring me so hard I don't even know if I would have put myself in that position. But he's still my alpha, and the thought of mouthing off at him doesn't sit well. So I say nothing.

Our little conversation has caught a lot of people's attention. Jasper is watching his dad with keen intent. Clayton is ignoring his lackeys, waiting to hear what the alpha will say next. Even Olivia is glancing in our direction, looking like she's just swallowed a bug.

"I'd like to make amends for this evening's little accident," Jericho says.

Accident?! Little? I know some people are questioning Jericho's authority, but somehow I don't think undermining my almost-drowning is the way to convince people you're fit to lead.

"There were six available spots in the emissary to the Rocky Pack. Our first- and second-place winners don't have mates." Clayton bristles; Olivia's eye dart to the ground. "Of course, our tied third-place holders and their mate"—he glances at Katie ever so briefly and I can feel her melt—"make the group up to five, which leaves an open space. It would give me great pleasure to invite you to join my son, and the others, on the trip to the Rocky Pack."

Clayton looks like he wants to try and murder me all over again. Jasper's eyes are wide and full of quiet fury.

"Max!" Katie squeals. "This is such good news!"

"Will you accept?" Jericho asks, sticking out his oversized hand for me to shake.

For a second I stand there like a dumbass. I glance at Aisha, who only raises her eyebrows and tilts her head as if to say, "Hey, it's what you wanted, right?"

And it is what I wanted—it is.

I shake Jericho's hand, grinning from ear to ear.

"I'd love to!"

"Very good," he says, and winks at me, which should be the coolest moment of my life but is actually a little disconcerting. "Enjoy the blood moon. I hope you make the most it."

When he releases my hand I have to wait a moment for the blood to flow back into the tips of my fingers.

I didn't win the race, but I'm still going to the Rocky Pack. I'm going to spend the holidays with Jasper!

"Congrats," Aisha says, and it only bugs me slightly that she sounds kind of skeptical.

"Max, this is so cool!" Katie says, rushing in and hugging me before I can remember that I'm kind of pissed at her.

When I glance over, Jasper has already stood up. I think he might come over and say something, but instead he turns and walks away. He nods at Clayton, who leaves his buds and joins him. Together they snake their way into the crowd and disappear into the shadows.

I WON'T BE HOME FOR CHRISTMAS

The house is dark when Aisha drops me off. I give her a little wave and she gives me a halfhearted thumbs-up before driving away. Figuring my parents are asleep, and not feeling much up to attempting the ten-foot-high jump back into my bedroom, I head for the front door.

Inside, I creep through the darkness up to my room, gently closing the door behind me, and am about to slide into bed when I see them.

A shadowy figure is sitting in my desk chair.

I scream as the person swivels to face me.

"MOM! You nearly gave me a heart attack."

Needing to fully convince myself I'm not about to become some serial killer's next victim, I flick on the light. I spin back to Mom, expecting her to make a quip about me nearly giving her a heart attack too and then shouting about how worried she was, but she doesn't say anything, just stares at me.

She isn't crying but she definitely doesn't look happy.

"Were you at the race?" she asks, as if it's hard to get the words out.

"Yes, but Mom before you say anything you'll never believe—I didn't win but this other guy, he tried to drown me, and so Jericho is letting me go with the envoy to the Rocky Pack to see the blood moon and—"

I stop. She's wringing her hands, twisting her mouth in a way that breaks my heart.

"I'm sorry," I say. "I'm sorry I snuck out, I know you must have been worried but I—"

"Was it something I did?" she asks. "Something to make you think you can't talk to me?"

"Something you did? What? No. I just really want to see the blood moon is all."

She scoffs. "You may be keeping some part of yourself secret for whatever reason, but I know you well enough to know that's a lie."

Her shoulders are slumped forward, like she's tired, like she's giving in.

"I just don't know what else to do." Her voice is all choked up. "I feel like I'm failing you but I don't know how to stop it."

I can't bear this. Mom and I have always been close. We have the same sarcastic sense of humor, we love watching singing competitions, and every Halloween she asks me what I want to be and makes me the most amazing costume. I drop to my knees and grab her hands in mine.

"You aren't failing me," I say. "You could never fail me."

My words hit me as I say them. She could never fail me—I know that—but there's another reason why I'm just not ready to come out to her, and I'm only just beginning to realize what that is.

"You could never ever fail me, Mom. The truth is"—part of me desperately wants to tell her everything and part of me knows that I can't, not yet—"there is something I'm going through. But I haven't quite figured it out for myself. And I know I messed up tonight but you need to trust me."

She lifts her head and looks at me with sad, tired eyes, but still raises a teasing eyebrow that says "Really?"

I laugh a little. "Okay, maybe sneaking out isn't the most trustworthy action. But I'm okay and I'm not like, doing drugs or crime or anything."

Now she laughs properly. "Believe me, if it was drugs I'd have known."

"Okay." I roll my eyes. "You look tired; can you tell me I'm grounded again in the morning?"

"Sure," she says, wiping her cheek, and rubbing my face with her free hand. "And just to be clear: whenever you're ready, your father and I are here for you."

"Thank you."

With a huff she stands and shuffles to the door.

"Light on or off?" she asks.

"Off is great."

"Don't forget to brush your teeth, kiddo."

"Okay, Mom, night. Love you."

"Love you too."

I slip into bed and let the heat from the blankets burn away any lingering chills from the water. Lying on my back, I stare at the glow-in-the-dark planets my dad stuck on the ceiling when I was a kid and I realize something I've known for a while now. The reason I haven't been able to tell them about Jasper has nothing to do with the fact that he's a guy. I know they wouldn't care about that.

The problem is Jasper. The problem is I not only have to tell them my mate is a guy, but he's also a dick who ignores me, and I'm embarrassed. Embarrassed because of how he treats me and embarrassed because even though he's a jerk I'm still chasing him. I nearly drowned tonight trying to prove a point. How can I tell my parents that?

This is supposed to be my big coming-out, but what am I coming out as? Some guy's boyfriend? That just seems lame. And not about me at all. I've been so obsessed with being Jasper's mate, I haven't stopped to think what this means about me, who I am. And before I tell my parents anything, I need to figure that out.

Mom and Dad insist on driving me to the airport. Of course, we're not taking a commercial flight, instead the lucky chosen few get to ride in one of the alpha's private jets, which means right now we're on our way to a private airfield somewhere on Long Island. It was touch and go whether I'd be allowed to come after I snuck out. But after our late-night chat, something has shifted with Mom.

She's chilled out so much, as if all she needed was the confirmation that something was up. I guess she just wanted to feel like she wasn't crazy, that she did still have some instinct about what was going on with her kid. And once she let up, Dad seemed keen to get everything back to normal.

I still catch her giving me these quizzical sideways glances—like the one she's giving me right now in the rearview mirror—but it's nothing like the piercing, questioning stare from before. I feel as if we've come to an understanding. She knows I have to tell her something, but she also knows I'm not ready and that's okay. At least for now.

"You're becoming a bit of a fixture at important pack events, Maxie," Dad says, leaning round from his spot riding shotgun.

"Huh, yeah."

I wish Katie was here with us to act as a diversion, but she said she was getting a ride with Todd and Simon. Plus we haven't exactly been texting at our usual rate since the race. It's been over a week, and I thought Katie might have called to apologize, but instead all I've received are some vague texts. We haven't even done half of our usual holiday traditions—like going to see the window displays at Macy's, or present shopping, or watching every holiday movie under the sun.

It's the middle of the morning and the weather is crisp and dry; the sun flits between the convenience stores and strip malls as we head through suburbia. Eventually we turn off and make our way down a long stretch of road. Chain-link fences—the kind I imagine surround Area 51—line a large, flat expanse of short brown grass cut through by a runway. A stout air control tower sits toward the left of the airfield, with some flat-roofed buildings situated nearby. We slow as we come to the entrance. A guard booth sits to the side of a security beam that's blocking our path.

"Uh, hello," Mom says, opening her window to speak with a cross-armed guard reclining in an office chair. "We're here to drop off our son for the trip to the Rockies."

"Name?" he grunts—definitely one of the pack's obedient security forces.

"Maximilian Remus," Mom says a little too proudly.

"Car park's on the right."

With another grunt he hits a button, the barrier rises, and we glide smoothly underneath.

As we turn into the parking lot I finally spot the plane sitting on the tarmac. It's this sleek, pearl-white jet sitting all alone in the massive airfield. There's already a group gathered next to it, while some of the airport staff move about with fuel hoses and luggage carts. I hop out and pull my duffel bag across the seat, slinging it over my shoulder.

I notice the full-on suitcases being lifted into the undercarriage of the aircraft and wonder if I've underpacked. It looks like a family of twelve is moving house. We're only going for a week, and other than one trip up a mountain, I thought we'd just be sitting in a cabin. Why could they possibly need that much stuff?

"Max!" Katie waves from across the tarmac, and I wave back, but she's immediately distracted by Simon and Todd pulling her in for a photo.

Olivia is there, staring at the runway, arms crossed, looking bored in a leather jacket and a pair of aviators. She might as well have come straight from the set of *Top Gun 3*. By the gangway, a couple of official-looking wolves in suits are holding clipboards, talking and pointing. They must be administrative types who work for the alpha, making sure everything is organized for us. Clayton steps off the plane in a preppy navy-blue sweater and white chinos, his hair perfectly quaffed, talking to someone on his cell. Without pausing, he brushes past the administrative types like they aren't even there. They bristle in his wake but get right back to finalizing their plans.

My attention is suddenly pulled left, where the door of one of the buildings has swung open. My breath catches in my throat as Jasper steps out onto the runway in a black turtleneck, black slim-fit jeans, and combat boots, a woman in a pilot's uniform following just after. They chat as they wander toward the plane, and Jasper looks every bit the conscientious prince, listening and putting his subject at ease.

"Well, kiddo," Mom says, pulling my attention away from Jasper, "it looks like everyone is here already. You better get going."

"Have a great time," Dad says, grabbing me up in a hug. "Make sure to take some pictures of that blood moon for us."

"I will," I say, letting him go and turning to Mom. "It'll be weird not being home for Christmas."

She can't help tearing up a little, her cheeks turning all rosy in the cold.

"It's just this once, and it'll be worth it, I bet," she says, trying to comfort me, herself, the whole family.

"I'm sorry I won't be there." Suddenly, I'm feeling super guilty. Not only have I been acting weird for months, and sneaking out, now I'm abandoning them for the holidays.

Mom pats me on the shoulder and gives my arm a squeeze. "It's all part of growing up, kiddo. You need to have your own experiences. There'll be more Christmases."

"And when I get back I can tell you all about it." I nod reassuringly, trying to tell her that I want to share everything with her, that I'll be ready soon.

"Can't wait," she says and pulls me into the tightest hug.

Oh Moon Gods, even I might start crying, and I can't show up at the plane with puffy eyes. I take one last breath of Mom's scent and let her go.

"You got everything?" Dad asks for the hundredth time, putting an arm around Mom and smiling in this half grin that dimples his cheek.

"Yeah, I'm ready." I turn to leave but have to turn back after a few steps. "I'll call you when we land."

"Go on," Mom says, shooing me away.

A breath and then I turn and make my way to the plane.

Everyone is boarding by the time I've crossed the airfield; Olivia is the last up the stairs and I get in line behind her.

"Hi," I say.

She turns and, without smiling, says, "Hey," then steps up into the jet.

I take one last look at my parents standing by their car with their arms around each other and give them one last wave.

The interior of the plane feels more spacious than it looks from the outside. The cabin is has cream walls punctuated by Tic Tac-shaped portholes. Leather chairs sit in pairs facing each other so that two people have to fly sitting backward, which sucks if you get travel sickness. Next to each high-end La-Z-Boy sits a polished oak table with gold detailing. Two crew members are moving through the cabin with hot towels and glasses of orange juice. *What, no champagne?*

Clayton has already taken a seat right at the front, facing the back of the plane. He's yabbering into his cell phone and Olivia, who has sat down in the opposite chair, is pulling on her headphones and scrolling through her phone, I'm sure looking for something to drown out that noise. I don't particularly want to sit next to either of them, so I glance to the back of the plane, where Katie is sitting facing me.

I try to catch her eye but Todd and Simon are fighting for the seat next to her, jostling each other into the aisle for prime position. I manage to squeeze past them and plonk myself in the opposite corner of a four-seat formation.

"Guys, come on, we can all move about during the flight," Katie says, swatting at them with an in-flight magazine. "It's not even that long of a trip."

"But I want to hold your hand during takeoff," Todd says.

"And I want to make sure you have gum in case your ears pop," Simon retorts.

Katie glances in my direction but I'm not in the mood to get involved, so I look away.

Jasper ducks through the door from the cockpit and swiftly takes in the seating arrangements. His glance lands on me and turns cold. He pulls out a large set of platinum headphones and sits in the seat closest to the door—the seat farthest away from me. The second he's sitting he closes his eyes. And I guess that's how he plans to stay the entire flight.

By the time the door is closed, Todd and Simon have managed to come to some kind of agreement, although they continue to nudge and provoke each other as the plane maneuvers onto the runway.

Katie is staring at me, so I return her gaze and she gestures with her head that I should go and sit with Jasper. There's no way I'm doing that—not in front of Clayton, not on this tiny soon-to-be-airborne vessel, not while he's acting like he wishes he was anywhere else.

With a huff I pull out my AirPods and nestle into the corner. I just hope we don't hit any turbulence.

A ROCKY START

Somehow, despite Todd and Simon's constant bickering, I manage to doze off during the four-hour flight. I'm woken by someone shaking my shoulder.

"Max," Katie says, her voice sounding distant, "we're here."

I blink and open my eyes to look around the cabin. It's still light outside and a sunny haze is drifting in through the open door. Jasper's seat is empty, he's already disembarked; Clayton is nowhere to be seen either. Olivia is stepping through the door, followed by Katie's jostling paramours.

"Come on," she says. "Cars are waiting to take us the rest of the way."

"M'kay."

Yawning and stretching out my back, I grab my bag and follow Katie toward the exit. She gives me this concerned look as she heads down the stairs. We're on a different airfield, but it's pretty much the same as the last one. The runway, a slightly different shade of gray, divides two patches of closely cropped lawn. A watchtower hovers nearby; some other buildings and a hanger or two sit across the field like an uninviting village. Only there's a crispness to the chill in the air, a freshness you won't find in New York.

Two town cars with blackout windows sit waiting for us. I spin my head from side to side, looking for Jasper.

"He already left in a car with Clayton," Katie says.

Of course he did. I'm only jealous of Clayton for a second because then it dawns on me. There are only two cars left and Katie is going to want to travel with her mates.

Over to my right, Olivia is opening one of the car doors; she glances at the remaining members of the envoy and catches my eye, does some quick math in her head, comes to the same conclusion I have, and sighs. We're stuck together.

"You could squeeze in with us," Katie offers halfheartedly, noticing my frown.

My shoulders slouch forward and I mumble something about it being fine then head over to the car where Olivia has already slipped inside and shut the door. I slide in next to her and she makes a point of turning up the volume on her headphones.

I can't for the life of me figure out why she's freezing me out. But if that's how she wants to play it, fine. There's a true crime podcast saved on my phone that's more inviting. I sure hope they're friendlier at the Rocky Pack.

Turns out the drive from the airfield is almost as long as the plane ride. Olivia and I sit in silence as the car makes its way into the mountains. We leave the small towns, with their retro diners and log-laden trucks, behind and begin our incline. Suddenly, we're enveloped on either side by steel-silver and snow-white mounds with jagged outcrops and no signs of life. The sun is beginning to set behind the mountainous horizon, casting everything in a peachy light.

Eagerly the town car plows on up a twisty mountain road, drifting way too close to the sheer edge for my liking. We snake our way higher and higher until I start to wonder if we're all going to need oxygen masks to survive the week.

Finally, in the distance across the valley, I spot the warm speckle of electric lights. Perched on a plateau carved out of the mountainside, the glow of civilization sits, warm and welcoming. I can almost smell the hot chocolate already. But there's a strange uneasiness in my stomach as we turn yet another corner and the settlement disappears from view.

We drive for at least another forty minutes until the twists are turning my stomach. The lights of the Rocky Pack occasionally flicker back into view, each time a little larger and a little warmer.

When we turn the final corner and arrive in a parking lot the size of a football field, my eyes can barely stay open the light is so bright. Fancy cars sit in rows sparkling in the glow of the Rocky Pack's headquarters: Porsches and Jags and Lamborghinis, plus a few pickups and a couple of coaches—the kind that ship human tourists around the country. The packhouse looks like the biggest, fanciest ski resort I've ever seen. Not that I've ever been skiing, but you know from films and stuff. The front wall is almost entirely glass, with logs the size of redwoods supporting the flat, angled, snow-laden roof. A wooden veranda protrudes above the doors, supported by stone pillars, and inside I catch a glimpse of a Christmas tree to rival Rockefeller's.

Tires crunch on gravel as the car pulls to a stop and Olivia jumps out. We've arrived but I need to take a quick breath before exiting the vehicle. I'm so far from home, in a strange stony environment, with no one except my best friend who I think I'm fighting with and a mate who wishes I was anywhere else. Maybe coming up here was a mistake—maybe this whole chase is—and now there's no way back. It's not like I can charter a private jet on my own, or call an Uber to come up here and get me. I'm stuck for the duration.

Well, you better make the most of it.

Jaw set, I clutch the strap of my duffel and step out of the car.

"How was the ride?" Katie asks, leaving Todd and Simon to deal with their bags and joining me as I head toward the glass doors.

"Pretty twisty," I say.

"Max, I—"

"We're going in."

A man in a black suit with a high collar and a little round hat has pulled open the front door and is ushering us inside. It's breezy up here and loose powder is flitting inside, so Katie and I hustle to join up with the others.

The warmth of the interior hits me like an unexpected bear hug, making my eyes water. Gentle music is playing from speakers I can't see. And it's... Yes, it's Christmas music: an instrumental version of "Sleigh Ride." Ahead, Jasper and Clayton are talking with two staff members wearing matching uniforms to the guy behind us. This is a packhouse, but they look like bellhops at a hotel. Clayton grins smugly as he slips a fifty-dollar bill into the coat pocket of one of the staff, patting their chest and watching as they take his many Louis Vuitton bags away.

"Sir, may I take your bag?" a squeaky voice says to my right.

I turn to find a short girl, barely older than me, in a matching staff uniform, smiling from ear to ear. Instinctively a light growl rolls in my throat. The last time an overly cheery attendant met me at a pack function I wound up her hostage.

"Sir?"

I've been staring too long. I'm sure this girl is the loveliest and not a mate-obsessed psycho, so I slip my bag off my shoulder and let her take it. Once the staff have taken everyone's bags, an older gentleman with salt-and-pepper hair peeking out from beneath his hat arrives with a tray of steaming mugs. The smell wafts into my nostrils and at once I'm giddy with festive cheer.

"Hot chocolate!"

We each take a mug, and as we remain standing in a huddle in the entryway, I sniff the hot chocolatey goodness and take my first sip. I've never in my life tasted hot chocolate this velvety and delicious. Whatever supplier they've managed to convince to travel all the way up here, it's worth the exorbitant price I'm sure they pay.

"That's so good," Katie says, looking first at Todd then Simon, then shyly at me.

I half grin but angle my body away.

The roof is stories above my head, a golden-beamed A-frame with a single sturdy rafter holding it in place. In front of us another set of glass doors lead into the main foyer, where a few Rocky Pack wolves are reclining on couches, sipping from the same mugs, looking cozy and chic in fair isle sweaters. Some kids, about the same age as Katie and me, walk past looking festively stylish, like they've stepped out of a department store's Christmas catalog. They stop under the ridiculous and gorgeous Christmas tree, and a tall boy with dark-brown skin, curly bleached-blond hair, and a slight overbite catches my eye. He grins and winks. I bury my face in my mug of chocolate and pretend not to have noticed.

"Hello Elite Pack!"

Another new voice, this time a little less perky, grabs my attention. A girl with bright-red hair and pale-white freckly cheeks has opened the doors to the lodge, looking like it's autumn and she's ready for the gram in a cream roll-neck sweater, blue jeans, and a pair of knee-high camel-suede boots.

"Mia, it's good to see you," Jasper says, approaching and giving her a European-style air-kiss on both cheeks.

My face grows warm. Gosh, am I jealous of her too now? Or maybe of the air Jasper is kissing?

I step to join the others but notice Olivia hasn't moved. She's hovering a step behind me, her sunglasses pushing her thick brown hair back, mug of hot cocoa in hand, and a look of terror on her face. Or maybe it's indigestion. But she doesn't look comfortable.

"You coming?"

She doesn't respond.

"Everything okay?"

"What? Huh?" Olivia shakes herself back into the room. "Uh, yeah, why wouldn't it be?"

She glares at me briefly, before marching to join the group. With a shrug I find a spot at the back.

"I'm so glad you could all make it," Mia says, her voice undulating like a lullaby, but with a bass note of power to it. "My name is Mia, I'm the eldest daughter of Alpha Morven—or Daddy as I call him. You all must be tired after your journey. Our staff will show you all to your rooms in a moment, but first I wanted to welcome you to our packhouse and extend my services to you for the duration of your stay. I'm here if you need anything at all; the Rocky Pack wishes you the jolliest Christmas and a spectacular blood moon. We have some amazing activities planned while you're here and I can't wait to get to know all of you so much better."

I swear she glances at Jasper when she says that last part. Glancing sideways and catching Katie's eye, I lift my eyebrows to say "She's really something," and Katie has to stifle a giggle. We may be sort of fighting, but we'll always get each other.

"So if you'd like to follow me…"

Mia turns with a flourish, and I wonder how anyone ever becomes that confident.

When we enter the foyer, everything is lit in this flickering warm glow from a fireplace the size of a bodega to our left. Everything smells of pine, cinnamon, and coal. It's warming and inviting and—I hate to say it but—the most Christmassy-smelling place I've ever been. Way more festive than Santa's grotto at Macy's, which usually has the scent of sticky five-year-olds and stale popcorn.

And then I spot the view. Beyond the lounge area is a wall of glass, and outside the Rockies are bathed in moonlight. It's like a painting, all the mountains rising on either side of a deep valley, jagged rock and smooth powder laid on top like a blanket. The moon is glowing down silver and blue, and I can only imagine what that vista will look like in the morning. Part of me is starting to get excited about sitting by the window, drinking more of this amazing hot chocolate, and watching the sunrise.

"This is the parlor," Mia says, floating between sofas like she owns the place, which I guess she does. "This is where we usually host dignitaries from other packs, or as you can see, it's where we like to gather before official pack dinners."

Some of the well-dressed wolves from around the room glance over. I smile awkwardly as a man wearing an actual cravat nods in my direction, while a woman in a purple ball gown raises a brow then continues her conversation.

"What do you think?" Katie says, sidling up next to me, eyeing our host. "Robot or mind control?"

I snicker.

"Definitely mind control. Oh no, do you think it's in the cocoa?"

We both feign terror but continue sipping our drinks.

"The private lodges are that way," Mia says, pointing to a hallway past the fireplace. "That's where most of your rooms are." She surveys the ragtag Elite Pack crew and finally rests her eyes on me. "I'm sure you'll want to change before dinner," she says, smiling too broadly. "The stewards will show you to your suites now so you can freshen up."

Four stewards appear to our left, ready to take us to our rooms.

"Get changed?" I whisper to Katie. "I only brought enough clothes for one outfit a day!"

She shakes her head. "Big mistake—huge."

"Jasper, Clayton, and Olivia," Mia pipes up before we can head off. "My father has graciously invited you to stay in our dignitaries wing, and I've been asked to personally see that you find your rooms."

"Excellent," Clayton croons.

"Thank you, Mia," Jasper utters.

"The rest of you, I'm sure you'll find our guest cabins more than adequate."

Mia nods to the stewards, who gesture for us normies to follow them. As we turn to leave the lounge, I glance back to see Mia taking Jasper's arm and leading him away.

"Hey." Katie nudges my side as we follow our guides through the halls of the Rocky Packhouse. "I'm sorry for not being supportive and then for being kind of awkward. I just... Well, there's something I need to talk to you about."

"Mystery, intrigue," I say, teasing. "Well now I have to forgive you; I'm hooked."

"Don't." She slouches a little. "I need my best friend."

Katie's brow is furrowed, so I link my arm through hers. "Don't worry, your best friend is here. He nearly died trying to get here but..."

Katie laughs and shakes her head. "And I know I've been flaking on our Christmas traditions, so maybe we can make some time while we're here and catch up. That is, if you're not too busy canoodling with Jasper in the hot tub."

So there are hot tubs?!

"That sounds awesome," I say. "And maybe you could help me out with something to wear?"

My room is a loft apartment on the fifth floor, nestled in the apex of the roof; it's the only room on this floor. Katie, Todd, and Simon are in rooms on the floor below me. A California king sits under the slanting roof, a bearskin rug—that's pretty creepy—laid out before it. There's a swish-looking en suite, a cozy armchair by a fireplace, and a wall of windows, with a door leading onto a small balcony.

As soon as I've refreshed myself, I head outside and take a deep breath, letting the cold mountain air fill my lungs. The view is just as, if not more, spectacular from up here. Out across the range, the moon, about two-thirds of the way through her cycle, looks like a cookie with a bite taken out of her. I know it's too early, but I swear I can make out just a touch of blood red creeping around one of the edges.

For a moment the breeze dies down and voices float through the canyon, pricking up my ears. To either side of me the lodge descends in levels, each a step down and out from the last. The windows are glowing yellow on the snow below, lighting up the balconies attached to each room. Way off to the right, about three floors below me, but in what might as well be an entirely different chalet, Mia is walking out onto one of the balconies. Her arms are wide like she's embracing the night air, and she spins, leaning back on the balustrade with her elbows.

Jasper follows her outside.

I can't make out the words of their conversation, just the melodies of their voices as they travel on the wind. Jasper joins Mia at the railing and gazes down at the valley. Mia arches her back and turns to face him, then runs a hand down his arm.

The muscles in my neck tense, my teeth clench, threatening to become fangs, and I growl louder then I mean to. Jasper's back straightens. Has he heard me?

Not wanting to be caught spying, I run back inside as fast as I can, shutting the glass door behind me and flopping into the chair. I don't think he saw me; I was too fast.

But was she flirting with him? They've probably met before, the kids of alphas at some interpack function. So maybe they're just friends, with history. Only that thought makes me feel worse. Maybe it was nothing.

Or maybe not. Maybe Clayton isn't the person I need to be worried about.

A DIFFERENT ALPHA

"Why did no one tell me that I'd need formal wear," I say, wriggling in a too-large button-down shirt Katie borrowed from Todd and/or Simon.

"It's not formal," she sighs. "It's smart casual."

"So why can't I be casual?"

I huff and look in the mirror. Katie is behind me lying on my bed, propped up on an elbow.

"I look like a kid wearing his dad's work clothes."

"It looks oversized, like it's meant to be that way. Here." With a huff she pops up and starts fussing with the shirt, tucking in one side, rolling up the sleeves and unbuttoning it almost halfway down my torso.

"There, you look trendy."

"I doubt it," I grumble. "But it'll have to do. Thank Todd or Simon, or whichever."

Katie is nibbling on the inside of her cheek—I can tell because it's making her mouth twist in weird formations.

"What did you want to talk about?" I ask, moving to the armchair to pull on my shoes, as Katie plops back down on the edge of the comforter.

She lets out a big breath. "It's about Todd and Simon."

"Oh, have you finally picked one?"

"That's just it: I thought by spending time with them both I'd figure out who I wanted to spend the rest of my life with—like it would be obvious. But the longer we're in this strange sort of threesome the more I think I... I like it that way. Like that's what feels obvious...to me."

"That's cool." I shrug and raise my eyebrows supportively.

"But is it?" She flings herself backward onto the mattress. "No one has two mates forever. It just isn't done. It's not normal. At some point I'm going to have to choose."

I finish tying my shoes and move to Katie's side. The mattress is soft and we tilt toward each other as it slopes in the center.

"I know my mate situation isn't exactly the best," I say, pausing for a snarky response and then continuing when none comes. "I know it's not exactly traditional or, you know, about to end in a happily ever after or whatever, but there's nothing I've learned about myself that I'd want to change. I kind of like that I'm not the same as everyone. And sure, the path forward is unclear and it might be difficult but I believe in the end it will all be worth it. That's why I'm here."

That *is* why I'm here, right?

"So my point is"—Katie leans her head on my shoulder and I rest mine on top of hers—"maybe you don't need to be what you're supposed to be. Maybe you just need to do what feels right. Which in your case is dating two men-children at the same time."

"Hey! Don't be a bonehead!"

She shoves me playfully, but we naturally come back together, our shoulders pressing against each other.

"They *are* being super annoying at the moment."

My silence is deafening.

"Okay, don't disagree with me."

"I'm sorry! They're probably just acting up because they still think it's a competition."

"Ugh, I need to tell them, don't I?"

"Soz."

"You know what? I was wrong about Jasper clouding your judgment. I think somehow all this is making you kind of wise."

"Seriously?" I raise an eyebrow. "I've come all this way and nothing has changed."

"We only just got here, give it time. Besides, who could resist the festive coziness and the mistletoe hanging from every doorway. In a couple of days he'll be snow melting in your hands."

I can only hope.

Katie and I are late for dinner, arriving as the food is being served. It didn't help that we got completely lost in a hall decorated with way too much taxidermy. Todd and Simon wave us over from where they've saved us two seats.

"You don't mind if I sit between them, do you?" she asks as we make our way over. "Otherwise they might shame the entire pack."

"Sure, no problem."

The dining room is rustic elegance to the max. Seventies-style stone pillars rise from four points in the middle of the room, and a large open fire crackles in the center. The walls are all glass and wood, with yet more ridiculously obscene views. Boughs of holly have been strung up, between red velvet bows. A long table faces the main entrance, connected on either end to two more tables which run the length of the room, creating a squarish U shape. The guests already in their seats—a mix of families and official-looking types—are dressed more smart than casual, with straight backs and slicked hair.

In the center of the table opposite the door, a large chair made of moose antlers and covered in furs sits conspicuously empty, with two, less grandly decorated, empty seats next to it. To the right of one of the empty chairs, Jasper is sitting, and to his right Clayton is leaning in, one arm resting on the back of Jasper's chair. I bristle as I head to my seat and force myself to look somewhere else...anywhere else.

The spots Todd and Simon have saved us are on the table to the right of the room, facing out toward the windows. They look unreasonably smug when Katie decides to sit between them, leaving me with the chair next to Olivia. I sit and she huffs, turning away to make small talk with some middle-aged man on her left.

As I glance across the dining room, that boy with the curly bleached hair from earlier is watching me with a gentle smirk. When I catch his eye, he does a little wave, which I return awkwardly. Luckily, a server arrives at my side to deliver a plate of food before things can get more awkward. My mouth floods with saliva at the sight of roast venison and mashed potatoes, with berry jam and carrots.

I glance up from my freshly delivered plate and notice Jasper speaking in a hushed voice to a staff member holding the same meaty plate of food. Guess they didn't know he was a vegetarian. *Take that, Princess Mia.* I wonder if they even have an alternative prepared. From the furs and antlers all over this place, I'd say they're pretty set in their carnivorous ways.

Once everyone has their plate, I pick up my fork and am about to tuck in when the lights dim. A horn sounds from somewhere overhead, which... Is that even safe with all these snowy hillsides around? Are they trying to cause an avalanche?

The doors swing open and in steps Alpha Morven Labraid, I assume. Every Rocky Pack wolf stands, so we do the same. When they rest a fist on their chest, we do the same. Morven is taller than Jericho but not as wide, with tanned skin—from all the skiing I guess—salt-and-pepper hair, and blue eyes that survey the room in a warm yet calculating way. He's wearing a cream sweater underneath a gray suit jacket, with matching pants and brown leather shoes. Less dressed up than most of the pack officials here, in fact, he looks downright relaxed, in a millionaire on vacation in Vale sorta way, but still. It's an alpha of a different color.

Morven reaches out his hand and is joined by a white woman around the same age, with coppery hair coiled in a bun, a maroon dress, and a black blazer draped over her shoulders. This must be Luna Astrid. She's tall and stoic, with a playful lilt to the corner of her mouth. Mia steps up to Morven's left side, her red hair—decorated with golden autumnal hair-pieces— contrasts with the green of her satin pantsuit.

Morven, Astrid, and Mia walk the perimeter of the room nodding cordially to their guests. Every eye follows them without wavering. Jasper stands when the royal trio reaches the central table. He shakes hands with Morven, bowing his head slightly, an impossibly serious expression on his face. He kisses the back of Astrid's hand and does the same European kisses on either side of Mia's stupid face as he did earlier. Finally, Morven takes his seat, giving Mia and his luna a kiss on the cheek. Mia takes the empty seat next to Jasper, of course.

"Welcome everyone," Morven says as we sit.

His voice isn't as resonant or deep as Jericho's. He has a casually confident tone I wasn't expecting from an alpha. Maybe this guy is all right?

"I am so thrilled you could all join us this evening, right on the precipice of such a wonderful and precious time of year. And I'd like to say a special welcome to the wolves of the Elite Pack, who have traveled to join us in celebration. You are most welcome in our pack and in our home. I trust you aren't too weary from your travels."

His eyes drift over us and I don't feel the same fear, the same innate need to obey, as I do when Jericho looks at me. Instead I feel a strange sort of warmth in my chest. Morven turns to his left and continues.

"A special welcome to Alpha Jericho's first born and heir to the Elite Pack, Jasper Apollo."

There's a light round of applause for Jaspy.

"It's a pleasure," Jasper says, the perfect representative for his father.

"How goes the search for your mate, Jasper? I hear it's been a little tumultuous."

For a second I wonder if Morven's forgotten the rest of us are sitting here listening, he seems so laid-back, so conversational.

Jasper's jaw tightens and his eyes roam the tablecloth. When he speaks his voice is caught at the back of his throat. "I'm yet to find my mate."

I stare at my lap. Even though I know he has to keep up appearances, it stings. Katie glimpses in my direction.

"Who knows, your presence here may prove to create a stronger bond between our packs than anyone was expecting."

Morven casually places a hand on Mia's back and I notice her stiffen. Is he suggesting what I think he's suggesting?

"Thank you for hosting my pack," Jasper says, ignoring Morven's inappropriately overt suggestion. "We are honored to accept your hospitality."

Morven laughs a little to himself, clearly amused by Jasper's overly serious tone. "You are most welcome." He returns his attention to the room at large. "Our ancestors have lived in these mountains for hundreds of centuries, although not always at the crest of the mountains as we do today. We were valley dwellers, roaming the shadows, struggling to survive, and it was only with perseverance, strength, and reverence for the Moon Gods that we were able to claw our way out of the valley to climb these lofty peaks. Now we sit at the top of the mountains, and this Christmas we will be given a gift: the gift of the blood moon—a symbol of who we are and where we've come from."

He holds his full glass of red wine to the sky. "Because of our connection to the Moon Gods, and our closeness to them, we must hold fast to our traditions and the beliefs that keep us from the shadows. This blood moon, let us give thanks to our Moon Gods, and pray for their blessing."

A few of the men around the room raise their glasses, nodding their agreement.

"I am most excited for our siblings from the Elite Pack to experience this one-in-a-lifetime event from our special vantage point." Once again his eyes find my packmates and he smirks. "Just be careful the blood wolf doesn't get you."

The wolves of the Rocky Pack chuckle and grin, nodding along at some joke that doesn't make any sense. I'd say you had to be there, but here I am and...nothing. I glance at Katie, but she shrugs—she's as confused as I am.

"I'm sorry," Morven says, chuckling to himself. "It was just a little wolf joke, there's nothing to be afraid of. I'm excited for the chance to share some of our culture with you. Now I have waffled on too long, haven't I? Shall we eat?"

Dinner is maybe the most delicious hour of my life. The meat is so succulent and rich, the vegetables perfectly cooked, and the dessert... I've never had an apple strudel that tasted quite like that!

Once the plates are cleared, I rub my full stomach contentedly, and the guests begin to leave. Some are heading back to their homes, and others must have rooms in the packhouse because the numbers dwindle quickly.

Olivia is off before they've even cleared her place, and I'm thinking about heading back to my room too when Morven approaches. Katie, Todd, Simon, and I stand to greet him.

"Hello, sir," I say lowering my head. "It's so nice of you to invite us."

"You must be the one who—what did Jericho say—fell in?"

He knows about that?

"Let's hope you have better luck on the slopes tomorrow."

My mouth drops open and I laugh awkwardly. "As long as there aren't holes in the mountain, I should be fine."

To my surprise, Morven laughs—maybe at my sort-of-joke, maybe at my complete awkwardness.

"The mountains may be holy, but they are free of holes. Enjoy your stay."

Morven leaves us in peace and Katie gives me her best sympathetic head tilt.

"Hey Elite Pack," Mia says, skipping toward us. "There's gingerbread and coffee in the den, if you want to meet some of the officers' kids?"

"Sure," Katie says, ever the extravert. "Max?"

"I dunno." I kind of want to go back to my room, maybe try and sketch something before bed.

"Come on, Mia says they have gingerbread; we can count this as our traditional gingerbread-house-building extravaganza."

"That sound cute," Mia says, and she has a point. This is the perfect opportunity to get back on track with our traditions.

"Fine."

"Great," Mia says, turning on her toes. "Follow me!"

We form a clump behind Mia and make to leave the dining room, but run into Jasper and Clayton at the door.

"Jasper!"

Mia catches him off guard, and his eyes snap to her before traveling to me. His brow is low, his mouth a straight line.

"Wanna come to the den for gingerbread and coffee? You too, Clayton."

"I'm in," Clayton says, clasping Jasper's shoulder.

"I...need to call my father," Jasper says gruffly. Mia looks disappointed and Clayton is a little surprised. "Sorry, maybe some other time."

Mia shrugs it off. "No problem, good night. See you on the slopes tomorrow."

"Good night," Jasper says, then darts off into the hall.

"Do you think he's annoyed because Daddy forgot he doesn't eat meat?" Mia asks Clayton, looking absolutely terrified.

"Of course not," he says laughing. "Jasper loves eating nothing but string beans and cabbage. He's just one of those early to bed early to rise types. Always has been." Clayton wraps an arm around Mia. "Me on the other hand, I don't plan on sleeping until *much* later."

Gross.

They lead us down to the den, which looks like the basement from every teen boy's dreams. A pool table is lit from above in the far corner, a jukebox glows and hums beneath a neon sign that says Cocktails in fluoro-pink cursive, there's a fully stocked bar, a dartboard with three darts sticking out at weird angles, and an array of squishy-looking leather sofas surrounding a coffee table.

A few Rocky Pack kids are already situated on their sofas. I nod to them as we enter, then my eye catches on the cute guy with the tight blond curls.

"Guys, these are the Elite Pack wolves," Mia says. "Make them welcome." She perches on the armrest of a sofa and gestures at the mountain of cookies and cups of steaming black coffee in the middle of the table. "Help yourselves, there's plenty, and get comfy."

Katie and her mates take a sofa and get cozy. Clayton goes behind the bar and starts inspecting the bottles of liquor. A couple of girls with remarkably straight hair are occupying one sofa, one lying with her feet on the other's lap; a big guy scrolls through his phone on another. A lanky guy with ginger hair, a girl with braids, and a girl dressed all in black have commandeered a corner sofa. The only spare seat is next to the cute boy with the adorable overbite. A gulp and I sit.

"Hey, I'm Mason," he says, giving me a smile.

"Hi, I'm Max."

"What do you think of the Rocky Pack so far?"

I pause for too long.

"Seems...nice. A lot of dead animals."

"Are you talking about the trophies or our parents?"

Okay, he's funny too.

"Don't worry," he continues, smirking. "It's not all dinner with the parents. Sometimes we actually have fun, too."

"Oh good." I rub the back of my neck.

Mason is... Mason is cute—and friendly. And from the way his knee is already nudging against mine, he's pretty forward, too.

"Right," Mia says, jumping up and clapping her hands. "The adults should be in bed by now. Shall we show these wolves what the Rocky Pack is really about?"

Okay, I thought Mia was like the ultimate Girl Scout, a princess as pack devoted as Jasper. Who is this?

The girl with braids jumps up and heads to the jukebox, and to my surprise, she unplugs it. The bigger guy looks up and starts tapping about on his phone. In a second, music is pumping from a Bluetooth speaker somewhere behind the bar.

"Mugs!" Mia commands, and the Rocky Pack wolves move their coffee mugs to the central table. With a dramatic flourish, like she's displaying a prize on a game show, Mia produces a polished metal hip flask and proceeds to pour something into the coffee. "What?" she says in response to our confused expressions. "It's not all official welcomes and diplomatic dinners. Oh Clayton."

He looks up from examining the label on a bottle half filled with an amber liquid.

"Daddy checks the levels on those," Mia says, then smiles at me. "I have a human contact in town who helps me out."

Mia is quickly turning out to be quite a surprise. And I'm not sure if this fun side to her makes her less of a threat or more.

Mason grabs his spiked mug of coffee and sits back on the couch.

"How do you like it here now?" he asks, and I roll my eyes.

An hour later, we're jumping on the sofas singing along to Olivia Rodrigo at the top of our lungs. I hate to say that I'm sort of proud of being off book for "good 4 u," and Mason watches smiling and clapping as I spit those lyrics like I'm starring in a music video.

"Bravo," he cheers when I poutily deliver the final lyrics. "That was amazing."

He grabs my hand to help me down off the sofa, and I fall back into it.

"This is the best gingerbread I've ever had," I say, grabbing a piece and shoving it in my mouth.

Mason flops down next to me and I realize I'm a little light-headed. Maybe it's the altitude, maybe it's whatever Mia poured into my drink, or maybe it's that I'm sitting next to a cute boy, our arms pressed up against each other. And for about thirty minutes I actually haven't thought about Jasper.

Across the room, Mia and Clayton are leaning on the bar having an animated conversation. Katie, Todd, and Simon are standing on the sofa opposite us, dancing in this sort of awkward but sort of natural three-person configuration. Some of the Rocky Pack wolves are also dancing, while the two girls with straight hair play pool.

"So, Mason, are you excited for the blood moon?"

"Did you really just ask that?" he responds, laughing.

"I mean it's a sacred event, right?" Am I slurring?

"Sure, just like the blue moon and the harvest moon and the jackal moon. Am I forgetting any?"

"Probably. There's so many moons!"

"Right?! And they're all the same—it's just extra energy making our wolf hormones go crazy. It's science."

I sit up and slap him in the chest. "That's what I said!"

"Our pack is super traditional," Mason says, less excitedly. "We're not exactly progressive, if you know what I mean."

He gives me this look like I should know what he means.

"I don't think I do."

"Oh, sorry I just assumed you were...like...you know."

"No, like what?"

Mason eyes me sideways and I can tell he's freaking out a little.

"Never mind."

"No wait," I say, watching my fun new friend drift away before my very eyes. "I do know what you mean I'm just..."

"You're still figuring it out."

I exhale and feel seen in a way that's completely knew—that I didn't even think was possible. Mason and I literally just met and we're relating in a way I never have with anyone before. It's not the same as knowing Jasper is like me. Because with Jasper it's all about us, about whether we're going to be mates or not, or tell anyone that we're mates, or be kidnapped and held at gunpoint because we're mates. It's never just about who we are, about what liking each other means about us.

"Yeah, I'm figuring out a lot," I say and sit back.

"Let me give you my number." He holds out his hand, so I pass him my phone. "Working this out alone can be really tricky. If you ever want to talk, just give me a text."

"Thanks."

He finishes adding himself to my contacts and hands the phone back.

"So," he says, grabbing an angel-shaped piece of gingerbread, "have you told your parents?"

"No," I say. "They're great and I know they'd be fine with it, but I just don't want to change the way they see me, you know?"

"I totally get it."

"What about you?"

"My parents? They're not as chill as yours sound. They're pretty high up in the pack hierarchy; my dad is Morven's beta."

"Oh, that is pretty high up, like about as high as you can get."

"Yeah," he chortles. "And I don't think having a gay son was ever on his to-do list."

I'm floored at how easily Mason is able to call himself gay, as if the word just rolled off his tongue. My parents don't sound anywhere as conservative as his and he's still able to say it, just like that. Now I feel extra bad for him.

"I'm sorry."

"It's no problem," he says, biting off the angel's head. "At least we haven't found our mates yet, right? That would be a whole other ball game."

I try to swallow the bauble in my throat but end up choking on it instead.

"Whoa, are you okay? You nearly panicked when I said... Oh shit. You've found him haven't you?"

Heat rises in my cheeks but I don't deny it. Mason clicks his tongue and leans back to get a better view of me.

"Well, he's a lucky wolf. Sucks for me though. You're cute."

More heat, more heat, more heat.

"Thanks."

"So why didn't he come with?"

My mind stalls, turning over, trying to come up with an answer that isn't "He's here!"

"The whole not being out yet thing; if we came together we'd have to tell people." It's only half a lie.

"Right, fair enough."

Thinking about all this has my mind well and truly back to obsessing over Jasper, so I decide to change the subject. I catch Mia laughing at something Clayton has said.

"Looks like someone else might be finding their mate on this trip."

Mason follows my eyeline.

"Not a chance," he says. "Mia's dad is hell-bent on her becoming Jasper's mate."

I spit out the alcohol-laced coffee.

"What?"

"Whoa, take it slow, that stuff is strong."

"What did you say about Mia and Jasper?"

He purses his lips and thinks for a second. "I wasn't supposed to tell anyone; Mia told me in confidence. Her dad wants her to try and seduce Jasper so that he'll choose her as his mate. Something about strengthening the bridge between the two packs. That's basically the reason he invited you all here. She's not super happy about it, but he's the alpha so she doesn't have much choice."

I stare at Mia, feeling all sorts of confused feelings. My wolf-self wants to shift and tear her apart or find Jasper and sink my teeth into his neck so that everyone will know he's mine. But on the other hand I feel sorry for her. She's just as trapped as Jasper was when his dad tried to force him to pick a mate.

Still, as long as she's trying to steal mine, I'm going to have to be on my guard. Screw the bridge between our packs and screw Alpha Morven. I came here to convince Jasper to be with me. And that's exactly what I'm going to do.

GOING OFF PISTE

I stomp through the halls of the packhouse, only a little tipsy and only a little lost. But feeling a steely sense of determination. For some reason—most likely whatever Mia had in that hip flask—I'm certain the best thing to do right now is find Jasper's room.

Just like in a hotel, there are dim lights keeping the halls illuminated, so at least I'm not stumbling around in the dark. But all I have to go on is the vague idea of where Jasper's room is based on the relation of our balconies— and the feeling in my gut, telling me he's getting close.

Slipping out of the party in the den was pretty easy. I told Mason I needed to use the restroom, and everyone else was preoccupied in some way.

I follow the tingling sensation in my gut down a series of long hallways, catching glimpses of the mountains as I pass the occasional window. Thankfully they're still on the left side of me, which means I'm heading in the right direction. The ceilings are taller in this part of the lodge, the carpets a little more plush, and the halls a little wider. Must be heading in the right direction because things are getting fancy up in here.

Finally, I find a door and know without a doubt that Jasper is behind it. I can smell his cherry blossom aroma wafting out from inside.

Without thinking about his neighbors, I knock three times. There's no answer, so I knock again and finally, the door swings open.

Jasper is in a navy toweling robe like the kind you get at exclusive spas. His hair is sticking up, and a yawn is escaping his mouth. He must have been asleep before I got here. No wonder he looks so grumpy, all squinty and scowly.

"What are you doing here?"

"It's not okay, you know," I say. "Saying you don't have a mate to everyone."

He rubs his forehead.

"You can't be here."

"It's a free country."

Jasper pokes his head farther outside his room and checks both ends of the hallway.

"You're being ridiculous."

"I'm being ridiculous?!" My head is spinning and I need to use the doorframe to stop myself from toppling over. "You're the one hanging out with a douchebag and being a jerkface."

"Are you drunk? How did you? Never mind. Look, it's not okay for you to be here. I told you it isn't safe."

"And I told you I don't—"

"Shh." He holds a finger to his lips and I shut my mouth. Why am I obeying him?

Voices echo down the corridor; maybe the party has moved from the den.

"That's Clayton." Jasper wipes his face with a hand and looks back into his room like he's making a really difficult decision. "Get in here."

He pulls me inside and shuts the door. It's dark in the short entryway, the only light a dim glow from a lamp beside his unmade bed in the main room. We wait in the darkness as the voices grow closer, arrive at the door, and then fade down the hall. Even when they're gone, we linger in the shadows, barely a foot apart, that familiar electric buzz holding us in place.

"What are you doing here, Max?"

Jasper is waiting for an answer, but with the tension broken I turn and wander farther inside.

"This your room?" I take it all in: the lounge area, the golden bar trolley in the corner, the massive flat-screen mounted in an open cabinet on the wall, the fireplace that my dad could drive his car through. "This is bigger than most people's houses."

Jasper traipses after me. On his bed the comforter is thrown back, a book lies open face down on the pillow, the sheets... They smell like him.

"Max," Jasper says, but I can't say anything back; I'm intoxicated, first by spiked coffee and now by the warmth emanating from his mattress.

"Max." Jasper's voice is suddenly a lot closer, and I spin to find myself face-to-face with him.

We linger in close proximity. Jasper's throat bulges like he's swallowing; I lick my lips and rise onto my toes slightly. I drift forward and so does Jasper, then he catches me by the shoulders.

"Max, you need to go now." His eyes travel from mine to the carpet and stay there. "If anyone catches you here they'll think—"

"What? That you like me? That you'd deign to speak to someone like me? The poor commoner, the pity invite? Is that so horrendous?"

"Keep your voice down."

"No one is going to catch us." I reach out and take hold of his robe, pulling him toward me.

Jasper's eyes find mine again and my jaw trembles. His breathing is shaky. His resistance is decreasing, the mate bond is taking over, fighting for supremacy and winning. He bites his lip, then pushes me away. I stumble a little, tripping over my own feet, but catch myself on the edge of the bed.

Jasper reaches out to help me up. "I'm sorry, are you okay?"

I slap his arm away, fully aware of how much of a brat I'm being, and stand. "You say you're ignoring me for my protection, but I think you're just ashamed."

"Max—"

"Do you know how it felt hearing you say to everyone you don't have a mate?"

He huffs and rubs his eyes. "I didn't have a choice."

"Whatever."

"You're acting like a child."

"Do you know how it felt?!"

"Of course I do!" he roars. "Do you get how hard that was for me? Being put on the spot like that. There are bigger things happening here than you and me, Max. This trip is important for the relationship between the packs. If Morven were to find out—"

"Stop hiding behind your father and the pack and your goddamn duty. This isn't about protecting anyone; this about you being a coward."

"Get out," he spits through clenched teeth.

I've overstepped. Suddenly, I have no idea what my plan was. To come here and seduce Jasper before anyone else could? If that was the idea, I'm doing a terrible job. Being called cowardly isn't exactly a turn-on.

"Jasper."

"Get out, Max." He stares at the rug and points at the door. "And don't talk to me anymore while we're here."

"That's ridiculous I—"

"I mean it: leave me alone."

I feel so stupid. I know this person: this is the Jasper who pushes me away and treats me like crap—the Jasper he apologized for being, the one he said was an act to keep me at arm's length. I don't even like this person, but I've followed him all the way to this overdressed ski resort.

With clenched fists I give in. "Fine."

I amble back to my room, deflated and sober.

I wish I'd closed the curtains when I managed to get back into my room last night. As it is, the morning sun is streaming like a spotlight through the windows this morning.

What did Mia have in that flask?

Somehow managing to sit up, I blink until the light seems less blinding, and my breath catches at the view. It was spectacular at night, all shimmery and silver, but in the day...woof! A golden sun in a perfectly clear blue sky shines down on crisp white mountaintops, black jagged rocks poke through the powder the lower down I peer. Drawn to the balcony, I make my way outside and take it in. I didn't notice last night, but off to the left, low in the valley, is a town, set amongst the rocks like it was carved out of the mountainside.

Automatically, my gaze drifts to Jasper's balcony. It's empty and suddenly I'm filled with regret. What did I think I was doing? I know Jasper, and there's no way showing up randomly drunk would ever win him over. And now he's pissed at me—more than usual.

There's a knock at my door and I have a feeling I know who it is.

"Happy Christmas Eve Eve!" Katie says, throwing up her arms and hugging me the second I open the door.

"How are you so chipper?"

"Must be this mountain air." She shrugs. "We're heading down to breakfast; I bet they have good breakfast."

If that strudel last night was anything to go by, I bet they have some wild pastries, and I could devour an entire cow's worth of sausages right now. I may be feeling all kinds of awful, but I don't want to miss this meal.

"Let me get dressed."

I slap some water on my face, attempt to fuss with my unruly hair before giving up, then head down to breakfast with Katie, Simon, and Todd.

"So where did you slip off to last night?" Katie asks as we saunter down a pine-scented hall.

"Well if the plan was to get his attention I think it worked."

"So it went well?"

Ah, Katie, if only...if only.

Breakfast is served in the parlor buffet style, and I've barely packed enough meat and pastries on my plate and sat down at a table by the window when Mia—accompanied by Jasper and Clayton—walks past.

"Max!" she shouts excitedly. *When did we become besties?* She hurries over to me while Katie shoots me a confused glance. "How are you this morning?"

Clayton and Jasper have followed Mia over, and I catch Clayton elbowing Jasper's side as if to say, "Who is this dweeb?"

"I'm all right," I lie, trying to will Jasper to look up for even a millisecond.

"Mason said he had a nice time last night."

I blush and Jasper, well, he doesn't look up, but his shoulders are suddenly tense.

"We're all going skiing after this," she says. "You're all coming too, right?"

Katie leans over me. "I'm not sure Max is up to extreme sports today—"

"We'll be there," I say, cutting Katie off.

Clayton snickers and raises a judgey brow, Jasper eyes me sideways, and I force a grin in his direction.

"Great! We can all get the shuttle over together! Meet us out front in an hour?"

"Perfect."

Jasper doesn't hang around a second longer, instead he plows toward the farthest table from us. Mia waves as she and Clayton move to join him.

"Are you sure you're up for skiing? I thought maybe we could watch *Home Alone* or make popcorn ribbons..."

"Oh I'm ready for skiing, just you wait."

Okay, apparently everyone here is a professional skier. While I'm standing in my little ski suit, wobbling about like a nervous flamingo, everyone is shooting past me down the slopes.

"Come on Max," Katie calls, shuffling to the ski lift.

It's insanely sunny, and the glare off the miles and miles of white is intense. Luckily, my hangover is wearing off. The coffee and pastries have done their job. I do my best to catch up to Katie and hop a lift.

After breakfast we quickly changed then headed to the front of the packhouse, where a sleek shuttle bus was waiting. Mia was excited to see us but sat up front chatting with Clayton for most of the ride. Jasper sat in the back row with Olivia, both of them hidden behind sunglasses, earphones in, listening to music. Todd and Simon played video games for once not fighting for Katie's attention.

Mason, on the other hand, sat with us and regaled us with fun facts about the mountains as we drove.

"That's Mistlethorpe," Mason said as the town I noticed this morning came into view.

Believe me when I say it is hella cute—like a Scandinavian dream, all pointed roofs, houses made of pine, and cobbled sidewalks. I must have missed the part where we traveled internationally.

When we arrived at the ski slopes, we were kitted out with suits, skis, and goggles by a handsome guy in a knitted sweater, with the whitest teeth I've ever seen. I thought Elite Pack wolves were attractive, but this mountain air really works wonders. By the time I was done fidgeting with my bootstraps and figuring out how to walk with two planks on my feet, Jasper and Clayton had already sped off, clearly practiced on skis; Mason and Mia waved and told us to catch up when we'd found our snow legs. And Katie told Todd and Simon to go ahead as well.

For a while, Katie and I messed around on the practice slopes, figuring out how to stay upright.

But now we're ready to take on a real hill.

As we make our way up the mountainside, I stare down at the skiers whooshing past and wonder where Jasper has gotten to. The paths are pretty curvy, dotted with rocks and pines heavy with snowfall. It all seems a little dangerous, and Jasper's words are ringing in my ears. Sure he's told me to stay away from him before, but this time there was something else in his voice, a tightness that's new. Still, whatever he's got going on, I'm allowed to be out here skiing, and if we bump into each other, that's not my fault—there's only so much mountain to go around.

"Let's go," Katie says the second we're off the lift.

She glides to the starting marker of the trail and turns gracefully, ready for the descent. I've grown up with her my entire life, and I know for a fact she has never gone skiing either. So why does she have a knack for it and I feel like I'm wearing clown shoes?

"Come on, Max, it's easy!" she calls again, turning and gliding gracefully over the first little section of slope.

With some degree of difficulty I line myself up at the starting marker and am about to push off when Clayton's voice reverberates across the hillside.

"You sure you got enough practice?" he says, and I turn to find him and Jasper heading my way.

Jasper is wearing an extremely well-fitting, all-black ski suit that makes him look like James Bond. He's the one who told me to leave him alone and yet here he is, everywhere I am. They sidle up next to me and Clayton slips on his goggles, smirking in my direction.

"Certain you're ready for this?"

I shoot him my most sarcastic smile.

"Okay, then. Don't hurt yourself."

He pushes off, sliding down the slope at breakneck speed, already passing Katie, who's stopped to wait for me.

Jasper locks eyes with me for a brief second, but neither of us say anything. Then he pulls on his goggles and follows after his friend. I stare as he dips and weaves across the powder. His butt looks stupidly good in his ski suit.

But I can't think about that now. I shake the dirty thoughts from my head and prepare to push off. I'm not going to be the one Elite Pack wolf who can't make it down the slope, and if Clayton thinks he can be so smug, he's got another thing coming. As the breeze picks up I take off.

At first, it's crazy awkward and I worry I'm going to topple over at any second. But then I find my rhythm and actually it's not so bad. I pick up speed and even manage to avoid a collision with a poorly placed tree.

Up ahead I spot Clayton and Jasper having pulled to a stop near a red flag, so I head in their direction. I've reached a sort of plateau with trees and a picnic bench; off to the right there are a few differently colored flags.

"Max!" Katie's voice calls to me across the slopes. Luckily, the terrain has flattened out enough that I can stop without too much trouble. Katie skids her way over. "Wait up!"

Katie's calls catch Jasper's and Clayton's attention.

"That's the advanced trail," she says. "The beginner's slope is over here."

Glancing back in their direction, I notice Clayton smirking and shaking his head.

"I'm fine," I say, turning toward the red flag. "I want to try it."

"I don't think that's such a good idea."

"It's just snow; how much can it hurt?"

"A lot."

Katie's last words are lost on the breeze as I make my way over to the start of a new slope. It's rockier than the last, the path has way more curves and turns, and oh yeah, it's wildly steep—basically like skiing down a sheer cliff face.

"You've got to be kidding," Clayton says. "I didn't bring anything to wear to a funeral."

His snide remark is enough to get my engine burning, so I dig my poles into the snow and take off.

At first it's not so bad: I can handle the turns and the bumps, and it's not so fast, except that I'm speeding up. My skis dig into the powder and the farther down I go, the faster I travel.

"Heads up!" Clayton calls from behind me. He and Jasper are on my tail and gaining speed.

I grit my teeth. There is no way I cannot stay upright right now.

"Make room," Clayton yells, spraying me with snow as he races past.

I shake the powder from my goggles as Jasper passes too. I can be thankful he doesn't spray me as well, although I'd almost prefer that to his cold shoulder—he barely glances in my direction before overtaking me.

I know this is dumb—they've probably been skiing since they could walk, and I am a literal baby at this—but I'm determined not to let them win. Maybe this'll be like the weird superspeed I get around Jasper, maybe I'll also be super good at winter sports.

I bend my knees, lower my head, and push harder.

Icy wind slices at my cheeks as I descend at an ungodly speed. Every little bump under my skis feels like a boulder, and the muscles in my legs are straining to keep the skis from sliding apart and tearing me in half. But somehow I'm making up ground.

I bend into the turns, lean into the corners as the mountainside disappears behind me. Below, the trees begin to thicken, and I think for sure Jasper and Clayton are going to turn off, avoid the obstacles, but instead they disappear into the forest. The terrain becomes rockier and boulders jut out from the snow—jagged protrusions, like spikes on a hedgehog. I dodge and weave to avoid them and the trees which are closing in on all sides. This must be what Han Solo feels like flying through an asteroid field.

Behind me is a whizzing sound growing louder as it approaches, and I turn slightly to find Olivia right on my tail. She's bent over for aerodynamic efficiency; her knees are angles and her poles are held tightly at her sides. Her eyes are hidden behind dark goggles, but for some reason I feel like she's glaring at me. And just when I've been staring too long, she lifts her head and I spin in time to realize I'm about to collide with a very frozen-looking pine tree. In a winter sports panic I try to swerve, but instead I flop onto my side and skid to a painful stop.

I groan and lie in the snow. I should be grateful nothing is broken, at least I don't think anything is. With a grunt I yank my head out of the powder and am greeted by the distinct sound of Clayton laughing—and yep, the asshat is standing a little ways down the hill, literally clutching his stomach. Jasper is with him, his expression unreadable.

Olivia skids to an effortless stop nearby, throwing her head back and lifting her goggles off her face. She appraises me like I'm roadkill, and once she's ascertained that I'm still alive, she pulls her goggles back on and glides away.

I watch her go; when she passes Jasper, he turns on his skis and pushes off behind her.

They all leave me lying in the cold, biting snow.

What a bunch of jerkfaces.

I beg the Moon Gods to let the mountain open up and swallow me whole.

HOT TUB TIME MACHINE

"Need a hand?" I look up and Mia is standing over me with her hand extended, her snow goggles pushed back over a sleek red braid.

"That would be great."

She pulls me back onto my skis.

"The shuttle is about ready to take us back," she says as we begin to ski-walk our way across the mountain. "Unless you want to stay out here longer?"

I laugh. "No, no I think I'm done."

Mia's pale cheeks are flushed rosy in the chill, but she seems completely at ease out here—calm in a way she wasn't back at the packhouse.

"First time on skis?" she asks.

"How could you tell?"

"You know you were on the most advanced trail, right?" She glances in my direction with a friendly smile. Anyone else might have been teasing, but she sounds sort of impressed. "For a first-timer I think you did pretty good."

"Because I didn't die?"

"Basically."

We trudge—well, I trudge and Mia glides—through the scattered pines until I can make out the ski shed across the way. We're almost back, and I can almost take these sticks off my feet.

"Have you been skiing for long?" I ask, instantly realizing what a dumb question that is for someone who was raised on this mountain range.

"My whole life," she says. "Actually, out on the slopes is my favorite place to be. There's nothing like the feeling of freedom you get when you're whizzing down a mountain at a hundred miles an hour. I dunno, it's cliché but being out here I can sort of forget about being the alpha's daughter and just...be. That must sound dumb."

She shakes her head and sighs a little.

"It's not dumb," I say, realizing there's more to Mia than I first thought. Maybe she's just as trapped in this system as Jasper; maybe she isn't a stuck-up princess trying to steal my boyfriend. Maybe I should give her more credit.

She looks at me sideways from under her precisely manicured brow. "Sounds like you can relate maybe."

Me? Relate to being stuck in a tricky situation and looking for anything to distract myself? Not possible.

"Huh, maybe."

Mia huffs, clenches her teeth, and starts digging her poles into the powder.

"You okay?" I ask.

She exhales through her lips, letting them flutter a little, and rolls her eyes like she's thinking. "It's nothing."

I don't expect her to tell me. We've only just met. But if I'm right and the reason she's acting all huffy is because of pressure from her dad, then maybe I'm in the clear. Maybe she's not even interested in getting with Jasper, and I have nothing to worry about.

"Sorry if I, you know, interrupted your"—I wave my hand around at the mountain—"free time."

Mia smiles then glides smoothly toward the shed once more.

"It's fine. Hey, you know what's really great after a rough day on the slopes?"

A shrug. "An overnight stay in the ER?"

"Un-uh." She shakes her head. "A nice, warm dip in one of the packhouse's hot tubs."

After we arrive back at the packhouse, I shower, change, and head down to the parlor. On the shuttle back Katie and I decided we'd use the afternoon to brainstorm which Christmas traditions we could squeeze into our trip. Jasper, Olivia, and Clayton weren't on the shuttle—opting instead to stay and ski longer—and Simon and Todd went straight to sleep the second we left the slopes.

Katie isn't here when I step into the lounge. She's probably still showering or giving equal attention to her twin lovers. A few of the couches are occupied but I spot a familiar face.

Mason, looking freshly showered, peers up from his conversation with two of the other officers' kids and smiles. Without thinking much about it I smile back, and he waves me over.

"Hey," he says, turning from his group, who are debating whether or not *Die Hard* is a Christmas movie and if Bruce Willis is actually a werewolf. "How were the slopes?"

"Don't ask," I say, rubbing my extremely bruised thigh.

"That good, huh?"

"Let's just say I don't think I'll be participating in the Winter Olympics this year."

"Too bad, you looked good in your ski suit."

Am I blushing? Oh Moon Gods, I'm blushing.

My mouth flaps open but no words come out.

"Sorry," he says, throwing his arms up. "I know you're a kept wolf, but I couldn't help it."

I rub a hand over my face. "Well, not exactly kept."

"Right." He gives me a knowing nod and taps his nose. It's hard to explain but it's like within two days of knowing each other we have this secret language, like we're just on the same wavelength. So, that's cool. "Sorry I didn't catch you on the shuttle back, I hopped an earlier one, had some stuff I had to get done for school. I'm all done now and we were about to go watch a movie in the den if you wanted to join?"

"I'd love to, but I'm waiting for my friend—we were..." My sentence trails away in a cloud of preemptive embarrassment. Mason looks confused. "So we're sort of big into Christmas, and back in New York we have all these traditions and things we do—silly things like going to markets, wrapping presents, drinking peppermint coffees, stringing popcorn... It's dumb. Anyway, since we're here, we can't do any of those things, but we thought we could see what we could squeeze in or retrofit so it isn't like we're missing all the usual stuff—and because she has two mates, we haven't seen each other much recently, and we both want to make sure we're still nurturing the friendship, and I don't know why I'm still talking..."

Mason chuckles and my knees go sort of wobbly.

"Okay that all sounds really cute."

There's that word again.

"Well I can help if you like. I know all the good stuff to do around here."

"That would be—I mean... If you don't mind... Yeah, that'd be great!"

I recognize the girl with the braids from last night as she turns and touches Mason's shoulder. "Mase, we're heading down; you coming?"

"Yeah, one second."

The rest of the kids meander off, but Mason stays with me, biting his right knuckle and doing a great thinking face.

"Don't hurt yourself," I joke.

His eyes light up. "I've got it. You said *markets*, right? Mistlethorpe has the most amazing Christmas market, and tomorrow is Christmas Eve so it'll be wildly festive. I can take you both if you want."

"I mean, that would be amazing!"

"Okay, and maybe we can get you some popcorn to thread from the kitchens, and I'll keep thinking if there's anything else we can do."

It doesn't escape my attention that he's inserted himself into this plan—and I'm not mad about it.

"Mason! You coming?" The girl with the braids is leaning through the doorway. Mason's friends have all disappeared.

"You should go or Hans Gruber won't be happy."

He snickers at my amazing pop culture reference.

"Okay, meet me here at like ten tomorrow."

"Can't wait!"

I take a seat by the window to wait for Katie. The mountainside swoops out below me, the afternoon sun is beginning to sit low on the horizon, and golden rays are shooting out from behind the permafrosted mountaintops. It's gorgeous, but if I've learned anything today it's how inhospitable these gorgeous terrains are. I feel like there's maybe a lesson in there, but I'm not sure.

Almost an hour goes by and Katie still hasn't shown. It's seriously dusky now, and dinner will be served in an hour or so. I shoot her a couple of texts but she doesn't reply. Maybe she fell asleep. I guess this is payback for all those times I slept in and kept her waiting in the past. The view is so pretty I almost don't mind; I just wish I'd brought down my sketchbook.

A gust of cold wind blows through the lounge and I turn to see Jasper, Clayton, and Olivia arriving home. They strut through the entryway like royalty, fresh from conquering the slopes, paying me no attention as they pass through.

I sigh and shoot Katie one more text. The longer I sit still, the more the pain in my leg from where I fell intensifies, and I remember what Mia recommended. The hot tubs.

I figure I'll wait another fifteen minutes for Katie then go check them out. After ten Olivia strolls back into the lounge, sees me, rolls her head back, and turns in the opposite direction, disappearing from where she came.

There's something up with her and I have no idea what it is, but I don't care. She's being rude, and her rudeness, plus Katie's absence, plus my fall and the consequent humiliation, are putting me in a foul mood. I gather up my stuff, ready for a bit of me time.

If the ski slopes are Mia's fortress of solitude, then maybe the hot tub can be mine. Clutching a fluffy white towel, I make my way down a stone staircase, my flip-flops thworping on each step. Down I go past an indoor gym, a pool, and a sauna to a set of glass doors. I must be on the lowest level of the packhouse. The hot tubs are sitting outside on a balcony with a stone ledge, like four bubbling cauldrons, each with steam pouring out.

Not imagining I'd be heading outside, I've only worn my swimming shorts and an old T-shirt, and as the cold air hits me I feel like I've face-planted in the snow all over again. I can't wait another second to be in that hot, soothing water.

Glancing around quickly to make sure there's no one else out here, I drop my towel at the base of the tub nearest to me and pull off my shirt. Then speedily I kick off my flip-flops and climb in. At first the water is so hot my little feet feel like they might boil off, but as I lower my whole body into it, I breathe a massive sigh of relief. It's like every muscle relaxes at the same time, and every stress of the last few days (months?) drifts away. I rest my head against the smooth edge of the tub and look out at the view. *That darn view.*

Not five minutes into my soak, the sound of the door swinging opens pulls me from my steam-fueled reverie.

"Oh," he says before I can even turn my head.

Behind Jasper the door is swinging shut, leaving him standing, towel over his bare shoulder, in just his swimming trunks (black, obviously), out in the cold.

Gulp. Big gulp.

Even though I'm mad, and even though he told me to leave him alone but doesn't seem to be able to follow his own advice, I say, "Hi."

"I didn't think anyone would be here," he says, still not moving.

"Clearly," I say. "I'd also like the record to show that I was here first, just so you don't think I'm following you around or anything."

His face is expressionless.

"I should go." He doesn't move. Why isn't he moving?

Little goosebumps are beginning to pop up all over his arms, his shoulders, his...chest, until I actually can't take it any longer.

"Would you just get in? It's like fifty below out there."

His teeth beginning to chatter, Jasper actually moves toward the hot tub. I make room on the side closer to the steps and sit back as he lowers himself in. For a split second as his chest enters the water, an almost calm expression crosses his face. He closes his eyes, untenses his brow, and lets his bottom lip hang a little loose. For a moment I see a glimpse of the Jasper from the beach.

When he opens his eyes, he catches me staring and I swiftly glance away.

"These mountains are something," I say, ever so awkwardly.

"Yeah, I guess."

I force myself to keep my eyes focused on the valley, singling out one rocky outcrop and staring at it intensely.

"I'm sorry," Jasper says. "For what happened earlier. Are you okay?"

"You mean when I barely escaped death only to fall on my ass?" I say, staring at him deadass and tensing right up.

"Yes, I shouldn't have... I'm sorry. I hope you're okay."

He seems genuine, so I relax, sit back in the seat, and try to not to clench my fists underwater.

"It was pretty shitty leaving like that," I say. "But I'm fine."

"I know it was shitty, but I couldn't with the others around... I—"

"Right." I let my chin slip into the water. If I could dive under and stay there I probably would.

The bubbling sound of the water fills the silence that lingers between us. I shift uncomfortably while Jasper sits up straight, his eyes on mine.

"You know I didn't think it was possible," I say.

"What?"

"Your buddy Clayton, he's even more of a jerk than you."

It's a joke, but Jasper doesn't laugh; he breaks eye contact and lowers his head, like he's ashamed.

"I know."

"Okay, so why do you hang out with him?"

"His family and my family go back generations. Our relationship is important to the pack, it's..."

Jasper stops when he sees just how much I'm rolling my eyes.

"So he could be the biggest dick in the world and you'd still be his friend because it's important to the pack, but I'm—"

"Max, you don't have to worry about Clayton...in that way."

I huff.

Without looking at him I know that Jasper has edged forward on his seat, a little closer to me than he was before.

"And what about Mia?" I ask, knowing how sulky I sound. "You know the only reason any of us are here is because her dad wants to strengthen the packs by mating her to you?"

Jasper tenses in the water but remains where he is.

"If the pack is the most important thing to you then—"

"Max." Jasper's hand finds my arm just beneath the surface; he holds me tightly. "You don't have to worry about anyone like that. I..."

I feel the slight tug of Jasper's hand and slowly angle my body back in his direction. The steam wafts between our sweat-dotted faces.

"I may not be able to say you're my mate in public," he says, pulling me closer, and I drift helplessly through the tub and my confusion. "But there will never be anyone else that I..."

Can this dude ever finish a sentence?

Jasper purses his lips, and I drift a little closer, my eyelids drooping on their way to being shut. It's warm, but my entire body is covered in goosebumps. I drift another inch closer...and then I hear the door swing open. We pull apart fast and conspicuously, splashing water onto the balcony floor.

"You boys better stop splashing when I get in there," Mia says obliviously, shutting the door behind herself and heading toward the tub. "This is a place of relaxation."

Jasper settles uncomfortably back onto his perch, his arms crossed over his chest. I laugh awkwardly—half at almost being caught and half at the idea that Jasper and I were having some kind of bro-y water fight.

"Room for one more?"

Mia drops her robe to reveal an emerald-green bikini and the most rocking bod I've ever seen. It's well below freezing out here, but she is hot!

I glance at Jasper as she steps into the tub and find him gulping. Did he notice too?

WHAT'S THIS?

I can't seem to get the image of Jasper's face as Mia stepped into the hot tub out of my head. Even as we walk through the ridiculously picturesque streets of Mistlethorpe. Seriously, this place could have been packaged up in the Swedish countryside and shipped over intact. The streets are cobblestones, the buildings are golden pine and chocolate-brown logs, with delicate woodwork features, painted gables and windowsills. Multicolored string lights are dangling between streetlights that would look at home in a fairy tale. The sky might be overcast and the air chilly, but the shop windows are glowing.

Roasting chestnuts, popcorn, and cinnamon scents floats from street vendors and cafés. People wearing wooly hats and mittens are lingering in the town square beneath a Christmas tree, not as big as the one at Rockefeller but with more natural charm. I wouldn't be surprised if Olaf showed up asking for warm hugs.

On either side of the street these market huts that look like human-size cuckoo clocks are lined up. We pass a doughnut stall, a mitten stall, a vendor selling hand-painted ornaments, and another selling whittled wooden animals.

Yet despite all of this festive scenery, it's the lump in Jasper's throat, the panic in his eyes that I keep picturing. His eyes that couldn't seem to tear themselves away from Mia's smoking hourglass figure.

I know I'm not into girls, at least not in *that* way, even if I don't seem to be able to say the word for what I am. But I've never considered how it is for Jasper. Could he be into girls too? After we nearly kissed in the hot tub—*that is what happened, right?*—I know he's at least somewhat into me. But does that mean he's into other guys, too, or just me because I'm his mate? I kind of assumed he had a thing for Clayton, but maybe he was telling the truth about their friendship being just another of his pack-related duties. Then again maybe not. And what if he's into both?! That would be cool. Except what if I'm in competition with Clayton and Mia? And I'm the only option that doesn't bolster the pack? Where does that leave me?

These are the thoughts running through my mind as Katie, Mason, and I wander through the festive hubbub. Luckily these two have been too busy getting to know each other to notice my inner panic.

"So you've got two mates?" Mason asks Katie. "And you're into them in the exact same way?"

Katie takes a bite of her candy apple and a minute to consider the question.

"Well, no, not in the exact same way," she says. "It's different for each of them. Todd is sweet and spontaneous—he makes me feel excited and adventurous. Simon is calmer and thoughtful—he makes me feel at ease. So I like different things about them, but equally. Does that make sense?"

"For sure," Mason says, nodding and stepping over a frozen puddle. "I never really got how we're supposed to get everything from one person. Like, isn't that a lot to expect?"

He glances at me.

"And, actually, that's kind of the beauty of it," Katie continues, sounding more excited. "Why should we have to choose just one and miss out on so much? Why not have two?!"

"I totally get it," Mason says. "So you're polyam?"

"Polyam?" Katie asks. "What's that?"

Mason screws up his mouth and laughs. "Wow, you Elite wolves are kind of sheltered. I thought you'd be all up with the human terms, being from the big city and all."

"Sorry," I say, feigning incredulity. "Guess we were just busy not being stuck on a mountain; we didn't have time to brush up on our human vocabulary."

"Okay," he replies, nudging me playfully.

We reach the town square and Mason gestures to an empty bench next to a bush that's been carved into the shape of a reindeer.

"*Polyam* is short for *polyamorous*," he continues. "It's like someone who dates more than one person at a time—at least that's what I've read."

"Like cheating?" Katie asks.

"No, that's the point: if you're polyam it means you're honest with your partners."

"Oh." Katie sits back, her eyes wide, focused on the star at the top of the Christmas tree. "That does sound like me."

Mason and I sit for a moment and watch as Katie takes in this new term, this new identity, waiting to see whether it fits or if she'll reject it.

After a long, quiet pause, Katie closes her mouth and, slowly, a smile creeps into her expression.

"I like it," she says. "And what's even better, now I know what it's called I can explain it to Todd and Simon. Maybe if they understand better they'll know this is what I want long-term...and act less like territorial wolves."

"I'm glad I could help," Mason says.

"You have! Thank you!" Katie wraps him in a big hug and I grin, happy to see Katie embracing this new terminology. I wish I was this comfortable with labels, with my label.

"In fact," Katie says, standing, "you've helped so much I think I'm going to find those two and talk to them right now. Todd said they were going to check out a hockey game in some bar. Wish me luck!"

With an excited squeal, Katie is off. Mason and I call out as she goes, wishing her the best.

"Maybe I should be a therapist," Mason says.

Our eyes meet and I'm suddenly aware that we're alone in the most festive setting possible. I think Mason notices it too because he pushes off the bench.

"You want to walk a bit more?" he asks. "I know you're supposed to do all your Christmas things with Katie, but there's this café that sells the best peppermint coffees."

"Uh, sure."

Amblingly, we wander through the square toward where a group of carolers have set up. I'm thankful for the noise because I suddenly have no idea what to say. Why have I forgotten how to talk?

We pause for a moment to listen to their rendition of "Sleigh Ride," but move on the second we hear the first line of "All I Want for Christmas Is You." That song is a classic but it's way overdone.

"So," Mason says, dragging out the vowel sound, "you're really into Christmas, hey?"

I stick my hands into my coat pockets and shrug my shoulders.

"I guess... I mean back when Katie and I were kids, Christmas was everything—the most exciting time of year. Now I think it's more like tradition, like we're just trying to keep that magic alive, you know. Because..."

I pause and watch my breath puffing out in a cloud before me. I've never really stopped to think about why we still do all this silly stuff. Sure, it's fun. But I can't pretend this year doesn't feel different.

Mason tilts his head to look at me, as if to let me know it's okay to say what I need to.

"So much has changed in the last year," I say. "Katie and I, we've both changed...*a lot*. I don't know, maybe we're just holding on because we're scared of losing our friendship."

"Fair," he says. "But I don't think you two have to worry."

"I hope you're right. It's just now Katie has her two mates and I have my...whatever, and soon school will be finished and sometimes I feel like everything is moving so quickly. What if I look up one day and I don't even know who I am anymore."

"I have a feeling you'll figure it all out," Mason says, pointing toward a vine-draped archway that leads to a snow-covered park. "This way."

Someone has cleared the paths, thank goodness, but everything else is snowed under. Up ahead, some playground equipment is giving igloo vibes.

We wander through the park toward a frozen duck pond without ducks; we get halfway across a cute bridge and stop to lean against the railing.

"I know how you feel though," Mason says. "Why you'd hold onto childhood traditions and all that."

He leans over, staring at his fractured reflection in the ice.

"Mia and I used to be really close, but ever since she turned eighteen, Alpha Morven has been on her back about taking over the pack. My dad's been on my back as well but, well, he's not a great communicator."

"I'm sorry. Being the future beta is a big responsibility."

He snorts. "Yeah and like, I couldn't care less about battle strategy, or border control, or any of it. I just want to read comics and watch baking-competition shows forever."

"That sucks."

"Then there's the whole being gay thing; I can't imagine Daddy Beta is going to take that very well."

I gulp at the word, but force myself not to panic. Mason is opening up to me: he needs a friend, not a flake who's dealing with their own internal bullshit.

"I'm sorry that's so hard," I say. "I know we're only here for a little while, but you can always talk to me. You have my number now, so…"

Mason eyes me in a sort of amused, questioning way, then spins around so that his back is resting on the railing, and grins.

"Hey"—he bumps shoulders with me—"I'd like that."

I'm suddenly really glad I went through all the drama to get here, because if nothing else comes of this trip, I think I'm leaving with a new friend.

"Come on, I could do with a coffee after all this deep and meaningful chat." Mason leads the way once again, and we head to the exit on the other side of the park. "So, what about this mate of yours?"

"What about him?"

"I know you said he wasn't out and whatever, but can't you do some of this Christmas stuff with him?"

I scoff. "I don't think peppermint coffee and mistletoe are really his scene."

"Well, then it's a good thing he isn't here."

We've stopped outside of the quaintest, most adorable coffee shop on the entire planet. A small veranda wraps around the outside, complete with poinsettias and holly boughs; the shop front is painted in this adorable baby blue; big windows sit on either side of the door, decorated with fake snow, hanging stars, and tinsel; and steam is fogging up the glass, making the inside look cozy and mysterious.

"You never told me who he is," Mason says, opening the door and letting me enter first. "What's his name?"

Barely a foot inside the café I stop, my back arching, a snarl rolling in my throat. And it's not the delicious smell of coffee or nutmeg that's stopped me in my tracks. It's Jasper, sitting at a cute corner table, across from Mia, sipping a peppermint latte.

"Whoa, you okay?" Mason asks, following my eyeline. "*Oh.*"

THE BLOOD WOLF

The moon is especially bright tonight as I make my way down a rocky staircase carved into the sloping mountainside. It must have been made for giants because I basically need to jump from step to step. Apparently it's a tradition here before a blood moon to head into the depths of the valley and light a bunch of bonfires—something about the Rocky Pack's ancestors who lived in the valley, before they ascended to the peaks, who lit fires to call to the Moon Gods and were blessed with prosperity. At least, that's what I was able to take in when Mason was telling me about it on the way back from town.

The whole journey back, he kept trying to distract me with pack customs and legends, but all I could think about was Jasper and Mia, sitting in that café, looking like the leads in a Netflix Christmas movie.

Mason was pretty cool about the whole thing. When I said I wanted to leave, he took me straight back to the packhouse in a shuttle van. And I think he could tell I didn't want to talk about it because he didn't ask any questions. He didn't say much about it at all—which, as I head toward the orange glow deep in the ravine, is starting to worry me. What if he ran back to his pack to tell them the juicy gossip? Or worse, what if he told Mia, or Alpha Morven, so they could strategize about the best way to get me out of the picture and marry off the heirs? Mason seems cool, and like, chill, but why would I assume he's more loyal to me than his pack?

Distant voices echo off the mountain walls as I reach the bottom of the staircase. A gravel path leads toward some densely packed trees; I can just make out the flicker of flames between the branches.

I haven't spoken to anyone since I came back from town—not even Katie, so I have no idea how things went with her coming out to Todd and Simon as polyam. I'm assuming no news is good news, but who knows when there are territorial teen wolves involved.

Snow crunches under my feet as I snake through the forest, eventually coming to a clearing. Four pyres blaze before me. The flames are tall and shaped like witches' hats, their smoke trailing into the sky, draping itself across the light of the moon. Still, she glows bright, on the brink of fullness, and just a little pinker than usual. The blood moon is on its way.

Rocky Pack wolves are huddling around the fires, passing round steaming mugs of something that smells spicy and festive. It's a sea of pom-pommed woolen hats, puffer coats, and boots. I wander between the groups, looking for a familiar face, and can't help thinking people are glancing at me, shooting me strange looks—looks that say, "I know."

Finally, I spot Mason standing with a group by one of the fires. For a moment I stop and wonder whether I should go over. What if he's already told them? What if he doesn't want to be my friend anymore now that he knows my mate bond is an obstacle in the way of strengthening his pack? Or what if he isn't interested in spending time with me now that he knows my mate is here? Not that anything would ever happen, but we were definitely acting on the flirtier side of friendly. Maybe he's not interested now that he knows I'm completely off the table.

To my surprise, he catches my eye and smiles, lifts his brow in a way that asks, "Are you okay?" and waves me over.

"How are you?" he asks when I arrive.

I don't really know how to answer so I sort of huff, tilt my head, and make a weird in-between expression.

"Right," he says, nodding. "Let's find somewhere we can talk."

Mason excuses himself from the group and takes me over to where a woman is ladling out whatever spiced concoction everyone is drinking from a steaming crockpot. She passes me a mug, which I take and cradle in both my hands, warming them, then she refills Mason's and he nods in the direction of an empty log near one of the farther-away fires.

I take a long whiff of the drink as I sit; it smells delicious, rich and fruity, and oh so festive.

"What is this?" I ask.

"It's glühwein; it's a German thing. You haven't had it before?"

I take a sip and it instantly warms my throat and chest, coating my mouth with this citrusy, tangy, sweetness.

"No, but I love it!"

Mason grins and so do I, but quickly his gaze darts to the ground and a somber expression lowers his brow.

The bonfire is warm on my face and the light from the flames is flickering against the snow and rock, but the shadows are darker on the periphery too. I squeeze my lips together and clutch onto my glühwein for dear life, waiting to hear the verdict from Mason.

"About earlier," he says, still not looking at me. "I just I want you to know I would never tell anyone."

I take a short gasp of a breath, shocked and relieved, and a little confused.

"It must be difficult for Jasper," he continues. "All that pressure and feeling like you can't live up to people's expectations."

"Yeah, must be real hard for him," I grunt.

"And I can't imagine how hard this must be on you."

Oh.

"Seriously, I think I would have gone completely mad by this point. I don't know how you're not a complete mess."

I laugh. "I have been pretty messy."

"Well"—he places a warm hand on my knee—"I'm here for you. If you need a friend."

Just then I look up and spot Jasper walking between the fires with Clayton at his side. He doesn't notice me; they just walk across the field until they're out of sight.

"Why are you being so cool about all this?" I ask, grateful to have met someone like Mason.

"The thing is," he says, "people like us, we have to stick together—despite pack borders or ranks or whatever, we have to have each other's backs. Because it's hard for everyone."

"And you're not worried about your pack? Aren't Mia and Jasper supposed to be the bridge that brings our packs together?"

"Nah." He nudges me with his shoulder. "People like us...we're our own pack."

"There you are!" The girl with braids, whose name I've learned is Halle, is peering around the bonfire. "It's almost time; what are you doing?"

"Time for what?" I ask, but Mason is already on his feet.

"You'll see," he says, extending a hand and helping me up.

Back in the clearing, a large circle has formed in the middle of the fires. Anyone lingering by the periphery is making their way to join the formation. I spot Katie stomping toward the group and catch her eye. She doesn't look happy.

"Hey, how'd it go?" I ask as she joins me and Mason.

Katie glares at us.

"That good, huh?"

"Ugh, they're like a couple of greedy pups who don't know how to share."

I do my best sympathetic smile.

"It's like here I am telling them about this big revelation I've had about myself, and all they can think about is how they can win me over—like I'm a freaking game show prize."

"Where are they now?" Mason asks.

"I don't know and I don't care. I told them if they were going to react like that then I needed space."

"Fair enough," he says.

"Anyway, what's happening now? Why does it look like we're about to do a group rendition of 'Kumbaya'?"

A couple of Rocky Pack wolves shuffle sideways to let us into the circle.

"It's a Rocky Pack tradition: we all gather in the base of the valley—like our ancestors before they conquered the mountains—and we make a plea with the Moon Gods to protect us from the blood wolf."

The blood wolf.

I have no idea what this is, but Morven mentioned it at dinner the first night we were here. I thought wolves all shared their superstitions, but maybe this is Rocky Pack-specific.

"What's a blood wolf?" Katie asks.

"You don't know?" Mason replies.

We both shake our heads.

Our circle has formed around a large, flat boulder in the center of the valley, and as Mia steps forward, the group goes quiet. She steps onto the surface of the boulder to the sound of fire crackling and nothing else.

"Wolves," Mia says, flames glinting in her eyes, the same color as her hair, "in three nights we will encounter a blood moon: this is a signal to remind us that the Moon Gods are watching us."

The circle is watching Mia, enraptured by whatever this is. I find Jasper on the opposite side, of course, with Clayton, but he's watching Mia intently, his expression as stoic as ever.

"Yes, they are watching," Mia goes on, "and during the blood moon they will pass judgment. Should you be judged worthy, you and your family will be blessed. But should you be judged unworthy..."

Mia spins with her arms outstretched, making eye contact with every member of the circle. A suspenseful silence holds the crowd in its grip; a chill runs down my spine as her gaze meets mine.

"Should you be deemed unworthy by the Moon Gods, you will be cursed."

Um, excuse me?

"For on the blood moon, it is said, one wolf will be transformed." Mia has stopped spinning and gestures like a witch conjuring a spell over her cauldron. "This wolf will be haunted by a million voices, driven to madness, bloodthirst, and a hunger for violence. This is the blood wolf."

Fire cracks and I swear the pyres burn a little higher. Everyone is staring at Mia, their mouths drooping open, as if frozen with fear.

"It is said that in times gone by," Mia continues, "the blood wolf, crazed and wild, devoured entire packs, destroyed ancient bloodlines, and colored the earth with the blood of wolves."

It's Christmas Eve, so why does this feel like a Halloween story?

"Why does it want our blood?" someone calls from across the circle.

Mia turns to them, grinning wickedly. "Because the only thing that will calm the madness of the blood wolf"— she spins, once again eyeing the crowd until her gaze lands on me—"the only thing to quench his insatiable hunger, is the flesh of another wolf."

Gulp. A few people gasp, others bury their faces in their scarves. Some people are giggling nervously. Katie glances at me with concern.

"Is this for real?" I whisper to Mason.

"What? Nah, it's just an old superstition," he says. "Like Krampus or something."

I'm glad that Mason doesn't seem to have bought into all this, but from the petrified looks on some of the pack's faces, not everyone is so chill.

"There is one thing we can do to stave off the curse of the blood wolf," Mia says. The eyes of the group watch her eagerly. "Howl to the Moon Gods! Ask them for your blessing. Beg for their mercy!"

Some dude to my right immediately lets loose an earsplitting howl.

"Yes!" Mia cries, her face alight. "Howl with me now! Howl so you escape the curse of the blood wolf! Awoooooooooo!"

Mia howls and the group explodes into a symphony of wolf cries. A couple of people even start to shift a little: one girl on the left has sprouted wolf hair, making her look like something out of a B movie, and another guy has extended his claws.

To my right, Mason lets out a massive howl, and I grin at Katie, who's finding this equally as silly as I am. Never one to not join in, Katie shrugs and releases a cry. She probably needs a bit of tension relief anyway.

Across from me, the only other person not lifting their chin and wailing to the moon is Jasper. Amidst the howls, our eyes find each other's, and it should be a sweet moment, where we smile knowingly because of course we're the only two not joining in; and of course we've found each other in the crowd. But I'm too annoyed to find this moment adorable, so I send my best scowly vibes his way. In return, Jasper furrows his brow questioningly.

When finally the howling stops, my attention is pulled back to Mia.

"Now let's have a good time!" she shouts, and there's a cheer from the crowd.

The circle disbands, people gravitating back to the fires and to refill their mugs. A few members of the Rocky Pack, amped up by the howling, whip off their clothes in the shadows and shift into their wolf forms, running off into the darkness.

"They're really going for it," I say as Mason, Katie, and I make our way to a hexagonally shaped arrangement of logs.

"Oh yeah, it's like I said: that extra lunar energy around the blood moon."

"It's kind of like the Blue Moon Festival all over again," Katie says, suggestively arching a brow in my direction.

"Sure," I mutter. I've lost sight of Jasper since the circle broke up.

"So you guys have never heard of the blood wolf before?" Mason asks as we sit.

Katie and I both shrug in response.

"Is it true?" I ask. "I mean, is it just a superstition or has the blood moon really made someone go crazy?"

"Well, I can't say for sure if this was because of the blood moon or a curse from the Moon Gods, or just a coincidence, but there was one guy, about twenty years ago—a Rocky Pack wolf, a gamma, one of my dad's subordinates—who went up to Wolf Point to see the blood moon, and when he came back..."

Mason pauses.

"What?" Katie asks.

"He was never the same."

"What happened to him?" I ask.

"I'm not sure—my parents never really told me the full story. I think he probably left the pack, went rogue."

"That's so sad," Katie says.

"He was probably just some guy who needed help," Mason says, "and we just didn't know how to give it to him."

Mason goes quiet, staring into the flames. I wonder if he's thinking about whether his parents would accept his differences if they knew about them. Accepting wolves who deviate from the norm is not a pack's strong suit: it's not in our nature.

I notice Mason's cup is empty.

"Hey, you want a refill?" I ask, pulling Mason back from the brink.

"Sure," he says, then turns to Katie. "While he's gone, let's come up with a plan to get your mate situation back on track."

I wander in the direction of the glühwein, and I have to be honest, I'm kind of amazed. Mason is so thoughtful—he just wants to help me and Katie, who are struggling with our mate situations, even though it can't be easy for him. I guess he's right: we are like our own pack, even if we're separated by territories and alphas. And we need to look out for each other, or we could end up like that gamma, alone and packless.

"Two refills and one more cup, please," I say to the woman sitting next to the crockpot.

While she fills our mugs I turn and immediately spot Jasper sitting in a circle, Clayton to his right chatting to some girl, and Mia on his left, leaning against him, with his jacket draped over her shoulders.

That's it!

If someone like Mason, the kid of a high-ranking wolf, can be so cool and supportive, why can't Jasper? Why do I have keep finding him looking all flirty with someone else? Someone with an agenda.

"There you go," the glühwein woman says, but I've lost my thirst.

"Sorry, I just remembered I have to...go." I turn and run straight into Olivia, who's just appeared out of nowhere holding an empty mug.

"Ugh, watch it," she says, glaring at me like I've just rammed her Porsche with my rusty pickup.

"What is your problem?" I ask, loud enough that people stop their conversations to look. She's been a dick to me since we bumped into each other at the Plaza, and I've had it. "Seriously? What is up your ass?"

Olivia's face falls but she doesn't respond. She drops her mug in the snow, turns, and walks away—as if I'm not worthy of her presence, not worth an apology.

More faces have turned to watch and now I feel like all eyes are on me. Mason and Katie are watching with concerned expressions. Clayton is scoffing, enjoying the show. Mia looks kind of unimpressed, and when she whispers something in Jasper's ear I can't take it anymore.

Screw the glühwein, I need to get out of here.

I stomp out of the clearing and away from the bonfires, ignoring the pitying glances, heading back through the trees and up the giant staircase, toward the packhouse. When I reach the top of the stairs, huffing on the outside and raging internally, the glow of the packhouse shines through the glass doors onto the snow—a golden welcome mat—but I turn and look back down into the valley.

Shadows dance across the mountainsides, a wolf howls in the distance. Everyone down there is playing a game, telling spooky campfire stories about made-up monsters, howling at nothing so they can be blessed like their ancestors who walked up a mountain one time. They're reveling in fake superstition, pretending their lives could be anything but perfect, and turning people who aren't like them into the enemy.

I glance up at the moon and I swear it looks fuller than before—redder, too.

MERRY FREAKING CHRISTMAS

I'm woken by a knock at my door. Blearily, I wrap a sheet around myself and roll out of bed.

"Merry Christmas!" Katie says, holding a long sock stuffed with presents.

"Ah!" I wrap my arms around her and give her the best best-friend hug I can muster at whatever ungodly hour it is—I haven't even looked at my phone yet. "Merry Christmas, Squishface."

"Here, take your stocking!"

Katie hands over the stuffed sock and I take it gleefully. This is one of my favorite traditions we have. Around the time we both turned thirteen, our parents decided we were too old for stockings—a travesty of the highest degree. So Katie and I decided every year our gifts for each other would all come stuffed in the biggest, longest, wooliest sock we could find.

"Aaaaand, here's yours!"

I run to the cupboard to grab out Katie's stocking. The good thing about stocking presents is they have to be small, which means it was easy enough to shove them all in my duffel bag. And wrapping them each individually, as is our custom, was a great way to take my mind off Jasper and the whole blood wolf thing when I got back to my room last night.

"Gosh," Katie says, squeezing my dad's old football sock in different places, "so lumpy."

"Can we open them?"

"Absolutely!"

We jump onto my bed and pull out each little parcel, unwrapping them one by one. My first gift from Katie is a stress ball that looks like the moon. That one will definitely come in handy. There's a long, thin one that I know is a pencil, and I can't believe it when I unwrap it to find *Katie & Max 4eva* etched into the side in gold lettering. There's also a Pop-it Fidget Mat, a cool ring with this trippy stone that I bet Katie found at a flea market, some chocolate, a pair of gloves I mentioned I wanted once when we were scrolling through the winter collections at our favorite stores, and finally, at the bottom, a flat rectangular present. I unwrap this last gift and I cannot believe it when I reveal two tickets to see the New York City Ballet company's production of *The Red Shoes*.

"These must have cost a fortune!" I shout as I tackle Katie into the pillows. "And so sneaky shoving them all the way at the bottom."

Katie sits up but keeps holding my hands.

"I know we haven't really gotten as much time together to do all our normal Christmas stuff, so I wanted to get you something that we could go to, just us."

"Thank you so much." I pull her into another hug and notice an unwrapped present on the mattress.

"You haven't opened your last present?"

Katie bites her lip, grins, then grabs the tube-shaped parcel.

So far, Katie has unwrapped a kitschy bracelet I found in a vintage shop that Aisha took me to in Brooklyn, some chocolate and Santa-shaped marshmallows, a new glittery phone case because her old one isn't so glittery anymore, a moisturizer I know she loves that costs way too much, and a squishy, peach-scented Disney plushy.

She gives me an excited look and opens her final present. Tossing aside the budget wrapping paper, she carefully unscrolls the piece of paper. For a moment she stares at it, tears brimming in her eyes, then she looks at me, smiles, and says, "Max, it's beautiful."

Even though I drew it, she holds it so that I can see—which is ridiculously cute. "It's us."

I've drawn Katie and me from a photo we took almost a year ago now, standing on the Red Steps in Times Square—a photo from before the Blue Moon Festival, before mates, and before Jasper. We look young and really happy.

"Thank you!"

We hug and chat for a while. A glance at my phone lets me know that it's still only six in the morning. I'm not usually an early riser, but I make an exception on Christmas Day. When it's finally late enough, we call my parents, and lying next to each other on the bed, we chat with them for the better part of an hour. I'm glad Katie is here so I don't have to field too many anxious questions from my parents. I know if it were just me and them, they'd stare at me with concerned faces, wondering if today is the day I let them know what's going on. This way we can all pretend like everything is normal and there isn't this big announcement hanging over all our heads.

Next up is Katie's mom, who's rushing out to see Katie's grandparents so can't chat long, but has enough time to tell us this hilarious story about Katie's aunt who had a little too much eggnog at their family Christmas party. It's so nice lying here, for a moment I almost forget that we're high up in the mountains, in a strange and unfamiliar pack, and that our mates are here with us, but no one is getting along.

"Yikes, we should probably get ready soon," Katie says, after saying goodbye to her mom for the nineteenth time.

"Wait, why? What's happening?"

"Mason told me after you left last night: there's this Rocky Pack tradition where they go up to Wolf Point and leave offerings for the Moon Gods."

"Of course there's another tradition," I say, rolling my eyes.

Katie tilts her head and holds my arm with both of her hands.

"It'll be nice to get some air, and don't you want to see Wolf Point?"

"We're going there in like two days."

"Come on, it'll be like when I come over to your place the day after Christmas and we go hiking, only with more people."

"People I don't want to see."

"Mason is going," she says. "Come on it'll be fun."

I don't really want to spend all of Christmas locked up in my room, or sitting in an empty chalet, so reluctantly I agree.

"Fine, let me just grab a hoodie and we can head down for breakfast."

I go to my cupboard and pull out my hoodie.

"What's that?" Katie asks, pointing to the wrapped gift on the floor next to my shoes.

"Oh, it's a present...for..."

"Jasper?"

"Yeah, it's dumb. I probably won't even give it to him."

"Maybe you should bring it on the walk?" she says, her voice lilting suggestively.

"Maybe you shouldn't push your luck."

"It's cold!" I say, shouting to be heard over the roar of the wind.

"There's supposed to be a snowstorm coming tonight," Mason yells back.

We've been hiking for close to two hours, up through the mountains, along winding stony paths, with little shelter from the gale.

"Are you sure it hasn't come early?"

"Morven will turn us around if it isn't safe."

I stare daggers at Katie for making me come on this walk, and she smiles exaggeratedly, trying to be encouraging.

Up ahead, Jasper is walking beside Mia, where he's spent the entire trek. Clayton was with them, too, early on, until he was distracted by Halle and her friends and left Jasper to be a creepy slimeball.

Todd and Simon are here, too—both of them looking back occasionally to glance at Katie and huffing when she refuses to join them.

"I get that they might need some time to adjust," Katie says. "But I told them I'm not changing my mind."

"You go, gurl," Mason says. "You got to be true to yourself."

Katie seems buoyed by this sentiment, but Mason and I glance at each other, sharing a moment of knowing just how hard that can be.

"Sooo," Katie says, bumping into me on purpose, "when are you going to give Jasper his present?"

"You didn't..." Mason says, open-mouthed.

I roll my head and groan. "I might have."

"What is it?" he asks.

"He won't tell me," Katie says.

"Come on."

"Stop pestering me, you kids," I say, throwing my hands back. "Besides, you might not have to wait too long to find out."

"What?" they ask in unison.

"Look, he doesn't deserve it, and I know—I *know*—he won't have gotten me anything in return. But I figured I'd rather just give it to him and not have to look at it anymore than be stubborn. And if he doesn't like it I can just offer it to the Moon Gods instead."

"You brought it with you?" Mason asks.

I unzip my jacket about halfway, revealing Jasper's gift, the golden bow flapping in the wind.

"Gorgeous wrapping, with a ribbon and everything," Mason says.

"Thanks," I say, knowing that even in these subzero temperatures my cheeks are flushing extra pink.

"So when are you going to give it to him?" Katie asks, bounding up and down. "Now? Is it now?"

"No, I just need to find the right time."

"We're nearly there," Mason says. "Maybe you can make your own offering at Wolf Point."

The last part of the trek is more of a rocky scramble than a hike. The incline of the mountain sharpens intensely, and the terrain becomes shaley. I'm worried I might slip and slide all the way to the bottom of the mountain. After fifteen minutes or so of clinging on for dear life, we scramble to a plateau. The mist up here is dense and white, like walking through a cloud, but it rolls back as we wander along the peak of the mountain, revealing a series of massive boulders arranged in a circular formation. It's too intentional not to have been built by wolves, but how on earth they got these boulders up here, let alone positioned them, is beyond me. Maybe our wolfy ancestors had even bigger muscles.

"Why is there less snow up here?" Katie asks, glancing at the ground, where only small patches of powder are dotted across grass.

"This spot was chosen because it has a direct link to the moon—something about the magnetic field of the rocks in the mountain, I think," Mason says. "But of course, our forebears assumed this meant the Moon Gods were closer here or something like that. Basically, more sunlight reflecting off the moon means warmer temperatures. Wolf Point has its own microclimate."

It's sort of wild. For days I feel like all I've been staring at is rock and snow, a white blanket draped across the world. But up here there's green grass, and even these delicate white flowers sprouting up about the place.

As we step into the circle of rocks I feel the increase in lunar energy like I'm stepping into a heated pool. It washes over me, straightening my spine, stimulating my senses. My hearing and scenting abilities are almost as heightened as if I was in wolf form. And the others are feeling it too. All the Elite Pack wolves are standing in wonder: Olivia's eyes are closed like she's basking in warm sunlight; Todd and Simon are quiet for once, turning to look at the stone structure; Jasper is staring at the sky, fists clenched.

I step farther toward the center and my teeth are vibrating, tingles running through my muscles. My feet keep moving without my meaning them to, my eyes traveling over the smooth, gray surface of the rocks surrounding me. To my right and left, two stones have been placed close together, with a third placed on top to make a doorway-like configuration. I turn around and find Katie grinning while she spins as well. And when I complete my circle I find myself standing face-to-face with Jasper.

"What are you doing?" he asks, more casually than normal.

I'm used to running into him, but he usually calls me Bonehead or scowls. This time he almost seems amused—he seems...calm.

"I...don't know. I didn't even realize I was moving."

Has the lunar energy brought us together? Is the power of Wolf Point doing what I haven't been able to for months?

"It's remarkable, isn't it?" Jasper asks, his voice trilling like a thousand bells in my ears.

For a moment the other wolves in the circle fade away, the wind quietens, and the clouds stop moving. It's just me and Jasper on the top of the world.

"It's wild."

Jasper's face twitches, a muscle under his eye moves, and to my great surprise he almost smiles.

"Hey, I"—my hand is moving to the zipper of my jacket without me meaning it to—"I wanted to give you something."

Like a blissed-out Christmas zombie, I retrieve the present and offer it to Jasper.

"You didn't have to," he says, coming the closest to blushing I think is possible.

"I wanted to," I say as his hand reaches out. "Merry Christmas."

"Max, I..." His fingers close around the gift and I feel a surge of electricity pass from him to me, as if the gift is a piece of metal completing the circuit. "I didn't...thank you."

Neither of us can let go—the sensation is too overwhelming, and then...

"Wolves!" Morven booms, breaking the spell. Jasper retracts his hand, turning away, and I'm left holding his present. "Welcome to Wolf Point. We will now make our offerings to the Moon Gods."

Everyone is back—not that they went anywhere really, but I'm suddenly very aware of the other wolves in the circle. I notice Clayton giving me a strange look, and then find Katie coming to join me. Without thinking, I stuff the present back in my coat.

We gather around a flat stone in the center of the formation.

"For the safety of my pack," Morven says, holding a basket full of fruits, baked goods, an expensive-looking bottle of wine, and a silver chalice, "I make this offering to you, Selene, Nannar, Mani, Igaluk, and Tsukuyomi."

Gently he places the basket on the stone and steps back. One by one, the Rocky Pack wolves approach the stone and place their offerings in the pile. Some say a few quiet words of prayer, others take a minute of silent contemplation before stepping aside. When Katie and I approach, she goes before me and slips the two pearl earrings she's been wearing out of their holes, closes a fist around them, and holds it to her lips. She whispers something quietly, then kneels down to place them safely in the pile.

Then it's my turn. I step up to the mound of offerings, clasping and unclasping my hands. My plan was to wait and see if Jasper accepted my gift, and if not I would offer it to the gods. But he was about to accept it, right? He looked almost...touched. So what am I supposed to do now? I haven't got anything else to offer. People are waiting behind me, watching to see what I've brought their gods. I smile awkwardly and reach my hands into my pockets.

There's nothing in my pockets except my phone—which I am not sacrificing—a balled-up gum wrapper, and my ChapStick.

Nothing. I have nothing else.

Reluctantly, I unzip the top of my coat and pull out the present, laying it gently on top of the pile. *Sorry, Jasper.*

As I move away from the central stone, hands shoved in my pockets, Katie catches my eye. She saw what my offering was. She reaches out a hand and loops it through my arm. When everyone has finished making their offerings and wondering at the strange aura emanating throughout the stone circle, we begin to make our way back down the mountain.

The scramble down is less daunting than on the way up, but I have to sit and shuffle on my butt some of the way so that I don't topple forwards and plummet to my death. When I'm back on my feet, I linger a little behind the rest of the pack.

Jasper is toward the front of the group, but as a breeze blows across the hilltop, he glances back—only for a second—and I realize I've made a mistake. I'm pretty sure I don't even believe in the Moon Gods. And Jasper knows I got him a present. So what happens later, when we're back at the chalet? He'll be expecting something, and I'll have to explain I left it at the top of the mountain.

It's dumb and I'm overreacting, but still my feet stop walking.

I glance up to the mountain peak. It will only take me a second to scramble back to the top and grab the present. I can leave something else as my offering. The Moon Gods probably love ChapStick and gum wrappers!

Katie stops and calls back to me: "Max, what are you doing?"

"I...I think I left something up there; I'll be right back."

"Max!"

Katie's call drifts away on the wind as I'm already turning and running back up the slope. The rocky scramble is treacherous, but this time I don't crawl—I plow ahead, my speed keeping me from slipping, and I make it back to the top.

Entering the stone circle feels exactly as it did the first time, like walking into a warm bath. I head for the pile and, looking around to make sure no one has followed me—I don't want anybody thinking I'm stealing from the gods—I grab Jasper's present and shove it back in my coat.

Biting my lip, which already feels dry, I pull out the ChapStick, quickly apply it one last time, then hold it to my chest.

"I'm sorry," I whisper to the Moon Gods. "But I know you'll understand. Besides, this is cranberry flavor, you're gonna love it."

Swiftly, I wedge the ChapStick between two more impressive offerings and back away, only a little scared I'm about to be hit by lightning.

Mission accomplished, I turn back toward the exit, and the second I leave the circle I notice the wind has really picked up. The mist has thickened into a dense pillow of cloud, and I can barely see two feet in front of myself.

Better hurry and catch up, or I'm going to get lost...

CAUGHT IN THE STORM

I'm stupidly lost—like, completely turned around, no idea where I am, absolutely screwed lost. And to top it all off it's started snowing.

Managing to descend the scramble, I find myself staring at the mountainside wondering which way we came from. All I can see is a bank of cloud; the descent is masked entirely, and with the snow falling faster and heavier by the minute, any path that exists is about to disappear. With only the vaguest sense of the direction we came from, I start making my way down.

"Katie!" I call, almost slipping on the suddenly unsteady ground. "Mason! Guys, wait up!"

I hug my chest, trying to fortify myself against the wind—which is whipping so hard I'm scared of losing my favorite beanie—and feel the squishy package stored inside my coat.

Jerk Jasper, if I'd just left his present I would have stayed with the group.

Jerk me for going back.

It's not like he was expecting a gift, and it's definitely not like he'll have one waiting for me back in the warmth of the chalet. Yet here I am putting myself in danger for him again. *What am I doing?*

The snowfall has graduated from flurry to full-on blizzard as I clamber over some awkwardly placed boulders and continue my descent. Shimmying across a particularly frozen patch of ice, I nearly slip, but catch myself on a jagged rocky edge nearby, pulling a muscle as I hang on for dear life.

Eventually, the land evens out a little, and instead of stone beneath my feet, I trudge through fresh powder about two feet deep. I wander between snow-laden trees that bend in the wind. The forest rises around me until I'm encased by boughs straining under the icy weight on top of them. Even surrounded by firs, the wind batters me. My legs are getting tired. My face is raw from the cold, and my lips are chapped. *Damn, I could really use that ChapStick right about now.*

I glance back the way I came to find my tracks are already gone. The snow is like a curtain of white, and even at this altitude the mist is thick. When I go to move off again I'm not sure which way I was heading. The trees all look the same—everything is white, and frozen, and blustery. They say each snowflake is uniquely formed, no two are identical, but right now they're all pretty freaking similar.

Panic sets it, my jaw is chattering, my whole body shivering. I don't remember ever being this cold. And I have no idea which way to go. The wind is a roaring ocean in my ears, and my runny nose is a rushing river. I spin in circles, hoping for a glimpse of light, some sign of civilization, but it's all cloud and snow and storm. My head swims and I suddenly feel faint. I trudge to the nearest tree and collapse into the snow.

How long will this blizzard last? And how long can I survive out here?

Knees pulled in close, I try and make myself as small as possible to keep my chest warm. I can't help it when the tears start to come. All I want is to be home in Stony Point, sitting at the dinner table with my parents, eating turkey, or curled up on the couch with a blanket watching *Lord of the Rings* or a live-action Disney remake, stuffing myself with chocolate. I don't want to be here. I wish I hadn't come. I wish I hadn't chased Jasper up here... I wish I hadn't chased Jasper...

"Max?" his voice cuts through the roaring wind.

I look up, wiping my snotty nose and straining to see through the snow curtain. Was that really him? Or am I experiencing some sort of frostbite-related hallucination? Is my body diverting too much oxygen from my brain trying to keep the rest of me warm? Am I dead? Have I frozen to death out here and his call is Death's, luring me to the afterlife?

"Max!"

Nope, that was definitely real. I wipe my eyes and shake my head, trying to reawaken my senses. Blood pumps in my system and I already feel a little warmer.

"Jasper?" I can't see him, but I know I'm not hallucinating. Pushing on the tree for support, I lift myself back to standing. "Jasper?!"

"Max!"

Finally, he comes into view, arms wrapped around his sleek black puffer, bracing against the wind. Even he is struggling to make his way through the storm. His jaw is set, his eyes glazed over with determination and then...relief.

He sees me.

"Max!" Jasper trudges toward me. "What is wrong with you?"

"I wasn't expecting a blizzard!"

"Are you hurt?"

"What?" I can barely hear him over the rush of the storm, plus I totally wasn't expecting him to be that concerned.

"Are you injured?"

"I'm fine."

"Okay." He takes a second to look at me, as if he needs a moment to assure himself that he's found me—*he found me*—and that I'm actually okay. He nods. "Okay, good. We need to get out of here."

He pulls my arm and turns back the way he came, taking me with him.

"Do you know where you're going?" I yell-ask, following him and *very* aware of his hand wrapped around my arm.

"I passed a ranger station a little ways back; we can hole up there until the storm passes."

Jasper leads me through the storm, and as we walk into the oncoming wind I realize I don't feel cold anymore.

We bust through the lock on the door of the old ranger station and slam it shut behind us.

"Ugh, when was the last time someone cleaned up in here?" I ask, glancing around.

The place is more than decrepit. The drawn blinds hang at awkward broken angles, there's a ratty couch with stuffing pouring out from one of the armrests, a desk to my right might as well be made entirely out of dust. Filing cabinets hang open; the floor is littered with papers, ceiling panels, and leaves. The cold seeps back into my bones.

Jasper flicks the light switch, but nothing happens. "I think it's been awhile since anyone's been in here at all."

"Great."

I wander farther into the room. There's a distinct musty smell, but luckily it's muted by the cold. I don't want to know how pungent it would be on a sweltering summer's day. Thankful to be inside and out of the storm, I hug myself to keep warm, but don't complain.

"We should be fine in here at least until the storm passes," Jasper says. I turn and find him watching me. "You're still cold."

Damn, he noticed the slight shiver in my shoulders.

"Ya-huh."

Jasper moves about the room as if he's searching for something. He pulls out drawers and opens cabinets, but whatever he's looking for, he's coming up short. Then, shoving a stack of magazines—probably dated 1990-something—he uncovers a battered army trunk.

"It's locked." I point at the rather obvious combination lock.

Jasper takes it in for a second, then tears it right off with his bare hand. He lifts the metal lid and begins to pull out what look like survival supplies—a couple of blankets, some cans of food, a can opener, a gas-powered lantern, and some matches.

"Here." He tosses me a blanket, a little too hard, then goes about lighting the lantern.

With the blanket wrapped around my shoulders I watch as my personal Bear Grylls manages to strike a match that's past its prime. A dull orange glow emanates from the lantern once it's lit, casting long shadows across the floor, but making our shelter just a little more cozy.

"Thanks," I say. "For finding me."

Jasper sighs and lets his head drop.

"You need to be more careful," he growls lowly.

"I—"

"You're lucky I found you before you froze to death. What were you thinking?"

Not this again. I'm sick to death of Jasper policing my actions, as stupid or reckless as they may be, he's not my guardian.

"Look," I spit back, "I appreciate that you came and found me, but just because you decided to save my ass doesn't mean you get to speak to me that way."

"You're ridiculous. You keep putting yourself in danger when all I'm trying to do is keep you safe."

"Well, maybe I don't want to be safe!" Anger is heating my veins and I don't need the blanket anymore, so I throw it off my shoulders. "If being safe means ignoring this"—I gesture between us frantically—"then I don't want it!"

"It's more complicated than that. You're not the only one involved here."

"You don't get to choose when it's convenient to be involved, Jasper. This isn't a voluntary position."

He runs a frustrated hand through his hair. "Why did you even go back up there? I don't understand."

"For this." I pull his present out of my jacket and toss it at him. He catches it and holds it out in front of him like he's never seen festive wrapping paper before.

"This?"

Okay, maybe he hasn't seen festive wrapping paper before. He looks so confused.

"Yes, I left your present as an offering to the Moon Gods, but I knew you knew that I had it and I felt bad not giving it to you so—"

"So you went back up there to get something for me?" He huffs. "This is exactly what I'm talking about, Max. You keep putting yourself in danger and all I want is to stop that from happening."

"What danger?!"

His hands fall to his sides. "It's complicated."

I gesture at our surroundings. "We have time."

Quiet settles between us. I think we're done arguing for now.

"Fine," Jasper says eventually. "Sit down and I'll explain."

"Okay." I gather up my blanket and move to the couch. "But wait…"

He looks at me strangely as he sits across from me.

"Aren't you going to open it?"

With an affectionate roll of his eyes, Jasper pulls at the ribbon and lets it fall to the dusty floor. Carefully, he peels away each hastily applied piece of Scotch tape. I'm more of a rip-the-thing-open type of guy, but this makes sense for Jasper. He unfolds the package and lets it rest in his lap.

"Well?"

He pulls out the maroon scarf with one hand and runs the other along it, feeling the soft wool.

"It's…great."

Smug, very smug.

Jasper wraps the scarf around his neck, then glances up as if to ask, "How does it look?"

"Perfect," I say, admiring how the red brings out the green in his eyes. "Now explain."

Jasper settles back into the couch. "When the rogues attacked my father's house, it sent a message: the Elite Pack is weak, susceptible to invasion."

"My dad said something like that, too, that it made people question Jericho—your dad's leadership."

"Yes." He nods, a grave expression cast across his features. "But not just to Elite wolves. Word moves quickly between packs, and now every alpha whose territory neighbors our border knows what happened."

"So? I thought we got on with the other packs."

He scoffs. "'Get on' is a bit strong. We have peace because there's a hierarchy. The Elite Pack is one of the oldest in America; our territory is vast, and so is our wealth, our military. People can covet what we have all they want, but they won't do anything about it if they know they can't have it. The rogues opened a hole in the wall, revealed a chink in our armor."

"And your dad is worried that other packs might try and take some of his territory."

"Not some," he says, glancing up at me, "all."

I swallow the baseball in my throat.

"But we can improve our position. The other packs will think twice if we have powerful allies."

Dots begin to connect in my head.

"This trip is about more than friendship, or blood moons," Jasper continues. "It's integral that I cement our allegiance with the Rocky Pack while we're here. They're our only ally with the resources to hold off a combined attack from our neighboring packs."

Suddenly, I feel sort of guilty. Jasper's been given a monumental task. He came out here to help protect the entire pack from the threat of invasion. I came because I thought we might make out.

"Why didn't you tell me any of this?"

"Because I meant what I said on the beach. You're safer the farther you are from me. The less you know, the better."

"But if you'd just told me, something, anything, I might not have followed you out here. I might not have entered that race. If you'd just talked to me you could have done your mission and not had to worry about me skiing off the side of a mountain."

"Maybe you're right." He lowers his head.

"I am right." I sit up straighter. "I'm sorry—I know I'm a pain but, Jasper, you kissed me and then ghosted. I hadn't heard from you in three months. What did you think was going to happen?"

He laughs a little, but a sad sort of laugh.

"I hoped you'd get the message."

What? I try to shake off the shock of what he's just said, but his words are like a cobweb I've walked through.

"Even now you think us being apart is the best solution."

"Max…"

The wind has picked up again outside and is rattling the windows.

"And what? You thought you'd come here and flirt with Mia—hell, maybe even choose her as your mate—just to save the pack, and it wouldn't matter because I'd be better off? Why do you have to be the one to save us, Jasper? Huh? Why are you the only one responsible?"

"I told you I would never with Mia."

There's a loud thump outside, as if a good chunk of snow has just fallen from the roof.

I huff and jump back to my feet. I can't believe what I'm hearing. I stomp away from him, holding the back of my head in my hands.

"Then how come I saw you two being all coupley in town?"

"What?" He looks truly confused, but I know he's not that dense.

"I saw you in that coffee shop. You looked pretty cozy."

"It was just coffee."

He stands, and the windows start shaking so hard I'm worried they're going to fly off.

"And I saw the way you looked at her in the hot tub, and how you've been letting her hang off you."

Jasper rounds the back of the sofa, coming toward me. "It's not what you think."

"Sure," I huff.

Jasper stops, rubs his forehead, then glares at me from under his bangs. "And what about you?"

"What about me?" *Where on earth is he going with this?*

"You and that Mason kid."

"Mason?"

Why is he bringing Mason into this? The wind is so loud we might as well be in the direct path of a wintery hurricane. The whole shack is shaking, vibrating under the force of the wind.

"What are you talking about?" I ask. "What's Mason got to do with anything?"

"You haven't exactly been subtle."

My mouth falls open and I stare at Jasper in shock. Is he...jealous?

"It's nothing. We're friends."

"Are you?" Jasper is speaking through his teeth, almost growling.

"Of course, I—"

"I can sense you, Max!" Are his fangs getting longer? "I may not know every little detail, but I know it's not nothing."

For a moment I'm speechless. I shake my head in disbelief. Where is this coming from? Sure, I may have liked flirting with Mason just a little. But nothing was ever going to happen with him. Besides, once he knew I had a mate, he pretty much backed off. What I have enjoyed is having a friend who knows what it's like to go through the things I'm experiencing, someone who can relate to what it feels like to be...to be gay, a gay werewolf.

"Mason is my friend," I say, somewhat forcefully. "I needed a friend because—believe it or not—this whole thing, being mated to you, is not so easy. And he understands because he's like us."

Jasper sneers. "I'm not like him."

"Whatever." I roll my eyes. "This is exactly what I'm talking about. You froze me out, Jasper! We could have figured this out together but you pushed me away. You don't get to be jealous!"

Jasper's chest is heaving, his hands are clenched. Maybe my safety is the reason he told himself he was pushing me away, but maybe he's been struggling more than I know.

"So you do like him?" he mutters.

"No, Jasper! I like you!" My shouts rise over the sound of the storm, filling the cabin. "I want you! Do you think I came all this way just to give up on this? To be distracted by a cute guy? Don't you get it?"

Jasper stares at me, intensity blazing in his emerald eyes.

"I made a vow that I would chase you to the ends of the world if I have to. And you can push me away all you want, but I'm not giving up, I'm—"

Before I can finish, Jasper closes the distance between us in less than a second. He pulls me into him with one hand, holding my head with the other, and presses his lips against mine.

Like a snowman in spring, I melt into him. I can't tell if the storm has passed or if I just can't hear it anymore, because the world is falling away, until we're the only beings left in existence, floating in a void. He kisses me, unleashing all the pent-up energy, the repressed emotion, the secret desire he's never let me see. And I return his kisses with all the urgency and hunger of a marathon runner refueling after a hard-won race.

We kiss for a long time, protected from the prying eyes of the outside world, hidden in our wintery fortress, reveling in the privacy. I love how his hair slips between my fingers, how his back is firm under my palm, how his chest is warm against mine. Our breathing syncs. Our hearts race as one. And finally we pull apart, just enough to look at each other, without letting the other go.

"I'm sorry," Jasper says.

"Why?"

"Because I was wrong."

He smiles slightly, and I try to take in each minute detail. His cheeks are flushed, as I'm sure mine are. I trace his subtle freckles with my gaze, like I'm marking out constellations. I lick my lips and he does the same, biting one corner with his still-elongated fang. Then he pulls me in once more and this time our kiss is slower, less desperate, more assured.

I never want to leave this cabin.

When we pull apart this time, Jasper runs a hand down the side of my face.

"Can you hear that?" I ask.

"What is it?"

"Nothing. The storm must have passed."

"Max, I—"

"What the...?" We pull apart at the sound of someone else's voice, and turn to find Clayton and Mia standing in the open door of the cabin. "Dude?!"

START SPREADING THE NEWS

"Dude," Clayton says, staring open-mouthed at Jasper and me. "What the hell?"

Mia is a step behind him with this confused look on her face.

I glance from them to Jasper, who pulled away as soon as we were interrupted, and is standing a foot away from me, rigid like a reindeer in headlights.

"It's not..." Jasper says hurriedly, trying to collect his thoughts. "We weren't—you don't—I..."

He runs both hands through his hair, completely lost for words. Swiftly, he glances at me and I can see the cogs turning; he wants to deny everything, but he can't while I'm here, because he knows how much that would hurt. And, besides, from the disgusted look on Clayton's face, it's probably too late for denial.

"We came to rescue you," Clayton says. "Not to see whatever that was. Are you...I mean...with him?!"

Jasper takes a breath and steps forward, as if he's made some secret decision.

"Clayton."

"No way, man. That's wrong on, like, so many levels."

Clayton leaves the cabin, pushing past Mia and disappearing outside, where the sun has already broken through the clouds.

"I have to..." Jasper looks at me, gesturing to the door.

I nod, letting him know I'm fine, I understand, and he runs after Clayton. Who knows what he's going to say. But I think Jasper might be done denying. If Clayton is a real friend, he'll support Jasper. Though I doubt he is.

Mia is leaning against the doorframe now with her arms crossed and this sort of impressed look arching one of her brows.

"That was quite the surprise," she says, grinning.

I rub the back of my neck. "Yeeeaaaah."

"Happy Christmas to me, I guess," she says. "Come on, let's get you back to the packhouse."

We haven't been walking long before Mia turns to me and asks, "So you want to tell me everything?"

We're heading back uphill—I guess I wandered farther into the canyon than I realized—between a line of bare trees. The sun is reflecting brightly on the crisp snow. Jasper went ahead after Clayton, and they must have made quite the head start because there's no sign of them. It's just me and Mia, and she's waiting for me to dish.

I feel a little bad for her. Up until about five minutes ago, she was probably thinking she and Jasper might end up mated. But I also don't owe her anything. I don't need to poor out my whole sob story just because she caught us—a feeling I think she gathers from the look on my face.

"Hey, look," she says, shrugging her shoulders. "You don't have to tell me anything. But if you want to, you should know it's totally cool. I know Mason is into guys, and I'm assuming you and Jasper are mates, which if that's the case I'd be nothing but happy for you guys."

"Really?" I stare at her in shock, trying to figure out if she's being genuine.

"Of course. Why wouldn't I be?"

"I thought your dad wanted you and Jasper to...you know...be mates."

"Yeah, that's what my dad wants. But I'm not about stealing someone else's person. That's not my scene. And, well..."

She trails off, lifting her hand to her mouth and nibbling on the skin around her thumbnail. There's something else she hasn't said.

"What is it?"

"Ugh!" She throws her head back dramatically. "I hate all this pretense, I'm a heart-on-my-sleeve kind of person. I can trust you, right?"

I'm getting some serious whiplash from this conversation.

"You know my biggest secret, so..."

"True, in that case..." She stops, planting herself in the snow like she's about to make a declaration. "The truth is I'm bi."

"Oh." Not what I was expecting! "That's cool."

"I like guys, but I tend to find girls more interesting. And seeing as I haven't found my mate, I was happy to go along with Dad's plan. A girl could do a lot worse than Jasper." She elbows me in the side. "But actually, you and Jasper being together is kind of perfect, because now I won't be stuck wondering if there's some awesome chick out there I've missed out on."

She smiles big and wide, and so do I. All this time I'd been thinking Jasper and I were the only ones like us. But coming here I'm realizing we're everywhere. And I love it.

Plus, she just said Jasper and I are together, and for the first time I'm thinking that might not be too far from the truth.

"I'm really glad you felt okay telling me," I say.

"Um can we be, like, friends?"

I laugh. "Yeah, like, for sure."

"Cool!" She squeals a little and hugs me. "Okay, so now will you tell me everything?"

For the rest of the hike I tell Mia the whole story. When finally the packhouse comes into view, she stops, pulling my arm so I turn to face her, and her expression is seriously earnest.

"Before we go in," she says, "I want you to know that I won't tell a soul. Not until you and Jasper are okay with people knowing."

My heart drops a little. I hadn't thought about the larger ramifications of being discovered together. The big secret could ostensibly be out. If Clayton tells people, the truth about me and Jasper could soon be public knowledge. Somehow I can't imagine Jasper being too cool with that outcome. And with the mountains looming above, the chalet perched like a hovering fortress, I'm not sure if I'm ready for that either. How will people react? Will they stare and whisper about me as I pass? Or will they be like Mia and Katie and be cool about the whole thing? All this time I've been chasing Jasper I haven't even thought about what it would be like if I caught him.

"Thanks," I say, unsure of what I'm about to walk back into.

"And if that dick Clayton has told anyone, I'll be here," she says. "I'm on your side."

Feeling a little less terrified, I let Mia link her arm through mine and together we ascend the final steps back to the chalet.

I've almost forgotten it's still Christmas when I walk inside to find Rocky Pack wolves sitting around the lounge area exchanging gifts, poking around at the base of the Christmas tree, and drinking delicious-smelling drinks.

"Max!" Katie leaps up from the table where she's sitting with Todd and Simon, to come running over. "Are you okay?"

"I'll leave you to it," Mia says, grinning, then heading to some of her friends by the window.

"I'm fine," I say to Katie. "Jasper found me and...I have so much to tell you."

"Let's get hot chocolate and go to your room and you can tell me everything."

"Okay but first, have you seen him?"

"Jasper? No, not since he left the group to go find you."

"And Clayton, have you seen him?"

"Mmm, nope."

I glance around the room. Clayton and Jasper aren't here, and so far no one is paying me any attention, they're too occupied with wrapping paper and sugar cookies. So, the news isn't out...yet.

"Okay let's go."

Up in my room, Katie and I lie on my bed dipping gingerbread people into our hot chocolate while I tell her all about the cabin, and the kiss, and Clayton. Of course, I don't tell her anything about Mia and her being bi—that's not mine to tell.

"So what do you think will happen now? Do you think Jasper will be cool with everyone knowing?"

"I can't imagine it, but if Clayton lets it slip, then he won't have much choice. He'll have to deal with it."

"And Clayton seems the type to out people for fun."

"You should have seen his face." I stare into the white drops of icing denoting the eyes, nose, and mouth of my gingerbread man. "He looked like...like he'd been betrayed." I snap off the head and shove it in my mouth.

"He's a dick; Aisha was right about him."

I roll over and sit up, facing away from Katie, rubbing my neck.

"You know I'll be here," she says, shuffling over so that she's beside me. "If Clayton does tell people, I'll be here."

"Thanks, Squishface."

"We have a bit of time until the pack dinner—"

"Oh no!" I throw my face into my hands. "I forgot about the dinner. Do we have to wear fancy clothes?"

"I'm afraid so," she says, rubbing my back, playing along. "And I heard there might be dancing afterward."

"Nooooooo!"

"I know it's not your idea of the perfect Christmas night, but that's why I was thinking we have just enough time for a movie."

We turn to look at each other and say in perfect unison, "*The Grinch*!"

Instantly, we spring into action. Katie builds a pile of pillows for us to sit up against on the bed, while I grab my laptop.

"Okay, Whoville, let's go," I say once we're situated on the mattress. And I'm about to hit Play when there's a knock on the door.

With a questioning glance at Katie, I hop up to see who it is.

"Oh, hey," I say, shocked to find Jasper standing on the opposite side of the door—*my door*. He's already dressed for dinner in a tailored black suit, with satin lapels, a white turtleneck, and patent leather shoes.

"Hi."

Instinctively I step toward him, and he backs up ever so slightly, glancing down both ends of the hall.

"It's fine," I say. "I'm the only one on this level."

He presses his lips together awkwardly. "Can I come in?"

"Sure."

Japer follows me in, shutting the door behind him, but stops when he spots Katie. He clears his throat.

"It's okay," I say, a little sharply. "She knows."

Gently, Katie shuts the computer.

"I'll give you two some space," she says, sliding her legs off the bed.

"You don't have to," I say, sort of pissed that Jasper backed away from me after what happened in the cabin, and that another of mine and Katie's traditions has been interrupted.

"I need to get ready for dinner anyway," she says. "I'll see you downstairs."

She shoots me a knowing look then slips past Jasper.

"Have fun."

As soon as the door shuts I realize this is the first time Jasper has come to find me, in my space. He's in my room and I don't know what to say. Part of me wants to walk up to him and kiss again, just like we did in the ranger station. But the energy is different and I'm worried if I do he'll reject me.

"I'm sorry—"

"How's Clayton—"

We speak at the same time and then fall awkwardly quiet. Jasper looks around, probably taking in my scent. His eyes linger on my sketchbook, open on the reading chair, then land on the pile of clothes spilling messily out of my duffel.

"I spoke to Clayton," he says finally. "He won't say anything."

"How did you manage that?"

Jasper grins a little. "Clayton's family holds a lot of influence. But I'm still the alpha's son."

"Right, so you commanded him to keep quiet."

Jasper rolls his eyes ever so subtly.

"Max, I can admit that keeping you at a distance wasn't the right thing to do. But that doesn't change the fundamental reason for that decision. If people knew about our connection, our"—he swallows—"relationship, it could endanger the pack and us. No one can know."

He reaches for my hand and I pull it away.

"So...what do you want then?"

"I don't know," he says, taking a step toward me. "All I know is that when we're alone, it's all I can do to control myself."

I stare at him and once again he steps to me and kisses me, taking my face in his sturdy hands. It feels as good as ever. I love the way his scent emanates off him, mixing with mine and changing the chemical makeup of the air. But something is off this time. I pull back and he gives me the cutest damn look of confusion.

"What is it?" he asks.

"I guess, I just don't know where I stand. Are we...like...together?"

"We can be," he says, nodding as if he's confirming something to himself. "But it would be better if no one knew. Can you do that?"

"Be your secret"—*gulp*—"boyfriend?"

"I know it's not fair to you but—"

I press my thumb to his lips to stop him talking.

"I can do that."

There's something sort of exhilarating about having a secret—the thrill of knowing something other people don't. And for the first time I actually feel like Jasper and I are sort of on the same page. He's not just my mate, as declared by the Moon Gods, he's my boyfriend. My little secret. This advancement is enough that I'm positively giddy as I make my way down to dinner.

Jasper didn't stay long in my room; in fact he seemed pretty keen to be on his way. I guess he was just worried someone might hear us. So even though it's totally cringe, I'm excited to see him again.

Every person I pass, I glance at and smile. Being in a covert relationship has put me in a really good mood and for once I'm actually feeling outgoing.

Just about everyone is in the dining room when I arrive. Katie is there already, sitting between her mates, who are hunched over silently while she leans back in her chair, arms crossed, an expression that can only be described as *fed up* on her face.

"What's up?" I ask when I arrive, but I'm only half-present.

The rest of my attention is on Jasper, who's sitting to the right of Morven's empty chair. He nods ever so subtly in my direction and I just about pass out. But the jelly-wobbles in my legs stop the instant I spot Clayton, one seat to the right, staring daggers in my direction.

"These two," Katie begins, and I seize the opportunity to break eye contact, slipping into my seat and hiding behind Todd, "who were being so nice earlier, brought Christmas presents for me, but because they're being dumb and jealous, they both thought it would be funny to steal what the other person brought and destroy it."

"Oh," I say.

"I'll buy you a new plushie," Todd says.

"He destroyed the necklace I bought first," Simon replies.

"Enough," Katie says, shuddering with rage.

"Tough times," I say.

"How did things go with Asper-Jay?" she asks, deciding to ignore her mates completely.

"I'll tell you later."

The horn sounds again, announcing Morven's entrance. The alpha looks ever so suave in a proper tuxedo. Astrid and Mia enter after him, the luna in a maroon dress, and Mia in a tartan gown that's totally giving Merida from *Brave*. On their way past, Mia shoots me a cheeky wink.

Before we can eat, Morven gives another speech all about the blood moon and how lucky we are to be in such a privileged position, and in such good company. Because he can't help himself, he makes a number of subtly suggestive comments about the growing bond between our packs, while grinning wildly at Jasper and Mia.

We get it! You're obsessed with your daughter boning my boyfriend.

I want to roll my eyes but don't want Morven to see and feel disrespected. Plus, the whole time he's speaking I can feel Clayton's unyielding death stare boring into the side of my head. Not wanting to give him the satisfaction, I pretend like he isn't trying to drill a hole through my skull with his eyes. I keep my gaze focused on Morven. Besides, I'm not the one who pulled rank and commanded he keep quiet.

The food they serve is ridiculously delicious. Honey-glazed ham, roasted potatoes, turkey, stuffing that I could eat for days, brussels sprouts, gravy, and so much more.

There're dishes I don't even know the name of, let alone think of as Christmas fare.

Katie's stalemate with her boys cools off a little during the meal, and finally the four of us are able to chat and have a nice time.

Between courses I risk a glance at Jasper, who is talking animatedly with Mia. Yesterday—hell, this morning even—this would have filled me with jealousy. But now I'm glad he has someone nice to talk to at that end of the table. As I move my attention back to the conversation at hand, I'm once again caught in the icy glare of Clayton, who is holding his knife upright in one hand and stabbing a piece of meat with the fork in his other.

Damn, am I that interesting?

For dessert we have traditional Christmas pudding, which isn't my cup of tea, and sherry, which despite being underage, we get to partake in. The alcohol makes my chest and cheeks warm. By the time dinner is over I'm worried I'll need to be rolled back to my room.

"Everyone," Mia says, standing and clapping her hands to gather our attention. "I hope you've brought your dancing shoes. When you're finished, we're hosting a little soiree in the Bjørn Labraid Ballroom. I hope to see you there and celebrate this Christmas with music and dancing!"

Roll me to the dance floor then, I guess!

Dinner guests stand and make their way back through the lounge toward an area of the lodge I've yet to explore.

"Let's go," Katie says, huffing at her mates, who glare at each other threateningly. "Fine, stay here. Max and I are going to dance."

Katie takes my arm and we leave with the river of Rocky Pack wolves heading for the ballroom.

Up a winding set of stairs we ascend to the next level of the packhouse and come to a wide pair of oak doors, through which music and light comes flooding out. Katie and I enter the ballroom, which must have been named after Mia's great-grandfather, and wander a little ways into the expansive space. Heavy iron chandeliers hang from a lofty beam; much like the dining room we're surrounded by golden wood and rocky columns. One wall is entirely made of glass with doors leading out to a wide balcony and through which the mountain range glimmers in the moonlight.

"May I?" I ask, taking Katie's hand and bowing.

"But of course."

I lead Katie out onto the dance floor and spin her around like I'm Beast and she's Belle and the teapot is singing. As we make our way around the floor, I take in the crowd of well-dressed wolves. Mia is standing by a table off to the side and raises a glass in our direction when we swish past. Mason and one of his friends are dancing, and we nearly collide with them while spinning too fast. I'm shocked when I even spot Jasper dancing slow and gracefully with Olivia.

I want so badly to be the one dancing with him. If I close my eyes I can almost pretend I am, except Katie's hands are way too small to be Jasper's. But I know that's not an option, so I try and push the thought away.

After a song or two, Todd and Simon approach us slowly. Simon clears his throat and Katie and I come to a standstill.

"We were hoping..." Simon begins.

"That you might..." Todd continues.

"Dance with us."

Katie looks between her mates in astonishment. Then she glances at me as if to ask "What the f is going on?"

I shrug.

"You mean both of you?" Katie asks.

"We were thinking…" Todd says.

"Since it's Christmas…" Simon elaborates.

"We could stop being jerks."

"Not that we're giving up, but think of it sort of like a cease-fire."

"For now," Todd finishes up.

Katie smiles at me. It might not be the forever response she was hoping for, but she looks like all her Christmas wishes are coming true. And who am I to stand in the way of a Christmas miracle. I gesture to the floor as I back away. Todd and Simon each extend a hand to Katie, and the three of them begin to move—surprisingly gracefully for a throuple—across the boards.

Everyone I know is either dancing or chatting, and I think I could use a little breather after the last few days, plus I'm feeling sort of pulled outside, so I head toward the glass doors and out onto the balcony. The cold air is instantly refreshing, and I take a deep breath as I head to the wooden railing. The moon is almost full and looking more purple than I've ever seen her. The tinge of redness that's been creeping up has engulfed her but is still thin enough that it's mixing with the silvery-blue opalescent color I'm familiar with.

I think back to that night at the festival when I looked up and saw a bloated, taunting face, and realize how much has changed in such a short time. Although I've been persistent, there has always been an undercurrent of resentment in my pursuit of Jasper. But looking up now, I don't resent the Moon Gods—if they exist; I'm glad they challenged me. For the first time, I feel hopeful.

"How'd you do it?" a gruff voice says behind me.

I turn and find Clayton standing between me and the doors. His shirt is half-untucked and his usually so perfectly quaffed hair is ruffled, messy strands falling limply over his eyes.

"What?" I ask.

"How did you do it?" He steps toward me. "How'd you trick him into thinking he could be mated to someone like you?"

There's so much venom in his words as he spits them through clenched teeth.

"I didn't trick anyone."

He takes another step, dropping a bottle of whiskey as he does. Glass smashes and scatters across the stone floor.

"Have you been drinking?"

"He was supposed to be a great alpha; he was supposed to be strong and continue his family line. He was supposed to be a powerful leader...and I was supposed to stand by his side."

Clayton is now within a couple feet of me. I back up until I'm pressed against the wood between me and the side of the mountain. A quick glance over my shoulder and I can't even see the bottom of the valley—just a pit of never-ending darkness.

"You... You can still stand by him," I say, my voice quivering.

"No...I can't...because you ruined him."

Clayton's face has twisted into an ugly, pained expression. He clenches his fist and takes another step.

"You ruined him!"

He pulls back his fist, and I brace for the impact of his punch.

AN INEVITABLE THAWING

I squint and wait for Clayton's fist to make contact with my face, but it doesn't come.

For a second I wonder if he's so drunk he missed me. Then I open my eyes properly and find Jasper, claws out, fangs elongated, having just thrown Clayton backward onto the ground.

Clayton groans and tries to stand.

"Stay down," Jasper growls.

People are crowding at the doors, drawn over by the commotion.

"Don't touch him," Jasper warns the prostrate Clayton. The ruffled Adonis doesn't submit just yet, growling in return and baring his teeth.

The crowd is spilling from the ballroom onto the balcony, their eyes darting from Clayton to Jasper to me.

What do they think is happening right now?

Mason is among them, watching me with concern. Clayton's growl intensifies and he readies himself to launch at me once more. Jasper widens his stance, ready to defend me. Mason steps forward, but surprisingly he's pushed aside as Olivia charges through the crowd. Without hesitating she grabs Clayton by his jacket collar and pulls him backward, throwing him against the wall. The crowd of onlookers jump aside so as not to get hit.

"Submit," she commands, and I have no idea if she's defending Jasper or helping him defend me. She's been a colossal dick to me since the Yule Ball; why would she be jumping in to save my ass now?

Clayton snaps his jaw, which is beginning to look more and more wolflike as the situation escalates.

"Submit!" Olivia bellows.

Katie, Todd, and Simon come running out onto the balcony, quickly taking in the situation, and—bless their cotton socks—the bro twins position themselves in front of Clayton as well, claws at the ready.

Clayton twists his muzzle, clearly thirsty for my blood, but surveys his position. He's ridiculously outnumbered, and with a final whimper, he begins to settle. His features shrink back into human form; he retracts his claws and loosens his muscles.

"Take him to my room," Jasper says. "I'll deal with him there."

Todd and Simon each take one of Clayton's arms and walk him through an opening in the crowd. He doesn't struggle—in fact, he looks a little weak on his feet. Maybe the liquor is running its course.

Jasper turns to me, clearly distressed. He takes a step in my direction, then glances at the wolves still lingering in the doorway. There are too many eyes on us—he stops far enough away that he can't touch me.

"Are you okay?" he asks.

"Yeah, I... I think he was drunk."

"I'll deal with him."

Olivia steps up to Jasper's side. "Go," she says. "I'll stay with him."

Maybe Jasper catches my shocked expression, because for a moment he hesitates.

"You're sure you're okay? He didn't hurt you?"

"No, I'm fine."

"Okay, thanks," he says, giving Olivia a nod. Jasper walks through the remaining crowd, ignoring their stares, as if they aren't there.

"You want to sit?" Olivia asks, and for the first time in weeks, she resembles the girl I met at the Blue Moon Festival.

"That'd be great."

"Max," Katie says coming over, accompanied by Mason. "Are you okay? What happened?"

"He looked pretty wild," Mason adds.

"I'm fine, you guys should go enjoy the rest of the dance. Don't let that dick ruin it."

"I should probably go see if Todd and Simon have made it back safely. You're sure you're fine?" Katie asks.

"I got him," Olivia says, continuing to bewilder me with how nice she's being.

"I'll make sure he doesn't leave his wing of the compound," Mason says.

"Thanks."

It's kind of cool that everyone's got my back—no, actually it's really cool. And it makes me start to think that maybe Jasper and I don't need to be a secret, if this is the way people react. I'm especially impressed with Olivia as she gives a nod to my friends and leads me toward a stairway off to the side of the balcony.

We leave the glow and music of the ballroom behind as we descend to a round platform with waist-high stone walls and a bench. It's the perfect lookout spot for stargazing and taking in the mountains.

"What an asshole!" Olivia says as we plonk down on the seat. "I've been waiting a long time for a reason to wail on him."

I laugh. "Oh really?"

"Growing up in the alpha's circle, you don't get much choice who your friends are going to be. That piece of shit has been pissing me off since we were kids."

Olivia is leaning back on her hands, staring out at the view. She seems chill, completely content in my company, and completely ignoring the massive elephant that's followed us out here.

"Thanks," I say. "For jumping in like that."

She takes a deep breath.

"You know," I continue, "I was starting to think you hated me or thought I was an asshole."

Olivia drops her head; she knew this moment was coming.

"You're not the asshole," she says into her chest. "I am."

Excuse me?

I sit quietly. I know I don't need to ask the question. An explanation is required—Olivia probably just needs a second.

"I've been acting pretty shitty to you, haven't I?"

"Just a bit."

"I wouldn't be surprised if you think I'm a bigger bitch than Clayton, to be honest."

"Okay, so why then? Did I do something?"

"No, you didn't do anything." She stretches her legs out in front of her and crosses her ankles.

I'm just now realizing how cold it is out here—the adrenaline must be leaving my body.

"I did something though."

My hands find the edge of the bench and I lean forward; Olivia doesn't turn to face me.

"I knew"—she takes a breath—"I knew you and Jasper were mates, when I agreed to let him choose me. He told me and I wasn't happy about it, but I knew and I still agreed to do it."

My heart is beating a little faster. I hadn't really thought about whether or not Olivia knew what she was doing when Jasper tried to break our bond. I guess I was more focused on the whole losing-my-mate thing. But hearing it from her now, I can't help but tense my jaw and shorten my breaths.

"It was an asshole move and I know it," she says. "I'm a complete jerk."

I can't disagree.

"So why did you agree then?"

In my mind I can picture the conversation I walked in on. Olivia and Jasper talking in hurried, hushed tones, neither of them looking particularly happy, Jasper desperate and Olivia reluctant. But she still said yes, she still betrayed me.

"It seemed like a good solution, at the time."

"Solution to what?"

Olivia leans forward and runs her hands over her face. She looks more pained than I thought was possible—she's always been so strong, so statuesque and invulnerable.

"That's what's so fucked-up about what I did. I knew what I was doing to you, because I'm...the same. I'm gay too."

Whoa!

Once again I'm caught off guard learning that there are other people like me and Jasper out there. I'm not sure why they all seem to feel comfortable coming out to me—I must have one of those friendly faces or something. But I'm glad. I just wish I was able to do the same thing and talk about myself so openly.

"You're...?"

"I'm totally into girls. And I thought..."

I can see how pained she is, how remorseful, and I want to intervene, because I understand, don't I?

"You thought if you mated with Jasper, it would go away and you wouldn't have to deal with it anymore."

"Pretty dumb, hey? Thinking lying to everyone would change something that's in me, part of me."

"We're all struggling," I say. "The thing I don't get is why you've been freezing me out…"

"Ugh, I guess I thought I deserved your hatred or something, like I didn't deserve to be friendly with you. So, I acted like I felt, like an asshole. And I guess I thought if I let you get close enough I'd have to come clean, so I kept avoiding you."

"Didn't work, did it?" I say, laughing a little.

Olivia sits back and finally looks at me; there's relief in her expression—and regret.

"Can't fight something that's inevitable," she says. "And while we're coming clean…"

She rubs her hands, palms down, on top of her thighs. What's coming now?

"You're not the only person I've been avoiding."

I tilt my head, scrunch my face up.

"What do you mean… Who…?"

Olivia arches a brow and my mouth opens in a gasp of realization.

"Your mate!"

She nods and buries her face in her hands again, but more like a shy puppy this time.

"Um, okay dish, who is it? Someone from back home?"

She bites her lip nervously and shakes her head. I'm desperate to know who her mate is, but I'm also enjoying seeing this softer side of Olivia. She's always been badass, but she's kind of a sweetheart too. I guess love makes a fool of us all.

"Someone from here?" I hazard a guess.

Olivia nods.

"Who is she?!"

I'm almost bouncing out of my seat, causing Olivia to shush me and hold me in place.

"Be quiet, I… I don't want them to know. I don't think I'm ready for…all that."

For a second I'm back on the balcony, Clayton with rage in his eyes and his fist raised. There might be more queer people about than I first thought, but there are haters too.

"I get it," I say. "You don't have to tell me who it is."

This strange giddy expression crosses her face, and I recognize it immediately. She wants to tell me, to speak the person's name, and speak the mate bond into existence.

"Let's just say," she begins, being all coy, which is weird coming from Olivia, "I can understand your predicament better than you'd think."

For a second I don't understand. My mind starts reeling through Rocky Pack girls like I'm scrolling through contacts in my phone. Then I land on a name and suddenly everything makes sense. The way Olivia reacted when we first met her. The way she hasn't been spending that much time around Jasper…

"Mia?" I ask.

She flutters her lips as if expelling pent-up energy, then nods.

"Oh my Moon Gods!"

"Calm down! I still don't know if she's even into girls."

I press my lips together. I want to tell Olivia so badly, but it still isn't my place to out Mia.

"What are you doing?" she asks, and I wish I was blessed with a better ability to lie. "What do you know?"

"I can't say," I snap frantically. "Just…don't ask."

She side-eyes me questioningly. "Okay."

We both sit back against the bench and turn our gazes to the sky. The moon is hanging massive and low, staring us in the face.

"I can say one thing," I offer. "If we've learned anything in the last fifteen minutes, it's that you can't avoid the inevitable."

"Ain't that the truth."

I turn to Olivia.

"So stop avoiding her."

The packhouse is strangely quiet when we head back inside. The festivities of the evening, not to mention the food and sherry, have wiped just about everyone out. We make our way to the parlor, which is lit only by the dying embers of the fire and the multicolored string lights on the tree.

"Okay," Olivia says. "You'll be okay getting back to your room?"

I kind of like the idea of having Olivia as my personal bodyguard but I can take it from here.

"I'll be fine, thanks."

"Okay and...thank you." Olivia pulls me in for a very rigid, too-tight hug that catches me completely off guard. Once the shock has worn off, I hug her back.

As she heads off toward the royal suites or whatever they're called, Jasper emerges from the shadows. He looks tired, his hair is a little mussed, and his white button-down is untucked, loose at the collar.

"Hey," he says.

"Hi."

He looks worse off than I feel, and I was the one who was attacked. My chat with Olivia has left me feeling strangely upbeat. From Jasper's expression, I don't think he's sharing my optimism.

"I'm sorry, Max. I should never have let him get that close to you... I..." Jasper sighs and rubs his eyes. "Are you alright?"

"I'm fine—I had Olivia. What about you? What's happened to Clayton?"

"Clayton has been confined to his room; he'll be sent back to the pack in the morning. He's actions are...inexcusable."

"Okay, great."

The lights from the Christmas tree are reflecting on Jasper's cheeks, lighting one red and the other green. Tonight Jasper came to my rescue, he protected me like he said he's meant to this whole time. But here he is, five feet away, and I feel more distance between us than ever before.

"Are you—"

"This is what I meant," he interrupts. "This is why we can't be... We can't be together."

"Jasper—"

"No, Max. Imagine if more people found out—more people like Clayton. I can't put you through that."

"Put *me* through that?"

The embers in the hearth crackle as more of them die and turn to ash.

"I thought maybe there was a way we could make this work. But it's obvious now it won't."

"Because one drunk asshat took a swing at me?"

"It won't just be him."

"I don't care, Jasper. You protected me, Olivia protected me, Todd, Simon, Katie, Mason. We have friends, we don't have to do this alone."

My voice has risen and echoes in the rafters. Jasper looks stricken; his eyes glance to the exits—he's terrified someone might hear us.

"We *are* alone," he says. "I'm sorry. I know… I know this isn't what you wanted."

My jaw starts quivering, and I want to argue, to tell him he's being a dick, acting like the jerk from the summer. But I don't say anything. It's one U-turn too many. I can't keep fighting, keep chasing him.

"Is that how you really feel?" I ask, voice trembling.

"Yes."

"Then so be it."

Jasper looks up, shocked, as if he has any right to be. I'm giving him what he wants. I'm backing down.

Before he can say anything else I turn and leave. Passing the fireplace, I notice the embers have gone dark. Soon they'll be cold too.

WHERE YOU STAND

"What's up?!" Aisha says, her face beaming through my phone screen. "Merry Christmas, dude. How's that mountain air treating you?"

The sun is shining too brightly through a gap in my curtains, I rub my eyes and lie back on my pillows.

"Merry Christmas," I croak. "The mountains are...wild. How are things with you? What did you get up to yesterday?"

There's so much I need to tell Aisha, but for the moment I just want to hear her talk and pretend like I'm back in New York.

"It's pretty chill here to be honest. My parents took Troy and me out for dinner in the West Village, and look what Troy got me."

She holds her wrist up to the camera so I can see. She's wearing a delicate silver chain with a sparkling wolf charm dangling from it like a Christmas bauble.

"Ohhh pretty," I say.

"Isn't it gorge? He's the best."

"And what did you get him?"

"He thinks we need to spend more time together, so I got us tickets for a couples cooking class."

"Fun."

"So lame, right? He also got a new Xbox game, because, you know, straight guy so..."

I laugh and for a second I'm glad someone is in a normal, happy relationship.

"But enough about me, what's going on with you? Is Jasper behaving himself?"

I give her a look and immediately she knows something's up.

"What's that donkey done this time?"

For the next fifteen to twenty minutes, I give Aisha an in-depth account of everything that's been going on. She *oohs* and *aahs* as I tell her about our kiss in the ranger station and purses her lips as I tell her about what came next. When I tell her about Clayton attempting to lay into me, her expression changes, her nostrils flare, and she stops blinking.

"That guy is so damaged," she says, fuming. "He's lucky I wasn't there. If I caught him acting up like that I'd have ended him for sure."

It's hard to explain, but there's an edge to the way Aisha acts when I bring up Clayton—like just the sound of his name is enough to tighten her jaw. That he nearly sucker punched me has her incensed. She looks like she wants to jump through the phone and mess him up.

"Jasper stopped him and he's being sent back to the pack."

"Good." She nods. "You need to stay as far away from him as possible. And what about Jasper? Have you spoken to him since?"

My dumb body completely betrays me, and as strong and in control as I want to act, tears spring to my eyes.

"He says it's just more proof that we can't be together."

"That ass."

I wipe my face and sniff back my emotions. "It doesn't matter. I'm over it."

She lifts a brow. "Ahuh."

"Anyway, we have the blood moon ceremony viewing thing tonight, then we're coming home, so…"

"I'm sorry, Max."

Troy enters the video frame. "Whoa, is that Max?" He approaches, wrapping an arm around Aisha. "Hey man!"

"What's up, Troy?"

"Ah you know, just eating well and treating my girl." He kisses Aisha on the cheek, but she's watching me with concern in her eyes.

"Sounds nice," I say.

"Actually"—he turns his attention to Aisha—"we gotta go. My folks will be at the diner in fifteen and you know they hate waiting."

"Okay, just let me say goodbye," she says.

"No problem. Hey Max, happy Christmas, dude."

"You too, Troy."

He exits the frame and Aisha leans a little closer to the camera. I wait for her to speak.

"It's okay if you're not over it," she says finally.

I take a deep breath in through my nose and hold it. "I don't know if I have much of a choice."

Aisha looks to the side, running something through her head. "Can I be honest about something? I was worried about you going up there. I didn't know if Jasper would ever be able to get over his bullshit and open up. But from what you've told me, it sounds like he's doing it—or at least, his version of it. It sounds like progress."

"Nothing's changed. I'm right back where I started."

"I'm just sayin', that boy has a truckload of trauma to work through. He's doesn't have the support you do. Hell, his best guy friend is freaking Clayton. He might need more time to process."

"And I'm just supposed to wait around."

"No, not if it's making you unhappy. But do you think you'd be happy giving up?"

My shoulders drop and I sigh, with a slight roll of the eyes, because my stupid self—my traitor of a heart—knows the truth: there's only one thing that will make me happy.

"Right," Aisha says. "So, maybe don't give up just yet?"

"I can't keep chasing him though. It's...too much."

"That's fair. You gotta protect yourself."

"So what am I supposed to do?"

"What if you stopped chasing? And see what happens."

I shoot her a confused look. "So, do nothing then?"

"You're a special kid, Max, and whether he's ready to admit it or not, Jasper knows it too. Maybe he needs a second for his head to catch up with his heart."

"Maybe."

Aisha glances off to the side, where I can picture Troy holding her coat and gesturing for her to hurry up.

"I gotta go," she says. "Remember where you stand and don't forget yourself in all this."

"I miss you," I say.

"Happy Christmas, Max."

"Happy Christmas."

She smiles at me and I give my best attempt at a smile back.

"Okay, go!" I say, swishing my hand as if I'm shooing her away.

"Laters!"

We hang up and I let my phone flop onto the mattress.

I head down to breakfast with my head in a swirl. Is Aisha right? Will giving up just make me more miserable?

Or is this a lose-lose situation? All I know is that I need to start putting myself first. What do I want? What will make me happy?

If I stop chasing Jasper, will he ever come around?

The parlor is busy this morning. I guess more Rocky Pack wolves have arrived for the blood moon. Heading to the pastry table feels like wandering through a hotel lobby. I load up my plate with apricot Danishes and apple strudels and look around for a place to sit.

I'm shocked when I spot Katie, Todd, and Simon sitting by a window—not because they're together, that's pretty standard. But because Katie is holding hands with both of the boys and they're not fighting or throwing things at each other.

"What's up?" I ask, taking the last seat at their table.

Katie grins at me like she's trying not to smile too wide.

"Hey bruh," Todd says.

"Sup, dude," Simon adds.

"You're all acting very strangely," I say, biting into my apricot pastry.

"We have some news," Katie says, like she's about to explode with joy. "After the dance we all sat down and talked and—"

"And we're going to try this polyam thing," Simon finishes for her.

"Wow, quite the development! How did you come to this arrangement?"

Todd still looks a little unsure, but Katie nods to encourage him to explain, as if saying it out loud will help him adjust.

"We always have a great time hanging out, the three of us, and when that dick came after you last night, Simon and I realized...we make a pretty awesome team."

"Yeah and if there's one person in the world I don't mind sharing with, it's my bro," Simon confirms.

Todd puffs up his chest a little. "And we're man enough to be confident that even if we have to share, it doesn't diminish what we have with Katie."

I shake my head in shock. "That is a very mature thought."

"It's still going to be hard," Katie says. "We'll need to make sure we're communicating with each other, and there will be times when jealousy makes us do silly things, but they know I love them both."

"And that's enough," Simon says.

"My gosh," I say, sitting back and taking in this cute little arrangement of people. "I'm happy for you all."

"We also know you'll want to spend time with Katie," Todd says, like that was even in question. "And we respect that."

It must be a Christmas miracle, or maybe it's the thin air up in the mountains, because somehow the bro twins have developed emotional intelligence. Or maybe they just care enough about Katie that they're willing to do what it takes to hold onto her. Is that what I should be doing? Or am I Katie in this analogy? Do I just need to lay my cards on the table and wait?

"It'll be a nice time for you two to be able to hang out as friends and not rivals, too," Katie says to her twin boyfriends. "Plus I was sort of lying when I said I liked watching you play video games, so you can do that when I'm with Max."

"Sounds good," Todd says.

"You're so smart!" Simon says.

From the corner of my eye I spot Mason passing through the parlor. His shoulders are hunched over and he looks tired. I watch as he moves to the breakfast tables, stares at the food, then turns back around and leaves. What's up with him?

"Well, I'm happy for you guys," I say. "I've got to go check on something. But I'll see you before we head out later."

"Are you okay?" Katie asks as I get up.

"Yeah, I think so."

Right now it's not me I'm worried about.

I follow Mason out, along a corridor to the den, then down some stairs and onto a balcony. Mason mustn't know I'm following him because he doesn't stop; instead he takes a path leading off into the snow-covered mountainside.

Without a coat the cold already has me shivering, but something is up with Mason—I don't know how, but I can just tell. I follow his tracks until I spot him sitting on a rock, staring out at the mountains.

"You'll catch your death out here, you know?" I say, and he turns but doesn't seem shocked to see me.

"You didn't need to follow me out here," he says in a monotone voice, not his usual peppy self.

"Is something wrong?"

He huffs and turns back to the mountains. Without waiting for an invite, I take a spot next to him on the rock.

"You don't need to babysit me," he says, and I have no idea where this is coming from.

"Who said I was babysitting? I happen to like freezing my ass off."

"You should go if you're cold."

"Did I do something?" I turn to him and notice his set jaw. "You can talk to me."

"Sure."

Why is he being dismissive? I grab him by the shoulder and turn him so that he has to face me.

"Mason, what's going on?"

"Nothing." He shrugs me off. "At least nothing you can help with."

"Why not?"

"I just get down sometimes."

"Yeah so does everyone."

He shakes his head. "You don't know what it's like to be me, so don't pretend you do."

I feel like I've been slapped. Have I been pretending I have more in common with Mason than I thought? He's one of the first people I've met who I can relate to.

"If you want me to go I'll go. But I'd rather stay."

"Well that's just it, you're not staying. Tomorrow you'll be gone back to your pack, and you can hyperfixate on your mate without me getting in the way."

Okay, now he's being ridiculous.

"In the way? You're... Mason, we're friends. You could never be..." I stop and watch him wringing his hands together, then I reach out and grab them with mine. "Hey, just because I'm leaving tomorrow doesn't mean we're not going to stay friends."

His teeth are chattering, a tear rolls down his cheek.

"You know I was so happy when you first arrived," he says. "Finally, I thought, someone like me. For a second I even thought we could be mates, because you're the only other gay wolf I've ever met. And I know you have your own shit going on, but you have no idea how lonely it's been up here. And now you're going."

I shuffle my butt along our rock bench so that we're sitting a little closer.

"I can relate to that, the loneliness, it's—"

"But you have a mate."

"Jasper's not exactly great company."

"But he loves you. Anyone with the most rudimentary gaydar could see that when he tackled that asshole last night. He'd do anything for you."

"Anything but spend time with me."

"I know," he says, wiping his frozen tears away. "I know he's a dick and it's not perfect, but at least it's something."

I wrap my arm around him.

"There's someone out there for you too."

"Whatever."

"Are you serious?!" I sit back and look at him like he's being the most ridiculous person in the world, because he is. "You're amazing. You're friendly and clever and funny and super cute. Maybe they aren't in your pack and maybe they hate winter sports, but there is a wolf out there somewhere who is going to be obsessed with you—like head over tail wildly obsessed with you. You don't know that about yourself?"

He takes a breath and sits a little straighter. "Not really."

"Okay, well you need to start learning that about yourself. Because you're like, literally, the best. And if you think we're not texting every day from now on you're insane. We're friends forever."

He laughs and finally cracks a smile.

"And I'm hard to get rid of," I joke. "Just ask Jasper."

Mason's laugh turns into a full-on cackle and I'm so relieved to see the light in my friend's eyes return.

"You are pretty clingy," he says, and I shove him, harder than I mean to, so he slips off the rock and falls into the snow.

"You little!"

He scrambles up, cupping snow in his hands and throwing it in my face.

"Oh no you don't!"

Before I can retaliate he's up and running. I chase him, gathering snow into a tight ball before tossing it and hitting him in the shoulders. He stops and turns, grabbing at snow, readying to strike again. I run at him and tackle him into the powder and we topple over.

"Okay, okay," he puffs. "You win."

Gasping for breath, we lie on our backs in the snow.

"You're so annoying," he says.

"Aw, you're okay too," I say, knowing that I've made a friend for life.

"I'm sorry for being a mopey sad sack. I just get like that sometimes."

"Hey"—I roll onto my side—"if you ever want to talk, I mean it, you text me, or call whenever you want."

He rolls over as well and grins.

"Thanks. And I'll want all the juicy goss when Jasper finally figures out what he's missing. And I mean details, I want aaaaaall the details."

I shove his shoulder gently.

When eventually we head back inside, I give Mason another hug. I'm so happy to have found a friend like him—and so excited for him to discover what I'm learning, that we're not as alone as we think. People like us, gay people, queer people, we're everywhere, even if we're quiet or sad or completely wrapped up in our own drama; we're here and we need to be there for each other.

The day passes slowly. I spend some time with Katie while her boyfriends are having designated bro time, then I do some drawing and call home. When it's finally time to get ready for the trek out to Wolf Point, the sun is setting, and the sky has turned this intense shade of pink. Ripples of peach and violet cloud roll in, and gradually the pink turns to maroon, then purple. By the time I'm dressed in my hiking gear, it's dark outside; the clouds have covered the sky, and behind them the moon must be rising. If the weather stays like this, we might not even catch a glimpse of the blood moon. But I don't care. This trip has been well worth the journey.

As I finish lacing my boots, there's a knock at the door.

"One second," I call, finishing a double bow then running over to see who it is.

I open the door, and no one is there. I glance side to side; there's no one down the hall either. I wonder if I imagined hearing the knock, and then I notice a package at my feet.

It's a small box, wrapped in silver paper, with a red velvet bow tied neatly on top. A gift?

Taking the present back inside, I sit on the bed and stare at it. Who would have left this here? Could it be...? No, that's too wild.

Christmas was yesterday, so there's no reason not to open it right away. I tug off the bow and tear into the paper. As I open the parcel, a faint hint of cherry blossom escapes. Inside is a what looks like a jewelry box and a note.

Sorry it's late.

It can't be...

The box snaps open easily to reveal a silver signet ring; pressed into the face is the seal of the alpha. There's only one person this could have come from.

Cold metal slips easily over my finger as I slide the ring on, and I examine it for a moment, watching it glint in the light. I leave the ring on and slip my mittens over top.

As I head downstairs to join the hiking party I'm distinctly aware of the ring's presence on my finger. But what does it mean?

Why has he given me this now?

Maybe he felt bad for not having anything to give me in return for his present and regifted a piece of his own jewelry. But Jasper doesn't wear rings. So he must have bought it specially. And why the alpha's seal unless... Unless it's supposed to suggest...

Once again, Jasper the king of mixed messages has sent my head swimming.

When I arrive outside to join the hiking group, Jasper is the first person I see—somehow the crowd parts so that I can take him in. He's standing casually in the middle of the group, hair swept to the side, in a sleek black puffer jacket, one hand in his pocket. Peeking out from the top of his zipper is a flash of red fabric. The scarf I gave him. He's wearing it.

He meets my eye and I know...the chase is still on.

THE BLOOD MOON

"Ready to freeze your ass off?"

Mason appears at my side, a green beanie perched on the back of his head and a festive thermos clasped between gloved hands. I glance back at Jasper, but he's not where he was a second ago.

"Earth to Max, what's going on?" Mason asks.

"Uh, nothing."

Jasper must be somewhere, but it's okay, I don't need to go looking.

"What's in the thermos?"

"Hot chocolate, what else?" Mason responds, grinning. "This isn't my first midnight hike—you'll thank me in an hour when you're shaking in your little boots."

"I'll take you word for it."

Out front of the packhouse, snow is falling, drifting sideways in the wind. It's not as intense as the storm I got caught in yesterday, but if this wasn't some sacred once-in-a-lifetime event, you better believe I'd be turning around and heading back to my room to watch *Housewives*.

Katie, Todd, and Simon arrive in the foyer, and I wave them over.

"This is so exciting," Katie squeals.

"You sure you're going to be warm enough, babe?" Simon asks.

"I brought an extra pair of earmuffs if you want them," Todd says, making Katie blush.

"And I brought a hot-water bottle, just in case," Simon adds.

Katie looks between them, then at me, and I can tell she's just the tiniest bit embarrassed. This throuple thing is going to be an uphill battle. And speaking of uphill... Alpha Morven and Mia have just appeared in the hall.

"A fantastic turnout!" Morven says, walking through the group.

Mia lets him go, instead looking around and finding Jasper.

He's off to the side with Olivia, and as Mia approaches, Olivia's face turns this sickly shade of olive green. She quickly excuses herself. Mia looks a little confused but swiftly moves on, smiling and linking an arm through Jasper's. I can't help the pang of jealousy, even though I know Mia isn't going to make a move on my mate, and even though Jasper and I are both wearing the presents we gave each other. So I guess nothing is going to take this feeling away.

"Could I have everyone's attention for a moment before we head off?" Morven says, and every eye is suddenly upon him.

"Years ago, when our ancestors climbed out of the valley, they did so with us in mind. They rose from the shadows to build the foundations of our pack on top of the mountains—so that we could have the best. And tonight we are so fortunate to be the only pack with access to Wolf Point. So let us remember our ancestors as we make the trek out there tonight and are blessed with a blood moon. We give thanks, to the wolves of the past, who rose from nothingness to the peak of civilization."

A murmur passes through the crowd as Rocky Pack wolves nod in agreement or bow their heads in reverence.

"Now wrap up warm, stay close to the group, and let's make our way to Wolf Point."

Morven's speech is met with a small round of applause as the doors are flung open. Cold wind sweeps into the foyer, bringing with it spinning currents of snow and ice. It hits my face and steals my breath.

Mason was right: We're about halfway up the mountain—or at least I'm praying we're halfway—and it is cold. Colder than cold. I cup the silver thermos lid between my mittens and sip hot chocolate. Under our feet the snow is icy and crunches with each step. The mountain range is rolling alongside us, jagged and brutal. Overhead, clouds are blocking out the moon, lit by the occasional spark of lightning.

"That's really good," I say, handing the thermos across to Katie.

Mason smiles proudly. "It's my mom's recipe, plus I added a little whiskey to give it a bit of a kick."

My mouth drops open in exaggerated shock. "Are you trying to get us drunk out here? So that we fall off the mountain?"

"Exactly," Mason says, "and you've fallen right into my trap."

"That's one delicious trap," Katie says, wiping her lips and offering the thermos to her mates.

"Right? And anyway, if I were you, I'd be less afraid of falling off the mountain and more afraid of the blood wolf," Mason says.

"You said that was just an old superstition," I shoot back.

Mason grins devilishly. "True, but superstitions have to start somewhere, don't they?"

A fresh shiver rolls down my spine. I turn back to the path ahead and try to speed up ever so slightly, wondering if one of the wolves here could be the one to turn wild.

The turnout for the hike is larger than I expected—there must be at least fifty wolves. My little group is somewhere in the middle of the pack. Jasper has been walking up ahead with Mia this whole time, and despite not feeling an urgent need to rush to his side, I've made sure to stay close enough to keep him in my sights. Part of me wishes we could be walking together. Sharing these kinds of experiences is what mates are supposed to do, right? But another part of me is happy to be with my friends, sharing a thermos of spiked hot chocolate.

A little of to the left, Olivia is walking alone. Earlier I waved at her, and she waved back but kept to herself. I feel bad for her. I may not get to share things like this with Jasper, but she doesn't even have the support of friends like I do. No one is offering her hot chocolate.

"I'll be right back," I say, and pick up my pace.

Catching up to Olivia has me huffing and puffing, and she glances at me when I arrive at her side.

"You having an asthma attack or something?" she asks.

"Just...need...one...sec..."

"How are you the same guy who nearly kept up with me during the Race of Fire and Ice?"

"It's the incline," I joke, breathing almost normally again. "How are you?"

Olivia exhales through her nose and keeps her eyes on the mountain path.

"Why don't you go over and say hi?"

Jasper and Mia are only a little ways ahead of us now, laughing about something Mia just said. *She must be hilarious to make him laugh like that.*

I shake myself out of my thought spiral—I'm trying to help Olivia.

"I... I can't," she says, but from the way she's glancing in their direction, I know she's tempted. "What would I even say?"

"You could start with 'Hi, I'm Olivia.'"

"That's lame. She knows who I am."

"Or how about 'Nice mountains, come here often?'"

"You're dumb."

"Look, I thought Mia was a bit uptight at first, but it turns out I was wrong about someone, yet again. She's great and she's not going to think you're dumb or lame. And you might want everyone to think you're the biggest, baddest wolf in the world, but you're not fooling me."

Olivia glares sideways at me.

"You regret a hundred percent of the chances you don't take."

She rolls her eyes. "Get that from a greeting card?"

"My dad says it when we go bowling."

Olivia huffs; she's clearly torn.

"He's not wrong though," I continue. "And what's the worst that can happen? You strike out?"

"Strikes are good in bowling."

"Okay so it's win-win!"

I'm even starting to confuse myself with these sports analogies. And Olivia is looking even more tempted, staring at Mia, biting her lip, but she's not sold just yet.

"Jasper is with her now—he'll have your back."

Words I never thought I would say about Jasper, but it's not untrue. He may push you away, treat you like garbage, but when the shit hits the proverbial fan, he's somehow always there.

"I don't know."

Man, what is it going to take to get this girl to act!? Wait—

"I have an idea," I say. "One second."

I run back down to my little group. They're all looking at me like I'm being weird, which—well, yeah.

"Can I borrow this?" I ask, snatching the thermos from Mason's hands before he can respond. I jog back up to Olivia and hand it to her.

"Here, offer them some of this. There's no way you'll throw a gutter ball with this."

"You're annoyingly persistent," she says, but I know I've beaten her down.

"That's what they tell me. Now go."

I give Olivia the gentlest of shoves as she heads up to join Jasper and Mia. At first they're a little shocked to see her; Mia especially looks quite taken aback. Maybe she's had the first whiff of her mate. When Olivia holds out the flask, Mia smiles and takes it graciously, and the two of them fall easily into conversation. Jasper glances back in my direction and nods ever so subtly, acknowledging that I've helped his friend.

Falling back to my group, I'm met with confused glances yet again.

"What's going on?" Katie whispers into my ear.

"Sometimes you just have to be persistent," I say and grin.

The wind has dropped away and the night is calm when we reach Wolf Point. The sky remains overcast, gray clouds hanging so low I think I could touch them, but stepping into the circle I suddenly feel warm. Like I'm standing in front of a roaring fire. I whip off my mittens and unzip my coat.

Quietly we move around the circle, feeling the lunar energy crackling like static between us. We really are closer to the moon here. Morven has stepped up onto the central rock where we left our offerings. There's no sign of the pile of gifts. Did someone come and collect them or...? No, that's ridiculous—they probably just blew away.

"Wolves!" Morven speaks, and we gather around him. "The blood moon is a symbol, a sign, representing the blood we share with all the wolves across the globe. Tonight every pack is joined by our connection to the moon."

That he's neglected to include rogues in his definition of "all the wolves" doesn't escape me.

"So as we wait in the hope that these clouds will part and the moon will bless us with her presence, take a moment to remember your family, your pack, and open your mind to the wolves of other packs. Despite the boundaries that separate us, we are one pack in the eyes of the Moon Gods. One pack under the moon."

At the end of the speech, all eyes are on the clouds. How cool would it be if, after Morven's declaration that we're all one pack, the clouds rolled away and we were bathed in red moonlight? Only that doesn't happen. Morven steps quietly down and we mill around the space.

Some of the older wolves move to the stones and place their hands against them, heads bowed, eyes closed, lips twitching in silent prayer.

Others stand facing out onto the mountain range, feet planted, palms forward, ready to accept the blessing of the moon the second she shows up.

But she doesn't show up—at least not for the next hour or so.

After wandering around for a bit, then chatting with Katie, I head toward the edge of the circle and sit. It's like sitting at the Earth's end. I pull my knees up to my chest and stare at the low-hanging clouds. Morven's words echo in my mind.

I can't get past the way he excluded rogues when he was talking about all wolves being connected. Because we have to be, right? Connected to them in some way. Just because they don't have a pack doesn't mean they aren't still wolves. And then I start thinking about the connections between wolves, because when you break it down, what separates me from any other wolf on the planet?

I'm an Elite Pack wolf, but why? Because of where I was born? Because my parents are? Because years ago some alpha won a war and claimed our territory and gave us a name.

If what Jasper said is true and our territory is under threat, what's to stop us from being conquered? What pack would we belong to then? Would we be rogues? And would that change who my friends are? My family? My mate?

It's all made-up. Someone named us the Elite Pack, someone called this the Rocky Pack, they called the people without homes rogues and left them in the shadows of the valley.

And then there're the new connections I've been making—to Mason, Mia, Olivia. Off to my left, Mia is leaning against a boulder while she chats with Olivia. They haven't stopped talking since Olivia went to offer her hot chocolate, so that's going well. Mason is laughing with one of his friends form the Rocky Pack; he looks happy and relaxed. And I realize that even though we're different from other wolves, and from each other, we're connected in our otherness.

And there are more wolves like us out there—who knows how many? Wolves who don't fit into this mold we're supposed to.

Would Morven have included us in his definition? If people knew, would they still want us in their pack? Maybe, maybe not. But that's why the connections we've made have to mean something. That's why I'm so happy to have met Mason and why I can't give up on Jasper just yet. Because he doesn't know, that we're part of this amazing undefined pack—he doesn't know that he's not alone.

"Mind if I join you?"

I look up and there is Jasper. His jacket is unzipped and his scarf is fluttering in the wind.

"You're not scared someone will see?"

"It's just sitting; we're not going to make out."

I laugh, but just a little.

"Anyway, I realized on the walk up here everyone who knows us, kind of knows already." Jasper takes a seat next to me.

Oh yeah... Katie, her mates, and Olivia know, plus Mia and Mason. And the Rocky Pack wolves don't know Jasper and I aren't friends. With Clayton gone, the only person who might have a problem with us is Alpha Morven.

I mean of course I'd prefer it if Jasper would want to sit with me even if some people who might care didn't know about us, but this is new for him, so I'll allow it.

"You're wearing it," he says, looking at my hand.

"Yeah, thank you."

"You're welcome."

"The scarf looks good."

"Max, I—"

"It's starting!" someone yells, and suddenly everyone is moving to the edge of the cliff. Jasper and I glance at each other, knowing there's more to be said, but it'll have to wait. The crowd gathers behind us as the clouds begin to roll away. Patches of onyx sky have appeared in the gaps, and at last, the bank blocking the moon is shifting. A ruby-red glow emanates in beams like a religious painting, as a swollen, dusty-red moon is revealed.

My chest becomes tight and my lips quiver. It's beautiful and potent—full of meaning, even if I don't know what that meaning is. My heart and soul feel full with purpose.

Blood-red light spills across the stone circle, turning every face crimson. Each wolf here is watching, transfixed, connected in our shared experience.

Morven was right, though he didn't go far enough. We are *all* connected, to whatever energy, whatever life force we receive from the moon. Whether alpha or rogue, we are valid and whole—siblings, family. One pack under the moon.

And from somewhere in the sky, I feel like I can hear the voices of this all-encompassing pack. Every wolf on Earth whispering in the clouds. Some are singing in Lupine, some are telling secrets, some are reaching out with a greeting, some are howling in pain.

Tears spring to my eyes and I feel as if my feet could lift from the ground. My body has become weightless, my chin rises, my shoulders pull back. Blood is pumping through me a mile a minute. I rise onto my toes, pulled closer; I could take off right now and fly into space.

Then a hand slips into mine and squeezes tight.

Jasper is still at my side, and almost like he knew I was about to take off, he's taken my hand, tethering me to Earth.

His face is glowing this rusty-orange color that brings out his freckles and contrasts with his eyes.

Our gazes are locked, but the moon is reflecting in his irises—Jasper and the blood moon combined. My jaw trembles and Jasper's lips move, forming the shapes of words. But I can't tell what he's saying because the symphony of voices has risen to a roar. The shade of red cast across the mountains intensifies and my skin graduates from tingling to burning. My muscles begin to spasm as the world turns the color of blood.

"Max," Jasper's voice breaks through, louder and sharper than the others. "Are you okay?"

I pull away from him as my arms and hands tense. A flash of light blinds me and sends a searing pain to my brain. I stagger backward, my leg muscles cramping and my shoulder blades feeling like they're about to explode out of my back.

The crowd turns to face me, horrified expressions pulling on their faces. Why do they look scared—like the terrified villagers in an old-school monster movie? Behind them the blood moon is humongous, overbearing, it's taking up too much space.

I slam my eyes shut and all I can see is red, like I'm looking at the inside of my eyelids, only it's a whole universe. Sparks of yellow energy are fizzing and zapping from a central point, jittering outward in crackling lines.

A ripple runs down my spine and suddenly I know what's happening. My claws elongate, fangs tear from my gums. I grow, expanding so quickly I explode through the back of my jacket. Before it can slice through my finger, I pull off Jasper's ring and toss it into the snow.

Bones crack and muscles tear, the sound reverberating through the valley. Despite trying to suppress it with every ounce of my being, I'm shifting. Fur sprouts all over my body and I drop onto my front paws.

As my wolf takes over, I lift my muzzle to the blood moon and let out a bloodcurdling howl.

MONSTER IN THE MOONLIGHT

I start up in bed, gasping for breath. My forehead is covered in sweat and my heart is racing. The room is spinning around me. I clutch the bedsheets and shut my eyes, trying to steady myself.

"Max, you're awake." Katie's voice feels distant but too loud. "It's okay, take your time. Slow breaths. You're okay."

Eyes closed, I try and steady my breathing as the room gradually stops spinning, and I'm left feeling exhausted and parched—like I'm the most hungover person on the planet.

How strong was the whiskey in that hot chocolate? But it can't just be Mason's concoction, because I don't remember feeling drunk.

Finally, I open my eyes. Sunlight is gently emanating through the curtains. I'm in my room back at the chalet.

"What happened?" I ask, my own voice thumping in my head.

Katie is kneeling at the side of the bed and reaches to take my hand, but I pull it away from her.

"It's okay, it's over."

My jaw trembles. "What's over?"

"You don't remember?" she asks, trepidation wobbling in her voice.

"I... I remember..."

The last thing I can remember is Jasper taking my hand as the clouds rolled away to reveal the blood moon, then it was like something inside my head exploded and took control. And then...then...

"You shifted," Katie says. "Remember?"

Growing increasingly terrified, I shake my head, biting back tears. "What's going on?"

"Sit back, let me get you some water." Katie stands and makes to move, but I stop her.

"No! Tell me what happened."

She turns back to me with fear in her eyes.

"Please," I say, softening.

Her shoulders rise and fall as she considers her options and sighs, resigned to being the bearer of bad news.

I wince and sit back against the headboard, unable to ignore the ache in my muscles or the pounding in my brain. For a second I feel dizzy and worry I'm about to collapse on the pillows.

"You sure you're okay?" Katie asks.

Through gritted teeth I try to fake a smile. "Tell me."

"Okay." Katie sits on the edge of the bed and for some instinctive reason, I make sure not to let her hand brush against me. "So, the clouds finally went away and the blood moon came out. And for a second nothing was wrong, we were all just taking it in. It was really intense, but beautiful."

An image flashes in my mind. A giant red moon looming above the mountains. I grunt and clutch the mattress.

"I can stop if you—"

"Keep going."

"And I'm not sure if it started right away because I was looking at the moon—we all were—but suddenly you were backing away and making all these horrifying sounds, like you were in pain, and then...you shifted. You turned into your wolf form, but it wasn't like your normal wolf form. You seemed—I don't know, it's hard to explain—confused maybe? It was like you weren't in there anymore. Like your wolf was a separate entity and it had control. Max, you seemed...wild."

"That's not possible." I wince. "Only rogues are like that. I'm not a—"

"Max, you snapped at me." She won't look me in the eye, just stares at a loose thread of her sweater she's tugging at. "I recognized your wolf and so I tried to approach you to calm you down or ask what was wrong, and when I did you came for me."

"What? No, I would never... Katie, I... I'm so sorry." A pain erupts in my back and I jerk to the side. Katie flinches. "I'm sorry. You know I would never."

She takes a breath. "No, I know you wouldn't hurt me, but it was like you were gone and it was some strange wild wolf. Anyway, Jasper shifted too; he stepped in front of me and growled at you—you know, in that alpha-command way he can. And you stopped attacking but you didn't back down. You growled right back at him. And when it looked like you were about to attack again, he tackled you."

"He what?"

"He had to. You fought him, Max. You fought Jasper's wolf."

"I did? I..."

Suddenly, I'm very aware that I have no idea where Jasper is.

"Did I...?"

"Jasper? No he's fine; he stayed on the defensive, trying to keep you away from the group."

"And did I... Did anyone else get hurt?"

"No. Morven started telling people to run, to head back here, then he shifted too. I think even in the state you were in you knew you couldn't take on Jasper and an alpha, so you ran off, down the mountainside. Jasper went after you and Morven sent a couple of his wolves to follow."

"And what happened then?"

"I don't know. Jasper said he found you in the morning in the ranger station. You'd shifted back and were curled up under a blanket. He thinks you must have passed out at some point."

My face is burning, sweat is dripping off me like a waterfall. I don't understand what happened—is still happening, making me feel out of control in my own body.

"Max, do you remember anything?"

I try, I really try, to think back to last night, but the last thing I remember clearly is Jasper's face: he was saying something, only I couldn't hear what he was saying. Then everything went red. I close my eyes and shake my head.

Katie reaches out and takes my hand, and instantly a searing pain shoots through the right side of my brain. I cry out and pull my hand away.

"What is it?" Katie asks, backing away.

"Nothing, it's..." I try to explain it away, but I can't; I have no idea what's happening to me. Why can't I touch my best friend? And why does she look so scared of me?

As she backs away, the pain decreases until I finally feel like I can breathe again.

"Why do you look so terrified?"

"I'm sorry. You just scared me." She stays where she is, back against the wall.

"I'm not going to shift," I tell her. "It's not like last night; I don't know what it is but I think that part is over."

Katie eyes me suspiciously and I feel a different pang of hurt, this one in my chest. Cautiously, she comes forward again, but she doesn't sit back down.

"Thank you, for staying with me," I say, starting to feel a little calmer, a little less like my brain is about to dissolve.

"I've actually only been here a little while. Jasper wouldn't leave your side. He's been here all night."

Oh.

"He was so worried, Max. He didn't say but I could tell. I don't think he even slept; he looked pretty wrecked when I popped in just now."

"Where is he?"

"He just went to call his father. I think they're getting ready to take us all back early."

As if on cue there's a knock at the door, and without waiting for an invite, Jasper pokes his head in.

"You're awake."

Katie is right: he looks rough—ruffled hair, bags under his eyes, T-shirt wrinkled, collar askew. But his expression is pure relief. Then he steps into the room.

I clutch my head as an agonizing explosion erupts in my brain.

"What's wrong?" Jasper says, coming to my side. The pain, which would only flash before, remains, throbbing. "Max?"

Through gritted teeth and squinted eyes I can tell just how worried he is. But the pain is only getting worse.

"Need...space," I choke out.

"Give him some room," Katie says, and Jasper looks between us like he's going mad. But he moves away from the bed, and as he does the pain decreases.

"Is that better?"

"A little. What's going on?"

"We don't know. I've spoken with Morven's healers and they've prescribed a sedative and painkillers." It's only then I notice the paper bag scrunched in Jasper's hand. "I want to get you home so our healers can take a proper look at you. But…"

I glance at Katie and she looks to Jasper. *But what?*

"But there's a snowstorm expected later today, and we won't be able to fly out until tomorrow."

I grunt and grimace. "I can't wait until tomorrow."

"Here, take some of these." Jasper fishes out a sheet of painkillers. It might as well be normal aspirin, and he sees me eyeing it dubiously.

"It's wolf strength," he says.

There's no way painkillers will be enough. Whatever is happening, it's in me. Somehow I know this isn't a normal headache.

"They won't work and I can't wait until tomorrow."

"Just try them," Jasper says, holding out the painkillers. He takes a step forward and the pain intensifies.

"Stay back."

He tosses the painkillers onto the mattress, and even though I know they won't be enough, I chuck two in my mouth, washing them down with the glass of water on my nightstand.

"It won't be enough," I say.

Jasper runs a hand through his hair, he doesn't know what to do and he's panicking.

"Tomorrow, we'll be back in the Elite Pack and then…" He trails off as our eyes meet and he takes in the gentle shake of my head, because the truth is nothing will change at home. Morven is just as rich and well connected as Jericho—maybe richer. If his healers don't know what's going on, why would ours?

"I'm so sorry, Max," Jasper says, his eyes dropping to the floor.

Another knock at the door interrupts the growing tension. The door swings open halfway and Mia leans in.

"Sorry," she says, "I don't mean to interrupt but..." She stops. *Can anyone finish a sentence right now?*

"What is it?" Jasper asks, a tinge of hope in his voice.

"I just spoke with Father and he told me what the healers said."

"That they're bad at their jobs," I huff, the pain making me more than grumpy.

Mia slips inside and closes the door quietly, as if she's undercover and doesn't want anyone to know she's here.

"I'm worried they're not considering all the options."

We all look at her like we have no idea what she's talking about.

"Why wouldn't they?" Katie asks.

"Because we're a modern pack... We have traditions, but our medicine is contemporary, closer to that of humans. They wouldn't consider—"

"Consider what?" I grunt.

"The blood wolf."

"What?!" Jasper, Katie, and I say at the same time.

"Hear me out," Mia says, stepping closer, making me grimace. "I know it's an old superstition, a ghost story, but it has to come from somewhere. What if it's real? What if the blood moon has done something to Max?"

"What like it's changed him?" Katie asks.

Mia pauses. "Or brought out something that was already there but hidden."

I lie back on the pillows, the thudding in my skull as strong as ever.

"What are you saying?" Jasper asks, fists clenched, anger rising in his voice.

"Max, you were feeling fine until the blood moon came out last night, right?"

"Yeah."

"And when it did you shifted; can you remember what happened next? Do you remember attacking Katie?"

I glance at Katie, who avoids my eyeline.

"No."

"You would never do that normally, would you? The blood wolf is summoned by the blood moon and—"

"And they become destructive, they turn wild." I finish Mia's sentence and Katie's eyes snap to mine. *Wild*, that's the word she used to describe me.

Jasper groans and rubs his eyes. "So what are you saying? Max has been cursed?"

"No, but maybe there's something about the blood moon that affects wolves—not every wolf obviously, but what if it can trigger something in us, like taking a drug or—"

"You think I'm some kind of monster?" I ask, nostrils flaring.

"No," Mia says, "but I think what might be happening to you has more to do with last night's lunar event than some might think."

"So," Jasper says, clearly exasperated by this line of thinking, "what are you suggesting we do?"

"The healers here and back at your pack won't know how to deal with this—they're too scientific."

"Should we call a priest?" I joke, even though talking is pretty damn painful.

"Maybe," Mia continues. "Or...there is someone else who I think might be able to help."

Mia stops talking, color rising in her cheeks, and she turns her toes inward. Why is she scared to tell us who this person is? We stare at her, waiting for her to continue.

"I could get in big trouble if I—"

"Mia," Jasper interrupts, "if you think this person can help Max then you have to tell us."

Mia's shoulders drop. "Okay. You didn't hear this from me, but there's a woman who lives in the valley. She's a healer but not like we have today; her methods are more old school."

"She's part of your pack?" Jasper asks.

Mia bites the inside of her cheek and shakes her head.

"A rogue?" Jasper's lip turns up at the suggestion, and Mia, hesitantly, nods. "You would place my mate's future in the hands of a rogue?"

Even in my pained state I look up, shocked when Jasper outright calls me his mate.

"She can help," Mia says.

"How do you know she wouldn't kill us the first chance she got? How do you know she isn't a charlatan?"

"Because she saved me when I was little. Father doesn't know, but when I was a child I ran away—I was upset because he told me that one day I would need to find a mate, and I didn't want one. So I ran into the valley and it got late and I was so cold, and finally it was so dark that I couldn't see and I tripped on a stone and fell. I was only a kid, but even I knew I'd broken my leg. The bone was completely out of place. I was alone at the bottom of the valley and I couldn't walk. But suddenly this woman appeared out of nowhere and took me to her house, and the next morning my leg was fine."

"It was probably a sprain," Jasper interjects.

"It wasn't," Mia shoots back. "Do you think I'd forget what it looked like? My leg was at a right angle, in the wrong direction."

Jasper presses his lips together.

"She healed me and she sent me home. And ever since then I've visited her, once or twice a year. Her pack left the valley decades ago, but she stayed. That's why she's a rogue. She's peaceful, she only wants to help. She *can* help."

Mia's eyes are pleading with Jasper but he still looks unsold on the idea.

"Let her help," I say.

Jasper's head lolls about on his shoulders. He's clearly had enough.

"Max, you can't go running into a rogue's nest based on some superstitious nonsense."

"She might be able to help me," I say. "And you'll be with me. Nothing bad can happen."

Jasper grinds his teeth but gives in. "How do we get there?"

"There's a road—it's narrow and icy, but it'll take you where you need to go," Mia says. "You can take my car."

"Thank you," I say, half pointedly at Jasper.

"No," Mia says, grinning kind of sheepishly. "Thank you." With a fresh blush in her cheeks, she leaves.

"This is a bad idea," Jasper says.

"If there's a chance this woman can fix whatever's happening to me, I don't care. Sometimes you have to take a chance."

I stare Jasper down, and finally he relents and follows Mia out.

The second he's gone, the pain eases off a little. The muscles in my chest release and I can breathe easier.

"You don't really think this blood wolf thing is real, do you?" Katie says, coming forward. "It seems a little, I dunno, spiritual for you. You don't think that you're—"

"What?" I ask. "A monster? I don't know. But we're about to find out."

THE ROADS WE TAKE

The blood wolf. Could I be? Am I the monster from the stories?

My head is consumed with these thoughts as we speed down the mountain road. It's already dusk again, so I must have been asleep for most of the day. And somehow I'm still exhausted. Golden light is peeking over the mountaintops, and the shadows in the valley are becoming long and dark.

Jasper hasn't spoken since we started driving. His knuckles are white on the steering wheel, his focus intensely locked on the road ahead. Mia must have given him directions and warned that driving on these icy roads is dangerous, because we're going a lot slower than I'm used to when driving with Jasper. Even still, every narrow turn I'm scared we're about to go sliding off the edge. At least we're heading into the valley, so each twist and turn is bringing us closer to the ground.

It's hard to tell if the pain in my head is lessening or if I'm just getting used to it. The painkillers must be doing something, but it's never gone. It feels like there's a knife sticking out of my forehead, just sitting there, and somehow I'm able to talk and walk around. If I close my eyes it's a little better, so I rest my head against the window and try to sleep.

"How are you feeling?" Jasper's voice is rough and unsure.

"Tired."

"And the pain?"

"Still bad."

Jasper speeds up a little, although I wish he wouldn't. If I had the strength to argue I might, but instead I continue leaning against the glass. My insides feel bruised, and even with the heat pumping in the car, I can't help shivering.

For a while I drift in and out. The snowstorm that kept us grounded sweeps in, making visibility tricky. Jasper can't keep driving at the same speed and decelerates.

I open my left eye ever so slightly so I can watch him. A single bead of sweat trickles down the side of his head. He's more than stressed. I wish I could do something to calm him down; I wish I could reach over and touch him and tell him it'll be okay. But every time I get too close to him the pain becomes worse. Not an ideal situation considering we're fated to be together forever.

So I try to act calm: I tense so I shiver less, keep my groans as quiet as possible, and I watch him to see if it works. I focus on his face, his eyes, and suddenly I'm pulled into a vision. I suck in a breath as the world melts around me, whipping past like I've gone into hyperdrive. When the whooshing stops, I'm somewhere new—the cool blues of the mountains and darkness of the valley replaced with yellow sunlight.

I'm still in the passenger seat of a car, only it's a different make. An old song is playing quietly on the radio. Lush green fields sweep by on either side.

Sitting in the driver's seat is a beautiful woman—a woman I've never met, but who I recognize. Her jet-black hair is tied up in a loose bun and the sun is dancing across the speckling of freckles just visible on the bridge of her nose. She looks just like him.

"Do you like this song?" she asks, smiling as she turns the radio up. Gently she hums along, finger tapping the steering wheel, and she laughs. Her laugh is like music itself, a happy trill that warms my chest. "It's a good one."

We're traveling through farmland. I wonder where we are. Up ahead is a water tower that looks weirdly familiar, but I can't place it. Across a cornfield, another road runs parallel to this one, and a couple of cars are speeding along it, keeping pace with us.

"When we get home what are you going to say to Daddy?" she asks, glancing at me, her green eyes full of love. "Will you tell him how brave you were talking with all those grown-up wolves?"

"Will he be there?" The words come out of my mouth, but I don't know why; my voice doesn't sound like mine.

"Of course, Daddy will be waiting for us when we get home. He's going to be very proud of you for visiting the rogue township with me. Almost as proud as I am."

"Why didn't Daddy come?"

"Your father is the alpha, Jasper. He has a whole pack to take care of. That's why we have to help him."

"The rogues are weird."

She tuts and shakes her head. "What have I told you? The rogues are just like us, but they don't have some of the things we have—like our pack—and that's why we need to help them."

"They're still weird."

"Just because someone is different it doesn't make them weird. We could learn a lot from the rogues."

The woman glances at me again, but her eyes catch on something behind me. Clouds roll across the sky and suddenly everything is gray. The golden sunlight is gone and dread seizes my gut. I remember where I know that water tower from. I saw it in the newspaper once, in a photo on the front page.

"Jasper, honey, sit back and hold onto the door handle."

I grip the plastic handle and press my back against the seat. We're coming up to an intersection, to the point where our road and the road running parallel to ours meet. The cars that have been keeping pace with us are gaining speed. I gulp down a glob of saliva and take one last look at the woman.

Her eyes are stern and focused, and as we arrive at the intersection, she spins the wheel sharply to the right. The car swings around and glass shatters as one of the other cars crashes into us; I'm thrown sideways and wake up screaming.

Jasper slams on the brakes.

I clutch the door handle and my chest as the world comes back into focus. The windows are intact. We're back in the mountains. The woman and the water tower are gone. But the impact I felt is still reeling through my body.

"Max, what's wrong?!" Jasper shouts as the car careens forward.

His foot is all the way on the floor, but the road is icy and we're sliding. He tries to steer us to the right, to get us back on the tarmac, but he's already lost control. We drift sideways toward the next turn, where we're surely about to go flying off.

I'm still screaming as we approach the edge, picturing our fiery deaths, while Jasper tries desperately to regain some control over the car. But as we drift off the edge, land rises to meet us. We've reached the bottom of the valley, and instead of falling, we screech to a stop.

Remind me to stop letting Jasper drive.

"What's wrong?" Jasper says, turning with fear in his eyes.

"Nothing, it was... I just..." But I can't explain it.

What was that? A vision or a dream? And how am I supposed to tell Jasper that I saw his mom—that I was in the car with her when she... When she... I lift a hand to my mouth, staring wide-eyed at Jasper. Because he was there too.

Jasper was in the car with his mother when she was driven off the road.

"Say something," Jasper says, his face as white as the snow outside.

"I'm fine."

He reaches out a hand and another stab of pain radiates through my brain.

"Don't."

He pulls back.

"I'm... I'm sorry."

"It's okay," he says. That's a change—I was expecting him to chew me right out. "It's lucky we weren't farther up. We must be close now."

He turns the key in the ignition but it won't roll over; he tries again but the car makes this unhealthy noise, then sputters out.

"Crap," he says.

We sit for a moment, taking stock of our situation. We're stuck at the bottom of the mountain, in a car that won't drive, with no heating, in the middle of a snowstorm, and oh yeah, the blood moon has messed me all the way up.

A knock at the window sends us both jumping out of our skin. Behind Jasper, a guy in a puffer jacket with a fur-trimmed hood pulled tight is tapping on the window. A little ways behind him, what looks like a snowmobile is standing at an angle, headlights on full beam.

"Need a ride?"

By the time we arrive wherever we are, I'm starting to pass in and out of consciousness. As if living through two car crashes—one in a vision and one very much real—wasn't enough, seating space on the snowmobile was extremely limited. I spent the entire ride with Jasper holding onto me. His grip was the only thing that kept me from falling off, but wherever our bodies touched my skin felt like it was burning.

I'm lifted from the snowmobile, Jasper's arms strong beneath me, and carried into what looks like an oversized ice-fishing hut. Inside the wooden cabin the lighting is dim, but it's warm and there's a calming scent in the air like incense or spices.

"Over there," our rescuer says, and Jasper lays me down gently on a bed.

I try to sit up but can't, and Jasper holds my shoulders, keeping me still.

"Agatha," the puffer jacket guy says and disappears through a curtained doorway.

"We're here," Jasper says, placing a hand on my cheek before backing away.

The rustle of a beaded curtain tells me that someone has arrived in the space, but I'm too weak to look up. My eyes won't open all the way, and what little light there is diffuses in my vision like I'm seeing through a screen.

"So, this is the blood wolf?" a woman's coarse voice asks.

"Can you help him?" Jasper replies.

"I will try, but you can't stay here."

"I'm not leaving him."

"You are his mate?"

There's a long pause and then Jasper says, "Yes."

"You want him to be in more pain?" the woman asks bluntly.

"Of course not."

"Then you leave us be and I will see what can be done for him."

"I'm not leaving him."

I sit up at the sound of scuffling. The guy in the puffer is holding back a red-faced Jasper by the shoulders. Coming toward me is an older woman with big, frizzy hair and deep wrinkles. Her eyes are this glowing shade of gold. She has a knitted shawl draped over her shoulders and is carrying a tray loaded with clay pots and bowls, bundles of dried herbs, a kettle, and some other instruments I'm scared to ask about.

Our eyes meet and she gives me a nod.

"Jasper," I say, and he stops fighting. "I'll be fine."

"I'm not leaving you."

The woman places the tray down on a table next to the bed and takes a seat on a wooden stool.

"Your mate is more stubborn than an oil stain."

Even though I'm in pain, I can't help but huff a little laugh. She's not wrong.

The woman turns to face Jasper. "I promise you, I will do everything I can to help him. Any friend of Mia's."

"Max," Jasper says, struggling against Puffer Coat Guy.

"You're making it worse, my man," Puffer Coat says.

Jasper stops struggling and stares at the guy like he just insulted his father. Then he looks at me, desperate and pleading. But I know they're right. Whatever pain I'm feeling is worse when I'm near Jasper. He needs to go.

"I'll be fine," I say, and keep my eyes on him, because he needs to let me take this risk.

Finally, he relents. "I'll be right outside."

Puffer Coat Guy takes off his coat and offers it to Jasper. "You might want this."

Jasper snatches the coat and ducks through the door, slamming it behind him.

I flop back onto the bed and the woman leans over me.

"I am Agatha," she says. "And your mate is a jackass."

I laugh then wince.

"Don't worry," she says, picking up a bowl and mashing some seeds with the end of a blunt piece of stone. "You are not the first blood wolf I have met."

She goes to work mixing her concoction, adding herbs and spices and mushing them up with the seeds, sniffing it, then adding whatever else she needs. I close my eyes.

Was she joking when she called me a blood wolf? Or is she for real?

And why does being the blood wolf mean that Jasper—the person I've wanted to get close to for so long—is the person whose closeness causes me the most pain?

It's almost too ironic to bear.

"Here, drink this."

I sit up as best I can and take the mixture, which she's decanted into a stubby ceramic cup. "What is it?"

"You wouldn't drink it if I told you."

I shrug, knowing whatever she said wouldn't have mattered. I can't take this pain any longer. I sip the brew, but reel back at the foul taste. She lifts her brow as if to say, "Go on." So I pinch my nose and down it in one.

"Good boy," she says. "That's just the start. Lie down and close your eyes."

I do as I'm told, and I don't move as she begins rubbing something soft and cool onto my skin.

It doesn't take long until the pain starts to subside and I drift off to sleep. But the last image I remember is Jasper's face as he left the cabin. The look of sad resignation, regret. Will this pain go away completely, or will Jasper always be the thing that hurts me most?

IN THE SHADOW OF THE VALLEY

When I wake up, the wind has stopped howling and the world feels still. I place a hand gingerly on my forehead: my skin is dry, and the pain is gone. Rubbing my face, I open my eyes and wait as they adjust.

My body is tired and heavy as I sit up and take in the room. The door is ahead of me; between me and it are a crooked old table and chairs where a vase of dried flowers sits amongst a mess of strewn books, mugs, and used plates. A basic kitchenette is to the left of the door, and a tapestry hangs beside me with some sort of swirling circular inscription woven into it. In the opposite corner are an armchair and a lamp with a stained-glass shade.

What is this place? It's rustic and chaotic, eclectic, and yet it somehow makes sense.

Something is scratching at the back of my neck, and when I go to rub it I realize it's a piece of string. Hanging on my chest is an emblem made of bent sticks and straw—a circle with what looks like an eye, or maybe it's a mountain, or a wolf's head, in the center.

From what I can see, nobody's here. Next to the bed is a glass of water, and as I gulp it down I realize I'm starving.

"Hey? Hello?"

In the next room comes a banging sound, then a rattling, and then a guy steps though the beaded curtain. I squint at him. I've seen him before, he's Puffer Coat Guy. Only he isn't wearing his puffer now, because he gave it to—a vague memory pops into my head and then it's gone. He's a lot younger than I thought, around my age. His dark hair is closely cropped, he has amazingly intense bushy eyebrows that almost meet in the middle, and wonderful blue eyes. He's wearing waterproof pants and a white T-shirt under a blue flannel that's covered in dark oil stains.

"I didn't know you were awake," he says, his voice deep but warm.

"Where is...?"

"Agatha had to go into town."

"Jasper."

"Oh, him." The guy rolls his eyes. "Probably still wandering about in the snow."

I shake my head, trying to figure out what's going on, and the guy just stares at me like he doesn't know that he should be explaining, double-time.

"How are you feeling?" he asks.

Not what I want from him, but not inconsiderate I suppose.

"Okay, my headache is gone, I'm just a bit tired."

"Takes a lot of energy to cope with that much pain. You slept for a long time though. It's nearly nine-thirty."

"At night?!" Immediately, I try to swing my legs out of the bed but am overcome by a dizzy spell and have to lean back. The guy doesn't move to help, just sort of laughs and shrugs a little.

"You should probably stay where you are."

He eyes me kind of seriously and something in me clicks. I have no idea who this guy is, or Agatha. I don't know how long I've been out and I don't know where Jasper is. Who knows what's happened since I passed out.

"I have to see Jasper now," I mutter as I manage to swing my legs out and attempt to stand. Stumbling forward, my feet and legs not ready to hold me upright, I tumble right into the guy's arms—which are surprisingly strong.

"Hey, I meant you should rest."

He helps me back to the bed, and as he lowers me down our gazes meet. I don't know why, but something is telling me I can suss this guy out, so I squint a little and look into his eyes.

"Are you okay?" he asks, looking amused but not bothered.

A warm feeling spreads in my chest and suddenly I'm not afraid anymore. Something tells me I don't need to worry. I settle back against the pillow and the guy moves to the sink.

"You want some tea?"

"Can you get Jasper?"

"It's probably best if we wait a little longer—you know, so the medicine can take effect." Why is he grinning like the medicine is working just fine and he wants an excuse to let Jasper stay out in the cold? "Now, tea?"

I cross my arms and huff. "What kind?"

The guy makes me a cup of peppermint tea and pours himself some other infusion that stinks like a campfire. He brings over the cup and pulls up the stool next to the bed.

"What's your name?" I ask.

"Omar," he replies, blowing to cool his drink.

"Well, thanks, Omar, for the tea."

"No problem." He grins and sips.

I do the same and burn my tongue a little.

"Are you in pain?" he asks, suddenly looking ultraconcerned.

"No," I say, lisping with my burnt tongue hanging out the corner of my mouth. "Juss bur—my tun..."

He nods. "Good."

"You some kind of healer too?"

He eyes me with this weird, content sort of smile. "No, I'm a traveler. Agatha was kind enough to let me stay for a few months during the winter in exchange for some help fixing up the cabin."

"But you are a werewolf, I can smell that much."

He laughs again and smiles brightly. "That bad, huh?"

"Not what I meant."

"I know. Yes, I am a wolf."

"A rogue?"

He bites down and his jaw twitches, the smile crinkles next to his eyes suddenly gone.

"It's, like, cool if you are," I say. "I know it's not true, everything they say about rogues."

His stare softens and he bows his head. "Yes, I am a rogue."

Maybe it's because I'm sitting in a bed, unable to stand and feeling vulnerable, but I don't have any qualms about asking a follow-up. "What happened to your pack? If you don't mind me asking."

He sighs and lifts his brow.

"Well, it's pretty simple really. I found my mate, I told my parents about my mate, they told the alpha, and we were both told to leave. No more pack."

"What? Why?"

He tilts his head as if to ask, "Isn't it obvious?"

"Why? Because my mate was a man, like me."

My heart sinks and my face turns cold. "That's horrible."

"Yes." Omar's shoulders slump just a little, but he sips his tea as if what he told me wasn't the most outrageous thing I'd ever heard, like it was inevitable.

"I'm so sorry. That's like, the worst thing ever."

"It was. But that is how the packs work."

"Not all packs," I say. He raises an unconvinced brow. "At least you had your mate—what's his name? Is he traveling with you? Is he here?"

Omar takes a breath and sits quietly for a moment. "His name is Mateo. When we were told to leave the pack we were given a choice: we would be allowed to stay if we rejected each other. I chose to leave. He chose to stay."

Instinctively, my hand rises to my chest. I want to say something but no words are coming to mind. My mouth flaps open and closed but there's nothing I can say for how terrible this is.

Omar takes a minute, cupping his mug between both hands in his lap, then lifts his head.

"But that was more than a year ago now. It's just how it is."

"It shouldn't be," I say, trying to put every ounce of disgust and sympathy I have into those three little words.

"No"—he shakes his head gently, then looks up—"but it could be worse: I could be stuck with a bullheaded macho type."

His cheeky smile lets me know exactly who he's referring to. I scrunch up my face, trying not to smile, and go to slap his arm but miss.

"Okay so you said you were a traveler; where are you going?"

His eyes become distant, almost like he's picturing someplace in his mind.

"I heard from some wolves farther south there is a place—a sanctuary for rogues—where we can live like we belong, with community and kinship, and there are no alphas and no borders."

"A rogue sanctuary?"

He shrugs. "Sounds too good to be true, doesn't it?"

"I dunno."

The only rogue colony I've been to is Rogue City, and it wasn't much of a sanctuary, more of a hideout. But I hope for Omar's sake there is someplace better.

"I don't know either. But we'll see I guess. When the winter passes and Agatha has everything she needs, I'm going to travel back down south. Maybe it will become my new home, or maybe I will keep walking until I find something else."

I reach out and place a hand on his forearm. His bronze skin is warm.

"You'll find it."

With a bang the door opens and Jasper staggers in looking like the Abominable Snowman. Frost hangs from the fur around his head and rests on his shoulders; ice sticks to the soles of his boots.

"You're awake," he says, whipping off the hood and smiling. "How do you feel?"

I glance at Omar, who rolls his eyes in a sneaky but friendly way, and then smile at Jasper. That warm feeling is in my chest again, only this time it's spreading to my limbs and my face. I'm so lucky, because even though it's been escaping me this whole time, I know what home feels like.

Half an hour later I'm strong enough to walk around, and Omar has lit a fire outside.

Jasper and I sit on a log and let the heat soak into our bodies. I have a blanket over my lap and a sausage on a stick that I'm rotating slowly for a perfectly even cook. How charming is this?!

Overhead the stars are twinkling like they're on the front of a Christmas card, and the moon has begun to wane ever so slightly, its rosy tint almost entirely gone. I can't look at her for too long without feeling a small bubbling panic rise at the back of my throat, so instead I focus on the sausage.

"In the morning, we'll figure out a way to get back up the mountain," Jasper says.

Omar didn't have any vegetarian sausages, so Jasper opted for a cheese sandwich, which he ate in about three seconds.

"Where will you sleep?" I ask, assuming I'll be heading back to my cot after dinner.

"That guy said he has a tent and a heater with an extension cord." Jasper doesn't sound too happy about this arrangement, but he's not complaining.

"His name is Omar," I say.

"Is it?"

The fire pops and I think my sausage is finally ready. I pull it out of the flames and take a bite. It's hot and juicy, and with each bite more strength rushes back to me.

"Did they explain what they think happened?" I ask.

"No." The fire is dancing in Jasper's eyes, and I wish I could know what he's thinking. Then I remember something.

"Jasper, back in the car before we... Before we stopped, I had a dream or a vision or something. I don't know what it was."

"And?"

"And I saw...your mother."

Jasper flinches. It's the tiniest movement, almost imperceptible, but I see it.

"You were there with her, weren't you? The day she died."

Jasper's lips press together, his hands clench and shake, and his eyes gloss over.

"Yes." He breathes. "I was there with her that day. They left me out of the stories in the papers—my dad made sure of it, wanted to save face or something. But I was there."

Jasper's shoulders rise and fall.

"I was in the car when those rogues drove her off the road, and I'm the reason..." He pauses, the fire crackles in his eyes, his lip trembles ever so slightly. "She swerved to save me."

I remember the look of resolution, of determination, in his mother's eyes as she spun the steering wheel.

"If it weren't for me," Jasper continues, "she'd still be here, still be alive."

I drop my stick and the half-eaten sausage falls into the fire, sending sparks swirling. How can he blame himself? He was just a kid. She was just doing what any mother would: trying to save her child.

"Jasper"—my hand drifts toward his, but every muscle in him tenses and I stop—"I'm so..."

A pair of headlights beam through the misty air, lighting the snow and blinding us momentarily. Agatha pulls to a stop on the snowmobile and hops down, pulling off a frost-covered helmet and sliding a pair of goggles from her eyes. She lifts the seat and pulls out a waterproof backpack, then sidles over to us.

"Feeling better, blood wolf?" she asks.

THE MONSTER AND THE MYTH

"So you really think I'm the...the blood wolf?" I ask hesitantly, fingers fiddling with the wooden pendant hanging from my neck.

Agatha is sitting across from me at her rickety table, her wild hair held back by a tie-dyed headband. One hand cups a mug of tea, each finger adorned with a chunky ring, while her other arm is slung casually over the back of the chair. She lifts her eyes as if to appraise me. I glance toward Jasper, who's sitting to my right, and then to Omar, who's fiddling with some piece of machinery over by the cot.

Agatha shrugs and leans forward. "Who can say?"

"But the stories, the blood moon... Something has changed in me, I can feel it."

Despite the medicine and the protective charm I'm wearing, I know the strange pain the moon caused is still inside me, like a thousand pieces of string trying to float out of my every pore. But what is it reaching for? And why has the blood moon affected me like this?

"True, there are a lot of stories about the blood wolf—so many it's hard to know what is reality and what is myth."

"But in the stories," Jasper says impatiently, "the blood wolf is created by the blood moon."

"Created," Agatha says, a questioning lilt in her voice, "or drawn out?"

Jasper bristles, and I reach over, place a calming hand on his wrist. He settles and I continue.

"You think the blood moon drew something out of me, like it was already there to begin with?"

Agatha releases her mug and nonchalantly tosses her hand into the air. "The blood wolf is a myth. But myths have to come from somewhere. They say the blood moon drives the blood wolf insane, filling its head with the voices of other wolves—from every pack in the world. Millions of voices all yelling at once. Enough to drive anyone a little loopy, no?" She grins at her little joke; clearly she enjoys her isolation. "Are you the blood wolf? It depends."

I lean forward, covering my mouth with both hands.

"You're right, something has changed within you. All wolves have a connection to each other. Time was we could all speak to each other without using words. Our ancestors used to use this form of communication to hunt, and to ensure the safety of their packs. Over time these connections have become dulled, we have become more human; their languages, their methods of communication, their smartphones, have permeated our culture, our way of life, and they have rendered most wolves incapable of communicating with their own kind without words. These sensing abilities are now reserved for the strongest wolves, those with the most powerful connections to the past."

"Like alphas?" I ask, remembering again the way Jericho is able to sense every member of his pack, and Jasper's meditation practice.

"Yes, like *alphas*." The word clearly doesn't taste all that good to Agatha. "What I believe happened to you, Mr. Max, is an opening of a sort. For some reason the energy from the blood moon has removed the barriers that have evolved over time, allowing you to sense the inner workings of wolfkind."

Suddenly, I'm light-headed, my limbs are weightless.

"What are you saying? I can read minds?"

She purses her lips. "In a way. Think of it as a spiritual connection, a link to the minds and souls of other wolves."

"But why does it hurt so much?"

"Your body is not used to its new ability. Think of it this way: imagine all your life you've been living in a cave, it's dark and quiet, then all of a sudden you're pulled into the light, the sun is blinding and the world is full of animals squawking and grunting. It would be a lot, no?"

"Yeah." I nod, thinking about how sometimes in New York all the noises and the hustle can be overwhelming for my heightened senses.

"You will need time to adjust. Your body needs to learn what to do with all of this new information. The herbs I've given you will help close off those connections, but it isn't a permanent solution. You must learn to control when you let the voices in."

I gulp and glance at Jasper. "Why is it worse when I'm near certain people?"

Jasper glances at me but his eyes dart quickly away.

Agatha leans forward, clasping her hands together in front of her.

"The sensation will be stronger depending on your connection to another wolf. So sadly in this case, the pain will be worse—"

"The closer I am to someone."

Jasper lifts his gaze to meet mine, and the look of guilt on his face is devastating.

"So, to answer your question," Agatha says, throwing both hands up. "Are you the blood wolf? If what you mean is, 'Am I a monster, the boogeyman from the stories?' Eh, I'm not so sure. What I do know is this." Her eyes bore into mine, and I can almost feel her thoughts, as if they're tickling my brain. "Whether you like it or not, you have inherited a great power, and once you have control of it, you will be capable of a great many important things."

The tickling sensation becomes a scratch, an electric pulse fizzing and burning at the edges of my consciousness. Agatha leans forward even farther and I wonder for a second if she's trying to press into my mind. Darkness grows at the edges of my vision, blooming into a maroon cloud, as a wall of energy presses against my brain.

I squint a little and grip my chair, trying my best to close off my thoughts, to resist the invasive sensation. I push back with all the energy I have left, and finally the pressure subsides. Agatha leans back, again draping an arm casually over the back of her chair.

She surveys me with narrow eyes for a moment longer before smiling.

"I think you'll be just fine," she says, grabbing her tea like nothing happened. "It will take work. But you will be fine."

I sigh a breath of relief. Was she testing me just now? Agatha has given me some clarity, but questions still swirl in my brain, and along with them a sense that things have changed irrevocably.

"It's gotten late," Agatha says, pulling me from my thoughts. "You must be tired, little blood wolf. At least I know I am. Maybe it's just my old bones, but I will say good night. Omar will take care of your sleeping arrangements."

Agatha gets up, and as she waddles toward her bedroom I stand and reach for her hand.

"Thank you," I say.

She eyes me once again, nodding slightly, and pats my hand. Without saying another word, she drifts off behind the curtained doorway. Jasper is watching me keenly from where he sits, and I force a smile.

"Jasp—"

He stands, interrupting me. "We should get some sleep."

"Yeah...okay."

"I can get that tent and heater set up for you," Omar says, jumping up from his makeshift workshop. Clearly he's been listening this whole time.

"That would be great," Jasper replies and follows Omar outside.

Around ten minutes later the door swings open again and Omar comes back in, shaking off the cold as he hangs his puffer on a hook by the door. I'm sitting up in my cot with a blanket over my legs.

"Oh," I say, when Jasper doesn't follow him.

"I'd tell you he said to say good night, but..." Omar shrugs.

Omar kicks off his boots and starts gathering blankets from a basket in the corner. "I know he's your mate and all, but that dude needs to learn how to chill." Omar tosses the blankets onto the armchair in the corner. "Suppose a night outside in a tent might do him some good."

I scrunch up my sheets in my fingers, unable to shake the image of Jasper's guilty face from my mind.

Omar plonks himself down in the armchair, pulling the blankets over his legs. *I guess we're sharing a room then.*

I should have figured this cot was where Omar usually slept.

"Jasper has a lot on his shoulders," I say, but the words don't quite come out right. My statement turns into a question before I can finish it. By trying to defend him I've fallen into the same trap as everyone else, giving Jasper the benefit of the doubt just because he's under a mountain of pressure.

"Hey, it's your life, cuz."

"Yeah it is." I huff and pull the covers up over my shoulders, rolling onto my side to face away from Omar.

"All right," he says, and I hear him shifting about. "Time for sleep."

He flicks off the light and the room goes dark. Down here in the valley there isn't much light to begin with, and without the soft glow of the electric bulb, I can barely see a thing. The only illumination a dull-blue light, coming from the digital clock on the oven.

Scrunched into a ball, I try to close my eyes and sleep, but thoughts keep racing through my mind: my vision of Jasper's mom, the guilty look on his face, the way his hands gripped the steering wheel when we slid off the road, how he reacted similarly when we burst a tire on the way to Rogue City in the summer. Is this why Jasper has been pushing me away? Telling me he's trying to protect me? Because he blames himself for his mother's death?

And then there's this whole blood wolf situation. Have I changed completely? Why did the blood moon pull this out of me? Was it there to begin with or was it random? What am I now?

I sigh and roll onto my back. Tingles tickle the side of my face and I have the distinct feeling I'm being watched.

"Can't sleep?" Omar asks, his voice low.

With a huff I lay my forearm over my eyes. "Nope."

"Has the pain come back?"

I think over Omar's question as I stare at the ceiling. The intense physical pain is definitely not back, but this sense of uncertainty is almost worse. I shake my head and a long pause stretches out for what feels like minutes.

"This may not mean much to you," Omar says finally, "but in my old pack we believe in the blood wolf too."

"Great," I say, unable to stop the sarcasm from busting out.

"Only in my pack we don't tell stories of a monster, a wolf driven crazy."

I roll onto my side and find Omar watching me intently with generous, caring eyes.

"To my people the blood wolf is sacred—a being who is able to commune with all of wolfkind. They symbolize that we are all born of the same mother, blessed by the same gods. Even if alphas have put up walls to keep us separate."

"One pack under the moon," I whisper in response.

"What was that, cuz?"

I press my lips together. "Mm, nothing." I roll back flat on the cot.

"Okay, we should sleep now anyhow. I just wanted to share that with you, in case you thought you were some kind of monster or whatever."

"Yeah, thanks."

Omar shuffles around a little, getting comfortable again.

"Wolves like us know what being misunderstood feels like," he says, sounding sleepy and withdrawn all of a sudden. "I just don't want you to worry."

"Okay," I say, not sure what a proper response is.

"Night, cuz."

"Good night."

Omar is asleep in a matter of minutes, snoring gently in a way that's sort of adorable, but I can't get comfortable. The cot is stiff underneath me, the quilt too scratchy, my pillow not the right height. And out there Jasper is alone, in the cold, feeling responsible.

The last words Omar said play on a loop in my brain: *"Wolves like us know what being misunderstood feels like."* Have I misunderstood Jasper this whole time? Have I misread his intentions?

I roll onto my side and Omar sniffs and moves but doesn't wake up. With the bed creaking beneath me, I push up into a sitting position. My shoes are at the end of the mattress, and I slip them on as quietly as wolfily possible. Holding my breath, I sneak past Omar—not sure why but certain I don't want to wake him—and make my way to the door.

Ice-cold wind wraps me in a freezing torrent and flakes of snow whip my cheeks the second I step outside. I shut the cabin door behind me, hoping I've not disturbed anyone's sleep. Jasper's tent is only a few yards from where I'm standing, but in the blizzard that's picked up it's hard to see, obscured by a foggy curtain. From inside the tent, a soft-orange light is emitting a warm glow. I wrap my arms around myself, brace against the cold, and head toward the light.

My teeth are chattering by the time I reach the tent, and my fingers are already so numb I fumble with the zipper trying to make my way inside. Suddenly, the zip slides open, pulled easily by Jasper, who lifts the flap and stares at me like he's just discovered a wild bear tearing at his shelter.

"What are you doing?" he asks, but I can't respond, I just stand and shiver.

Despite my silence and the look on his face, Jasper opens the tent further and I slip inside.

There's no room to stand, so I end up crawling into Jasper's space and find myself sitting, knees pressed to my chest, on a swathe of blankets and pillows. A lantern sits in the corner, casting warm light and deep shadows across the tent walls; in the opposite corner a small space heater is whirring away, the cord stretching back out through the door. And in front of me Jasper is sitting up, his legs buried in a sleeping bag and the pile of quilts, his hair mussed, his cheeks rosy, and a confused, stern look in his eyes.

"Is something wrong? Are you in pain?"

I laugh a little and shake my head. "No."

"You shouldn't be here," he says. "You shouldn't...be near me."

"Jasper—"

"No, Max. I saw the way it hurt you, the way I hurt you just by being close to you. I swore I would never and...I'm the reason you—"

"You're not, though. You aren't responsible for any of it. You couldn't stop the blood moon, just the same as you couldn't stop me chasing the thing I want most in the world. It was my decision to come here. It was my decision not to give up. Yeah, you've been a jerk and you've done things that have made me feel not great, but nothing is going to feel as bad or hurt as much as not getting to see you."

I pause, my chest heaving, fingers trembling. I edge forward slightly, closing the gap between us.

"Not getting to be near you."

I reach over and place a hand on top of Jasper's.

"Not getting to be with you."

I bite my lip as Jasper's gaze drifts from our hands to my face.

"Jasper—"

His lips meet mine with force, precision, and purpose. He steals my breath and my words, and I return his kiss.

When we break apart, puffing, and rest our foreheads against each other's, our breath is visible, little clouds of steam mixing in the small space between us.

"I don't want to hurt you," Jasper says.

"You won't."

"There's always a risk...if you're with me..."

I sit back just a little, keeping him held in my arms. "There's always a risk with anyone. But it's my decision if I want to take that risk."

Jasper's head leans gently into my palm, and I run my thumb along his stupidly perfect jaw.

"If I lost you..." he says, his eyes traveling everywhere but in my direction.

I lower my head and force him to meet my gaze. "You won't."

Jasper is shaking, his whole body shivering like he's freezing, even though the electric heater is working just fine. His mouth twitches and his chest rises and falls too quickly. I pull him closer and support the back of his head, squeezing him against my shoulder and holding him fast.

We sit like this for a while until Jasper has stopped quivering, then without saying anything we slide under the blankets, lying on our sides like a cozy set of cutlery. Jasper wraps a strong arm around me, rests his chin lightly on my shoulder, and presses his chest firmly against my back. Wind pummels the tent as the heater whirrs in the corner. And with Jasper wrapped around me, a protective cocoon, we drift off to sleep.

It's the best night of sleep I've ever had.

MORNING IN THE VALLEY

The pain is back when I wake up.

Not quite as intense as it was before Agatha worked her medicine yesterday, but still not great. Somewhere between a really bad headache and a knife wound to the skull. I moan and curl my legs up.

"What is it?" Jasper says sleepily, his arm shifting on top of me.

"Ah!" The movement heightens the pain and I cry out. "Max!"

Immediately Jasper is up, shuffling out of his sleeping bag and quilts and fumbling with the tent's zipper. Through waves of nauseating agony I hear him opening the door to Agatha's cabin and calling out for help.

In a moment the tent is pulled open and three bleary-eyed faces are staring down at me.

"Good morning, sunshine," Agatha says.

Omar and Jasper help me up and back into the cabin. I plonk into a chair at the small, round table and Omar slides a steaming mug of tea to me.

"My herbal remedies will only keep the pain at bay for so long," Agatha says, coming around the table nonchalantly and sliding into a chair herself. "But it will get better with time and practice."

"Practice?" I grimace.

Jasper is standing off to the side watching me with his arms wrapped around his shoulders and worry contorting his features. I know he's trying to keep his distance, but all I really want is for his arms to be wrapped around me.

"Yes, practice," Agatha says, nodding once. "You'll need to learn how to tune out the noise."

"Or you will go insane," Omar says from where he's leaning on the kitchenette, a blanket wrapped around his shoulders, smirking.

"Very funny," I say and take another sip of tea. From the corner of my eye I catch Jasper's confused expression.

Already I can tell this miracle concoction is going to work; the sharpness of the pain is growing dull, the throbbing less constant.

"Think you'll be strong enough to make it back up the mountain, blood wolf?" Agatha asks cheerily.

I down the rest of the tea, wiping my mouth with the back of my hand.

"Yeah, I think so."

"Speaking of," Omar says, stepping forward, "I was gonna go check out your car this morning, see if it still works."

Omar heads over to a wonky set of drawers next to the cot and pulls out a knitted sweater.

"You think you can fix it if it doesn't?" Jasper asks.

"Haven't met a machine I couldn't revive," Omar says, letting the blanket around his shoulders drop to the ground. Underneath he's wearing a white tank top. "Agatha is a miracle worker for healing wolves. I work miracles with cars—give me an hour or so and she'll be up and running like new."

Omar turns and is about to slip on the sweater when out of nowhere Jasper growls. He must have spotted something, because he's staring at Omar, his lip curling back to reveal an elongated fang. And I don't think it's just because Omar looks really good in a tank top.

"Whoa, cuz, what's up?" Omar asks.

"What is that?" Jasper says, and I suddenly see what he's talking about.

On Omar's shoulder is a familiar tattoo: a circle with a wolf and a lightning strike running through it.

"It's just a tattoo, man."

"Who are you?" Jasper takes a step toward Omar, causing Agatha and me to jump to our feet.

"Jasper," I say.

"Who are you?!" Jasper repeats, his voice turning into a roar, as he comes face-to-face with Omar.

"Whoa, man. What are you talking about? It's just a tattoo."

"The rogues who broke into my father's house wore that insignia." Jasper is close enough that Omar can probably smell what he had for dinner.

"I don't know what to say," Omar shrugs, shaking his head. "It's just a tattoo. I got it from some wolf in Texas when I left my pack. I just thought it looked cool."

Jasper eyes him dangerously, questioningly, clearly not satisfied with this answer.

"That's quite enough," Agatha says sternly.

Jasper, unfortunately, is very close to losing control, and without thinking he turns and growls at Agatha.

"You are a guest in my house," she thunders. "And Omar is my lodger. There are no alphas or their sons in the valley."

I think Jasper must realize that he's insulted the woman who's helped me and let us stay with her, because he instantly pulls back, a tiny whimper escaping him. "I'm sorry."

"Omar," she continues, although calmly now, "I think you'd better go see if you get can that car up and running."

With a dark look in Jasper's direction, Omar pulls on his sweater and heads for the door, grabbing a box of tools and his puffer as he goes.

"Now Max"—Agatha turns to me—"why don't you calm down your mate while I put together a flask of tea for you to take with you?"

I nod and she does the same in return.

Jasper doesn't move, not even when I'm standing right next to him. His jaw is tight, his hands are clenched, and a single bead of sweat is running down his temple.

Gently, I take hold of his arm with both hands, sliding the bottom one down until I'm cupping the base of his palm.

"Hey," I say, "Omar isn't like that."

"He has the tattoo."

"I bet lots of rogues have that tattoo; it doesn't mean he was one of the people there that night."

"It doesn't matter; he's just like the rest of them."

"He's not," I say, letting go of Jasper's arm.

Finally, he turns and actually looks at me. "How do you know?"

"I spoke with him last night. His family kicked him out because he's queer. That's why he's a rogue: because he's like us."

Jasper's eyes flash with some spark of emotion. Is it panic or recognition? Maybe it's because for the first time I've identified something about him that he hasn't been able to yet.

"He is?"

"Yahuh," I say. "So stop acting like a bonehead."

He rolls his eyes.

When it's time for us to leave, Agatha loads me up with a couple of thermoses worth of pain-relieving tea, along with a crystal, a book on meditation, and of course, my wooden necklace.

She stands in the doorway of her cabin and I can't help but give her a big hug.

"Thank you," I say.

"You'll be okay, blood wolf," she says, patting me on the back. "That mate of yours will be a handful though."

I grin so that only she can see it.

"Thank you," Jasper says, coming forward and extending his hand; I step back to let him through. "And my apologies again. I should never have snapped like that."

Agatha shakes his hand and smiles. "You were being protective of our little friend here. I understand. Though, you should try relaxing every now and then, you might like it."

Blush rises in Jasper's cheeks. "Yes, well, thank you again."

Omar, who came back from fixing the car and went straight to work on something else, is now packing up the tent behind us.

He eyes Jasper for a moment as he gathers up the cable connected to the heater. I nudge Jasper's side. He steps forward awkwardly.

"Listen, I'm sorry for earlier," he says. "I shouldn't have made assumptions."

"No, you shouldn't have," Omar says, unimpressed.

"And thank you for everything you've done. I hope... I hope you find your people."

Omar takes a breath and I can tell he's rolling his eyes in his mind.

"Okay, you're forgiven. Don't drive too fast on your way back; I don't want you crashing and showing up back here."

They both laugh, sort of.

"It's a deal," Jasper says.

"You gonna be okay, cuz?" Omar says, looking in my direction.

I join him, and Jasper steps away in the direction of the car.

"I think so," I say, and hold out a scrap of paper. "Here—it's my number in case you ever want someone to talk to about stuff or whatever."

He studies the paper, then smiles and pockets it.

"It was a pleasure to meet you, Max."

"You too."

"Don't let him be an ass to you, okay?"

Now I laugh. "Okay."

"C'mere."

Omar drops his cable and pulls me into a tight hug. He smells like petrol and oil, but underneath that, the scent of freshly mown grass, cinnamon, and coffee.

"There's going to be someone else out there for you," I say before I know what I'm doing.

We pull apart and Omar shrugs. "Maybe. Maybe he'll be as cute as you."

I nearly choke as my face burns red-hot.

"Hey, don't go all blood wolf on me now."

I swallow and take a breath. "I'm fine," I say. "Thanks again. Bye."

"See you round."

As I turn to leave, I can't help but notice the tiny throb of pain at the back of my skull.

Jasper and I trudge back to the car quietly, and I'm relieved to see it's already facing the right direction, ready to speed back up the icy mountain road. We jump into our seats and Jasper flips the engine on.

"Pump the heating," I say, rubbing my frozen little hands together. Jasper turns the knob then sits back in his seat. "What's up?" I ask. "You feeling okay to drive?"

"When we get back," he says, staring at the steering wheel, "is it okay if we... I still think it's probably best if—"

"If we don't tell everyone," I say, finishing the sentence for Jasper, as much as I wish I didn't have to.

"I just think it would be best until things with the packs are a little more settled."

I twist my lip and let out a short breath, but I was sort of expecting this. It's not ideal, no way, but I'm clued in enough to know one night in a tent wasn't going to change everything. Down in the valley things are different—we could just be—but back on top of the mountain, the rules change, and there are people watching us.

"It's okay," I say, snapping my seat belt into place.

"You're sure?" he asks and turns to look at me, his mouth open in concern but his eyes shining with relief.

"Yeah, it's okay. We can wait to tell people."

As Jasper shifts the car into gear and begins to roll up the steep path, I'm left wondering two things:

What is it we're waiting to tell people? That we're together? Is that where we're at? Are we...boyfriends?

And if we're waiting to tell people...how long will we have to wait?

A ROCKY FAREWELL

Walking back into the Rocky Packhouse feels like walking outside for the first time on a sunny day. I hold my hand above my eyes as if I'm shielding myself from the light, only I'm shielding myself from the noise.

The whole pack, it seems, is waiting in the parlor when we return. Jasper and I stagger through the doors, unwashed and unkempt, feeling particularly haggard in the pristine surroundings. Everyone is fresh-faced, in comfy-looking sweaters, with neat, freshly washed and styled hair. We might as well be a couple of yetis.

And despite Agatha's medication and the charm around my neck, the voices push in at the edges of my consciousness. Already the overwhelming pain is subsiding, like a sour candy once you've sucked the acidic powder away. Now, the intrusive sensation is more like a muffled wave of sound, lapping at my brain. Everyone's thoughts—their concern and relief, and curiosity, and even a little bit of disdain—are audible to me, albeit muffled by one serious herbal remedy.

I grumble quietly and Jasper places a hand on my back.

"You okay?"

With my lips pressed together I glance at him and nod.

"Max!" Katie rushes forward, and I'm so happy to see her.

Mason is a step behind her, followed closely by Olivia and Mia, who are conspicuously keeping close with one another. Gritting my teeth through the discomfort, I only have to force my smile a little.

"How are you feeling?" Katie asks.

"I'll be fine," I say.

"That's a shame," Mason says. "I thought you were going to go septic and take out the whole pack."

I laugh a short, sharp cackle.

"It's good to see you," he says.

"How good is Agatha?" Mia says quietly enough so that only those closest to us can hear.

"Seriously, a miracle worker," I say. "And great taste in scarves."

"Ah, you're back!" Morven's voice rises over the noise in my head as the crowd parts for him to make his way through. "Thank goodness. And you're feeling better, I take it? We weren't sure where you'd run off to."

"I just needed some space," I say, not sure how much Morven knows about his daughter's trips to the valley.

"We're so happy that no harm has come to an Elite wolf on Rocky soil," Morven continues, looking especially rosy-cheeked. I wonder if he was stressed about the ramifications of harming an Elite Pack wolf. "Please, you must stay one more night; the mountain air will do you, well, a mountain of good, and you can fly back tomorrow."

Right now all I really want is to sit down and have some hot chocolate and maybe do a drawing, so it doesn't matter to me when we leave. I glance at Jasper, who nods.

"We'd love to stay one more night," I say, suddenly speaking for the entire Elite envoy.

"Fantastic!" Morven claps his hands together enthusiastically. "And tonight we dine in your honor, Max!"

"Okay."

I rub the back of my neck and blush.

Up in my room, the press of the voices is almost gone, just a tickle at the back of my skull. And Jasper leaves me so I can nap and rest for a while. But I lie in bed with light streaming through the curtains and can't seem to sleep. So I text Katie.

"Wait, let me just make sure I've 100 percent understood," Katie says, reclining on her side and nibbling a piece of gingerbread. "You and Jasper spent a night in a tent together and *nothing* happened?!"

I shove her shoulder gently.

"No, nothing happened." Why is it suddenly so hot in here?

"But like...did you want it to?"

Grabbing a pillow, I roll onto my back and proceed to smother myself.

"Nuhah! You can't hide from me!" She whips the pillow away, leaving me exposed and blushing.

"It...wasn't like that, it was more intimate."

"What's more intimate than sexy time with the alpha's son?"

I shoot her an eye-rolling glare. "It was more like we just, I dunno, finally understood each other—something just clicked. It was nice."

Katie pouts and grins like I've just said the most adorable thing. But I can't take it so I laugh and flop about.

"Staaaahhhp!"

"No, it's sweet." She swats to get me to stop rolling. "I'm really happy for you."

"I mean"—I lift a brow—"it doesn't mean I never want more to happen, of course."

We both giggle, and I realize this is just the distraction I needed, a little bit of normalcy.

"You also haven't asked me anything about how I'm like, spiritually connected to all of wolfkind," I say.

"Okay," she says, taking another cookie from the plate sitting on the mattress between us. "What's that like?"

"It sort of keeps changing. Agatha said it was hurting because my body was overstimulated, but now that I'm all numbed up, it's more like when you're in bed on a Saturday and your mom keeps yelling at you to get up, so you throw the covers over your head and then you can only sort of hear her. You know she's still calling but it doesn't feel as urgent."

"And do you, like, know what I'm thinking?" She looks hesitant, like she isn't sure she wants the answer, like suddenly she's tempering her thoughts.

"No," I say. "I don't think it's quite like that. I'm not Professor X all of a sudden. It's more like voices. Like if you were saying something loudly I could maybe overhear it, or if you were trying to tell me something I could probably hear that, but it's almost more like a sensory thing—like there's a presence and I can tell what emotion it's feeling. At least, that's sort of what it felt like with everyone downstairs, and with the people in the cabin. I even had a vision."

"Excuse me?"

"I don't know if Jasper was thinking it, but I saw…" I stop myself, unsure if this is my story to tell.

"What?"

"I saw something personal."

She sits back, scrunching her mouth up like she's a little disappointed.

"But it made me realize something about Jasper I'd never known before."

She sits forward again. "Almost like your power or gift or whatever was letting you in on something that would help you."

"I dunno, maybe. I don't know if it's as intentional as that but...sure."

"Wow." She polishes off her second gingerbread wolf. "So my best friend is like a superhero."

"Ha! Not even." I grab a pillow and whack her with it softly.

"I'm just happy you can still be around me."

For a moment I sit and watch my friend as she fiddles with a folded-over triangle of quilt. She looks older, more mature than the Katie I used to lie with on her pink fluffy rug and listen to music. She seems calmer, more content.

"You're really glad Todd and Simon sorted that shit out, aren't you?" I ask, catching Katie off guard.

For a moment she lowers her eyes and studies me as if I've just read her mind. Then she relaxes and rolls onto her back.

"You were more worried about it than you let on," I continue.

"I just knew I wasn't going to be able to make a choice," she says. "Like I would have been denying myself if I had. But that things could only end one way—with a fight or like this. And I'm so lucky that my mates cared enough to want to figure things out."

"I'm glad you're happy."

Katie doesn't look at me when she says, "Thanks." She just stares at the ceiling, and I worry I overstepped. "Don't get too perceptive on me now, okay?" she says.

"I don't think you have to worry too much," I say. "I'm just as oblivious as always."

She does this little half-laugh exhale through her nose and keeps staring upward. I wait for her to say something but she doesn't, so I lie down next to her and stare at the same ceiling. Because what I said wasn't exactly true. I have changed, so has she, and I think we both know it.

Before heading down in the evening I gulp a cup of cold tea and ready myself to block out the noise.

At dinner I head to my usual seat but find it occupied by a Rocky Pack teenager I haven't met. I glance at Katie, flanked by her mates, and she shrugs.

"Over here!" Mia calls, and I notice Mia and Jasper have swapped sides and there's a spare seat between them, one seat away from Alpha Morven's place setting. She waves me over enthusiastically.

I half grin at Katie, then make my way to the head of the table.

Jasper stands when I arrive, which is, like, wildly gallant for him, and I take my spot between him and Mia.

"Hey," I say, leaning forward and spotting Olivia to Mia's left. She nods in return.

"Daddy wanted you to have a prime spot for your celebration dinner," Mia says, wrapping her arm around mine. Then leaning a little closer, she whispers in my ear: "And I thought everyone might enjoy a new seating plan."

I lean back and catch her grinning. She mouths the word *thanks*, then turns to Olivia and continues whatever conversation they were having before I arrived.

Jasper clears his throat awkwardly. "Hi," he mumbles.

"Hey."

It's almost adorable how bad he is at this, as if he's spent so much time pretending not to be interested he's forgotten how to act like a normal wolf. I used to think he was always so suave, always knew how to act, but clearly I'm seeing a new side to my mate.

"How are you feeling?" he asks.

"Fine," I say, fiddling with the pendant beneath my shirt. "I had more tea before I came down. Hey, when we get back do you think—"

"Morven is here," he says, breaking me off midsentence.

As always a horn sounds announcing Morven and Astrid's entrance. When they arrive at their seats, Astrid sits and Morven holds the attention of the pack.

"This last week," he says, "we welcomed members of the Elite Pack into our home, our land, and we shared with them a sacred bonding moment." His blue eyes beam out at his people. "Of course, as things in the Rocky Pack often go, not everything has been smooth sailing." He glances in my direction, giving me a subtle nod. "But I have faith that this week has brought our two packs closer together than ever before. And I foresee a glorious future where our packs continue to work together and grow."

Staring out from the head of the table at the faces of the Rocky Pack, they dart their eyes from Morven to Mia to Jasper, as if there's some secret they all know that I don't. Pressure builds at the front of my mind, the overwhelming sense that the wolves before me are thinking the same thing. Their collective consciousness prods at my brain, and I do my best to resist it, pressing my lips together and clutching at my thighs beneath the table. But it's no use. The group energy is too much, and an image penetrates through my defenses. The image flashes in my mind, painful and unbearable. I wince as I work to shut it out. Jasper looks over, concerned, and I stare at him questioningly.

"Now," Morven continues, "let's eat!"

After dinner the kids gather one more time in the den. There's dancing and music and even spiked hot chocolate. But through it all I can't concentrate. Even Mason twerking and jumping about like he's performing at the VMAs can't pull me from the funk dinner left me in. So I excuse myself and head to my room.

When I get there there's a folded-up note on the floor. Someone must've slipped it under the door. I lift my nose and catch a hint of cherry blossom in the air. Jasper was here.

Carefully, I unfold the note:

Sit with me on the plane tomorrow.
Sleep well, Bonehead.
X

Maybe I'm stressing myself out, and there's nothing to worry about. After all, the image I saw during dinner didn't come from Jasper. It was just a stupid idea cooked up by a misinformed alpha and fed to his pack. I shouldn't worry.

I hug Mason one more time and tell him as firmly as I can, "Text me the second I get in the car."

"I'm already drafting the perfect goodbye message."

"It's not goodbye, remember, you're going to be so sick of me you'll beg me to stop calling."

He hugs me back, then kicks at the snowy gravel.

"I'm really glad you came," he says.

"Me too."

It's early in the morning and only a handful of people have come to see us off. The storm has passed, but it's still cold and misty out front of the chalet. To my right, Mia is hugging Olivia and whispering in her ear; Mia's eyes look red and I don't think it's because we all got up stupid early. I feel like I have something of an idea of what they're going through. The uncertainty, the pain of not knowing when you'll see this person you feel so connected to again even though you've just met.

I shake Morven's and Astrid's hands, and when Olivia, steely eyed behind a pair of blackout sunglasses, ducks into our car, I head over to Mia and say one last goodbye.

"You're a star," she says. "I'm rooting for you."

I laugh and grin. "And me for you."

Katie, Todd, and Simon are already in their car waiting to leave, and Jasper is saying one last goodbye to Morven, doing his diplomatic best, so I wave to Mason and Mia and hop in my car.

Somehow we've ended up in the same formation we did on the way out here. Only this time Jasper will be riding alone. Or maybe not...

Just as we're about to leave, the front door of the car opens and Jasper hops inside.

"Let's go," he says, half to the driver and half to no one in particular.

I stare at the side of his head, and I swear he grins just a little.

The plane feels emptier than when we first set off, even though the only person missing is Clayton. Once again I'm the last to board. Olivia has taken my spot from the way over in the back of the plane and is wearing big headphones while texting. I wonder to whom! Katie takes a spot with Todd and Simon.

"You want to join us?" she asks.

But then I see Jasper across from me and I smile and shake my head.

I take a seat next to him and he looks up.

"You excited to get home?" I ask. "I bet Jodie missed you over Christmas."

He laughs. "I think she was too busy playing on the new trampoline my dad bought her."

"Nah, she'll be over the moon to see you. I bet you missed her too."

He taps his armrest as his face turns thoughtful.

"What about you and your parents?" he asks. "Excited?"

I think for a second about his question. I am excited to see my parents—I've never not been around them at Christmas before. But then I start to think about the conversation I think I'm ready to have with them, the conversation I *want* to have with them. And nervous moths start flapping about in my stomach.

"Yeah, it'll be nice," I manage.

"Are they picking you up?" he asks.

"Yeah."

"Text them, tell them not to," he says confidently. "I'll drive you home."

"Sure."

Face flushing, I pull out my phone and text Dad. When I'm done, the plane is taxiing out to the runway, about to take off, and Jasper is pulling out a laptop.

"Do you mind?" he asks when he spots me staring at it. "I have college work I'm behind on."

Okay, I wasn't expecting we'd chat for the whole flight, but maybe more than two minutes.

"Ah, sure," I say.

The plane speeds up, bouncing a few times on the tarmac as we're lifted into the air. As we ascend into the clouds, I sit back in my chair and think about everything that's unresolved and all the questions that may or may not be answered when I get home. Jasper has never been more comfortable around me, and yet there's still a strange distance between us. Will I ever be able to bridge the gap?

Finally, I start to feel the pull of sleep. We were up early so we could fly out before another storm passed through. I lie back and let my mind relax. Just as I drift off, the image from last night's dinner replays in my mind. My fingers dig into the armrests of my chair and my feet curl inward.

In my mind, Jasper and Mia are standing at the head of the Rocky Pack's dining table. They're dressed like they're attending the Oscars—Jasper in a tux and Mia in an emerald-green gown. The rest of the pack is staring and applauding—beaming at the wolves before them. Because they're holding hands, smiling, radiant with the glow of a freshly formed couple. It's obvious they're in love—mates. And for both of our packs their coupling is a cause for celebration. They've united our two peoples. Everyone is happy. And Jasper isn't mine anymore.

COMING HOME

The drive home is quiet—the gentle hum of Jasper's sports car rolling beneath the silence that lingers between us. It's late in the afternoon, but the clouds overhead are so thick and gray it's hard to tell what time of day it is. They hang low and heavy, as if they're pressing down on us, compacting us, a reminder of all the things we need to figure out and everything we're not saying.

As the houses of Stony Point drift by, I let out a little sigh. I'm not sure why. But it's out before I know to stop it. Jasper glances at me. I give him an encouraging smile, and he does his best in return.

Finally, we slow to a stop at the end of my parents' driveway. The house sits quiet and still, the lights of our Christmas tree twinkling from behind the blinds. It looks the same as I left it, of course—we've only been gone the better part of a week—but it feels like so much longer. So much has changed, I guess I was just sort of expecting that change to be reflected in our surroundings.

A shadow moves about somewhere behind the glass, and I wonder if my mom is in there, and if she's seen us. I shrink a little lower in my seat. For a second I think about opening up my mind and seeing if I can hear them or feel their thoughts. But I'm scared that will let the pain back in, so I focus hard on keeping myself closed off.

"Happy to be home?" Jasper asks, pulling my attention away from the windows.

"Huh? Oh, yeah." Halfhearted doesn't even cut it. I mean, I'm not *not* happy to be home, but being here means I don't know when I'll see Jasper again. And I have zero idea if he's thinking the same thing—if he even cares.

"I..." he starts then stops, twisting his hands on the steering wheel. "Is it okay if you don't tell them?"

I shake my head a little to rid myself of the shock.

"Yeah, of course. I won't tell anyone, not until you're ready."

A lump bobs up and down in Jasper's throat as he tries to swallow. What if he's never ready? What would that mean? For us? For me?

He lowers his head. "Thank you."

"Well, I should..." I unbuckle my seat belt and go to open the door when Jasper's hand lands on my knee. I freeze.

"Max, I'm sorry."

I stare at him, wondering what he's trying to say.

"I'm sorry this isn't what you want. That I'm not..."

The muscles in his jaw are twisting about. I take his hand in mine, and he doesn't pull back. Our fingers slide between each other's.

"We'll figure this out," I say, nodding, trying to convince myself. "It may take time, but we'll be fine."

I smile at Jasper and he tries his best to reciprocate. With a squeeze, I let go and open the door.

"Max," he says, before I can slide out, "my father is hosting a New Year's Eve party. Aisha and everyone will be there. Will you come?"

As if there was any other answer. "Yeah, I'd love to."

"Good. I mean...I'm glad."

One more time I smile at Jasper and step out of the car. Then I think of something.

"Where is it?" I ask, leaning back down to see into the car. "The party?"

"The packhouse. I'll make sure your name is on the guest list."

"Okay."

I grab my bag from the back seat and stand to watch as Jasper drives smoothly away. *The packhouse.* Our packhouse isn't like the welcoming winter lodge in the Rocky Pack. Ours is a high-rise in the middle of Manhattan; the only wolves who really go there are the ones who have a reason to—officials, businesspeople, important wolves. I guess now I have a reason, too. A little flutter flitters in my stomach.

Turning back to the house, I take a moment, let my chest rise and fall, and hold my shoulders back. I knew this moment was coming, and I know I can't wait anymore. It's time to let my parents know who I am.

"Hello!" I call from the open door, dropping my bag.

"Honey!" Mom says, appearing in the hall, a mug of coffee spilling over in one hand and a magazine in the other. "You're home!"

I whip off my coat, dropping it onto the floor as she fumbles to put her drink down, and we meet in the middle of the hall. She pulls me into a hug that says how much she's missed me, and I give her one back. From here I can see through to the living room, where a small pile of gifts sit untouched beneath the tree.

"Is that Max?" Dad calls, followed by the banging of the kitchen door. He wanders into the living room, his outfit complete with gardening gloves and a pair of pruning shears. Without putting them down, he joins the hug.

When finally we're all hugged out, I take a step back.

"Hey, can I talk to you guys?"

Mom and Dad glance at each other, and I think Mom might explode with joy.

"Of course," Mom says. "But do you want to get unpacked first? Maybe take a shower?"

"No," I say, shaking my head vehemently. I don't want to wait. I can't hold off any longer, I don't know if I'll ever be able to do what I'm about to. "Can we talk now?"

"Whatever you want, bud," Dad says, ushering us to the sofas.

When we're situated in the living room, I hop up one more time just to move the pruning shears away from Dad's immediate vicinity. Not that I think I have anything to worry about, but you never know.

As I sit back down, fear erupts in my gut. My parents are watching me expectantly, waiting. My feet are suddenly freezing, I can't stop fidgeting with the zipper of my hoodie, my face is on fire.

"I—"

"Just take your time—"

Mom and I speak at the same time, then laugh awkwardly.

"Whenever you're ready," Dad chimes in calmly.

"Okay," I say. *Here goes!* "So I know you've noticed that I've been changing, and you're right—I have, only I also sort of haven't."

They squint, and I can see them trying to make sense of the convoluted mess that is my sentences.

"What seems like change is actually more like, I guess, a discovery—like I'm sort of figuring out something that's been true all along."

They nod as if they're sort of getting it.

"And the thing I want to tell you is that...I'm gay. I'm into guys."

There it is, out in the world.

Silence descends on the living room, and I study my parents' vacant expressions. *Please just give me something...anything!*

Finally, Mom tilts her head and smiles. "Sweetie," she says, her voice thick with love, "thank you for feeling like you could share that."

Dad nods in agreement, tears springing to his eyes.

"Is that... Um...are you... Is that okay?" I ask, shrugging, completely unsure of what I'm supposed to say next.

Dad looks even more confused. And without saying anything he stands, plants himself on the cushion next to me, and pulls me into his side. Mom hurries to join him on the other side.

Mussing up my hair, Dad says, "You never have to worry if who you are is okay, buddy. You got that?"

"We are so proud of you," Mom echoes, squeezing me tighter.

We sit in this warm little ball for a second, everyone's cheeks damp. And a part of me begins to wonder if they're overcompensating somewhat, like maybe it isn't as okay as they're making out, but they don't want me to feel bad. So I open up my mind just a little and let the buzzing of voices that have been pressing on the edge of my brain seep through. And even though my head is suddenly full of noise, there isn't any pain. None of the sharp, stabbing pangs from the mountains. There's just this warm, sort of glowing sensation, like a protective blanket wrapping itself around my heart.

When finally my parents sit back, dismantling their Max sandwich, Mom laughs a little and wipes away a tear. She grins at Dad and I know she's relieved.

"Told you it was nothing to worry about," Dad says, and Mom swats at his arm.

"So how did you, you know, discover this about yourself?" Mom says, curiosity getting the better of her.

I knew this was going to be the tricky bit, how to explain things without outing Jasper at the same time.

"I sort of started to realize over the summer, at the Blue Moon Festival."

They share a knowing glance.

"Does that mean...?" Mom asks. "Did you find your mate?"

I roll my eyes, because even though I've wanted to say this for the longest time, it's still embarrassing.

"Yeah," I say.

Mom does this happy squeal noise and Dad pats me on the back.

"Who's the lucky wolf?" Dad asks.

"The thing is I...can't say. He's not out yet."

"I see." Mom's tone is empathetic, like she knows how hard it must be for him.

"Well, if he ever wants to come over, I'll be happy to make him a steak sandwich," Dad says.

"Is that why you didn't want to tell us sooner?" Mom asks.

Ha! If only she knew.

"Sort of, I guess. But also I was still figuring things out. And to be honest I didn't know if I was gay or if I just had a guy for a mate. And what I've learned recently is that this is me, I have this identity, and whether I'm with him or not, it's important for me to know who I am and be true to that. And that's why I wanted you to know, because actually this isn't about having a mate or whatever, this is just...me."

Mom leans back, fixing the cuff of my hoodie, which turned inside out during the group hug, and when she looks back up she's crying again.

"What?" I ask, laughing.

"It's just... When did you get so grown-up?"

I can't help it; I roll my eyes again. "Sometime between turning twelve and now I guess."

My parents stare at me like I've just graduated law school or won the lottery, which I guess I have in a way, to have such supporting folks. But this mushy scene is getting too much, so before this can become even more of a cheesy daytime movie, I stand up and head back toward my bag, still sitting in the hall.

"I'm going to unpack."

"You hungry, buddy?" Dad asks. "Want me to make you something?"

"Yeah that'd be great."

I hoist my pack over my shoulder and make for the stairs.

"Max," Mom calls before I can disappear, "thank you for telling us."

I smile back at her, feeling stupidly grateful, and then I remember, there's another massive change I should probably tell them about...

"Oh, I nearly forgot there's something else..."

Concern etches itself across both their faces.

"Have you guys heard of the blood wolf?"

"Yeeeees," they say together, stretching out the vowel.

"So I'm sort of that...as well."

"What?!"

THE PEBBLE IN YOUR SHOE

Aisha comes leaping toward me, a pastel-purple box in her hands, her high-pitched squeal shattering the silence of the theater's foyer.

"I am so proud of you!" She wraps one arm around me and squeezes the air out of my chest. "You've done so good, kid."

"Thank you," I say, pulling away and rubbing the back of my neck. It's not like Aisha to squeal and hop, but I guess telling her about my coming-out has got her all excited. A true ally.

"These are for you," she says, holding out the box. It has the Magnolia Bakery logo printed on top and inside are six perfect, colorful cupcakes.

"I mean, thanks! What are these for?"

"They're coming-out cupcakes!"

If I'd have known there'd be baked goods, I would have come out sooner.

"Okay come sit; I only have like fifteen minutes till I'm supposed to be backstage. These two-show days are killing me."

Aisha pulls me over to a rectangular leather-covered bench. I wish we had more time to hang out, but her company is neck-deep in their Christmas season.

We sit and she leans back, appraising. "So how'd it go? Tell me the whole story, paint me a picture."

"It was all pretty chill, they were really great about it."

"And how do they feel about having the prince of pensive stares as their new pup-in-law?"

"Oh I didn't tell them about Jasper—he... He's not ready for people to know...just yet."

She raises an eyebrow.

"But the thing is I'm glad I haven't told them about him yet; this way it's more about me and not all about him. You know?"

A semi-smug but very happy grin spreads across her face.

"You know what? That's actually perfect. And they were cool?"

"Yeah, I'm really lucky." I think about the other wolves I've met, the ones like me who aren't as lucky. Omar springs to mind. His coming-out was the reason his pack disowned him. "Actually, they were more confused about the whole blood wolf thing."

"Oh, so you're just straight-up calling yourself that."

I shrug. I know it seems like a lot, taking on the mantle of the sacred—or cursed, depending on how you look at it—blood wolf from the myths. But I don't know how else to explain it. It feels right.

"So tell me more about that. How does it work?"

"At first it was like, wildly painful; now it's just a mild headache and I can sort of feel people's energy buzzing around my head."

"Like we're a bunch of flies?"

"It's more that I know everyone is there, like I can feel my connection to everyone. And if I focus really hard I can sort of hear everyone."

One of her eyebrows hits the ceiling. "You can read my mind?"

"Why does everyone think I've become some kind of wolfy superhero? I wasn't bitten by a radioactive moon."

She leans in conspiratorially. "But really, can you?"

I bite my lip; the leather cover of this bench is getting sweaty under my hands. "Maybe. I haven't really tried. I don't really think I want to."

Aisha mushes her lips together and squints like she's thinking something over.

"Is it weird?" I ask.

She thinks for one more beat, then with certainty she says, "No, it's not weird. It's an amazing gift."

I try to laugh but it comes out more like a sigh.

"And you know what they say about great power?" Aisha says, lightening her tone and nudging my arm.

"It comes with great responsibility?"

"Heck no! It comes with great clothes and medical insurance."

Aisha is the best.

"Jasper invited me to the New Year's party at the packhouse tomorrow. He said you'd be there."

"Hold up. Jasper invited you to a party, but he doesn't want anyone to know you're together?"

"Yeah, that's why I was hoping you'd be there."

"Is Katie going?"

I tear at the corner of the cupcake box. When I asked Katie if she was going, she replied to say she was. The thing is, that was the only reply she's sent to any of my texts since we got home.

"Yeah but she'll probably be hanging out with Todd and Simon," I half lie.

"I have a show that night," Aisha says, and my shoulders drop. "But I'm coming after."

I breathe a sigh of relief. "Okay, that's amazing. So I'll only have to pretend to fit in for a couple of hours. I just hope Clayton isn't there."

Aisha's expression turns dark; she crosses her legs and shakes her head.

"He better not be."

I raise a questioning brow.

She huffs. "Ever since he came back from the Rocky Pack, I've been hearing rumors about some of the shit he's been saying. Some people think he's trying to poison his parents against Jericho."

"Why would he do that?"

"I dunno—to overthrow the alpha, maybe, so his daddy could take over the pack."

This all seems like a lot for how casual Aisha is being. "Could that really happen?"

"I hope not. Jericho still has his allies. If he can keep them sweet, I've got to believe he'll be fine. Plus, why anyone would listen to that slimeball, Clayton, is beyond me."

Something has been tugging at the side of my brain, like a loose thread hanging from a shirt.

"Why do you hate him so much? I mean, I get that he's the worst, but every time I mention him to you, you go all...storm-cloudy."

"Let's just say I know Clayton better than most." Something zaps at the edge of my consciousness. "I've seen what's under the pristine veneer and, dude, it's nothing but rot."

Aisha is focused on the toe of one of her combat boots. The fizzing at the front of my brain increases and I lean forward, studying Aisha, feeling like there's more to the story—something dark and intense, screaming to be heard. For a second I wonder if it would be okay to let my guard down slightly. I almost want to, like the thought is calling to me.

But then Aisha stands, brushes her hands on her pants, and smiles.

"I gotta get back to warm-up."

"Oh, okay. Are you alright?"

"I'm great!" she says almost convincingly.

"Okay, well if you have to go. Do you want to take a cupcake at least?"

She pushes the box back toward my chest. "Nah, those are yours, to celebrate." Suddenly, she wraps both arms around me tight. "I'm so happy for you...really."

When we pull apart Aisha is already moving.

"Have a safe trip home, dude."

"See ya," I say, waving back as she disappears through a door marked Stalls.

For a moment I sit in the foyer. Through the glass doors it looks cold and blustery. Usually when I'm not sure who to talk to I simply call Katie, but her lack of correspondence is giving me a weird vibe. Soon the evening crowd will start filing in, so I pull on my woolly hat and head out.

As I wander back uptown, I glance through the windows of restaurants, cafés, bars. My eyes catch on a table in this supercute, supertrendy coffee spot. I stop in the street and stare through the window at two guys sitting under a blackboard menu, smiling at each other over two steaming cups of coffee. Instinctively my hand reaches for my phone.

"Um hi!" Mason's voice is bright and welcome. "Gosh, you're obsessed with me!"

I burst out laughing. "Yeah I just couldn't hold myself back any longer."

"Well, it has been what, two and a half days?"

"A lifetime!"

I leave the cute couple to their coffee and continue walking toward the station.

"How are you?" I ask, and there's a longer pause than I'd like.

A sigh. "I'm good."

"Really?"

"Well, almost. It's not like I've been face down on my bed, locked in my room, crying and overdosing on leftover Christmas chocolate since you left or anything."

"Sure."

"It has been quiet since you all went. Now that the fancy New York wolves have vacated the packhouse, it seems the whole pack has gotten bored of each other and disappeared back to their houses."

"Packhouse dinners not quite doing it for you then?"

"Hardly." He laughs a little bitterly. "Mia has basically disappeared into a lovesick void and barely notices anyone who isn't the messaging app on her phone."

"Mmm, I wonder who she's talking to."

"I blame you for this, by the way. It's your fault she's got a hot beta mate and her old beta best friend is rereading comics and almost excited to get back to school."

I wait at a crosswalk for the light to change—not a very New York move, but for some reason traffic is whirring by this afternoon.

"Maybe I can come visit when it gets a little warmer, or you could come here?"

"Yeah maybe, that'd be cool," Mason says. "Oh! I forgot. You won't have to wait too long to see a different Rocky Pack queer."

"What do you mean?"

"Mia is heading to New York tomorrow."

My heartbeat speeds a little in excitement. "How come?"

"Her dad was invited to some New Year's Eve party your alpha is throwing—guess she's going as his plus-one."

Suddenly, the traffic light turns green and I, along with the crowd around me, pour across the street.

"You still there?" Mason asks when I reach the other side, and I realize I haven't responded. The truth is I'm not sure if it's the crowd around me or the crowd of thoughts in my head that have me distracted.

"Why were they invited?" I ask. "We were just there."

"You got me," Mason replies.

Something isn't sitting right.

"Maybe it's just like an alpha thing, like a thank-you for the blood moon trip—you know, political back-scratching."

Aisha was just telling me about how Jericho would need his allies close to him, and suddenly I'm legit worried. Is something going on?

"You there or has some devastatingly handsome New York wolf stolen your attention?" Mason jokes.

"I'm here," I say.

Only this new level of worry is making it harder to block out the buzzing at the edge of my mind. I can barely hear Mason as I reach Grand Central.

"Hey, I've gotta go," I say, pretty sure I just interrupted him midsentence. "I'll call you soon."

"You better," he says.

I hang up and head to the train, pressing a hand to the side of my head.

THE PACKHOUSE OF THE ELITE

The packhouse looms above me, a glimmering rectangular giant, a high-rise stretching to the stars. A cold breeze whips down the sidewalk as I stand gawking up at it. I pull the collar of my puffer jacket tighter to block out the icy wind. Underneath, I'm wearing yet another smart shirt and fancy jacket Mom helped me pick out—a maroon blazer and white button-down with black-accented buttons, and another ironic bow-tie.

Seriously, all these pack events are going to bankrupt me.

This time however, I've paired my dress pants with sneakers—a stubborn little signifier that I'm still myself.

Glancing up and down the sidewalk, I hope a familiar face might suddenly turn a corner, but instead the only people I see are older, wealthier wolves, heading through the automatic glass doors, ignorant that I even exist.

I've been in this weird daze since my call with Mason yesterday. Somewhere up there are Alpha Morven and Mia, and I have no idea why.

When I finally called Katie, she was friendly enough but told me she was going to the party with Todd and Simon. Aisha is still pirouetting downtown. And without either of them, curiosity is the only thing stopping me from turning and going straight home—well, curiosity and Jasper.

Knowing there won't be a response, I pull out my phone and check if Jasper has replied to the text I sent five minutes ago: *'I'm here.'* Yep, no reply.

I guess I'm on my own. Head up, shoulders back, I make my way through the entrance.

This isn't my first time visiting the packhouse. As kids we were brought on an educational outing organized by the alpha's team. Elite pups were bussed in from across the state and given a tour of some of the offices, the boardrooms, the cafeteria. For all intents and purposes, the building is just like any other flashy office in New York, like the kind that's owned by some megamedia conglomeration. But inside it's all wolf business: pack security, pack finances, interpack relations. I'm sure Clayton's dad has a corner office with a stupidly stunning view.

A purple carpet has been laid out to mark the path from the doors to the elevators, and the same woman from the Yule Ball, the one with the iPad and superior smirk, is standing by a potted plant, waiting for me.

"Good evening, sir, and welcome to the Elite Pack New Year's Eve Bash. Can I take your name?"

"Uh, it's Max, Max Remus," I say, rubbing my neck.

She squints over the top of her fashion-forward half-moon glasses before checking her list.

"Ah, there you are, Maximilian," she says, as if to a five-year-old. "Such a strong name. Please take the elevator to the function room on the ninety-ninth floor and have a wonderful evening."

There's a high-pitched ping as the elevator arrives, and I step into the brightly lit box.

"Happy New Year!" the woman calls as the doors slide shut.

Like a bullet I'm whisked up through the building. An LED screen on the ceiling plays a video that mimics my movement, only instead of traveling through an elevator shaft, I'm shooting through the night sky toward a glowing full moon. I'm just glad it's yellow and not red.

Another ping signifies my arrival, and as the doors open I have to take a step back. A wave of noise and warmth spews forth, flooding the elevator and my senses. And it's not just noise from the crowd of well-dressed wolves mingling by high tables, sipping drinks, dancing under a wolf's-head-shaped disco ball, or vaping on the terrace, furs draped over their exposed shoulders. It's mental noise. So many wolves all in one place. There's a fierce ricocheting pain in my head, despite my having downed what was left of Agatha's tea before leaving the house. The force of will it takes to block out the noise is so intense, I jam my eyes shut and press my shoulders against the mirrored back wall of the elevator.

Maybe this is too much, too soon. I've only just begun to understand my new ability. It was silly to think I could just hang out here where the wolves are the most entitled, where their thoughts are the loudest. I remember what I've been told about harnessing the power, and I think of Jasper sitting cross-legged on a rock in a clearing, his eyes closed and his breaths steady. I try and do the same—breathe in through my nose and out through my mouth, count to ten.

I need something to cut through, something to focus on. Knowing he's here somewhere, I channel my energy into finding Jasper, searching through the overgrown hedge maze of thoughts and feelings, searching for his unique wavelength. Finally, I catch a whiff of cherry blossom, and a calming sensation washes over me.

"Coat, sir?" a man's voice asks. Hesitantly, I open my eyes, and find that I can temper the noise. I build up my walls again and focus on the young guy in a cute uniform, with his arm outstretched. "Can I take your coat, sir?"

"Sure."

I hand the guy my well-used puffer jacket and step into the light of the party. The alpha's function room is expansive, set out across two stories with an atrium and a wicked glass sculpture suspended in the center. A swirling glass staircase leads up to the second floor, which stretches farther back until it's too dark to make anything out. Multiple bars, well-stocked with just about every liquor, champagne, and garnish you could think of, sit to the sides of the room. Everything is onyx black or shining reflective silver. It's garish and stark and looks like money. I scan the crowd, searching for Jasper.

Beyond a glass wall is a wide diamond-shaped terrace where people are huddled around tall braziers burning in what must be freezing New York winter air. Thinking some air might do me good, I head outside. A cool breeze pinches my cheeks, but somehow, even up this high, I'm not cold in my suit jacket. Wolves stand at tall circular tables, sipping cocktails and champagne. Set against the New York skyline, a stage sits surrounded by gold and white balloons, through which the infamous Times Square Ball can be seen. The jumbotron screens repeat their flashy advertisements, bright as all hell. On one of them a clock is counting down to midnight. Just three and a bit hours to go.

Through the crowd I catch a brief wisp of Jasper's scent and turn to find him chatting to a couple—the woman with a backless gown, the deepest shade of burnt orange, and the man in a full-on tuxedo. Jasper says something, and the woman, unable to help herself, runs a hand down his arm as she laughs outrageously. I know for a fact whatever he said was not as funny as she's suggesting.

Without hesitation I make my way over to him, and grin when he looks up and spots me. For the briefest moment he smiles back. But then his smile turns to muted panic. He glances at the couple in front of him, then he looks back at me, and gently shakes his head. It's a warning. *Not now.*

Is this dude serious?

He invites me to this dumb party, and immediately he doesn't want to be seen with me. Is he worried I'll say something stupid in front of some important wolves? Or is he just afraid that if we're seen together, people will connect the obvious dots?

With a huff and a sigh I head back inside toward one of the bars, desperately hoping they don't card in a place like this.

Halfway through the room I stop, the light of the glass sculpture bright on one side of my face. A painful niggle at the side of my consciousness is pulling me in another direction. It feels familiar, an energy I've interacted with before. And it's in trouble.

Turning swiftly, I make my way through the crowd toward a bank of high-backed booths and a dark corner of the room. I let my instincts lead, surprised at how quickly I'm becoming attuned to my new sensibilities. There's no one back here, but I spot a door marked *Fire Exit* and push through.

Outside in an industrial stairwell, voices float up from one floor down: one is distressed, the other angry. I head down and find Mia sitting on the top step of the next flight, her head in her hands, and Olivia standing next to her, her jaw clenched, one hand gripping the railing so hard it might bend.

"What's wrong?" I ask, and both girls snap their heads in my direction. Olivia breathes a sigh of relief to see me. Mia just stares at me with blood-red eyes.

"It's her father," Olivia says, spitting the last word.

Swiftly, I descend the last of the stairs to join them. "What do you mean?"

Olivia glances at Mia as if to say, "He's your father, you tell him."

Mia sniffs back some snot and wipes her face. The emerald of her gown is brilliant against the pink flush of her pale skin. "After you all left, my father could sense something was up. I didn't want to tell him just yet, so I was messaging Olivia in secret, but eventually he looked in my phone."

"That's horrible!" Anger flares in me at this invasion of privacy.

"He's a real piece of work," Olivia chimes in.

"He completely blew up," Mia continues. "Said I was responsible for the future of the pack. And that's why he brought me here."

Cold dread drips down my spine, and I have to focus a little harder to keep the voices at bay.

"Why did he bring you here?" I ask.

Mia locks eyes with me, her bottom lip quivers, and she shakes her head apologetically. "He's going to make a deal with Alpha Jericho: our support in exchange for a courtship."

I stare at her a little harder, wanting her to spell it out so there's no confusion.

"He's going to suggest an arranged mateship between me and Jasper."

Mia bursts into tears, holding her forehead in both hands. Olivia runs a hand down her back.

"We won't let him do that, guapa," she says. "We'll run away if we have to, we'll—"

"We can't run away!" Mia explodes. "He's not just my alpha, he's my father. What about the rest of my pack, my family, my friends? What about yours? We can't just give all that up. Where would we go anyway? And what would we become? Do you want to be a rogue? Do you know how people treat rogues?!"

Mia's head falls back into her hands and Olivia glances at me, most likely hoping for a suggestion.

I rack my brain, trying to think of something. In a lot of ways this is all too familiar. I think back to the Harvest Moon Celebration, when Jasper was ready to reject me to please his father.

But then I remember Jasper's apology and his promise that he would never try to break our mate bond again. Sure, he doesn't want to be seen with me in front of some rich wolves, but he meant what he said, right?

Even though there's a specter of doubt in my mind, I think I have an idea.

"Jasper won't agree to this," I say. "Let me find him; I'm sure he can talk to Morven or Jericho and sort this out."

"Really?" Mia says between sobs.

"I...think so."

Olivia gives me a grave nod and I run back upstairs.

The first familiar face I see when I make it back out into the party is Katie. She's wearing a figure-hugging, floor-length gown in this eye-catching pink. She looks like the most fully realized version of herself, a Pokémon in her final form. Todd and Simon are nearby, of course.

"Hey," I say, sidling up to her, having to shout to be heard over the music.

"Hi," she says, and then stares at me tight-lipped.

"Have you seen Jasper anywhere?"

"No, sorry."

I wait a beat, expecting her to say more, but she only tilts her head and twists her lips in a vaguely apologetic way.

"Is everything okay?" I ask.

She nods. "Mmhmm."

"You're acting kind of strange, and you haven't really been answering my texts or calls."

"I know, it's just I sort of needed some space."

"Okay." I run a hand down my forehead. I don't have time for whatever it is Katie is having trouble with right now. "Listen, I need to find Jasper."

Her eyes move in a circle, avoiding meeting mine. "Can't you just like...read his mind or whatever?"

"What? I...huh?" Is this what's bugging Katie? The whole blood-wolf thing? "That's not how it works... I... Katie..."

Her jaw moves and I can tell she's thinking something over.

"I think," she says, and tears spring to her eyes, "it's just maybe a bit too much for me."

I shake my head wildly. "What's too much?"

"All of this, Max." She waves a hand about, gesturing at nothing in particular. "I know you've been going through a lot, and I just want what's best for you. I really do. But I've been going through a lot too."

"Yeah, I know." I glance at Todd and Simon, who are pretending they're not listening in. "We've barely had a second to ourselves."

She blinks and shakes her head like a bug just flew into her mouth. "Well, yeah, because everything is about you and Jasper. He's not even nice to you, and all you're interested in is following him around. And now there's this blood-wolf thing and—"

"And what?"

She shrugs and stares at the floor. "Maybe we're just drifting apart."

My ears must be telling lies because there's no way my best friend just said that. But the way Katie is fidgeting with her purse and curling her shoulders in, I can see she means what she said.

"Katie, I... I don't want us to drift apart but..."

Across the atrium, Jasper passes through the crowd, catching my eye.

"But what, Max?"

As much as I want to stand and talk this out—as much as I want to make things right—I can't stop right now. Not when a couple of my friends are about to be torn apart.

"There's something I need to take care of."

Katie glances back and spots Jasper as well, and when she turns to face me, her eyes say it all: she's not angry, just disappointed.

"I'm sorry," I say, before darting into the crowd to find Jasper. I have to believe that my friendship with Katie is strong enough to withstand this—that running from her now to find Jasper isn't the nail in the friendship coffin.

When I reach the other side of the room he's gone. I turn in circles, but there's no sign of him—no whiff of his scent amongst the heavily perfumed wolves gyrating to some repetitive song. I spin again, and this time when I stop I come face-to-face with a giant of a person.

"Jericho," I say, and then remembering myself, I bow my head and add, "Alpha."

"Max," Jericho says, his voice cutting through the noise effortlessly. "I see little has changed since I arranged for you and my son to spend some time together."

Oh, if only he knew.

"I'm disappointed, Max."

His words hit me like a high-speed train, but instead of letting myself be run over, I give into the anger that flares in me.

"You're what?"

"I thought you would have the gumption necessary to tame a future alpha."

Maybe it's because my best friend has potentially just told me she doesn't want to be my friend anymore. Maybe it's because Mia and Olivia are stuck in a stairwell panicked they're about to lose each other. Or maybe it's just because this dude thinks I'm responsible for his son's complete inability to open up, but something inside me snaps, and I forget who I'm talking to.

"You know what?" I say, letting the floodgates fall. "I'm disappointed too! I'm disappointed that you've put so much pressure on your son to be a certain way, he has no idea how to behave like a normal teenager. I'm disappointed that you've let him blame himself for his mother's death his whole life. I'm disappointed that before you decided to set us up you tried to break us apart by forcing Jasper to mate with someone else. And I'm disappointed that no matter how hard I try to get Jasper's attention, he's too busy trying to get yours. Trying to show you he's worthy. Maybe if you'd stopped for a second to tell him how proud you are of him, how you love him, Jasper would be better adjusted, and he and I would be together already. Maybe if you'd been a better father, I wouldn't be responsible for making him feel okay about himself."

When I'm finished, I clamp my mouth shut. Alpha Jericho is towering over me, very much like how this very skyscraper did earlier. His face has turned an impressive shade of purple, veins are bulging on his forehead, and suddenly I realize... *Oh shit, I've just pissed off the alpha!*

HAPPY NEW YEAR

I turn and run, leaving Jericho steaming behind me. It's maybe the cowardly move, but I'd rather run and leave this party with my limbs intact than stick around.

I'm pretty sure I've just pissed Jericho off enough to sink his Jasper-Max ship and now I need to find Jasper more than ever.

My adrenaline is pumping so hard, I don't even feel the cold when I burst out onto the windy patio. I stand on tiptoes, trying to see over the crowd, and press my lips together, concentrating, shutting out the noise. In Times Square the clock has counted down another hour. *Already?* Time is ticking away.

For an instant I think I see a flash of black hair across the patio, so I head in that direction. When I reach the spot where I thought I saw him, Jasper is gone again. Maybe he *is* avoiding me. *Well, sorry Jasper, this is an emergency, and you don't have a choice.*

Back inside, I scan the bar areas and wonder if I can use my blood wolf senses to reach out to him. I close my eyes and let down just a sliver of the barrier I've been maintain. A trickle of sweat drips down my forehead as I content with my new power. My mind reaches out across the dancefloor, the tables surrounding it, to the upper level and the shadowy booths toward the back. *Nothing.* Is he blocking me out?

A warm, familiar presence materializes toward the elevators, and as the delicate ping of its arrival sounds, the doors open and Aisha wanders in. I put my barriers back in place and take a moment to catch my breath. Aisha is looking insanely gorgeous in a navy gown that drapes over one shoulder and flows in cascading layers to the floor. She spots me almost instantly, and for some reason she looks about as serious as I probably do.

"We need to talk," she says the second I'm within earshot.

"Yeah we do."

"This way."

She takes me by the arm and leads me past a bar and a blossoming cherry tree in a large planter—because, of course—to a small seating area off to the side. Black leather sofas surround an oversized, ornate copper vase, and mirrors reflect our faces back in all directions. The music and the lighting are lower back here making it the perfect chill-out area.

"What's going on?" I ask.

Aisha pushes a loose strand of hair behind her ear and puffs out her cheeks in preparation.

"Remember what I said about Clayton and those rumors?"

"That his family are planning to overthrow the alpha?"

"Turns out, they're not just rumors."

My head feels light and I have to prop myself up with one hand to keep from toppling over.

"What?!"

"Apparently, Clayton's dad has been positioning himself to take over the mantle for a while now—hoarding funds, gathering support from the gammas and high-ranking officers. I asked my father about it and he confirmed it. Walter has even been speaking with other packs."

"Crap," I say, wiping my forehead. "And he's planning on making his move soon?"

"Very," she says. "I heard Clayton has some information about the alpha that could be used as the final blow."

My eyes pop open. There's only one piece of information that Clayton could use to discredit the alpha, and that's...

"It's me and Jasper," I say. "That's the info Clayton has."

Aisha sighs and takes my hand. "I really hoped that wasn't the case."

"So what? You think he's planning on outing Jasper, and that will convince the other packs to help Walter with his mutiny?"

She shrugs heavily.

"That's disgusting. Do you really think the officers and the other alphas would be that narrow-minded?"

Aisha twists her lips, and all I can think of is Mia, crying in the stairwell. Her father is willing to marry her off to prevent her being with another girl. Maybe Jasper and I really are a danger to the pack.

"Morven is here," I say. "He found out about Mia and Olivia, and he's trying to convince Jericho to arrange a mate bond between Jasper and Mia."

"Jesus!" Aisha says, rolling her eyes. "Have you spoken to Jasper?"

"Nope, I've been looking for him but I can't find him. I don't know if he's ignoring me or avoiding me or what. I feel like I've been chasing him all over this stupid party."

"We really need to find him now," she says, standing up and smoothing out her dress. "Come on, I'll help you look."

Together we head back into the party. Thinking I've covered most of the downstairs area, we head up the illuminated glass staircase to explore the upper level. It's a little more subdued up here, and yet the air feels more pressurized. The guests are more smartly dressed, less flamboyant. They aren't drinking or dancing. Instead they're standing in small circles, discussing important matters, presumably, in hushed and serious tones. This must be where the dignitaries and officers come to talk shop? A cool draft pulls my attention further in, and I notice there's a set of doors toward the back of this level, leading out onto another, smaller patio.

"That's the VIP balcony," Aisha says. "They reserve it at functions for the highest-ranking wolves."

That's when I spot the beefy wolf to the side of the door, dressed all in black, sporting sunglasses and an earpiece.

"I guess there's no way we're getting out there..."

"Worth a shot," she says. "Whether they know it or not, you're kind of important now."

I take a second to register what Aisha means. It hasn't really dawned on me that being Jasper's mate might mean helping to lead the pack one day. I guess I've barely had time to imagine what an actual relationship with him would look like, let alone all the trimmings that would come with it. There's too much going on right now for me to spend any time focusing on this overwhelming revelation, so I push it to the back of my mind.

Aisha and I head to the doors of the VIP patio, but we're met with a stern grunt and the impassable outstretched arm of the security beefcake.

Never one to back down from a fight, Aisha begins arguing with Mr. Beefy, trying to convince him we should be allowed outside. But my eyes catch on something beyond the glass. Standing between two olive trees are three impressive-looking men: Alpha Jericho, Jasper, and Alpha Morven. They're huddled close; Jericho is slapping Jasper on the back and talking animatedly while Morven swirls the tumbler in his hand. Jasper is looking at the floor. But when Morven directs his next statement—or maybe it's a question—toward Jasper, he looks up and nods.

Morven smiles. He smiles as if he's just won something. And next thing I know, Morven and Jericho are shaking hands. They're grinning and nodding like they've just come to some kind of arrangement, cemented a deal. Morven extends his hand to Jasper next, and without blinking, Jasper returns the handshake.

I should turn and run again. But my stomach has become jelly and my legs feel like wisps of smoke. My feet are lead, unable to move. Alarm bells are ringing in my head so loudly they actually block out the noise of the wolves around me. Everything is fuzzy, like I'm hearing through cotton wool. It can't be happening again. Has Jasper agreed to sacrifice what we have for the sake of the pack? Maybe he knows about the Bridgerses' mutiny. That has to be it. Once again he's willing to give up everything for the greater good.

But then again, maybe it's not about the pack at all. Maybe it never has been. Maybe he's doing this to cover his own ass. If he knows Clayton is planning to out him, maybe he's scared of being exposed.

My jaw quivers, my vision blurs as tears build in my eyes, and my hands twitch.

The world moves in slow motion as I watch Jasper looking from Morven to his father, an expectant expression on his face, asking if he's done enough. Then just as slowly, his gaze drifts and lands on me.

Panic floods his expression as the world speeds back into real time. Our eyes are locked and he knows what I've seen. Before he can excuse himself, before I crumble to the floor, I leave Aisha arguing with the security guard, and run. I tear through the somber crowd of officers all sipping their drinks, looking too pleased with themselves. I race down the stairs, almost tripping over my own feet. When I reach the lower level, I look for the exit and spot an elevator arriving to deposit a gaggle of overdressed guests. Without pausing to reflect on the irony that, after all this time, I'm running *away* from Jasper, I head for the exit.

I push through the crowd, longing to be outside, back on the ground, in the cold winter air. I want to feel it on my face and remember that I have a whole life outside of this weird, elitist tower. The golden light of the elevator is calling to me, and just when I'm about to dive in, a strong, familiar hand grips my arm and pulls me away.

Jasper drags me to the side room where I just was with Aisha and doesn't let my arm go once we reach the quiet sanctuary.

"Max," he says, desperation in his voice, "whatever you saw, it isn't what you think."

I try to turn away, but he holds me fast.

"I know why they came here," Jasper continues. "I know Morven brought Mia with him because he wants us to unite our two packs. But I promise you that isn't going to happen."

"Whatever."

"Max, I swear, I told you I would never hurt you like that again."

"Then what was that?!" I explode. "He wants to mate off his daughter because she's into girls, and you were out there smiling and shaking hands with him. What else am I supposed to think?"

"I know how it looked but I didn't agree to anything."

"What do you mean? You shook his hand."

"We agreed to wait."

I reel back like the beefy security guard has just punched me right in the kisser. With all my strength I pull my arm out of Jasper's grip.

"You what?"

"Morven suggested the arranged mate bond, but my dad and I were able to convince him I needed more time, that I wasn't ready to be mated yet."

"Yet? So you will be ready sometime?"

"No that's not—we were buying time, so we can think of plan to get out of it without hurting the relationship."

"Without hurting the what…?" I scoff and turn away. "And what happens in a year or two when Morven doesn't want to wait any longer?"

"We'll have come up with a plan by then."

"You're joking, right?"

Jasper's chest is heaving; he's holding his hands out, palms up, like he's pleading with me.

"You may believe your dad has your best interests at heart, but there's no way when push comes to shove he won't do whatever it takes to retain his power."

Jasper takes a step toward me, trying to take my hand. "I won't let him."

"And what if you don't have a choice?" I spit, pulling back. "What if there's no way out? Huh? In a couple of years, if Morven is still hell-bent on this arrangement, how am I supposed to know you won't do what's needed for the pack?"

Jasper stares at me like he's confused or hurt or whatever, I don't really care, because the only thing I notice is that he hasn't answered. He hasn't said that he'll run away with me or do whatever it takes to keep me. He's stumped. And suddenly I know the answer to my questions.

"I'm not going to be strung along until the time comes for you to abandon me for the pack."

"I'm not asking you to!" Jasper comes forward once again, this time managing to take both of my hands. "It's just a Band-Aid so that we can figure something out without endangering the pack. It's what I need to do."

"You don't *need* to do anything!" I try to pull my hands away, but he holds on tight. "You just need to be honest."

"You know I can't do that."

Jasper's grip loosens and our hands slip apart.

"I've never asked you to be anything other than what and who you are," I say. "Can you say that much for your dad, the pack?"

Jasper rubs his eyes with his thumb and forefinger. "You know it's not that simple."

"I'm not saying you need to tell them about us—I'm not saying you need to tell them about yourself, or anything until you're ready. But I have been running around this party, trying to find you. I've been trying to find you for months. And I can't do it anymore. If we aren't in this together, if you can't be honest with me at the very least, then maybe we shouldn't be together at all."

Jasper's shoulders drop and dread fills his emerald eyes. He shakes his head, but no sound comes out of his gaping mouth.

My hands are shaking so much I have to cup them together to make it stop. I want to throw up and fall over and explode all at once. I've laid out the truth—my truth, at least. And even though it feels like my heart has been frozen and smashed into a million spiky shards, I know I'm doing the right thing. I also know I need to get out of here before I crumble completely.

"Max, it's just for now. I promise I will figure out a way to fix things with Morven."

"Don't bother..."

I push past Jasper and leave the room without looking back.

As soon as I'm back out on the dance floor, I feel like my chest is going to explode. My heart is beating faster than it ever has before. I can't catch my breath. Everything is spinning around me. I feel like I could cry or howl if only I could inhale. My fingers curl up like I'm a shriveling corpse. I close my eyes and try to breathe—in and out, in and out—but it isn't getting better. I need air. I need to get out of this stuffy, suffocating party. I glance at the elevator, but the door is shut, and there's no way I can wait long enough to get all the way back down to the ground floor.

So instead I head for the emergency exit and the stairs. It's already cooler when I burst through the door into the industrial stairwell. I wonder briefly if Mia and Olivia are still out here, but they were down a floor and I need to go up. I need to get as high as possible—to the roof, where the air will be freezing and I'll be able to breathe.

Hoisting myself up the banister, I stumble to the top of the stairs and find just what I need, the exit to the roof. *I freakin' love New York*. The door is a little jammed, so I ram it with my shoulder and tumble out into the night.

Immediately, I feel a little calmer. The drama and calamity of the party is below me now. There's no noise from the wolves, no incessant feelings intruding into my brain. To my right is a clichéd-looking water tower, to my left some large exhaust vents, and other than that just clear night air. I put Times Square, with its lights and crowds and countdowns, behind me and head over to the edge of the roof that looks out on Central Park.

It's dark down there, just the lights of the baseball field and the lamps lining the paths. I take a deep breath and let my mind drift up to the stars. I finally start to find calm.

But then the questions begin to bubble up: did I just break things off with Jasper? Did I do the right thing? Should I have listened and waited? Should I have given him one last chance? Or am I better off? Have I made the right decision in the long run? Is this really the end?

"Nice night," a smooth voice says from behind me.

I turn and find Clayton standing a little ways off, masked by the shadow of the water tank. He takes a step into the moonlight, a dangerous glint in his eye.

"What's wrong? Not enjoying the party?"

Oh no...

MEET ME ON THE ROOF

"What are you doing here?" I ask, pressing my back against the rooftop's railing.

Clayton scoffs and takes another step forward. His quaffed hair is blowing in the breeze. He's wearing a white suit jacket over a crisp button-down, with pants a deep shade of navy, and shiny boots. An undone bow tie hangs loosely around his neck.

"Me?" he says, grinning snidely. "I belong here. This... All of this"—he throws open his arms as if he's gesturing to the entire world—"is my birthright!"

"Oh yeah, then why are you hiding on the roof?"

He hisses and his lips curls back, his grin becoming a snarl.

"I know why I'm up here," I say, thinking I'm onto something. "Because you're right: I don't belong down there. That isn't my world. But that's all you have, it's all you know. And yet you're up here with me all the same."

His snarl becomes a growl, and the wind picks up, throwing a lock of hair across his face. I don't know if he's drunk or just mad, but I know I don't want to spend any more time up here than I have to. Unfortunately, Clayton is standing between me and the door. I may be fast, but there's no way I'd make it before he could get to me. And if I run I might provoke him. Better I try and keep him calm. Only, from the way his growl is turning into a manic laugh, I don't think I'm doing a very good job.

"You think you're so important!" he yells, spit flying from his mouth like a rabid dog's. "You think you've got it all figured out. You've managed to brainwash Jasper, and now you think you have a place in society—that you're worth more than me."

I shake my head. "That's not what I think."

"You think you deserve the life that was supposed to be mine!"

"No, Clayton. I'm not trying to take anything from you. All I did was show up."

Clayton takes another worrying step toward me, his hands at his sides, fingers splayed.

"You've done a lot more than show up and you know it. Don't deny it! But only an idiot would think I'd give up the life I was born into, the life I was destined for, without a fight."

He's lost his marbles, gone right off the deep end. I've done literally nothing to this dick, but for some reason he's interpreted my existence as a slight against him.

"I don't want your life, and I don't want to fight you."

"The fight started the second you sank your claws into Jasper."

Speaking of claws...Clayton's have started to extend from his fingertips.

"The day you showed up thinking you could have even a sliver of my birthright."

Man, he is obsessed with his birthright.

"But what you don't understand is you can't win." His maniacal smile is back. "Not against me or my family. We have been the real power in this pack for centuries, and now because of you, we're finally going to show just how powerful the Bridgerses are."

Is he talking about using Jasper and me to help overthrow the alpha?

"You think outing someone is going to give you power? You think this pack will just roll over and let archaic bigots like you win? You've got another thing coming."

Okay, Max, you were meant to be keeping him calm. Don't poke the bear!

Clayton raises a clawed hand as his fangs extend, his eyes glowing like a wolf's at midnight. "Maybe you need a taste of my power to believe me."

The metal rail is solid and cold against the small of my back. The door is impossibly far away and blocked by the approaching figure before me. There's nowhere to run or hide. I could try to shift, but even in my wolf form I'm no match for Clayton.

"If you hurt me, Jasper will tear you apart."

"Well wouldn't that be a shame... At least then the pack will know what sort of wolf their future alpha is. You think people will fall behind an alpha pathetic enough to love someone like you?"

"Yes! And not just because he's the alpha's son. Because he cares, because he's worked hard to be the sort of wolf that's fit to lead. He's made sacrifices." *Lordy, do I know he's made sacrifices.* "He's made the hard choices an alpha has to make. He isn't content to sit around and claim his family's power just because he was born into it. He isn't lazy or entitled like you."

Clayton's lips curl back again as his unleashes a fearsome growl, bending at his knees and preparing to strike.

"You want to know the truth?" he asks. "You're right. If I try to hurt you, Jasper would probably give up everything to save you. But what if it's already too late?"

Huh?

"You don't get it! You don't matter! You're insignificant to everyone except Jasper. And with you out of the picture completely, the prince will crumble."

For some inexplicable reason Clayton pulls off his jacket and tosses it aside, then throws off the loose bow tie and starts unbuttoning his shirt.

"No one else will care, but his true colors will have been revealed. The alpha's son will be labeled a coward, a weakling, unfit to lead! And I will walk away without a single consequence. In fact, I'll become the next in line to lead the pack."

Is he... Does he want to kill me?!

"What are you saying? That's...insane!"

He cackles and drops his shirt, then undoes his pants. "Poor little Maxie, has no idea how the world freakin' works. See, people like you disappear every day and no one bats an eyelid. While people like me...we get what we want!"

And with that, Clayton leaps forward, leaving his clothes in a pile and shifting, his claws extended in my direction. In a frightening moment, his wolf is revealed. Everything happens so fast—this manic, gnarly golden creature flies in my direction, fangs bared, eyes piercing into my soul. I have no time to shift, so I roll to avoid being tackled off the roof.

My shoulder hits the concrete, hard, and I barely have enough wherewithal to stagger to my feet before Clayton has turned and pounced.

He lands on me with a thud, sending my head crashing into the ground with a skull-splitting crack. With what strength I have, I push against his thick fur, trying to hold his snapping jaws at bay. Saliva trickles from his open mouth, spattering me in the face. I kick and thrash, but he's too heavy, too strong.

Narrowly missing a snap of his jaws, I twist to the side and notice his exposed belly. So I extend my claws and swipe. He rears back, howling in pain, and blood splashes the concrete. In that instant I'm able to push him off me and scramble for the door.

Before I can take more than three steps though, he's on me again, swiping at my back and tearing through clothes to shred my skin. I cry out as the pain burns and I fall.

In one movement Clayton catches the front of my shirt with his paw and, like I weigh nothing, he tosses me across the rooftop. I skid over the concrete, sliding to a crash landing as I collide with the wall. I try to stand but my leg is hurt, and the wounds on my back are searing with pain.

Clayton stalks forward, readying to attack once more. I need to shift if I'm going to have any chance of defeating him. But even as a wolf, would I be a match? Is it useless? In either form I'm too weak to beat him. He has the upper hand. He always has. There is no point letting my wolf out, because the result will be the same.

And in this moment of hesitation he pounces again. I groan as he hauls me up and holds me against the railing. The pavement seems miles away beneath me, the traffic streams past in miniature, headlights blurring as the wind tears at my face. I choke against the grip Clayton has around my neck.

He lowers his muzzle so he can stare into my eyes. He wants to gloat, to tell me he doesn't care if I die—that he'll enjoy watching me fall. I meet his gaze and know all this, and then realize...I can feel him. I can feel his hatred, his murderous intent, but more than that I can feel his discomfort, his loss, his displacement and feelings of inadequacy. And I realize I have a strength that Clayton doesn't.

With my eyes closed, I relax my body, falling limp in Clayton's arms. I sense a moment of shock but I move past it. I let my mind open, let the barriers fall, and reach out to Clayton, extending my consciousness like a net of blood-red electric pulses that stream into his soul.

At first everything is dark and I wonder if this is what Clayton's subconscious is—empty...nothingness. He's always been a dick, but recently he's verged into homicidal territory, so honestly it wouldn't surprise me. But then I see a glimmer up ahead, a shimmering light. I push forward, streaming through the currents of his mind. I travel instinctually, letting my senses lead me, and as I dive farther into Clayton's subconscious I know I'm heading in the right direction. The glimmer opens up, revealing a memory.

When I arrive, the world whooshes into place around me, until I'm standing in the center of a vision. My legs wobble, unstable beneath me, like it's taking energy to be this far in. The last time I experienced a vision it was an accident. I've never done it on purpose. It will be exhausting to maintain. But my blood-wolf senses brought me here, so I know I have to persevere.

A rose-tinted light filters through the oak trees overhead. I'm standing on grass, in the middle of a quad, with tall red-brick buildings surrounding me on three sides. Some kids in uniforms sit on the grass with workbooks open and backpacks tossed haphazardly to the side. This must be a school—a fancy one from the look of the place.

From behind a tree a wolf emerges. A wolf I haven't seen before from this viewpoint, but one I recognize instantly, because it's mine. My wolf-self saunters toward me, not lifting its head to make eye contact, but passing casually and continuing on. When it reaches the corner of a building, it glances back and I know to follow.

My wolf leads me through the expansive campus. From the look of the buildings I'd say we're somewhere in the states—maybe New England, or somewhere that's supposed to look like it, but definitely somewhere old. The buildings are grand, with ornate finishings, wrought iron gates, tall frosted windows through which I can't see, and strange pained-looking faces carved into the stone walls. Kids in blazers, woolly hats, and scarves run by on their way to class, holding books to their chests. A couple of boys are tossing a ball against a wall, jostling to beat each other to it.

Up ahead, the paths between four buildings intersect. Benches sit in a square formation facing a leafless tree under which a couple is talking. My wolf walks right up to them and I approach carefully, unsure if they can see me or not.

It takes a second for me to realize I know both of them. Clayton has rosier cheeks and fluffier hair, but looks basically the same, filling out his school blazer the way he filled out his suit jacket. He has his arms around Aisha, whose blazer is on the ground. Her hair is tied back in braids and her face is flushed.

Why is he holding her like that?

My wolf glances back one last time before vanishing. I call out to Aisha, but my voice is silent; my slow-motion-waving arm does nothing to attract her attention. I step forward, eager to watch this memory play out.

At first they seem playful, joking—almost like a couple, teasing and acting coy. Aisha is wriggling, trying to escape Clayton's arms, but he doesn't want to let her go. To the unaware observer it might almost seem sweet. Finally, Aisha manages to free herself, but Clayton catches her by the hand and pulls her back to him. Her playful smile becomes an annoyed grimace. Clayton leans in in an attempt to kiss Aisha, but she ducks her head to the side, evading his advance. He pulls back, looking confused but not dissuaded, then goes in for the kiss again, and this time Aisha tries harder to break away.

Clayton holds fast. The dick… *Let her go!*

Their playful energy is gone and now Aisha's grimace is a strained expression of panic. She doesn't want this. She braces herself against him with her forearms to put some space between them. Yet Clayton continues to hold onto her. I want to run to them and pull them apart. I want to help her. But I can't move. This is as close as the vision will let me get.

Finally, Aisha has had enough. She throws open her arms, breaking Clayton's hold, and pushes him away. He approaches again, yelling, and tries to pull her back to him. But she turns and slaps him across the face, hard.

Clayton holds his reddening cheek.

And for the first time I can hear their voices clearly.

"You bitch!" Clayton yells. "I'm your mate!"

What?!

Aisha never told me she was mated to Clayton. But now it's beginning to make sense, the way she warned me against him, the way she always bristled when he was brought up. They were mates once. But not anymore.

"I don't want to be your mate, Clayton," Aisha says, not missing a beat. "And you better believe I never will."

"You're confused. You don't understand what you're saying."

She stabs at him with an angry finger. "I know exactly what I'm doing. I reject you, Clayton. Do you hear that?"

He grips his chest.

"I reject the mate bond. Find someone else to claim."

Without another word or glance, Aisha turns and walks away. Despite the shock of learning Aisha and Clayton were mates, I want to cheer and clap, I want to jump up and down. Aisha really did that. She was destined to be with a jerk and a creep, and she said no. My respect for her skyrockets.

Back under the tree, Clayton's knees give way and he crumples to the ground. He digs his claws into the brick footpath and howls. Tears stain his blood-red face as he screeches to the clouds. So that's what it looks like when a wolf is rejected.

The world turns to liquid around me as the vision ends and I'm pulled backward—everything floats away, and I'm brought back to reality.

High-velocity winds tear at my cheeks as I open my eyes. Clayton's slick jaw is barely an inch from my face, his frenzied eyes boring into mine.

Aisha broke the mate bond with the most entitled dick I've ever meant. I can't help but think this has something to do with why he's so desperate to hold onto Jasper and his position in the pack. But none of that is very useful right now.

Clayton still has his paw on my neck; I'm still leaning halfway over the edge of the roof as traffic drifts by a hundred stories below. Clayton is still huffing hot, sickly breaths into my face, rage and violence shining in his yellow eyes.

With a growl and a roar he lifts me from the ground and readies to throw me over the edge.

NEW YEAR'S RESOLUTIONS

Aisha was mated to this monster, the wild animal clutching me in its paws and about to throw me off the roof of a hundred-story high-rise.

But she was strong enough to walk away. And I'm not about to let him hurt me anymore.

Clayton's claws dig into me as he lifts me higher, and I can feel the shift in the air as he holds me out over the drop. I grunt in pain but manage to lift my hands to the sides of his face. With all my energy I force him to look at me, and as soon as our eyes meet I channel his pain, the agony of losing his mate, the pang of rejection, that howling sensation that still sits deep in his subconscious. I pull that pain into myself—like blood I let it flood my veins, course through me, and I feel every moment of it.

Then I give it back, serving his pain to him like a fresh steak, hot off the grill.

I let Clayton's hidden feelings escape me and float, in glowing red tendrils of energy, back to him.

His eyes widen. His grip loosens. He stumbles backward.

Distracted and distressed, he drops me, and I flop onto the concrete of the roof. Safe.

Clayton huffs and spins. He shakes his muzzle.

Staggeringly, I'm able to push myself to my feet.

"You think we're different," I say. "But I've felt what you felt, and it's the same."

He stomps and claws at the roof.

"Your love is the same as mine. It's burns as bright. And it hurts the same too."

Finally, he lifts his nose and howls to the waning moon.

I wait and watch as he slowly collapses under the weight of his rejection, his grief. Gradually, Clayton shifts back to human form, until he's lying curled up on the concrete, naked, exhausted, spent.

I grab Clayton's suit jacket from where he tossed it and drape it over him.

"We're all powerless when it comes to love," I say. "The only power we have is in the choices we make."

Clayton doesn't look at me; he stays curled in on himself, shivering.

Suddenly, the door to the stairs bangs open and Jasper rushes out onto the roof. Aisha is close behind him.

His eyes dart between me and his former roommate.

"I felt—are you...?" he asks, coming toward me.

"I'm fine," I say, standing.

Jasper stops. I don't need to be a blood wolf to know he's desperate to reach out to me, pull me into his arms, hold me tightly against him, and make sure I'm not hurt. But he doesn't move.

I glance at Aisha, who is staring at Clayton, the wolf she was once mated to, taking in the pitiful sight of him. She doesn't look happy to see him like this, but there is this sort of resolute acceptance in how she doesn't look away.

At some point I'll need to tell her what I saw and hope that's she's okay with me knowing, but for now, all I want is a large box of chicken nuggets and my bed.

"Did he hurt you?" Jasper asks as I wander past him toward the door.

"He tried," I say.

"I'll get security," Aisha offers, pulling her attention away, happy for a reason not to be near Clayton any longer. Before she disappears through the door, she turns to me. "You sure you're okay, kid?"

Part of me wonders if I told her he was about to throw me off the roof, if she would change her mind about finding security and take matters into her own hands. But there's been enough drama tonight.

"I'm fine," I say.

She gives me the briefest of nods, like she's thankful not to stick around any longer. I return the gesture and Aisha disappears inside.

"You're bleeding," Jasper says, not caring to keep his distance any longer. He leads me to the side of an air-conditioning unit and sits me down on a concrete ledge.

"Take this off," he says, carefully removing my jacket for me and turning my shoulders to examine the scratches on my back. He pulls out his pocket square, a silk swatch of fabric with a tropical design, and lifts up the back of my shirt. Gently, he dabs at the wounds. "Does it hurt?"

I wince as he cleans the lacerations, unable to hide my discomfort. The adrenaline that was holding the sting of Clayton's claw marks at bay is wearing off.

"I'm sorry I wasn't here, Max. If I'd have known he was up here I—"

"You didn't know," I say. "This isn't your fault."

"I know but it is my fault you ran away. It's my fault—"

"Stop," I say, closing my eyes. "You haven't put me in any danger, at least none that I haven't chosen for myself."

"Max, I—"

"And it's fine," I say, gritting my teeth as I realize just how much pain I'm actually in. "I mean it. I don't mind. But I also meant what I said. I need to start choosing the path that's best for me."

Security guards rush through the door and Jasper points them in Clayton's direction. They lift him up, swiftly wrap him in a blanket, and carry him from the roof.

When it's just Jasper and me left up here, I look into his eyes. The moon is off to the side, fuzzy and unfocused. I wonder if the Moon Gods are up there watching us now.

I think back to that day on the beach when I vowed I'd do whatever it takes to cross the path between souls, the moonlit path across the water that would lead me to Jasper. But now I know there are different paths, loads of them. There are paths leading in all sorts of directions—all equally as valuable and worth crossing as the next. Paths to friendships and community. Paths to love, albeit rocky and marked with danger. Lonely paths, but where things are quiet and safe. Paths leading to the soul of every wolf out there in the world. And there's the path that connects me to my own soul. That's the path I need to take now.

"You need to do what you think is best," I say. "And whatever that is, it's okay because that's what you've chosen. I won't get in your way any longer."

"Max..."

He cups my face with one hand. I take it and hold it.

"And wherever your path leads, I'll be watching on from the sidelines, super proud. You're going to be an amazing alpha."

We rest our foreheads together and I hold back the tears threatening to explode from my face. With one last squeeze of Jasper's hands, I let go and hoist myself up.

Staggering just a little, I make my way back downstairs.

My back twinges as I put my torn-up jacket back on and push through the emergency exit. The music is still pumping, the festivities in full swing. Through the patio doors I glimpse the countdown to midnight—just a few minutes left. Not long to go now. I limp through the crowd as heads turn and eyes gape at me. Some faces are concerned, and others glare like I'm a vermin they'd rather avoid.

Katie catches my eye and comes running over.

"Max, are you okay? What happened? I'm so sorry about earlier. Let me help you."

"It's fine," I say, spotting Todd and Simon behind her, watching her, both as concerned as the other. "I'm heading home. You should stay here, have a great time. I'll call you tomorrow."

"Are you sure?" Katie asks.

I nod and she does this half-smile head-tilt thing before heading back to her mates. Whatever is going on between us, it can wait.

The elevator is sitting open, and I exhale as I finally enter the warm-yellow light within. The doors slide shut and I let myself collapse against the back wall.

Above, the LED screen shows the same video from earlier, only in reverse, and I sigh a little, happy to finally be heading back to Earth.

The foyer is empty. Everyone is upstairs, excited about the impending strike of midnight, the New Year and all its promises. I'm just happy to be going home—back to my single bed, in my cozy room, in my small but comforting house by the woods.

I step outside and realize I've forgotten my puffer jacket. With the adrenaline gone completely it's cold, but I can't face going back inside. With an arm wrapped around myself, I step to the curb and raise my free arm to hail a cab, laughing quietly about what they'll do with an old, discount puffer at the end of the night when nobody wants it.

Luckily, a free taxi pulls right up. I open the door and take one last look back up at the packhouse. It doesn't loom as large as it did before, and I can almost make out the noise of the party from the top floors. There is a life I could have had up there, it would've been big and flashy, and adventurous and wild. But also painful and rocky and uncertain. Resolutely, I place one foot inside the taxi. I'm about to slide into the back seat when I hear...

"Max!"

THE STROKE OF MIDNIGHT

The packhouse doors are sliding shut behind Jasper.

"Max, wait!" he calls again.

I pull my foot from the taxi and place it back on the sidewalk.

"Don't go," he says. "Please."

"Jasper, I have to. There's no place up there for me. I don't belong in that life, but you do. It's what you've been working so hard for, it's what you've wanted—"

"But what if it isn't," he says, and I stop talking. He takes a step forward, gulping. "Look, we don't get to choose who our parents are, and I can't pretend there aren't things I have to do simply because of who my father is. But I'm tired and I'm done."

I stare at his face, trying to read his expression. There's no noise coming from his mind; I must've wiped my blood-wolf self out redirecting Clayton's trauma. *Interesting.* But his eyes are set on mine, and his lips are steady, his jaw set. He means what he's saying.

"All my life I've been told that I am one thing. That I can only be one thing. The alpha. I've been told that I'm responsible for the fate of my pack, that I need to live up to my father and his impossible standards. And I've had to give up things, friends, family…" His jaw twitches. "I've sacrificed to prepare myself to be the strongest alpha I can be. But I've also let people push me around and tell me what to be. And not just my father. Weaker people, creeps like Clayton, I've let them dictate who I'm supposed to be and what my life is supposed to look like. And I'm done."

He beats his thigh with a clenched fist. The wind ruffles his perfect hair, bringing with it a whiff of his scent. Only it's different than usual. What is usually a gentle mix of mint, lemon, and cherry blossom, is now overwhelming cherry. The moon is reflected in his eyes.

"Why does being alpha mean giving up the things that matter to me? Why should I give up the things that make me happy?"

His bottom lip hangs open a little and he takes the tiniest step in my direction.

"A good leader should lead by example, but how am I doing that if I turn myself into a jerk and push away the people who mean the most to me, the people who have only ever asked me to be myself. The people I…love."

Another tiny step.

"When I become alpha I want my pack to be happy, but that shouldn't come at the expense of my happiness, should it?"

His hand finds mine, and he entwines my fingers with his.

"Won't a happy alpha make for a happier pack?"

His other hand slides over my hip bone and pulls me in closer. All of my senses start firing up—my body cascades with tingles and shivers.

"And you make me happy, Max."

He lets go of my hand to run a thumb down the angle of my jaw.

"I know it may not seem like it," he says, laughing a little, more relaxed than I think I've ever seen him. "I know I've been kind of an asshole."

I huff and roll my eyes but can't help the grin threatening to curve my lips.

"And as much as I've tried to push you away, to put distance between us, the only time I feel okay—*happy*—is when I'm with you."

He pulls me even closer, till our chests are pressed together, and my heart is beating faster than the speed of light. There is no breath left in my lungs.

"I can't lose you."

Jasper's lips find mine. He presses his mouth to mine gently but with certainty. And I relax into the kiss. I don't know what I'm going to do, but if this is our last kiss, why not enjoy it, right? As if he knows exactly where my body wants them to be, he slides his hands down until one is cradling the back of my neck and the other is on the small of my back. My legs are a weak cliché, my stomach is fluttering like a swarm of cotton-candy bats have just woken up. And there's a new sensation, too—a warmth, a feeling of real connection, like putting on your favorite sweater or reading by a fire—spreading from Jasper's body to mine.

When we pull apart, there's a tear just beginning to form in one of Jasper's eyes, and an easy smile on his lips.

"I could do that all night," he says.

"Ahuh," is all I manage to reply.

Then suddenly our romantic moment is shattered by the honking of a car horn.

"Hey, you getting in or not?" the cab driver yells. I'd forgotten he was there, idling at the curb waiting to take me home, away from Jasper and the path he's laid out before me.

"Max," Jasper says, taking both of my hands in his. "Will you be my boyfriend...again?"

I stare at him in wonder. I've never felt like this before, not even with him. This protective warmth, this sense of connectivity. But I know saying yes means more than it seems. Dating Jasper isn't the same as dating anyone else. It won't all be cute coffee dates, or holidays with hot tubs. There will be danger; there will be people—important, powerful people—who want to tell us how to live our lives. And there will always be that voice at the back of my mind wondering whether I'm the most important thing to Jasper, or whether there's something he cares about more.

"Buddy, you coming or not?!" the cab driver yells.

I gulp down the lump in my throat.

"It's almost midnight," Jasper says as we're whisked back up into the stars. "Here, take this."

He pulls off his jacket and hands it to me. Even without it he looks dashing, his shoulders wide, and his crisp white shirt tucked tight into his waistband. Before the elevator arrives I manage to swap out my torn and somewhat bloodstained jacket for Jasper's pristine, amazing-smelling one.

My heart hasn't stopped racing since Jasper kissed me. But as we ascend the levels of the packhouse I start to wonder if I'm making the same mistakes all over again.

He asked me out, which was kind of dumb, but also totally adorable. And maybe it's my blood-wolf senses or just a result of everything we've been through, but I want to trust Jasper when he says he's done bowing to the whims of others. That he's ready to put his happiness—and mine, by extension—first. But what if this elevator is only leading me into more trouble, more doubt.

Jasper wasn't just asking me out, he was asking me to take a risk. There's no guarantee he won't revert back to his jerky, alpha-focused self at the first sign of trouble. But I think, and I hope—I really really hope—the risk will be worth it. And after all, the paths we take aren't laid out before us, predetermined and set in stone; they're the paths we create. So before the doors ping open I decide to make a choice. Without sacrificing my own well-being, I'm going to trust Jasper and take this risk with him.

As we arrive at level ninety-nine, Jasper gives my hand one quick squeeze before the doors open, but as we step back into the still-thrumming party, he lets go.

I hesitate in the elevator, suddenly unsure, not knowing if I've made the right choice.

Jasper slaps a hand onto the metallic frame to stop the doors from closing.

"Are you coming?"

"I..." My mouth flaps open but nothing comes out.

Jasper steps back into the elevator and the doors close, giving us another quick moment of privacy.

"What's wrong?" he asks, holding me by my shoulders.

"I just—look, I'm not trying to rush you into anything. I know you won't want to tell people and that's fine—it's fine, it really is. That's hard and takes time and everyone's journey is different. But I just don't... I don't know if I'm ready for this—for all of this."

He laughs and grins and kisses my cheek. "What are you talking about?"

"I guess I've been chasing after this for so long, I sort of hadn't figured out how it would feel when I actually had it, and now it's here and I'm just... There's so much I'm not sure about..."

He levels his eyes with mine. "Are you unsure about me?"

"I don't know, maybe... People always say you have the world on your shoulders, and like, how could anyone not crumble under that much pressure and—"

He kisses me firmly and I know he's just doing it to shut me up, but it works.

"What can I do to show you there's nothing to worry about?"

But it's the wrong question because there's nothing he can do, not without me asking him to do something I know he isn't ready for. So I twist about to free myself from his hands, which suddenly feel too warm. In fact, the whole elevator feels too hot and there's not enough air and—oh Moon Gods, am I having a panic attack?

"Nothing, there's nothing," I say, pacing about as much as possible. "And I wouldn't expect you to, but there's just a lot I don't understand, and what if we're just making things hard for ourselves? And what if you realize it's not worth it?"

"And what if we realize it's worth more than we ever imagined?" he asks, and I can't help but think he's sort of enjoying seeing me freak out. "What then?"

"Well"—my heart rate slows and my breathing returns to normal—"that would be nice."

Jasper is finally able to take my hands. "It's going to be fine."

"There's just so much I haven't got figured out, and who knows how this is even going to work and—"

"So let's figure it out together," he says, and just like that the doors of the elevator open again. "Come on, I want to show you something."

This time Jasper doesn't let go of my hand. Instead, he leads me from the elevator through the crowd. Some people turn to stare, but Jasper's grip never wavers.

He pulls me across the dance floor, past his father's officers and business partners, past the entire upper crust of werewolf society. He doesn't let go as he leads me through the doors and out into the night air. With just over a minute until the ball drops, the patio is packed; everyone is outside to see in the New Year with a bang. More and more wolves are streaming outside to join the crowd overlooking Manhattan.

As we muscle through the masses, Jasper never letting go of me, I spot some familiar faces. Jericho and Morven are standing next to a potted plant, drinking from lowball glasses. Olivia and Mia are huddled in a corner. Katie is laughing at something Todd just said while Simon slaps him on the back. And Aisha, having already spotted us, is watching with a bemused expression.

Against the backdrop of Times Square, Tobias Volk is standing on the balloon-framed stage, holding a microphone.

"Ladies and Gentlewolves, there's only one minute left until the stroke of midnight, so find that special wolf before the clock strikes twelve and get ready to see in the New Year with a kiss!"

Before I know what's happening, Jasper is heading to the side of the stage and to my horror, up the stairs. Leading turns to pulling as he drags my ass onto the raised platform and in front of the ever-growing crowd of expectant wolves. I manage to tug my hand out of Jasper's before too many people can see. What is he thinking? If this many people saw us holding hands, they'd have questions for sure. He must be confused or excited, or… Oh no…

I try to stop Jasper from going any farther but feel the heat of a spotlight on my face and swiftly retreat into the shadows. Politely as ever, Jasper clasps a hand on Tobias's shoulder and whispers something in his ear. Despite a slightly confused stammer, Tobias graciously hands the microphone over to Jasper before exiting the stage.

"Excuse me, everyone! Can I get your attention?"

The DJ, or whoever, halts the music with an almighty record scratch, and every face on the patio turns to see what Jasper is up to.

"Thank you," he says, shielding his eyes from the light for a moment. "I'm sorry—I know there's less than a minute until the New Year, but that's why I wanted to... Before we start a new year together as a strong, united pack...I have an announcement I'd like to make."

Is this really happening? Please Moon Gods, say this isn't happening!

"But first I want to say thank you to my dad, Alpha Jericho—yes, go ahead, give him some applause."

The confused crowd goes along with Jasper's instruction.

"My father is an amazing man. He's strict, sometimes too strict"—Jericho is watching Jasper cautiously, and I very briefly notice his eyes flickering in my direction—"but despite how much of a hard-ass he's been to me growing up, I know that he loves me."

The crowd goes "Awww."

"He's a great father and an even greater leader. My father is an amazing alpha, and yes, there are some people out there—corrupt, power-hungry people—who would want to take his place..." I glance into the crowd and notice Walter Bridgers shrinking behind a standing heater. "But I know that with the right allies, this pack will continue to grow and prosper."

Jasper takes a moment to swallow and then focuses his gaze intently on Alpha Morven.

"And some of our allies are here tonight. Alpha Morven of the Rocky Pack, who was gracious enough to let a few of us come and stay with him recently." Morven lifts his glass casually as the patio gives him a spattering of applause. "I think you'll agree with me when I say that it's the differences between and within our packs that, when brought together, make us strong. And I hope that you and my father will have a long, healthy relationship, by understanding that difference is a strength."

Morven seems a little taken aback, a crack appearing in his spotlessly polished veneer. But Jericho has raised an eyebrow. Is he impressed?

I glance at Mia and Olivia. Mia is watching her dad's face intently, until Olivia slips a defiant hand into Mia's, prompting her to turn and smile at her mate.

"And finally," Jasper says, his voice catching ever so slightly in his throat. "There is something I want you all to know."

Silence falls across the crowd; somewhere in the distance a countdown has begun. Ten...nine...

"Recently, I met someone—someone I never imagined could exist. Someone who is funny and clumsy and stubborn."

Eight...

Seven...

"Someone who drives me insane and who can be a complete bonehead."

Six...

Five...

"Someone I never imagined I would end up with. But someone who makes me happy—truly, ridiculously, immensely happy."

Four...

"And I want you all to meet him."

Wolves in the crowd share bewildered glances as Jasper reaches back, takes my hand, and pulls me into the spotlight. For a second I'm blinded, squinting to make out the sea of confused wolf eyes staring back at me.

Three…

"Members of the Elite Pack, I want to introduce you to Maximilian Remus."

Two…

"My mate!"

One…

Fireworks explode all around us.

And in front of the entire pack, Jasper kisses me.

ACKNOWLEDGEMENTS

When I first sat down to write *The Alpha's Son* I had no expectation that anyone would read it, much less that a whole swathe of people would read it and find something in it to love. I'd been working in the universe of shifters and werewolves for a while, editing, ghost-writing, and immersing myself in this furry subgenre, and I saw an opportunity to use the hierarchical structures of the pack system as an analogous mirror to our world and how queer people—and in fact anyone outside of the norm—are often cast aside. As a queer person myself, I felt as if representation was sorely missing in this genre and I wanted to explore what being queer as a werewolf in a world where straight true mates were the status quo. So I sat down to write about two boys, one who represented that innate sense of rebellion I believe most queer people feel to some extent, and one who represented the system in its most concentrated form. From that sprung a cute, oftentimes frustrating, adventurous, and (I hope) boundary pushing romance. And I could never have imagined that my little experiment would touch so many people.

So first and foremost I need to thank you, the readers, my little wolf pack, those who read the first book in this series, who have shared it online, told their friends about it, requested it from their library, complained about *that* ending (I'm sorry Jasper wasn't quite ready for his HEA just yet! Stay tuned!), and who have stuck around to read this sequel. You have humbled me, made me cry actual tears, and warmed my little wolfy heart. This book is all about finding one's identity as a queer person outside of our romantic relationships and community is such a large part of that. The community of readers who have embraced Max and Jasper, rooted for them and their friends to find love and happiness, who I've interacted with online and who I've seen loving the world I've built are the shining light of this experience. I'm not much for online, I don't spend a lot of time on social-media (an author faux-pas for sure), but I see you and I'm so grateful. Thank you. I hope this sequel has lived up to your expectations and I hope you're as excited as I am to see where this story goes and how things will pan out for Max and Jasper. There is more to come and I'm so excited to share it with you. #jasmax forever!

This series wouldn't exist without Tiny Ghost Press. Massive thanks has to go to Joshua Dean Perry who saw the promise in
this series and has guided me through the continuation of the story. I know you're as invested in Max and Jasper's story as I am and I love having you as a partner in wolfy-crime. Huge, HUGE, thanks to Dana Keller, your edits and insightful comments have lifted this sequel to new heights and I'm so grateful for the work you've put in. It's still wild to me that people care about this world as much as I do and your care and attention is second to none. To the rest of the Tiny Ghost team—Reuben Davies-Hoare, Kylie Koews, Jeremy Gibson, Joana Podeszwicka, and Thomas Shah—you're doing amazing work, thank you so much for the time and effort you put into making this book the dream experience it's been.

I have to give a massive shout out to the friends and family who have supported me, bought a copy of *The Alpha's Son*, and been my cheerleaders throughout. I know for a lot of you gay, werewolf, romances aren't your first impulse when choosing a book, but seeing my book on your shelves and hearing your thoughts has been such a wild experience and I am honestly shook by the support you've given me. Thank you!

Max and his parents go through a learning curve in this book and I'm lucky enough to have two very supportive, accepting, and caring parents. Thank you for helping me achieve my dreams and never expecting me to anything other than the rogue I am.

To my partner, you are the bedrock of my life and the biggest supporter I could have ever asked for. I'm so happy the Moon Gods lit the path between our souls, lol. And to our most precious Taco, without whom our family would be incomplete, you are my constant companion, I don't know who I'd be without you near.

Finally, I just need to say thank you once again for reading these books and being part of the pack. I'm so excited for what the future holds and I hope you'll be there too.

ABOUT THE AUTHOR

Penny Jessup is the bestselling author of gay werewolf romance *The Alpha's Son*. She cut her teeth writing online on fanfic sites before beginning a career in ghostwriting and copywriting. She has a bachelor's in creative writing and lives in upstate New York with her partner and their dog, Taco. She loves anime, baking while listening to her favorite podcasts, and hiking in the woods near her house.

MORE BOOKS FROM
TINY GHOST PRESS

AVAILABLE NOW WHEREVER BOOKS ARE SOLD

FOR MORE SPOOKY QUEER STORIES SIGN UP FOR OUR
NEWSLETTER AND FOLLOW US ON SOCIAL MEDIA

WWW.TINYGHOSTPRESS.COM
@TINYGHOSTPRESS